Cyril Cook was born in Easton, Hampshire, but at the age of five was brought to live on a farm in Mottingham, Kent. Educated at Eltham College, he matriculated in 1939, joined The Rifle Brigade in 1940, and was commissioned and transferred to The Parachute Regiment in 1943. He saw considerable service in the 6th Airborne Division in Europe and the Far East where for a period he commanded, at the age of 22, a company of some 220 men of the Malay Regiment.

His working life was spent mainly as the proprietor of an engineering business which he founded, until he retired to start the really serious business of writing the six volumes of The Chandlers.

By the same author

THE CHANDLERS

VOLUME ONE – THE YOUNG CHANDLERS
Published in 2005 (Vanguard Press)
ISBN 1 84386 199 2

VOLUME TWO – THE CHANDLERS AT WAR
Published in 2006 (Vanguard Press)
ISBN 978 1 84386 292 5

VOLUME THREE – THE CHANDLERS FIGHT BACK
Published in 2006 (Vanguard Press)
ISBN 978 1 84386 293 2

VOLUME FOUR – THE CHANDLERS GRIEVE
Published in 2006 (Vanguard Press)
ISBN 978 1 84386 294 9

VOLUME FIVE – THE CHANDLERS ATTACK
Published in 2007 (Vanguard Press)
ISBN 978 1 84386 295 6

THE CHANDLERS

VOLUME 6

The Chandlers Win Through

Cyril Cook

THE CHANDLERS

Volume 6

The Chandlers Win Through

Vanguard Press

VANGUARD PAPERBACK

© Copyright 2007
Cyril Cook

The right of Cyril Cook to be identified as author of
this work has been asserted by him in accordance with the
Copyright, Designs and Patents Act 1988.

All Rights Reserved

No reproduction, copy or transmission of this publication
may be made without written permission.
No paragraph of this publication may be reproduced,
copied or transmitted save with the written permission of the
publisher, or in accordance with the provisions
of the Copyright Act 1956 (as amended).

Any person who commits any unauthorised act in relation to
this publication may be liable to criminal
prosecution and civil claims for damages.

A CIP catalogue record for this title is
available from the British Library.

ISBN 978-1-84386-296 3

*Vanguard Press is an imprint of
Pegasus Elliot MacKenzie Publishers Ltd.*
www.pegasuspublishers.com

First Published in 2007

**Vanguard Press
Sheraton House Castle Park
Cambridge England**

Printed & Bound in Great Britain

DEDICATION

This volume is dedicated to my daughter,
Ann, and her husband Bryan Lambert.
Throughout the six volumes of 'The Chandlers'
I have stressed the infinite value of 'family'.
I rate Ann and Bryan as being beyond value, as they
have shown all through these past years,
in word and deed.

MAIN CHARACTERS FROM PREVIOUS BOOKS

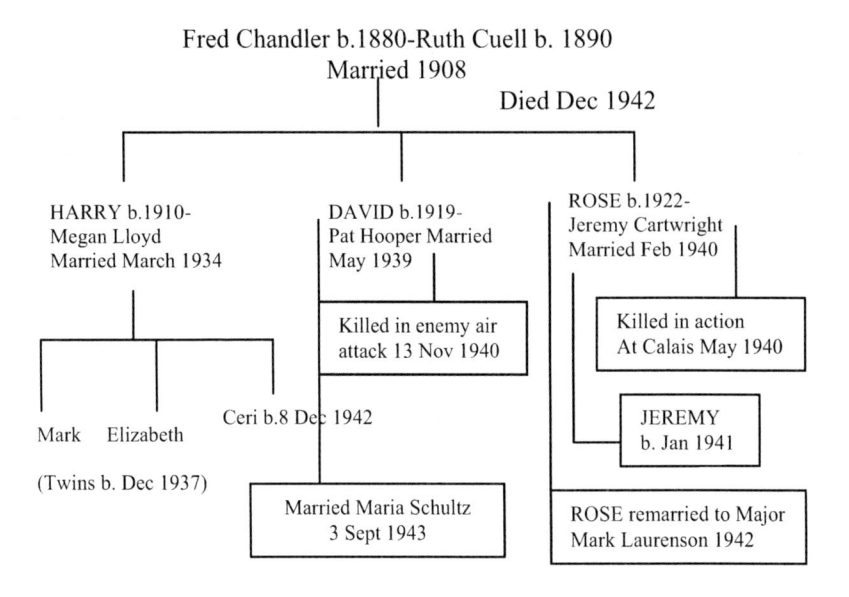

Fred Chandler b.1880-Ruth Cuell b. 1890
Married 1908
Died Dec 1942

- **HARRY b.1910-** Megan Lloyd Married March 1934
  - Mark   Elizabeth (Twins b. Dec 1937)

- **DAVID b.1919-** Pat Hooper Married May 1939
  - Killed in enemy air attack 13 Nov 1940
  - Ceri b.8 Dec 1942
  - Married Maria Schultz 3 Sept 1943

- **ROSE b.1922-** Jeremy Cartwright Married Feb 1940
  - Killed in action At Calais May 1940
  - JEREMY b. Jan 1941
  - ROSE remarried to Major Mark Laurenson 1942

OTHER CHARACTERS

JACK HOOPER	Now Sir Jack, Pat's father. Married MOIRA EVANS, Megan's Aunt. Moira is a Top Civil Servant involved in the Atom Bomb project. Son JOHN born August 1937.
TREFOR LLOYD	and Elizabeth. Megan's parents.
BUFFY CARTWRIGHT	and Rita. Baby Jeremy's grandparents.
KARL REISNER	Refugee from Nazi Germany now naturalised British citizen. Father of ANNI married to ERNIE BOLTON, David's boyhood friend and now Works Director at Fred and Jack's engineering company Sandbury Engineering.

DR KONRAD VON HASSELLBEK
and Elizabeth. Parents of David's great pre-war friend, Dieter, now fighting in a panzer division in Russia. All fervent anti-nazis. Also daughter, Inge, ardent Nazi married to Himmler's nephew. Dieter married cousin Rosa April 1940. Rosa subsequently confined to Ravensbruk concentration camp for six years, now released to work at Bruksheim Klinik as a doctor but still a prisoner.

CECELY COATES
with children Oliver, now 18, and Greta now 16 caught in England when Japs invaded Malaya. Husband Nigel and Nigel's brother Judge Charles Coates in Jap internment camp if still alive.

CHARLIE CREW
Son of Brigadier Lord Ramsford, David's previous C.O., and grandson of the Earl of Otbourne. Charlie is a great friend of the Chandler family. Engaged to Wren Emma Langham.

HENRY SCHULTZ
and wife Susan. David's parents-in-law whose son, Cedric, had been killed at the battle for Calais in 1940.

GLORIA TREHARNE
Lost her daughter and son-in-law in the Blitz. Now lives with Cecely Coates at "The Bungalow", along with Cecely's two children and her own two grandchildren, Eric 9 and Patricia 11. The Earl is very fond of Mrs Treharne.

MAJOR MARGARET COULTER. U.S. ARMY
Shortly to marry Fred Chandler.

Chapter One

When the occupants of Chandlers Lodge, and regions adjacent, awoke on New Year's morning in the Year of Grace 1945, some clear-headed, others not so clear, they found they were enveloped in a foot of snow which had silently descended upon them during the night. This produced paroxysms of delight from the children, hastily gobbling down their plates of Shredded Wheat as fast as they could so as to get out and build a snowman.

"Can I help?" Margaret asked.

Mark, Elizabeth and young John Hooper looked at each other. They really would have preferred if grown-ups were to mind their own business, but Margaret was soon to be Mark's new step-grandmother, and John had always been brought up to be courteous to grown-ups, which, allowing for occasional lapses he was, in the main. They therefore chanted together 'Yes of course.'

Three-years-old Ceri piped up.

"I want to come."

"You'll fall over in the snow like you always do," was Mark's immediate reply.

"If mummy says you can come out, you can come with me," Margaret told her, lifting her on to her lap. "Have you got your wellies with you?"

"Yes, and my scarf and my bobble hat."

Mummy said it was alright, but not to get her woolly gloves wet, so they all quickly got well wrapped up and moved out on to the large circular lawn at the front of the house. They built a 'hooge' snowman, as four-year-old Jeremy later described it over the telephone to his grandfather Cartwright in Romsey, the final ball of snow for the head having to be placed on the main body by Margaret, as the seven-year-olds could hardly lift it.

"Wait a minute," she called out to the children, and disappeared round the side of the house. Now children cannot wait a minute. You know that and I know that. They could conceivably wait five seconds, but a minute was too much to ask. With the exception of little Ceri, standing on a clear patch of grass which had previously been snow, but was now the head of the snowman, they scooped up handfuls of crisp white ammunition, and as Margaret reappeared she was welcomed with a salvo of snowballs, fortunately lacking in both accuracy and penetrative power. There then began a general snowball fight, with little Ceri and young Jeremy trying to take part but scoring little, until Margaret called out,

"Hold your fire."

They all stopped as she went over to the snowman, put two small potatoes in for eyes, stuck a carrot in for his nose and put an old cap on his head which had been in the lean-to at the back of the house and which had at one time been Fred's gardening cap. They all cheered, which brought the adults in the house to the big bay window of the drawing room to see what was going on.

"Come on in now," Megan called. They all trooped in, discarding their wellies in the back door porch.

"Now go on in and get warm, but don't put your hands to the fire or you will get chilblains."

It was a great start to the New Year, not only in Chandlers Lodge, Sandbury, Kent, but elsewhere as well in far flung places throughout the world.

In London the New Year's Honours List for 1945 was headed by the announcement that David Lloyd George, who had had an unbroken connection with the House of Commons since 1890, was to be made a Companion of Honour. Fred's comment to Jack Hooper went along the lines, 'If a randy old blighter like him can get a C.H. what must you be worth?' It was common knowledge that L.G. had run a mistress for over thirty years, kept a wife, and that no lady in her right mind would risk being in a room alone with him. Yet he had got away with it for decades, whereas in later years such antics would be considered political suicide.

There was good news from Burma to start the year, where the 14th Army, christened by themselves 'the forgotten army,' were beating the retreating Japs back to Mandalay under appalling conditions.

All at Sandbury were glued to the wireless as the news bulletins were announced. The Germans had attacked through the Ardennes in the middle of winter - considered in every staff college in Europe to be impossible - routing the American army opposing them, and were seemingly on their way to Antwerp. Heavy fighting was reported. The Germans had thrown in an estimated twenty-three divisions, including their best Tiger tank regiments, and reinforcements were being rushed to halt them. With the advantage of bad weather preventing the RAF and USAAF from mounting ground attacks against their armour it seemed they could cut the

British Second Army in half, leaving one part in Holland, the other in France.

But held they were. The 6th Airborne Division, of which David's battalion was part, was one of the units which eventually stopped their headlong thrusts. He and his company were now in reserve waiting for their next move.

Other good news came from Dover hospital where young John Power was recovering from his ordeal, having been entombed for two days in Betteshanger mine after a roof fall. John was a 'Bevin boy', one of ten per cent of young men of call-up age who were drafted to work in the mines instead of becoming soldiers, sailors or whatever. He had suffered no broken bones but had severe lacerations and abrasions resulting from crawling over sharp flints through the cavity the rescuers had scraped out which had enabled John and his three comrades to crawl out. Although in considerable discomfort he was on the mend. It was only a matter of time.

Harry's good news, despite the fact it had no direct bearing on their circumstances, came over the air waves in the form of a report that British carrier-borne aircraft had very successfully bombed an oil refinery in N. E. Sumatra at Pangkalan-Brandan, and shot down seven Jap fighters. The significance of this announcement was twofold. Firstly, the action was only two hundred and fifty miles from their hidey-hole in the jungle and secondly the Royal Navy was hitting back hard. An interesting incident, which only received publicity many years later, occurred at the aftermath of this raid. One of the British aircraft was hit, and had to ditch, first sending out 'Mayday' messages. These were picked up by HMS Whelp, the First Officer of which was a certain Lieutenant Philip Mountbatten which raced to pick up the pilot and gunner from their life raft. Many years later they all met up again at Buckingham Palace, which understandably was a much more sober affair than that which they enjoyed when Prince Philip went ashore with them when they eventually were landed at Fremantle, Western Australia.

Finally, Fred's good news, tempered as it was by the thought of an immediate parting, meant that in two or three weeks Margaret would obtain her release from the US Army, come to Chandlers Lodge, and be married to him. She had no qualms about this intended chain of events. The fact that Fred was over twenty years older than she was had never, in her mind, been a stumbling block. She had been attracted to him at first sight, his strong looks and capital sense of humour winning her completely. Now in a few weeks they would be wed. That part of the picture did produce a few qualms. She was a widow, but a widow with very little experience of matrimony.

Her husband had been a highly qualified engineer on an oil rig in the Gulf of Mexico. As a result, most of their time together had been in the form of a series of short honeymoons. Now this could have resulted in experiences to look back upon with longing and regret, but just as some new wives are a little disappointed at the outcome of their wedding night, so Margaret had been somewhat unsatisfied with the end results of her succession of honeymoons. But she loved her Glynn very much, and that was enough. Then after two years and eight or nine honeymoons Glynn was killed in an oil rig fire, she was a widow at just under thirty years of age, and since then had remained celibate, despite many offers to change that state.

Fred saw her off at Sandbury station on Wednesday 3rd January, with a big hug, a long kiss, and the words,

"It won't be long now."

She smiled at him, sunk her head on to his shoulder, and replied,

"Fred darling, I'm looking forward so much to being with you always." Fred hugged her in reply, but ever the realist, was dismayed at the certainty that 'always' was to be measured in a few short years. He would have to make those perfect for her as far as he could, he determined.

With a mild westerly wind, the snow had cleared by Thursday. As Greta was on holiday from Benenden, where she was now in the sixth form, she asked her mother if she could travel to Dover to see John Power, John the Younger that is. As she was getting herself ready to get the 12.10 train, the telephone rang. It was John.

"Greta, I've asked the authorities here if I can be transferred to Sandbury hospital now I am more or less mobile, and they have agreed. They are sending me in an ambulance after lunch, but as the ambulance has to go to Canterbury and Chatham first, I shall not reach Sandbury until about five o'clock. If you can bear the sight of my ugly face can you find out from Mrs Chandler, or should I say Sister Chandler, whether you can come and see me this evening?"

"Of course, of course - but you've a lovely face."

"You only say that because it's true."

They laughed together, and Greta hurried away to tell her mother of the change in plans. After a short silence between them, Cecely asked,

"You are not getting too serious with John are you dear?"

"By that question, my dear mother, do you mean am I sleeping with him?"

"Greta, where on earth can you have learnt to say a thing like that?"

"The sixth form at Benenden, mother, dear, has left me with no lack of knowledge of anything to do with the designs and methods of operation of horny young men. However, I can assure you this learning is still in the theoretical stage, and is likely to remain so for some while yet, and that applies to most of them there. You see, if your eyes are fastened, or have been fastened by your family, on Sir Humphrey, or Lord Bedpost or whoever, the old virgo intacta bit is a must. Mind you, I have to say this, there are one or two, if what they tell us in vivid detail is true, are going to have to perform feats of considerable magic to pass the acid test on the wedding night. I think, in the main, this means getting the husband somewhat sloshed and secreting a small bottle of red ink under the pillow for subsequent use after the conjugal bit."

Cecely looked at her in astonishment.

"So that's what you girls talk about in the evenings is it?"

Greta thought for a moment.

"Afternoons and mornings as well, quite often," she paused for a moment. "But never in front of the children."

"Never in front of the children? Oh, my goodness. Well I can see I shall not have to explain to you 'The Facts of Life,' as it used to be so succinctly put in my day." Greta smiled, put her arm around her mother's waist and replied,

"Just remember, if you want to know anything, just ask. Anyway, I must ring Megan and find out visiting times. I go back to Benenden on the fourteenth, so I shall only have a few days."

Megan duly contacted, visiting hours given, Greta busied herself about the house, whilst Cecely made her way to 'Country Style' where she helped Mrs Draper out for part of the week. Country Style had been owned by David's first wife, Pat, who had been killed by enemy action a little over three years earlier.

Moira, Jack Hooper's wife, went back to her War Department office on Thursday, having had two days off after New Year's Day.

On Friday evening she came home before Jack arrived from Short's at Rochester, where he was the chairman and, at present, managing director as well. She poured herself a large scotch mixed with a modicum of soda, to find, as she went to drink it, her chauffeur driven husband arrive. Jack bustled in, followed by Harold the chauffeur carrying his briefcase and a large box of documents of some sort.

"Hallo, what's all this? Do you see this, Harold, secret drinking at six o'clock in the afternoon?"

Harold smiled. "Good evening, m'lady." Harold was always precise in addressing Sir Jack and his wife. "Will that be all, Sir Jack?"

"Yes, thank you - shan't need you until Monday."

"Right. Good evening, sir, good evening, m'lady."

Harold departed, Jack turned to Moira.

"I suspect you have something to tell me."

"Yes, my love. I have to go to America again, probably for six months."

"When?"

"At the end of this month. We shall be flying."

"Is it to do ....?"

"Yes."

Jack was referring to a project he knew she had been on through a large part of the war. What he didn't know, and what she had suffered constant torment in not being able to discuss with him, was that she was one of a very small number of people involved in the atom bomb programme, already having visited the site out in the Nevada desert on two occasions for six months on each occasion. Knowing the immensity of the horror of this weapon, she had had to live year after year in the knowledge that the Germans, or the Russians, could be a month ahead of the combined US/British team. That thought was the subject of nightmares.

He hugged her up. "I shall miss you terribly again. Let's hope it will be the last time."

"I think it may well be."

It was the first time she had ever ventured a comment of any sort in respect of the work in which she was involved. He made no reply.

On Saturday evening they all met up at Chandlers Lodge.

"Got to cheer Fred up now he's been deserted," Jack boomed.

On that day the government announced the scale of devastation to private dwellings during the war. Four hundred and fifty five thousand houses had been destroyed and were uninhabitable; another four million had been damaged.

"When you think what that means in the loss of goods and chattels, precious family heirlooms and things of that nature, it makes you wonder how people will ever recover," Jack sighed.

"And with these V2s coming in thick and fast it's not over yet," Fred added. Nor was it. December '44 casualties had numbered 367 killed - 111 men, 192 women, and 64 children with another 847 seriously injured.

It was a gloomy evening, despite the hangover of the good news from the New Year, and the positive benefit of the Whitbreads Light Ale from under the stairs. However, the gloom did not extend to Sandbury Cottage Hospital where a delicately made-up Greta was shown into a side ward - the very same side ward David had occupied when he had been battered by the farm bull as a boy many years earlier - by Sister Megan. She chastely kissed John in front of the sister, and as Megan turned to leave John asked,

"Sister, could you lock the door behind you?" Megan gave the request some thought.

"How then would your visitor be able to leave?"

"That's the general idea."

"Any more bright ideas like that, my lad, and I'll move you into the men's ward. Oh, and don't forget I can see through the Venetian blinds on this side." She continued, addressing Greta, "You know, that used to be one of Harry's stock jokes. He used to say that Venetian blinds were the greatest invention ever. If it had not been for Venetian blinds it would have been curtains for everybody."

The three laughed together.

"I wonder what Harry is doing now," Greta meditated.

"It's the middle of the night there, so unless Chantek is digging her claws into his back, he will be fast asleep."

"Isn't it wonderful to have such a close association with a huge, beautiful wild animal like that?"

"Yes, and what a wrench it is going to be when he has to leave her to come home. It will break her heart to leave him; he at least has all of us to look forward to being with again."

"Do you know," Greta suggested, "I only knew Harry for a short while, but I wouldn't mind betting he will try and bring her home. What are the regulations for keeping a pet like that, do you know?"

"No, I'm afraid I don't and it frightens the life out of me to think about it. Anyway, get on with your visiting, and don't worry about the venetian blinds."

She gave the cord a tug and the blinds snapped shut. She smiled at them and left.

The snogging session John had envisaged prior to Greta's visit was not effected as competently as he would have liked, in that if she hugged him, she pressed on lacerations endeavouring to heal, which made him wince. On the other hand, if he stretched his arms to any extent, this in turn affected other injuries on his shoulders.

"If you were to lie flat, I could stretch out on top of you. That way you wouldn't have to move at all," she suggested.

"The very thought of that has started a certain movement already," he replied. She looked at him in feigned innocence.

"Mr Power, what do you mean?"

"Give me your hand and I'll show you."

It was just as well that the door opened and Megan appeared.

"You've more visitors," she said, as Ernie and Anni appeared, Ernie sheltering a half pint bottle of light ale in one inside pocket and a half pint glass in another. The days when one took grapes to anyone in hospital were long gone.

"Any news of David?" John asked.

"The news tonight said the 6th Airborne Division was fighting on the right flank of the Americans," Ernie replied, "but how old that information might be is anyone's guess."

The five minute bell rang prompting Anni to say, "Well, we'll be away and leave you two love-birds to say goodnight," and with that they departed with a 'thanks for the beer,' following them from the room.

As Greta walked back to The Bungalow, she mulled over the incident of 'the hand.' Up until now John had been what would be described in 'Peg's Paper' as a perfect gentleman. Although his prowess in the kissing stakes was in division one, which had sometimes produced results in the seventeen-year-old she had only known about through hearsay at her sixth form soirees, he had always thus far kept his hands to himself. A groper he was not. 'Oh well,' she told herself, 'no harm done,' and then, 'I wonder what it would have been like.' She gave a little shudder. Perhaps it was the cold night air, perhaps it wasn't.

The next two weeks passed very slowly for both Fred and Jack, Fred for obvious reasons, Jack because Moira, having to prepare for her six-month assignment in America, was working all hours in London to clear up matters in which she was involved there. They no longer had the evening Home Guard parades to attend. That left a gap in their social lives, since whilst Home Guard duty was a very serious business, or so they assured any who queried the fact, the drink or two in The Angel after parade had become part of the proceedings.

On the second Wednesday, Jack called in at Chandlers Lodge.

"Moira has to stay over tonight at Horse Guards," he told Fred, "why don't we have a trip over to the Prince of Orange at Mountfield? I've got some petrol in Moira's car. She won't be needing it."

"That's not a bad idea. I'll ask Ernie if he would like to come."

At the Prince of Orange they were welcomed like royalty, it having been nearly two years since they were last there. The pub was at the end of the lane in which was the farm where the Chandlers lived before their removal to Sandbury. Nothing had changed. The same faces, the same leg-pulling, even the same dart board, now very much the worse for wear.

"What's this we hear about you getting married again, Fred?"

"Getting married? Who the devil would have him?"

"Come on Fred. We hear it's an American lady and far too good for you."

They paused for a reply from a bemused Fred, and a laughing Jack and Ernie.

"Well, it's quite true, and if you promise to behave yourselves I will bring her over one evening to meet you all."

"Give Jimmy notice of that," little Mick Travers suggested, "he'll put a clean shirt on for a change."

They turned their attention to Jack.

"We hear you're a 'sir' now Jack, is that right?"

"That's right, Jimmy, but I haven't let it go to my head. You can still buy me a drink."

"And what about this OBE you've got, Fred?"

"Other Bugger's Efforts," Fred replied.

"Yes, that's what everybody says, but that Military Medal you got wasn't," Frank Lovell, the landlord chimed in. "Did you know he had an M.M. from the first lot?" he asked the customers in general.

They had a great evening. The regulars and Frank Lovell made them very welcome, Maureen, Frank's wife, even bringing out hot sausage rolls for the assembled company prompting the inevitable comment,

"Christ, Fred, you can come over every night. Maureen only does that if sir Oliver turns up, and he hasn't done that for ten years or more." Sir Oliver Routledge was the local squire and biggest landowner for miles around.

So their evening out broke the week up, and on Saturday a telephone call from Margaret told Fred she would be released on Friday 26th January and would arrive at Sandbury on the 4.22 train. In the meantime she would send some luggage on by Carter Patterson. In the event she nearly didn't arrive. Her friends and colleagues had arranged to give her a going away party on the Saturday evening after her telephone call to Fred. Rocket bombs, the V2s, had been arriving in London with awful regularity, a total of 220 to arrive in January alone.

The venue for the party was a restaurant in Richmond, on the banks of the Thames, a mustering point cultivated by US Army middle ranking officers over the past three years, now seeing its clientele being rapidly depleted as staff personnel were moved to the continent. As Margaret and three of her friends were driven through Chiswick there was an enormous explosion. The heavy Dodge in which they were travelling was literally lifted off the ground and moved laterally fifteen feet on to the forecourt of, of all places, a funeral parlour. The driver in the meantime was furiously applying the footbrake, not realising that for that action to be effective, the wheels had to be in contact with the ground which at this stage they certainly were not. By great good fortune the vehicle stayed more or less upright, hit the ground with a resounding bump and ran forward to demolish a waist high wall. Miraculously, all the glass remained intact and no-one was hurt other than one girl bumping her head rather hard. The driver, a young man from the mid-west, applied his hand brake, sat back, and announced, "For my next trick ....."

When they looked over to their right some 250 yards away they could see where the bomb had landed, hitting the end of a block of flats, leaving sitting rooms, kitchens and bedrooms exposed to the cold January evening.

"What do we do now, ma'am?" the young driver asked Margaret.

"Well, first of all, can you reverse out of this wall and get back on to the road, do you reckon?"

The driver, keeping his fingers crossed that the darned thing would even start - it had stalled on hitting the wall - pressed the button. No problem. It roared into life, the Dodge was built like a battleship. Gradually he eased it back out of the pile of rubble, cringing at the sound of the crackling of glass being further pulverised by his tyres, (or should we say tires?) glass which until a few minutes ago had been the forefront of the funeral parlour, glass which until only a few weeks ago had been covered in criss-cross adhesive paper, untouched throughout the blitz and the subsequent VIs, now lying in shards all over the forecourt.

With the aid of a couple of three-point turns they found themselves back on the highway. As they regained the road a police car came along side.

"You alright, sir?"

The car being a left-hand drive, Margaret wound her window down to answer the enquiry.

"Yes, we are all uninjured, thank you very much for stopping."

"Well, can I suggest you take that chunk of lamp post off the canopy of your truck? It was a good job it must have been horizontal when it hit you. If it had come straight down one of you could well have copped it."

Margaret and the driver jumped out of the cab to examine the piece of street furniture with which they had been decorated. They found a piece of tubular steel about seven feet long positioned almost diagonally across the canvas roof, the roof supports having prevented its penetrating the interior. It must have hit them during the noise and confusion of their ramming the wall. Margaret and the driver lifted it off. It was not heavy; it is surprising how lightly made lamp posts are.

"What shall we do with it?" Margaret asked the policeman in all innocence.

"Since you're a lady, I won't tell you," the copper laughingly replied, as they drove away.

They made their way over Kew Bridge to Richmond, where they arrived covered in dust, with a story that would be told and retold by the people there for years in many parts of the United States.

A story which frightened the life out of Fred when she recounted it to him the following day.

* * *

Chapter Two

When Nigel Coates and his brother Judge Charles were interned in Singapore in early 1942 they managed to keep together. After two or three months they were put to work clearing the bomb damage in Singapore City, then an assortment of tasks extending the airfield at Kranji and elsewhere. At the end of the year three hundred of them were marched to the docks at Keppel Harbour, crammed into the hold of a very old and rusty tramp steamer, to set sail they knew not where into the teeth of a tropical storm only one stage removed from a typhoon.

For three days they were brutally tossed about. The conditions were indescribable. The hatch covers could not be removed because of the storm, the temperature in the hold with the ship being only a degree or two from the equator was well up in the nineties, after a day and a half the drinking water ran out, they received no food. Combined with there being no sanitation, everyone being violently sick, three hundred people packed into a space in which one hundred would have been crowded, the weaker ones began to die.

As the storm blew itself out so the prisoners became aware the engines had stopped, a factor which added to their misery, since without power the ship was being bobbed around like a cork in the seas heaving from the results of the typhoon. On the fourth day the Japanese guards, themselves having been prostrated by the brutal weather, threw back the hatch cover to begin the task of sorting the dead from the living and heaving them overboard. Nearly a third were disposed of in this manner.

During all this time Charles and Nigel had wedged themselves in against one of the ribs of the ship. Although both had been violently ill, at least being out of the main crush they had not suffered the emissions from their companions to any great extent.

"What do you think has happened?" Nigel asked his brother.

"I'll ask Mac," Charles replied.

'Mac' - Captain Graham MacDonald was one of the very few who had not been violently ill, although despite his forty years at sea he had come very close to it - readily had the answer.

"The prop shaft has been bent in the storm. I imagine the propeller itself has lost a blade, possibly two. There is nothing they can do about it even if they have a spare propeller, which on an old tub like this would be unlikely."

Charles thought for a moment.

"And what happens if a Yankee submarine spots a sitting Jap duck through his periscope?"

"The answer to that my friend is, you won't know much about it."

For two days they bobbed about, the sea gradually becoming calmer. On the third day they heard the throb of engines nearby, a great deal of megaphone-type shouting in the shrill, throaty voices of the two crews, and in an hour or so the ship began to move forward, obviously under tow since no engines were running.

Charles' immediate comment on this situation was, 'the Yanks could get two for the price of one at this rate.'

The Jap soldiers had left the hatch cover off despite the occasional bursts of rain, a circumstance welcomed by those in the hold underneath the hatch as an opportunity to get clean, or at least, cleaner, swapping places with others so that each had a turn in the improvised shower.

"From the way we are heading, and from where I guess we were before the storm I reckon they are towing us to the Philippines," was Mac's view.

He was spot on. They originally had been scheduled to be sent, among hundreds of thousands of other civilians and POWs, to Japan to work as slave labour. The ship that had taken them in tow was heading for Manila, and that was how they ended up in that mass of islands known as the Philippines.

After landing at Manila in February 1943 they were put on to barges and towed south to the island of Mindoro where their first task was to build their own camp. That completed, they were put to work improving the very poor west coast road, never a main highway, now being attended to by American bombers at regular intervals.

Both Nigel and Charles had bouts of illness during 1944 - who didn't? - but although Charles was the older of the two, in his late forties, he seemed to be able to combat the various diseases they suffered better than Nigel, until as we have already noted, at the beginning of 1945, Nigel died. Charles and Mac buried him and put a simple bamboo cross at his head, to join a veritable forest of crosses which was beginning to grow there.

On the 15th of December the Americans landed on Mindoro. Three days after Nigel's death they overran the camp, the Japanese having retreated on to Luzon to make a last stand there, taking only American POWs with them, leaving civilians behind.

Speedily, American field hospitals were set up and the civilians treated for their diseases and disorders, and gradually brought back to being able to eat nourishing food again. At the end of January, a hospital ship, laden with wounded from the ongoing attack on Luzon, took Charles and Mac and some fifty other civilians aboard, and sailed for Brisbane, in Queensland, Australia. On the 8th of February they found themselves in a requisitioned hotel on the banks of the River Brisbane.

They had survived.

* * *

Chapter Three

John Power was discharged from hospital on the same day as Greta went back to Benenden. He was to be 'on the panel,' still off sick for two weeks, during which time he decided to go home to Hampshire with his parents. When he returned to Betteshanger he was given an office job for the time being, which meant he did an eight to five stint, no shift work. He came back to Sandbury on Saturday and Sunday, when again he met up with Greta, but there was no further familiarity of the description in evidence during that visit to the Sandbury Hospital side ward. Greta was a bit undecided as to whether she was sorry or not at this state of affairs.

On Wednesday 31st January the telephone shrilled at Fred's elbow.

"Major Coulter on the line, Mr Chandler."

"Thank you, Miss Russell."

"Fred, dear, my discharge is now on 7th February."

"That's a week today."

"Yes. Apparently the hold up was due to some papers being lost." She had originally been told her release date would be 26th of January. "So I will be on the 4.22 as before. Did the Carter Patterson stuff arrive?"

"Yes, two suitcases. I opened them but couldn't find any money in them."

"They were locked."

"I know, I had a lot of trouble with one of them."

"What about the box?"

"There has been no box."

"Oh well, it was sent two days after the suitcases so it will probably turn up soon." There was a silence for a few seconds. "Fred, darling, I am so looking forward to being with you."

"And I with you, my love. We must fix the date as soon as possible."

"Can't it be sooner than that?"

Fred met Margaret off the 4.22 on the 7th. They went into a huddle that evening, telephoned Canon Rosser at nine o'clock asking him if they could be married on Thursday afternoon 15th February at three o'clock. It would be a quiet wedding with just family and a few friends present, the organ but no choir, and a reception at The Angel. In the event, the word got around quickly and despite it being a Thursday afternoon, the church was crowded with Rotary friends, and others, including the Earl and Gloria, Dr and Mrs Carew and Lady Earnshaw. The bride was given away by Sir Jack, and Ernie, to his great pleasure, was asked to be best man.

The newly-weds stayed in London overnight before going on to Ramsford Grange, to which the Earl had invited them for their honeymoon. Fred had had a few qualms about the wedding night. This was to be the first instance of real intimacy between them. He was very conscious of their age difference. He realised he no longer had the body of a young Adonis, although to be fair he was trimly built. But at sixty-four you can't look twenty-four and he had a certain anxiety about that fact. Nevertheless, he was a practised lover, a quality which he now executed with tenderness, leading to excitement, leading to passion, then to complete fulfilment, a physical state until now not having been experienced by Margaret. As she lay, breathing great breaths of satisfaction against Fred's chest, she said,

"That has never happened to me before. Oh, Fred, you are a wonderful, wonderful man."

Fred held her close.

Twelve thousand miles away in Brisbane it was ten o'clock on a very hot, humid, Friday morning as Charles made his way to the local agents of the Hong Kong and Shanghai Bank. He asked to see the manager, told him of his release from internment and was made very very welcome indeed. He had had a substantial account with the bank in Kuala Lumpur prior to the invasion, along with a considerable sum on deposit at Coutts in London.

"Now, Judge, how can I help, apart from ready cash of course, which I will arrange straight away, along with a cheque book."

"You are a very trusting sort of a chap, if I may say so," Charles replied, smiling at the middle-aged, well-tonsured gentleman on the other side of the desk, who it must be said, had already checked on the visitor before arrival, in the pre-war Straits 'Who's Who,' to find his bankers were in fact HK and S. The gentleman in question shrugged his shoulders deprecatorily as much as to say 'think nothing of it,' when all the time he was batting on a pretty sound wicket. As you may be vaguely aware, Australians do play a type of cricket.

Charles signed a few forms, like most people going to a bank being only vaguely aware of what they were all for, shook hands with his new friend and left to make his second call.

His solicitors in London before his incarceration were Haskins and Wise, in EC1. He knew they had been bombed in the blitz and had moved, but could not remember their new address. However, he did remember their cable address, which he had used on numerous occasions, and assumed this would remain the same no matter where their new premises might be situated. He therefore made his way to Cable and Wireless (Australia) Ltd offices only a short distance away having been directed by his new bank manager.

"Ask for Bluey Rogers, he's a friend of mine."

Bluey turned out to be a carbon copy of his friend at HK and S.

"G'day, how can I help you?"

"I would like to send a cable to my solicitors in London and have them reply here. Would that be possible?"

"Sure thing. Here's the pad. Do you know their cable address?"

"Yes, it's HASWISE.LDN."

"Right, scribble away."

Charles then realised he had not written anything of consequence for three years. Getting his thoughts into action, his words into some sort of compact order, and getting them on to the form, one word in each block, presented him with a challenge he was unable to overcome. Bluey looked at him.

"Having trouble, mate?"

"I've just come out of a Jap camp. I can't seem to get my thoughts organised."

"Jesus Christ, mate, how long were you there?"

"Three years."

"Bloody hell. Here, come through here."

He lifted a flap on the counter and led Charles through into an interview room, other staff behind the counter looking on with curiosity.

"Look, if you tell me what you want to say, I'll draft it out for you."

Charles looked at him, and then felt himself brimming with tears. Bluey remained silent. Charles put his head on his arms on the table at which he had been seated and sobbed and sobbed. The recognition of his weakness, the fact that he was starting the procedure to tell Nigel's family they no longer had a husband and father, the fact that they had had to bury Nigel without even a blanket to wrap him in, all came back after weeks of bottling it all in. In a little while he became quiet.

"I'm sorry about that. My brother died just a few days before the Americans rescued us on Mindoro. I have to break the news to his wife and family in England."

"Well, it won't hurt to wait a few more minutes. Let me get you some tea or coffee, then we can draft something out."

"You're very kind. Thank you, coffee would be very acceptable." Bluey went to the door.

"Marlene, get us two coffees will you, there's a pet?"

The coffee and accompanying biscuits dealt with, they got down to business again.

"I want Haskins and Wise to try and find my sister in law, Cecely Coates. The only lead I have is a family in Sandbury, Kent, named Chandler. I can't remember the father's name, but the mother was Ruth. Not much to go on I'm afraid, but if they can't find them from a directory they must employ an enquiry agent to track them down, always assuming they haven't been killed in the bombing of course. From what I've read in the past two weeks that corner of England is getting a real pasting from the flying bombs and rockets."

"Right, let's make a start." Bluey started to write on the squares-covered pad.

HASWISE LDN.
MESSAGE FROM JUDGE CHARLES COATES MALAYA STOP PLEASE
LOCATE CECELY COATES STOP LAST KNOWN CONTACT RUTH
CHANDLER SANDBURY KENT STOP USE ALL MEANS STOP REPLY
C AND W BRISBANE STOP

"That OK, Judge?" Charles examined the written form.

"That's fine, Mr Rogers."

"Oh, no misters here, Judge, Bluey's the name."

Charles smiled. He was not used to smiling; he had had little reason to smile for a long time.

"In which case, no Judges here, Bluey, Charles is the name."

They laughed together, again an activity on Charles' part which had received little practice for, it seemed, as long as he could remember. Bluey pushed a button and Marlene returned.

"Get that off straight away, Marlene, will you, please?" Bluey turned to Charles.

"Now, all things being equal, since it's more or less midday here, that should be on their desk when they get in this morning. That gives them a whole day to try and get some information and get it on the wire back to us for tomorrow morning. Now, where are you staying?" Charles told him.

"Look, why don't you come out to my place for the weekend. We can phone the office in the morning, or they can phone us if they've got a reply. You'll be a lot more comfortable out there with my lot than in that hotel on your own."

"With your lot?"

"Well, we've got a biggish property. I've got two daughters in their early twenties and three teenage boys. My wife will be delighted to have you. We don't meet many English people; those that came out before the war are more Australian than we old stagers. And I promise I'll not let the lads pump you about the bloody Japs, so how about it?"

"You really are very kind, Bluey, you really are."

"Think nothing of it, mate. After all you've been through, nothing's too good for you." Charles came close to having another weep. Only a severely bitten lower lip and considerable willpower prevented it.

"Right then. I'll pick you up at four o'clock." They shook hands and Charles made his way back to the hotel, on the way having the remembrance of mind, if there is such a condition, to buy a nice bunch of flowers, their stems wrapped in a wet cloth in a waterproof bag, which he plunged into the sink in his room until he was ready to leave.

A little after four o'clock Bluey arrived.

"Blimey, you going to get me a bad name?" he joked with Charles.

"How do you mean, Bluey?"

"Well, you taking flowers home. If I took flowers home one of two things would happen. Either the roof would fall in or my wife would think I'd been out with another Sheila." They laughed together for the second time that day, as they climbed into Bluey's Ford V8 Pilot for the journey to Hamilton.

The family were all gathered to meet Bluey and their guest when they arrived. They were exactly what one would imagine to be a typical Australian family. Each one tanned, lithe, open faced, totally unpretentious without being disrespectful in any way. The house was a typical twenties Queensland single storied dwelling. Built in the days before air conditioning, it was raised on piles some five feet off the ground, provided with a veranda on the front and two sides, and beautifully proportioned. Being raised as it was, the air coming in off the river (they were only a few hundred yards on the uplands overlooking the River Brisbane) wafted beneath the flooring. This kept the living quarters cool, even if the space was sometimes invaded by one or another of those long limbless reptiles of the suborder 'Opidia' - snakes to you, of which Queensland has more than its fair share.

Bluey made the introductions. "My wife Jean, eldest girl Rhona, next Thelma. These two are getting married soon."

"Yea, Rhona to a Yank and Thelma to a blooming Pom," interrupted the thirteen-year-old Hector, known as Sandy for patently obvious reasons.

"Then we've got Jim, he's eighteen and goes in the air force for air crew training at the end of the month, and last the brains of the family Donald, known as Don."

"Like Don Bradman," chimed in Sandy.

"Who's Don Bradman?" Charles asked with a perfectly straight face.

"You never heard of Don Bradman?" Sandy almost shrieked the question.

"What does he do, is he a film star or something?"

All the others were smiling at this badinage from Charles, the oldest one there, to the youngest.

"No, he's a famous cricketer."

"Oh? Who does he play for?"

"Australia of course."

"Do they play cricket in Australia?" the 'play' heavily emphasised. Sandy looked at the rest of the family.

"He's having me on, ain't he?"

Automatically his mother reprimanded him.

"Don't say ain't." Well, mothers do, don't they?

Charles put his arm round young Sandy's shoulder.

"Only a little bit."

"You had me going there for a minute, Charles."

"Heh, not so much of the Charles, Judge to you," Bluey reminded him.

"No, please, I would rather be Charles to all of you if I may."

Sandy had now got the bit firmly between his teeth.

"You're a Judge, Charles? Like, sentencing people to be hanged and all that?"

"That's enough from you, young man," Bluey intervened. "Charles is here for a rest for the weekend, so you stop badgering him."

But Charles didn't feel badgered. It was his first experience of family life for over three years of absolute hell, of death, of disease, of filth, brutality, degradation and despair. Again the evidence before him of what life should be, and should have been like, brought a lump to his throat. Sandy looked up at him.

"Sorry," he said. Charles, with his arm still resting on Sandy's shoulders gave him a little hug.

"You can badger me all you like," he smiled at the freckled faced youngster.

They had drinks on the veranda, then dinner. Charles had warned Bluey that he was still unable to eat the sort of full meal to which they were all accustomed, which brought the inevitable comment from Sandy,

"Blimey, I used to eat more than that when I was five."

"One more rude remark like that, my lad, and I'll wallop you, big as you are."

Sandy looked somewhat crestfallen at being reprimanded in front of guests. He hadn't really considered he was being rude in any way, he had merely stated a fact. After a moment's gloom he grinned, looked at Charles and told him,

"He would have to catch me first," which had everyone laughing, including Bluey.

At seven o'clock the next morning the phone rang. The duty man at C & W reported a cable had come in for the Judge.

"Read it over will you, Jimmy?"

"It reads:

TO JUDGE CHARLES COATES STOP WELCOME BACK STOP SINCERE
GREETINGS ALL PARTNERS HASWISE STOP CECELY COATES AT
THE BUNGALOW SANDBURY KENT STOP AWAIT FURTHER
INSTRUCTIONS STOP WISE

Did you get all that, Bluey?"

"Loud and clear, Jimmy, as they say on the American films."

"Don't talk to me about the bloody Yanks; they smashed another shop front down here last night."

Brisbane was the Pacific Command centre of General MacArthur; as a result it was crowded with American troops and marines either stationed in the HQ or in transit to and from the various island fronts to the north. There was a great deal of hostility between local Aussies and the Americans, punch-ups resulting in many cases in the destruction of property as reported by Jimmy. There was a large contingent of Negro troops south of the river, mainly construction battalions. They were not allowed over the river into the town centre otherwise the problem would have been worse, as happened many times in the UK when white and black US troops were stationed near to each other.

Charles studied Bluey's handwriting.

"Shall I give you half an hour to compose a message, Charles?"

"Yes, please do, it's not going to be easy. You see, Bluey, my brother Nigel, Cecely's husband, died in the camp on New Years' Day. She will not have heard anything from him or about him for nearly three years, so she's probably been living in hope all that time. Now I'm the one who has to break the news to her and the children."

"The children?"

"Yes, Greta and Oliver. Greta's now, let's see, around seventeen, Oliver nineteen. I expect he will have joined up, knowing him. God, this is going to crucify all of them. They were a very, very close family."

"What about your family, Charles? I'm sorry; I didn't mean to ask questions."

"I have no family. I'm the bachelor uncle."

He stared into the distance.

"Why the hell couldn't the Good Lord have taken me and left Nigel?"

There was silence between them for a short while, broken by Bluey.

"I'll leave you to it and bring you in some coffee. There's writing paper on the side, there."

"Thank you, Bluey, you're a gem, you really are."

Charles, in his professional life, had been well acquainted with summing up reams of evidence into a few easily understood paragraphs for the benefit of a jury. The fact he was presently out of practice did nothing to help his need to tell his sister-in-law her husband was dead in the form of a cable, which did not allow for extended prose. He found difficulty in starting the message, difficulty in presenting the crux of the message, and difficulty in ending the message without it seeming abrupt. Several sheets of paper ended in the bin before he settled on what he hoped was a combination of fact and sorrow.

CECELY COATES STOP THE BUNGALOW STOP SANDBURY STOP KENT

STOP UK STOP AM LIBERATED STOP SADLY INFORM YOU NIGEL DIED

JANUARY 45 STOP WRITING IMMEDIATELY STOP DEEPEST SYMPATHY

LOVE GRETA OLIVER YOURSELF STOP CHARLES

Bluey came in with the coffee.

"Finished?"

"I don't think I could do better, Bluey. The fact that sickens me is the impact it's going to have on those people back there in Kent. They've lived in hope all these years only to be struck down when things look to be going our way."

"Well, if you're sure, I'll get it sent."

"It's Saturday today."

"C & W work twenty-four hours a day every day. That doesn't mean it will be sent straight away. There's a queuing system and the diplomatic people and the military take priority. Some cables have to wait a day or more. You were lucky when you cabled Haswise."

"Well, next week I am going to have to see how I can get to England, there will be so much to sort out. I shall be seeing my friend Mac on Monday; he will probably have an answer or point me in the right direction."

Charles thoroughly enjoyed his weekend, except for one small incident. On Saturday evening Rhona's Yankee fiancé arrived to take her to the Saturday night dance at Cloudland, a dance hall up in the hills, patronised mainly by Americans since they had petrol in abundance when it was strictly rationed to Australian civilians. It is well known that American service men in all war theatres were possessed of a ratio of one vehicle per man along with the necessary fluid with which to propel it.

Back to Rhona's escort.

We have already noted that Charles in his professional life had been adept at summing up evidence. He further had learnt many years ago not to judge an accused, or a witness, by his or her appearance. Even a narrow-eyed, scruffily dressed, smelly individual could well be telling the truth whereas an open-faced, well spoken, immaculately turned out person could be the biggest crook unhung. One went entirely by the evidence.

Rhona's escort, a Navy Lieutenant, was impeccably clad in white drill, his voice equable, his appearance prepossessing, yet Charles, contravening all his previous precepts, took an instant dislike to him. Bluey introduced him.

"Scott, this is Charles, Charles Scott Eberhardt."

The American shook hands, somewhat limply Charles considered, and immediately asked,

"And what do you do, sir?"

Charles was a little taken aback at the bluntness of the enquiry.

"Well, at the moment, nothing I'm afraid."

"Everybody should be doing something in time of war, even older people, sir. No one should be allowed to shirk."

"Yes, I suppose so."

Bluey, who had turned away to get the three of them a drink, heard the tail end of the exchange.

"What's he telling you Charles?"

"Your future son-in-law has firm ideas on the desirability of labour."

"I would call it duty, not desirability," the Lieutenant pronounced. At this Rhona appeared and took him away. Bluey looked at Charles.

"He having a go at you?"

"He asked what I did. I told him 'nothing at present,' hence the lecture."

"Rhona thinks the sun shines out of his fundamental orifice, we all think he's a pompous shit. To hear him talk he and General MacArthur have won the war for us, yet he's been stationed here in Brisbane since he was commissioned a year ago, he's never seen a shot, or a torpedo, fired in anger. We just work on the premise that one day Rhona will cotton on to what he really is, and nylons or no nylons tell him to sod off!"

The next morning the family went to church. Although not a Catholic, Charles went with them and offered a prayer for Cecely, Greta and Oliver in their great sadness. As they were leaving the church, Sandy sidled up to Charles and asked,

"What did you think of Scott?"

"What is it our American cousins say? I'll take the Fifth Amendment on that one."

"My dad thinks he's a right shit."

"You've just been to church!"

Sandy thought for a moment.

"Yea, I know. But he's still a right shit." Charles smiled as they walked home together.

* * *

Chapter Four

It was just after eight o'clock on the morning of the 20th of February as Cecely was leaving the warmth of her electric fire in the bathroom, she heard the doorbell ringing. Hurrying through the unheated passageway in The Bungalow, dressed only in her pyjamas and dressing-gown, she unbolted, then unlocked the door to find a telegram boy standing on the freezing doorstep. He handed her a cable.

"Come inside for a moment, you must be frozen." Although the snow had more or less cleared, it was bitterly cold. She opened the cable, worrying if it was bad news of Oliver in France, then immediately remembering bad news of casualties always come in small buff coloured envelopes. This was larger and had 'Cable and Wireless' printed all over it.

The telegram boy waited patiently. He had been carrying out this duty for over a year now and was well used to judging the contents of the message his small envelopes contained by the first changes on the face of the recipient. Despite his youth he had experienced everything from supreme happiness through to frenzied hysterics resulting from his handing over his innocent looking missives. He watched carefully, to see Cecely reach out and hold on to the hall-stand. He waited a short while.

"Will there be a reply, madam?"

Cecely looked at him blankly.

"Reply? Oh no, there will be no reply."

There was a sprinkling of loose change on the small sunken tray on the hall-stand. She picked up a shilling and gave it to the lad.

"No, there will be no reply," she repeated, as she handed him the coin.

"Thank you very much, madam, good morning madam."

She walked into the only other warm room in the bungalow, the kitchen, and sank down at the table. She put her head on her hands, but strangely did not cry. Not yet. Later, yes, she cried and cried. Her first thoughts were for Greta and Oliver. 'I must phone Benenden straight away' she resolved, 'and then the shop.'

She booked a call to the school. The bursar answered.

"Mr Kimber, this is Mrs Coates. I have just received a cable that Greta's father has died in the Japanese camp. Can you please tell her, and ask her to come home straight away?"

"Mrs Coates, please accept our sincere condolences. How terrible for you. I will get the Head and Reverend Thomas to tell her, and I will bring her home in my car myself. Will she be coming back here?"

"Oh, I am sure she will, Mr Kimber, in a little while."

"Then I should be with you mid-morning."

"Thank you so much, you are so kind."

Next she phoned a shocked Rose, asking her not to tell her father, Fred being on his honeymoon, but asking her to tell the rest of the extended family. She then booked a call to Lord Ramsford, only to be told, when eventually it was received, that the Brigadier was away for a few days and could not be contacted. A message would be given him to contact her immediately he returned. She then composed a short letter to Oliver to tell him the tragic news. She had virtually completed this when the telephone shrilled, making her jump.

"Mrs Coates? Canon Rosser here. I've just heard your bad news from Rose. Can I be of help in any way? Mrs Rosser asked me to say how terribly sorry she is."

"I don't think there is anything anyone can do, vicar, but I do so much appreciate your getting in touch. I think eventually I would like to hold a memorial service for Nigel. He was a wonderful man, and we shall never have a grave to visit. What wicked, wicked people those Japanese are."

"I think it highly likely we have no inkling of the depths to which they have descended, but time will tell, time will tell."

Greta arrived soon after half past ten, tear stained and terribly upset. The separation from her father had only increased the great love she had for him all their years together. She, her mother knew, would be the one to be most devastated by the dreadful news.

Shortly after Greta's arrival the telephone rang again. It was Fred.

"Cecely, I've just heard your news. Gloria and the Earl are very upset and have asked me to tell you how sad they are for you."

"But how did you know? I asked Rose not to interrupt you on your honeymoon."

"Well, the plan slipped up. Rose phoned Ernie at the factory. Shortly after I telephoned Ernie to see everything was alright, and to tell him of someone coming to see me today, whose name I hadn't put in my diary, and he said how sad he and Anni were to hear your tragic news. That's how we all know about it. Now, is there anything we can do to help?"

"No, thank you, Fred. Greta has just arrived home." She went on to tell him of Charles being released and sending the cable. They would be waiting now to hear further from Charles by letter in due course, ending with, "There is nothing we can do, nothing to be done, we must just try to carry on as we have been these last three years." As a final thought she added, "Harry will be very sad, they were very good friends despite their short acquaintance."

Late on Monday evening, Mac called on Charles at his hotel in Brisbane.

"Do you still want to get back to UK, Charles?"

"I certainly do, Mac, I certainly do."

"Well, I've been talking to the agent who represents my old line. He tells me that the Berentia, a sizeable cargo ship which also takes half a dozen passengers is sailing tonight for Liverpool via Fremantle and Cape Town. There is a vacant berth due to the passenger who had it being taken with a heart attack on his way to the ship. So I took a chance and booked you in on it."

"But I couldn't possibly get to Sydney tonight."

"I know, but you could get to Fremantle by the time it gets there. It takes just over a week to go south around Tasmania, across The Bight to its first stop, another eight days to Cape Town, and probably ten or twelve, depending on the route, from Cape Town to Liverpool. The accommodation is not your Queen Mary class, you know, just ordinary ship's food."

"After what we've had in the camps I don't think I shall ever complain about food again."

"No, you're right there, my friend."

"Mac, I'm totally indebted to you. I don't know how I will ever repay you."

"The boot's on the other foot isn't it? If you hadn't looked after me as you did so many times on Mindoro, I wouldn't be here today."

They were silent for a few moments, each thinking of the hell they had left, and the hell many thousands of their compatriots were still suffering. Mac broke the silence.

"I'll take you to the agent in the morning to get the passage papers."

"Do you know what it will cost?"

"No idea. He will tell you. You give him a chit then you can pay our people in Leadenhall Street when you get to London."

"So now all I've to do is to find a way to get to Fremantle in a week or less. I will start on that first thing in the morning, and thank you my dear friend for all you've done."

Three days later Cecely received another cable.

WILL BE WITH YOU APPROX ONE MONTH STOP LOVE CHARLES

This news cheered her as nothing could have done - but how agonising it would be to have to wait four whole weeks or more for that phone call to say he had arrived.

* * *

Chapter Five

David and Paddy sat in their cold company headquarters a few hundred yards back from the fast flowing River Maas in Holland. After their caper in the Ardennes the division had been bussed up to the front between Roermond and Venlo. The weather was atrocious, cold, snowing and frequent fogs. Fortunately it was just as bad for the Jerries sitting on the other bank three or four hundred yards away. With the swollen river separating them the only action from them was a regular stonking from artillery and mortars, and periodic bursts of machine gun fire traversing B company front, with the same entertainment being provided from the Paras to enliven their days.

As a result, nobody on either side was able to move in the open during the day.

They had travelled up on 3rd January, had taken over their positions from some Jocks during the night, beginning their strange existence of sleeping during the day, apart from sentries, and carrying out patrols of the sodden river bank during the hours of darkness, which at this time of the year was from stand-to soon after four o'clock in the afternoon until eight o'clock the next morning.

When they had been there for four days the company field telephone rang for David to go back to battalion HQ to see the CO, Colonel Gillespie. A little after it got dark David got into a jeep with which his company had been issued, and was driven by Angus back to a monastery, now deserted by its former occupants, where the colonel had established his headquarters.

"David, come in. Sorry I haven't been down to see you yet. I've left you until last."

"Someone always has to be last, sir."

"Ah, but in this case that's a compliment, I don't have to worry much about your lot. Now I've got two jobs for you." He spread a map out on the table.

"I want you to send a subaltern and three men over the river to find out what is going on in that building you can see nestling behind the woods right in front of your position, and secondly to establish how deep that anti-tank ditch is which is shown on this aerial photo. Oh, and it would be nice to grab a prisoner if possible."

"I'll detail Roger Hammick on that one, sir."

"Good. I'll get the IO down to brief him tomorrow night; he can then go on the night after provided there is no fog. Now, the second job. I've to send a major back to Corps HQ to sit on a Field general Court Martial for up to three days. I would like you to go. Now I know you have no service dress here but you are to wear your decorations, do you understand? You are far less likely to be pushed around by those Corps HQ bullshitters if you are showing you have been around a bit." Hamish Gillespie was well aware of David's reluctance to show off his ribbons.

"So, take Angus with you. Come back here before it gets light, travel tomorrow in daylight and you will then get a night's sleep there before the trials."

"Do you know what's involved, sir?"

"Haven't a clue, somebody flogging the rations I suppose, in which case a good kick up the arse would be better than spending all that time on pseudo-legal business."

But the proceedings were to be infinitely more serious than flogging rations as David was to find out.

David and Angus travelled back to their company HQ in the battered farm buildings on the river bank. David sent a runner to get Roger and told him the IO would be down to brief him regarding the patrol, handed over to his second-in-command, and prepared himself to move out before daylight. Once they were clear of Battalion HQ they could travel in daylight. As he was making his final preparations Paddy came in.

"Where have you been?"

"I've been having a walk along the river bank, sir."

"You look as though you've been walking in the river."

"It was a bit damp in places, sir. You see, a couple of Jerry patrols came over at this point the week before we arrived. I wanted to make sure we had got our wire out properly. Their mortars have knocked it about a bit."

"Well, Mr Hammick has to take a patrol over to them, not tomorrow night, the night after."

"Right sir, can I go with him?"

"You can't swim."

"Jesus and Mary, they're not swimming over, sir, are they?"

"No, they are going in the standard canvas boat I presume, but it could always overturn, or get holed by a branch floating down, or be perforated by an MG42 by some hawk-eyed machine-gunner over there."

"You trying to put the wind up me, sir?"

"Yes."

"Well, you've done a bloody good job. OK if I go, sir?"

"OK by me if Mr Hammick will have you," but David knew there would be no-one in the battalion that Roger would like to have more.

Angus carefully unpacked David's best battledress and boots from his valise and laid them into a canvas travel bag along with a change of underclothing, socks and in particular a spare tie, just in case 'his officer happened to spill something down the one he was wearing.' David had always had a little giggle at this quirk, thinking that if Angus took it to extremes they would end up carrying a complete change of clothing.

They left at seven o'clock, and reported to the IO at battalion headquarters to get a map and reference point of Corps HQ where the court martial was to be held, a distance of some thirty miles. The roads were appalling. Not being main roads in the first place their foundations and subsequent top surfaces were designed to carry light vehicles and farm carts. After a few forty-ton Churchill tanks had traversed them they had completely collapsed in many places. Pioneer Corps men, along with Royal Engineers manning bulldozers, were hard at work on the worst sections; even so travel by any other vehicle than a jeep would have been extremely difficult. As it was the thirty miles took nearly three hours.

The building in which the Court Martial was to be held was previously a boarding school. David reported to the front office with Angus in tow and was told he was billeted in one of the staff bedrooms. Angus would be housed in a school-room now converted into a barrack room. Lunch was at 12.30, a meeting with the other members of the court-martial would be at 3pm in Room Six.

At 3pm David duly reported to Room Six as directed and found to his surprise four other officers already there. Most courts-martial only have three officers; in fact, for cases of a less serious nature only two officers need to be those sitting in judgement.

David saluted the senior officer - a full colonel.

"You are Major Chandler? Let me introduce you to the other members."

The colonel, covered in red tabs, introduced him to a lieutenant-colonel, another major and a captain.

"You are the senior of the two majors, I believe, Chandler. Therefore you vote in the middle."

The procedure at the end of a trial would be for the captain to vote 'guilty' or 'not guilty' first, followed by the others in order of seniority, this system designed to prevent any undue influence being exercised by senior officers on their juniors.

"Right then. We have two murders and a rape case to deal with. A civilian lawyer from the Judge Advocate General's office will be in attendance to advise us on points of law and improper procedure, but the guilty or not guilty decision is purely ours. I repeat, he is not judging the cases, we are. He may give advice on sentencing if we call for it; otherwise that too is our prerogative."

"Is there any appeal procedure, sir?" David asked.

"No. Our findings go to Army HQ where the sentences are confirmed or where they can be reduced. If we find the accused not guilty that cannot be overturned by higher authority under any circumstances. I don't doubt an appeals procedure will be instigated one day in line with civilian law, but it doesn't exist at present." The colonel was prescient in this belief. Six years later a serviceman was enabled to appeal against conviction on a point of law, but it was to be over fifty years before he could appeal against sentence.

David spent the remainder of the evening after an early dinner - 'Corps HQ certainly do a hell of a lot better than we do' being his comments in the letters he caught up on to Maria, Fred and Harry.

At 0945 hours in army language, he reported to the courtroom annexe. At 1000 hours he filed into the courtroom to sit at the left hand of the presiding officer, the JAG lawyer sitting on his right hand. The lawyer asked them to stand and repeat after him, each holding a Bible.

"I solemnly swear to well and truly try the accused. So help me God."

The first accused was marched in, escorted by two extremely bulky looking military policemen, and the trial began. Apparently the soldier in question had taken part in a running argument with another man in his unit at a time they had been withdrawn from the line. Evidence was given that their section corporal ordered them to cease, which they did until the corporal was called away. The accused then said, "Hiding under the skirts of the corporal now are you? Sure you haven't been giving him a bit of bum while nobody's looking?"

At this the victim flew at his tormentor, punching him hard in the stomach. As the latter doubled up he grabbed his bayonet lying on the bunk, swung it round and caught the victim in a deep and fatal cut across his neck. There was no doubt he had struck the blow, there having been a dozen witnesses to the incident. The court retired to the annexe and in a discussion which lasted nearly an hour concluded he was guilty of murder, the argument being mainly concerned with the question of intent on the part of the accused.

The colonel announced the verdict of 'guilty.' There was no plea of mitigation, evidence from all witnesses had shown that the accused started the argument and pursued it over several days. His defending officer was not a particularly forceful person.

He received the death sentence.

The next day the court resumed to try a second murder case. It boiled down to a simple case of a private soldier shooting his platoon officer. The defending officer in this case was a solicitor in civilian life, therefore infinitely more capable than the officer in case one, however it must be said that a top London barrister himself would have had difficulty in saving his client in the first trial.

The evidence, such as it was, relied on the fact that the officer had had a 'down' on the lance corporal accused for the past three weeks. In the snow and fog two weeks before, the two of them, along with four private soldiers, were on a night patrol to establish where the enemy lines were. The day before, after being reprimanded yet again by the lieutenant, the lance corporal was heard to say by several of his section, "I'll get that bastard one of these days." During the patrol the fog came down and they lost contact with each other for a short while, during which a shot rang out. They all hit the deck, and a little later, the fog lifting a little, they saw the lance corporal standing over the body of the lieutenant.

"He's been shot," said the lance corporal, "he's as dead as a dodo." There was no sympathy in his voice whatsoever.

"We'll carry him back."

The evidence showed:

1) There was only one shot.

2) The bullet had hit the officer's head, had passed through, and was therefore not recoverable.

3) The lance corporal's rifle was not checked until the next day by which time it had been cleaned.

4) The only person near the officer was the lance corporal.

5) The other members of the patrol gave widely different views on from which direction the shot came.

6) The medical officer could not give an authoritative view of the distance the shot was fired from its target, nor the size of the bullet which caused the fatality.

They broke for lunch, heard two more witnesses and closing speeches from the prosecuting and defending officers.

The prosecuting officer made a lengthy and somewhat histrionic speech, which when boiled down proved the lance corporal was clearly guilty since:

1) He had previously made threats regarding the officer and that he would 'get that bastard.' He therefore had the motive.

2) He had been in close proximity to the officer, with no other witnesses nearby. He therefore had the opportunity.

3) There was only one shot fired. On a patrol if a shot is fired it would certainly be followed by others, had it been fired by the enemy.

4) As none of the other men on the patrol had fired, the shot must therefore have been fired by the lance corporal.

5) The fact that his rifle was clean when inspected cannot be considered in favour of the accused since he had had a whole day in which to clean it.

The defending officer said that in his view the case should never have come to trial. There was no evidence the NCO. had been anywhere near the officer at the time of his death, the shot was from an unknown distance, it was dark and foggy, and there was no proof the lance corporal's rifle had been fired. A not guilty verdict would therefore in his view be the only verdict possible.

The court withdrew. The colonel made a very creditable summing up, after which he invited the captain to give his verdict. The captain, a blunt speaking tank man from the Staffordshire Yeomanry replied,

"I think he's probably as guilty as hell, but nobody's proved it. Not guilty."

The first major, from the Duke of Wellington's Regiment just replied,

"Agreed. Not guilty."

Major David also gave a 'not guilty' verdict.

"In that case," concluded the colonel, we have a majority for 'not guilty.'"

The lance corporal was discharged, sent back to his unit, from which he was immediately transferred to another battalion.

On the third day, 11th January, they were given the papers regarding Private Roper. W. charged with 'Buggery of a fellow soldier,' namely Private Harris. P.

"Don't get many of these," remarked the colonel to JAG representative.

"No, and what's more, like civilian rape, damned difficult to prove, since it usually is one person's word against another's. Still, we mustn't anticipate the evidence."

At 1000 hours the court took their seats and the prisoner was brought in, securely handcuffed. The colonel waited for the handcuffs to be removed which the escort seemed to have no intention of so doing.

"Remove the handcuffs," the colonel ordered. The escort, two full corporals of the Military Police looked at one another. The senior of the two standing rigidly to attention replied,

"The accused has been very violent on each occasion the handcuffs have been removed, sir."

"Remove the handcuffs. If the accused is violent in this court he will be charged with further offences."

"Sir," and the six-feet-tall, fourteen-stone redcap freed the prisoner.

David in the meantime had been observing the accused closely, checked his name - Roper - and immediately recognised him as 'Piggy Eyes,' the youth who, along with three of his gang, had abducted David's girlfriend, as she was then. They had taken Pat, who was later to become his wife, and had been killed by enemy action on Sandbury airfield in 1940, to a barn, where they stripped her and were about to rape her when she was rescued. They each subsequently received seven years with hard labour.

David was seated next to the colonel, the president of the court. He leaned towards him.

"Sir, I know the accused."

"I see. Well, we had better adjourn for a few minutes to sort it out."

"The court will adjourn for a short while." They filed out.
"Well, Major Chandler, what's the problem?"

"The accused came from the small village I did. He and three others were convicted of the attempted rape of my first wife a short while before we were married. They got seven years hard labour."

The colonel turned to the JAG lawyer.

"Any problems regarding his trying this accused, Mr Stewart?"

"As he is not of your regiment, no. You," he added, facing David, "have sworn to truly judge the accused. Do you feel you can approach this case with an open mind, giving your verdict based on the evidence as presented?"

"Yes, I can do that."

"Then I think we can proceed." They retook their places in the court.

As the JAG man had said, these cases are very difficult to prove. The alleged victim was called to give evidence. To summarise answers to the questions the prosecuting officer put to him, he said that Roper was a persistent bully and braggart. He had boasted he had, when in Thurnhout, raped a Belgian woman and her daughter on the same evening. At this the defence counsel objected, saying it was irrelevant to this case. The prosecuting officer disagreed saying Private Roper had boasted of this in front of the witness and others and it was therefore evidence.

The court refused the objection.

Private Harris then continued by saying that when in reserve at Eindhoven Roper had persistently made suggestive remarks to him. Asked what those suggestions were he replied,

"Things like: 'you know you would like a bit of navy cake, wouldn't you?'"

"Will you tell the court what is accepted as the meaning of 'navy cake.'?"

"What queers do."

"What do queers do?"

"You know, sodomy, that sort of thing."

"Right. Go on."

"He said he'd fancied me ever since he joined the battalion. He said I'd got a lovely little bum."

"Anything else?"

"Yes. He said, in front of Private Durkin and Private Roach that one day he was going to have me over the barrack room table, it was what I was wanting anyway."

"And was it?"

"No, 'course not; he made me sick to look at him."

"Tell the court, have you ever had any homosexual experiences?"

"No, 'course not. It's disgusting."

"What happened on the night of 24th December?"

"We were in reserve billeted in an office block. I was in a small office with my mates Durkin and Roach."

"How was the room furnished?"

"We had palliasses filled with straw on the floor."

"Nothing else?"

"There was a desk there from when it was used as an office I suppose."

"What happened that evening?"

"My mates went out for a drink. I don't drink so I stayed behind reading. About ten o'clock the door crashed open and Roper stood there. He looked the worse for drink to me. I scrambled up..."

"What do you mean, you scrambled up?"

"I was sitting on the palliasse on the floor with my blankets over my legs; it was cold in the room."

"Right, so you scrambled up."

"Yes, and as I did so Roper picked up Durkin's rifle leaning against the wall by his palliasse, and hit me across the back of the neck with it. I must have passed out for a little while. When I came to I was face down across the desk and Roper was buggering me."

As Harris said this, David looked away from him to the face of the man Roper, expecting to see dissent, antagonism, rage even, there. Instead the man was smiling, his lips wet at the remembrance of the incident, along with clear evidence in the fly-button area of his battledress trousers that recollection of the night was exciting him all over again.

"What did you do?"

"I screamed and struggled and he must have finished and let me go. He pulled his trousers up and said, 'Now don't say you didn't enjoy it,' and laughed at me as he walked out."

"Was anyone else there or nearby at the time?"

"Durkin and Roach came back from the Naafi bar and met Roper in the passageway."

"How far would that meeting have been from the doorway to your room?"

"Half a dozen paces, sir."

"Could one see your doorway from the point where your roommates passed Private Roper?"

"Yes, sir."

"Then no-one else could have left your room after Private Roper left without they would have been seen by your roommates."

"No, sir."

Here the defence officer objected to that question and answer, which was sustained by the court.

Evidence was then given that the two comrades then took Harris to the MI Room where he was booked in by a lance corporal medic on duty. He then telephoned the officer's quarters on the direct line laid on by the signal platoon. The MO arrived some ten minutes later, examined Private Harris and immediately sent a runner for the Provost sergeant. He in turn, along with one of his section, arrested Roper and brought him to the MO for examination, who confirmed that not only could he give evidence that Roper had had recent sexual intercourse, but also that he had experienced anal entry.

It being then 1600 hours the court adjourned until the morning.

On Friday 12th January the court resumed. Other witnesses were called and cross-examined by the defending officer. By midday the prosecution case was completed. There were no witnesses for the defence and the defending officer declined to call the accused. In brief, the summing-up on the part of the prosecuting officer presented, as he stated, 'an open and shut case - the court would doubtless draw its own conclusions upon the fact the accused had not subjected himself to cross-examination.'

The defending counsel put forward the case that no independent witness saw the alleged offence; the two main witnesses were friends of Private Harris and were therefore to be considered unreliable. The fact that Private Roper had indulged in sexual intercourse that evening was not disputed but was with an unknown prostitute in the town.

At this the president of the court interrupted.

"If you wish that to be taken into evidence you must call the accused to put it forward and be cross-examined by the prosecution."

"I understand, sir. That concludes my case for the defence."

"In that case the court will retire to consider its verdict."

It did not take long.

"Can I vote last, sir?" David asked.

"Under the circumstances I don't see why not."

It was pretty clear what the circumstances were. He was as good as saying that Private Roper was as guilty as hell.

They voted in turn. Guilty, guilty, guilty, the colonel said 'guilty,' David added, 'guilty.' They returned to the court.

"All stand. The verdict of this court is that you are guilty of the offence with which you have been charged."

As the colonel ended the sentence Roper turned to make a run for it, but the MPs were ready for him, one putting a stranglehold on him while the other speedily re-fitted the handcuffs they had used to bring him to and take him from the court each day.

The colonel addressed the defending officer.

"Have you any plea of mitigation of the sentence we shall pronounce?"

To his astonishment the defending officer stood up and replied, "I am afraid not, sir."

The court looked one to another. Invariably a defending officer can find something about an accused which can hopefully be put forward to the court to get the sentence reduced. This could be that the offence was entirely out of character, the man was provoked, he would promise not to repeat the offence, and so on. Good defending officers could almost make courts cry, but here was a perfectly good defending officer unable to say a word for his accused!

When the court officers retired and examined Roper's conduct sheet, or should I say sheets, they could see why. Insubordination, absent without leave, dirty rifle, striking a junior NCO, theft of army property, damage to barrack fittings - they were all there. And now there was the big one.

The JAG lawyer advised them on the scale of the sentence for the crime committed. The colonel addressed them.

"Captain Cole?"

"Ten years penal servitude, sir."

"Major Humphreys?"

"Fifteen years penal servitude, sir."
"Colonel Black?"
"I think ten years, sir."
"With penal servitude?"
"Yes, sir."
"Major Chandler?"
"I think fifteen years penal servitude, sir."

"Then I have two of you suggesting ten years, and two of you fifteen. In which case, if you agree I will come down with twelve years with penal servitude. You appreciate this sentence must go through to Army HQ. I really can't see their reducing it though."

They resumed their places in the courtroom.

"The decision of this court is that you will serve twelve years penal servitude for the offence of which you have been convicted. Take him away."

The MPs bundled Private Roper away to serve the first two years of his sentence at Dartmoor, where later ... but you shall know about that in due course.

You shall also hear the sad story of Private Harris.

Ten soldiers were hanged and thirty-three shot for murder during and just after World War Two in the British Army.

* * *

Chapter Six

Whilst David was away on his legal duties Roger Hammick, accompanied by Paddy, took his teams across the swollen River Maas. It comprised the 'Recce' team, Roger, Paddy and three men, and a boat covering party consisting of a sergeant and three men.

They launched at 2215 hours over marshland flooded further inland by another five or six feet since the reconnaissance the previous night, The Rifles defence concertina having to be cut through to allow the canvas assault boat to get through. They crossed the swollen, fast-flowing river, feeling very lonely on two counts. Firstly, there is nothing to hide behind on a river if you are spotted, secondly, large chunks of tree were not uncommon floating down at some speed, often semi-submerged, which if in collision with the boat, would not do it a lot of good. Dressed as they were, if they ended up in the water their chances, even if they were adequate swimmers, would be nil.

The boat party did a good job in getting the recce crew within twenty yards of their intended land fall, where they all sat out for a while listening and keeping watch. Not hearing any activity, Roger then led the recce party up the river bank. His instructions were to move inland to a wooded area to establish what the building in there was being used for, in addition to establish the size and depth of an anti-tank ditch running along parallel to the Maas and some four hundred yards from it. On the way back if they could grab a couple of prisoners without making a noise and bring them back that would be a bonus.

They had only gone a few yards when they heard German voices approaching them. Roger gave the signal to freeze and three soldiers passed across their front only ten yards away without seeing them. The patrol pushed on, first having to get over a trench, flooded by the back-up from the river of a nearby stream overflowing into it. Fortunately, although this was close to the anti-tank ditch it had not flooded that. They were able to establish the obstacle was some twenty feet wide and twelve feet deep. First job done.

As they approached the wooded area, Roger tripped and fell over. The remainder instantly froze, but the noise of his sten gun hitting the hard ground was heard by a sentry only a few yards ahead. He came towards them, unslinging his rifle as he came as they could clearly see in the pale, snow-reflecting light. Paddy drew his fighting knife and with the speed one would not have associated with a man of his size moved the three or four yards to grab the man around the neck and before he could shout, with a clinically accurate upward strike of the fighting knife, plunged it into the sentry's heart. They pulled his body into some neighbouring bushes, removed his identification badges and took everything from his pockets for the IO to examine later.

"Well done, Paddy," Roger whispered.

"You alright, sir?"

"Yes, I tripped on a bloody root. Let's push on."

The sentry must have been an outlying picket; they still were some twenty yards from the wood, in which they could clearly hear voices coming from the building. They got very close to it but apart from getting a picture of its size and an approximate idea of the number of troops in it they could not establish what sort of unit it housed, or whether it was an HQ of any sort. They listened out for half an hour then made their way back over the anti-tank obstacle and the flooded trench to the boat party. As the three recce men were re-boarding Roger whispered to the boat sergeant and Paddy,

"We will paddle up river keeping in as close as possible to this bank. They will find that sentry any minute now, then all hell will be let loose."

It was hard work for the boat party to paddle against the strong current, but within ten minutes they appreciated the wisdom of Roger's strategy. The whole river became flooded with light as flares went up from the enemy defences, Spandau-fire on fixed arcs swept and re-swept the surface of the river from two machine-gun positions. To add to the kerfuffle Nick Dale, in reply, lobbed three-inch mortar bombs in a thoroughly enjoyable stonk to the enemy bank in an attempt to destroy the machine gun nests. For twenty minutes or so it was bedlam, while Roger tucked his party away under the shelter of a raised section of the bank out of harm's way. Well, almost out of harm's way. A couple of Nick's little playthings landed a bit too close for comfort, about which both he and Paddy would impart gentle remonstrances in due course to the boss of the mortar platoon.

They waited there for an hour while Sandy Patterson and the rest of B Company were biting their nails wondering if their comrades had been captured, killed, sunk, or whatever. At last Roger gave the word, "Right, let's go."

They then had to find their landing point, a task made difficult by a mist coming down, which while it gave them a little protection from the prying eyes of Jerry also made spotting the gap in their dannert far from easy. Roger cursed that he had not left a marker of some sort on it. They had to keep some distance from the present edge of the river. Having got this far the last thing they would want to do would be to foul some underwater fence or tree stump.

"I think we've come too far," Roger whispered to the boat party sergeant.

"I'll give it a few more yards, sir, then I'll turn back and we'll have another shufti."

He was just about to turn back when one of the paddlers called softly,

"There it is, sir."

They had made it, except for one small incident. As they made their way through the gap in the dannert, the side of the boat ran against a steel supporting angle holding the wire, which produced a two-feet-long slit through which flooded gallons of icy cold, filthy dirty and very wet water, which, in addition to immediately saturating the backsides of the men sitting on the canvas floor, rapidly began to fill up the boat. It literally sank slowly beneath them while they scrambled to their feet and one by one ended up in four feet of the River Maas. To add insult to injury, Jerry decided at that point to have another of his little firework displays which meant the men, to try to escape being spotted, had to crouch down almost up to their necks.

The Jerry pyrotechnics ceasing they reached dry land to be met by Sandy and his batman.

"Roger, Paddy, you look a trifle damp. Come on; let's get some rum into all of you and some dry clothes on. Then the IO wants to see you Roger, and there is a chap from Div. Intelligence with him."

"I didn't realise that Div. had any intelligence. If they have, from my experience at the sharp end, it's in very small measure."

Roger was only repeating the general view of subalterns regarding Div. staff upwards, their main purpose in life being, it seemed, simply to bugger people like Roger about at regular intervals.

They had another three weeks on the Maas until at the beginning of February David was called, along with the other company commanders to battalion headquarters.

Hamish addressed them.

"I know you will all be sad to have to leave this sodden place - I said 'sodden' not sodding, you will note. Correction, I know you will all be glad to leave this sodding place; the first news I am to give you - the good news - is that you are going back to the balmy bordellos of Bulford. The not so good news perhaps is that after a very short period of leave you are going to further the glory of The Parachute Regiment. No guesses what that means. I of course have not been apprised of the nature or place of the operation, but as there is only one big obstacle, namely the Rhine, between us and Berlin, it would seem you might get ten out of ten for guessing we are going to be the first into the great plains of Northern Germany. Advance parties from our old friends, the Cheshires, will come up tomorrow and get familiarised with the positions, followed by the take over on the night of 19th/20th. TCVs will then take us back to Ostend on the 22nd; we should be in Bulford by late on the 24th. No post will be sent from now on. That's about all for now. The adjutant will send you movement orders in due course and the QM will organise haversack rations for the journey. Any questions?"

'A' company commander asked how far was it to Ostend, getting a typical reply from Hamish, "Haven't a bloody clue, that's what I have an intelligence officer for. Do you know, David?"

"I would say about a hundred and thirty or so miles, sir."

"Well, I just hope the MPs escorting us don't get lost. We're going to be twelve to fifteen hours on those trucks as it is."

They arrived back at Bulford late on the Saturday night. It was close on 3am before David and Paddy and the platoon commanders got to their beds, having seen the men fed and settled in. At seven o'clock David, knowing that Maria would be awake with the baby having announced again its presence in the world, as was its morning wont, made tracks to the telephone. To his surprise it was Mr Schultz who answered it, a very tired sounding Mr Schultz.

"David, this is a surprise."

"A surprise for me too, father-in-law, don't tell me you've had a night on the tiles and you have just got home with the milk?"

"Well, first of all it's Sunday, so no milk, but secondly we have had a V2 at the end of the road about an hour ago and we have lost all our windows and a fair number of the roof tiles. Maria, Susan and the baby are all at the Bulstrodes in Loughton. I've just got back from taking them there. We were all unharmed, but it was a bit frightening with all the glass flying around, I don't know how many of the poor souls along the road were killed, two or three people you have met lived there." He sounded so sad. "Anyway, where are you?"

"We're back in England - can you let Maria know? We shall be getting a short leave then we are off on another job."

"I'll do that. The Bulstrodes aren't on the phone, so when I've made things as secure as I can here, and have cleaned all the mess up, I shall be going back to fetch them - probably late afternoon."

"Right, I'll try again this evening. We may know a little more by then."

But they did not. The day was spent on replacing personal ammunition, inspection of weapons, sorting out deficiencies, and all the usual tasks confronting a unit coming out of action soon to be back in it again.

That evening David had a long chat with Maria, promising to let her know on the morrow as soon as he was able what his future arrangements were to be.

"David darling, Daddy said you were only here for a short while before you go off again?"

"Yes, that's right, but it won't be long now before it's all over. With Warsaw liberated by the Russians, their forward troops less than a hundred miles from Berlin and with us over the Rhine they will surely collapse."

"So you are going to jump the Rhine?"

"We haven't been told that, but it seems pretty logical to all of us. It will be a piece of cake."

But it was far from being 'a piece of cake' as we shall find out in due course.

After talking to Maria David telephoned Chandlers Lodge, his call being answered by Margaret. They had a very friendly chat together until she said, "Oh, here's your father, just back from flogging the workers as usual."

David was so pleased to hear the obvious fondness in her voice at the mention of her new husband.

He had a long talk with Fred, ending with, "You will never guess who I bumped into in Holland."

"Oh, who was that? If I will never guess there's not much use my trying is there?"

"The Roper lad."

"Don't tell me. He's won a medal?"

"Nothing as gallant as that I'm afraid; he was on a court martial, at which I was a member.

"You mean he was the accused? What the hell for?"

"Well, this is strictly between you and me, although I suppose it becomes public knowledge once the sentence is confirmed."

"So what's he done?"

"He was convicted of buggery."

"Bloody hell. Was the other bloke a willing partner in the act?"

"No. Roper laid him out before he committed the offence."

"What did he get?"

"Twelve years penal servitude, subject to confirmation."

"Should have been life, would have been in my day."

"Well, I'll tell you all about it when I come home, and about the others."

Fred was left wondering what 'the others' were!

On Monday an 'O' group was called, and the company commanders were told that the unit would be going on leave in two groups, half of HQ company, all A company, and a platoon of B Coy, on Wednesday for seven days, the rest of 'B' and HQ Companies and all of C Company on Friday 6th March. There was to be a divisional exercise on the weekend of the 16th March, after which they would once more be incommunicado. David decided he would let Sandy Patterson and Paddy go on leave with Andy Gilchrist's 4 platoon first. He would wait and go with the other two platoons. It took a great deal of single-mindedness to arrive at this arrangement, when he could easily have pulled rank and gone first. It was a bit like having the resolve to keep the biggest strawberry till last, you enjoyed the taste more!

Chingford was not the only place receiving its share of V2s. They had already caused horrific damage during January, when in addition to its normal quota of domestic tragedies, the assault included a direct hit on a cinema, and a few days after that a convent, a hospital and two more cinemas. Many children were killed in this latter incident and over a hundred injured. In The House on the 2nd of February Mr Churchill was asked, 'If the

Germans use gas now that they are cornered, either in the field or against the civilian population, would instant retaliation be made?'

Churchill replied, "If the contingency indicated were to occur, tenfold retaliation would be inflicted on Germany," adding, "it is no doubt the realisation of this fact and not any moral scruples on their part that has hitherto procured us immunity from this particular form of warfare."

The V2s continued to rain in with deadly regularity, day after day. Yet another cinema was hit in early February, along with a clothing factory and a shelter, in both of the latter two incidents mainly women being killed.

On the 8th of February the Home Secretary announced the numbers of civilian casualties so far during the war. There had been 57,468 killed, 80,000 injured and hospitalised; the countless numbers of people injured and treated by the ambulance crews and voluntary bodies probably trebled those numbers.

The 6th of March finally presented itself. David and his two platoon commanders, Roger Hammick and Reggie Pardew, scrounged a lift on a twenty-five-hundred-weight truck going into Salisbury. They managed to find a first class compartment into which they prepared to settle, putting their baggage up in to the overhead racks, when Reggie nudged David. Pulled up on the adjacent platform, literally only inches away from their own window, was a train chock-a-block with German soldiers. David turned towards them; as he did so a senior NCO in the compartment immediately aligned with them, bellowed a command. The dozen or so packed in there, scrambled to their feet and stood as rigidly to attention as they could while the NCO faced the three officers and gave as Prussian a salute as any to decorate a Potsdam parade ground. David returned the salute, and indicated for them to resume their seats, which they did, although it must be said that packing twelve averagely bulky Fritz's in a carriage designed to seat six-eight at the most, was a bit of a squeeze!

Arriving at Chingford he was shocked at the sight of the Schultz's house. Most of the windows were boarded up, only the essential ones having been reglazed so far. Nevertheless all had been put to rights within. He spent two days, oh, and more importantly, three nights, there before they went off to Sandbury, where they received a royal welcome.

Jack arrived during the evening, making a great fuss of Maria as he invariably did. During the course of their conversations he said to David, "Have you heard that Ulm has been bombed twice in the past week?"

David replied, "No, I've heard little news. At Bulford, I was very busy."

"In the bar no doubt," from Rose.

"I'll ignore that remark, and when I got to Maria's house their aerial had been blown down in the blast and was only re-erected yesterday. I suppose there must be some factories at Ulm on warwork, but it would seem to be risking a lot for a small return somehow."

"Perhaps they're running out of targets," Ernie suggested.

"I think they must be," Fred suggested, "the Yanks bombed Basel in Switzerland a week or so back, and then Basel and Zurich a couple of days ago. That second bombing hasn't been confirmed yet. It was announced by Lord Haw-Haw last night."

As a result of this second bombing of the Swiss towns, general Spatz, the commander of the US air forces, asked the Swiss government to paint white crosses on the roofs of border buildings. Commenting on this, Fred considered this was so that the Yanks could hit them more accurately.

There was the usual mini-party on Saturday evening during which David and Maria were able to tell Cecely how sad they were at the news of Nigel's death. David asked, "How is Greta taking it now?"

"Well, she is back at school, which keeps her busy during the week. She comes home at weekends of course. I've persuaded her to go to the dance at the church hall this evening, so she will be calling in here later on."

"Still going strong with young John Power?" David queried with a grin.

"I'm afraid not. That's a taboo subject at the moment. He had a month's sick leave after he was discharged from Sandbury hospital, and went home to Hampshire to stay with his parents. When he reported back to Betteshanger he wrote what I believe our American friends call a 'Dear John' letter, only I suppose it should have been a 'Dear Jane' letter in her case."

Maria exclaimed "Oh no, poor girl."

"Yes. Apparently while he was at home he met a girl he used to go out with. She had given him the heave-ho before he met Greta, but had now seen the error of her ways and enticed him back. She apparently is the same age as John, that is, older, and probably more, what shall we say, more complaisant than our Greta has been? She's getting over it a bit now but it did give her a body blow at the time."

As she spoke, Greta arrived, accompanied by a young pilot officer.

"Mummy, this is Stanislaus Rakowski, he's a pilot in the Polish Air Force," she sounded quite bubbly in making this introduction.

"Well, my dear, since your friend has wings on his chest and 'Poland' on his sleeve he could hardly be anything else, could he?" Greta laughed.

"No, I suppose not. Anyway we met at the dance."

Cecely smiled at Maria and David, who each correctly interpreted that as John Power now being history. She introduced them both.

"Are you stationed here, Stanislaus?"

"Only for a short while I believe, Mrs Coates. Oh, and people call me Stanley, Stanislaus is a bit of a mouthful."

He spoke perfect English; no trace whatsoever of a continental accent.

"You speak excellent English," David remarked.

"Well, I have lived here all my life. My father is in the Polish diplomatic service."

"And what do you fly?"

David was in civilian clothes, and had been introduced as 'David Chandler.'

"It's an airplane not many people have any knowledge of." David looked at him quizzically. "It's called a Lysander. We call them 'Lizzies'."

"In which case, my dear Stanley, I am going to take you away from this young lady and find you the biggest glass I can, into which I shall pour a veritable torrent of Whitbread's Light Ale."

"May I ask why?"

"Because if you do what I think you do you damned well deserve it." Quickly he added, "With France liberated where do you go now?"

"Holland, Denmark, Norway even, although I haven't made the Denmark trip yet. David, may I ask what you are, or do you seem to have some knowledge of the Lizzie."

"My first flight ever was as a passenger in a Lizzie to France. That was nearly four years ago. I've never been so scared in all my life."

"You were an agent?"

"Well, sort of. But I mustn't tear you away from Greta or she will strike me off her visiting list. We'll chat another time. I'll get you that beer."

Gradually others came over to be introduced to Stanley; as a result Greta found herself to be part of the main centre of interest, which further resulted in one John Power being definitely relegated to Division Three in the league of past suitors.

It transpired that the young pilot was stationed temporarily on Sandbury aerodrome, training for a special job to be carried out in a month or so. When the evening ended he literally 'got on his bike' to go back to his quarters, the cycle in question having been loaned by a fellow pilot to get him to the dance.

"Well, not exactly loaned," he confided to Greta, "he's on a forty-eight this weekend, so I took temporary possession of it, you might say."

"You sound like a lawyer."

"I did make a start; I shall carry on after this all ends."

"Will you go home to Poland?"

"With the Russians now occupying it and their own communist government in Warsaw, I don't think there will be a place for my family there. I shall almost certainly stay in England. Still, I mustn't talk Polish politics to a pretty girl."

Stanley having stated publicly she was a pretty girl relegated John Power further down into Division Four, if there was such an institution.

"Then could you come and have tea with us tomorrow?" said oh! so casually casual.

"I'm sorry no, I'm flying tomorrow."

"On a Sunday?"

"'Fraid so. And we don't get double pay like the munition workers do. But I could come and take you to the flicks on Monday evening."

Greta almost blurted out, 'I'm sorry I shall be back at school,' then suddenly realised she didn't want this young man to know she was still a schoolgirl, a sixth former it is true, but still a schoolgirl. He would have to know soon, if they were to remain friendly, but for the time being she would let sleeping dogs lie, only in her case???

"I'm sorry, Stanley, I shall be away all the week, but I shall be back on Friday."

"Right, Friday evening flicks then. I'll meet you outside 'the Bug Hutch' - that is what the locals call it, is it not? - at 6.30, agreed?"

"Agreed." They shook hands and he pedalled off.

Returning to the sitting room she rejoined her mother, now talking to Margaret. They looked at her transformed face.

"Nice young man, Greta," was Margaret's opening gambit.

"He will do until something more suitable comes along," laughed Greta, "but David, what is all this 'Lizzie' business?"

"Well, Lysander pilots take agents to continental countries and land in hostile territory, and then bring others back. Since they do this usually at night, have to land in the dark by the light of a few torches, never knowing whether the landing zone has been compromised or not, they have to be first class pilots and extremely brave to boot."

Greta was silent for a few moments. "And to think I've been dancing with him all the evening and thought he was just an ordinary chap like all the others there."

"I expect that's how he would consider himself" David observed. Greta turned to him.

"David, you have never told us of your derring-dos. Now, what happened when you went to Yugoslavia for instance?"

"I can't tell you that with my wife here, can I now?"

"Well, we know about your exploits in Calais from Kenny. We know a little bit about your Lizzie trip to France, although we don't know what went on there. We know nothing about the trip to Portugal, or wherever it was you ended up at that time. We know something about the Normandy and Ardennes because it was all on the radio, but we know nothing at all about Yugoslavia."

"Well, I promise that one day I will tell you everything of interest that has happened to me. OK? It will take all of five minutes."

"I just do not believe you. Maria, can't you use your womanly wiles to wheedle it all out of him?"

Maria put her arm around Greta's slender waist.

"To tell you the truth, my dear, we see so little of each other there's not a lot of time for secondary occupations, such as conversation." The girls all laughed heartily. "But I will try when time permits, I promise," she added.

When she and David were alone - obviously he could not have the story inveigled from him with others present - she singularly failed in her plans. Well, as she had already made plain, conversation was unequivocally a very secondary occupation under such circumstances.

* * *

Chapter Seven

Sunrise did not arrive at Camp Four at the end of December as previously had been advised to Harry and his men. A further message came through the ether in early January saying their CO would be with them by the end of the month, bringing with him ten more mouths to feed. This cheered Harry no end, despite the fact they would have to train the newcomers into his ways, send them on patrols to get them used to the lie of the land, the approaches to the camp and teaching them many other aspects of living in the jungle.

When Sunrise did arrive, they immediately observed a difference in his uniform, to whit, a pip on each epaulette in addition to the crown he previously had displayed. Major David Lister was now Lieutenant-colonel David Lister. Harry gave one of his impeccable salutes and said, "Do we genuflect now, sir, or just prostrate ourselves as normal?"

Sunrise grinned.

"In King's Regs it states categorically that lieutenant-colonels are entitled to a double rum ration after having traipsed two hundred miles or more, so don't hang about, major, don't hang about."

"Major, sir? I am just a humble captain."

"Since the first of January this year you have been a major, though it won't reach the pay people in Delhi for at least a month. We could have told them over the air waves but they won't do a thing unless it's in writing. Tommy and Reuben have been given another pip as well. Personally I would make you all major-generals if I had my way for all the work you do here month after month."

"That would then make you a field marshall, wouldn't it, sir?"

Sunrise laughed. "So what about this bloody rum?"

Harry gave a big hug to Bam and Boo, his two aborigine friends, much to the surprise of the new contingent. Their communism did not lend itself to considering the orang asli as being equal to them in any way whatsoever; they were certainly not in the category of being hugged. Sunrise was then led off to Harry's quarters to a well deserved tot of rum, and a somewhat diffident welcome from Chantek.

"You're as lovely as ever, aren't you, Chantek?" Sunrise spoke softly to the leopard lying on a raffia mat at the side of Harry's bed. Chantek looked steadily at him with her beautiful blue eyes, from which, in the Malay language, she had got her name. She gave a little throaty growl of pleasure in being spoken to in the soft manner the colonel had chosen. Harry looked across at her.

"Come on," he said. She raised herself, moved across to his side, sat on her haunches and put her head on Harry's thigh. All of these movements were carried out with such grace and elegance as to combine into one fluid movement. She looked up at Harry just as she had in the drawing sent to Sandbury. Harry stroked her head and rubbed the side of her jaws, jaws which could tear the flesh apart of anything they seized upon. The colonel, fascinated by the love of this enormously powerful wild animal for her human friend, wondered what was to happen to her when 'all this lot was over,' but refrained from raising the subject.

After a good night's sleep the colonel held a meeting with the three officers and Choon Guan the next morning.

"I can fill you in with some news which will cheer you," he said, "last week, Super Fortresses flew from India, three thousand five hundred miles, and bombed the naval yard at Singapore. They also bombed the naval installation at Georgetown, Penang, in the process shooting down four Jap Zeros. So you see, the attack gets nearer and nearer. The Germans are on their last legs, they lost the best part of twenty divisions in their Ardennes attack, which means that in a few months now everything will be thrown in against the Japs. As it is, the 14th Army are knocking hell out of them in Burma, Mandalay will soon be ours, and the Aussies and the Yanks are taking island after island from them in the Pacific.

"Now, it doesn't need an aircraft designer's brain to guess, although I have no knowledge whatsoever of this, that with Burma recaptured as it will be in a short while, and with all the landing craft in Europe now surplus to requirements there, the next invasion will be right here. In the meantime therefore, we have to do all we can, until we receive specific operational orders, to disrupt communications, destroy electricity grids, railway bridges and signalling systems. But do it in different necks of the wood all the time. Have the Japs running from pillar to post. This will achieve two things. One, they will not be able to post troops north to Siam to help out their retreating forces there. Two, it is quite likely they will have to increase their presence here because they won't know where we are going to hit them next.

"The other three camps will be doing the same. I have marked out the boundaries of your operational territory on this map so that you don't stray into some other operation going on. With the area you have to cover it should keep you out of mischief for a little while. Start date for all camps is the first of March. We shall have seen the worst of the monsoon by then, and you will have had ample time to train the new people and get them welded into their groups. Any questions?"

There were numerous questions from an excited 'O' Group, at the end of which the colonel said, "Now, one thing I have kept until last. Each camp will be receiving in the next air drop a piece of equipment used to tremendous effect in Europe called a 'Piat' - Projectile Infantry Anti-tank. It is carried by one man, though I suspect you may have to make a harness and allow for two men to carry it. It will blow any Japanese tank off the face of the earth, and," - he paused here for effect - "one projectile into the guts of a railway engine will do everything you want without going near the permanent way. This will enable you to target troop trains without the risk of hitting the wrong target as you do with derailments."

The colonel and his small party stayed another five days, resting and recuperating from their long journey south, a journey made worse by the effects of a particularly heavy monsoon on the many streams they had to cross, streams which were now torrents in many places.

On 26th January they made an early start, seen off by the whole company, who burst into spontaneous applause at these brave people who moved from camp to camp up and down the spine of Malaya, keeping the groups in touch with each other.

A few days after Sunrise and his small party left, it was the 1st of February, the troops in Camp Four, training hard out on the parade ground, looked far up into the sky to see twelve tiny silvery objects. Tiny though they seemed they knew immediately they could only be Super Fortresses. A state of excitement broke out in the Chinese that Harry and Reuben had never before witnessed. There, up there, was proof that the Japanese monkeys were on the run. The rape of Nanking would soon be avenged. It did not immediately occur to their communist brains that those aircraft on their way to strike the enemy were being flown by members of the most capitalistic, most conservative, most anti-communist country in the world.

The next evening they heard from their radio that these same aircraft had made a one hundred and eighty degree turn to fly back over the old naval dockyard at Singapore, and had sunk the 50,000-ton King George V graving dock so kindly donated to the Japs at the fall of Singapore. The citizens of Singapore City some twenty miles away, the POWs in Changi Gaol only a little over five miles away, all witnessed or heard the aircraft or the bombing, it giving them too the assurance, or at least the hope, that delivery from their oppressors was in sight.

By the end of February they had received their air drop, and in addition to the important items, i.e. the mail and the rum, they received their Piat with twenty four projectiles to use with it.

"You realise of course, we are not going to be able to fire the blasted thing until we do it in anger," Harry stated to his 'O' Group, "added to which have we got anyone with enough strength to carry the blasted thing?"

At thirty-six pounds, along with two cases totalling six bombs, projectiles, missiles, whatever you would like to call them, weighing another eighteen pounds, they were no light weight to lug around, particularly under jungle conditions. Nevertheless, there was competition in the camp as to who should be the 'Piat Man.' The thought that with one pressure of the finger he could blow a train off the permanent way, snuff out a tank and its contents, or totally shatter a three-ton lorry and anything or anyone on it more than compensated for the sore shoulder, aching arms and occasional whack on the head when the tube-like piece of metal got caught up in the jungle vines. Being Number One on the Piat was a position of considerable importance.

On Sunday 4th March Harry called an 'O' Group.

"I've been looking at possible targets," he announced, "they are at different distances from here, but we will hit them at exactly the same time, or as close as we can make it."

"You are going to split the force?" asked Reuben.

"Yes. There will be four patrols of ten men, leaving just half a dozen men in the camp with Matthew and the other HQ people. They will be:

No 1 party. Reuben, with Piat, to hit train on narrow gauge railway at Jeranut, thirty miles north of our previous hit on that railway. Second target the post and telegraph station there.

No 2 party. Tommy. Blow up water tank and railway workshop at Kalumpang on the main west coast line.

No 3 party. Choon Guan. To raid the Rest House on the north side of Frasers Hill, a little way out of the town. It will be full of very killable senior Jap officers.

No 4 party. Myself. Destroy main grid transformer station at Behrang, ten miles south of the Slim River bridge.

"Now, they will all take place on the Saturday/Sunday night 17th/18th March. Each of you will make your own plan, bring it to me for approval, and then practise like mad as usual. You will probably want to be at your target on the night before so as to get a good sighting of it in daylight before you attack. If you see anything else to have a crack at, do so, as long as, and I repeat, as long as, it does not jeopardise the operation. Keep a tight hold on the men, particularly the replacements."

They worked on their plans. They were fortunate in that there was at least one in the company who knew the villages they were to attack, and in the Frasers Hill operation they had two brothers who had actually worked in the Rest House and knew the place, and the approaches to it, like the back of their hands. I have always wondered about that expression. Who the devil ever studies the back of his or her hand enough to be able to differentiate it from anybody else's?

Reuben suggested he would need an extra day to get to Jeranut. Harry agreed.

Choon Guan suggested that as far as possible each of his men should be armed with a tommy gun. Rifles would be an encumbrance in the close confines of a building. Harry was able to find him six by denuding himself and others who would be unlikely to be at close quarters with the enemy.

Tommy Isaacs assured Harry that he would not do a repeat of his Trolak venture. In December 1943 he had been given a similar assignment in respect of the huge water tower at this main line station. He had set the explosive on the leg of the water tank, and fitted the detonator and fuse. It failed to go off. Instead of waiting at least fifteen to twenty minutes he was impatient to get away and after only three or four minutes decided he had better have a shufti at it. Which was where he, in army terms, dropped a bollock. The blasted thing went off; thousands of gallons engulfed him and threw him, fortunately, against a wire mesh fence. He learnt the lesson the hard way.

Reuben moved out on the Thursday morning 15th March, reached their target area by late Friday afternoon, and were able to carry out a detailed reconnaissance. They realised they were going to have pot-luck in respect of the type of train they would hit. They had selected a small, scrub-covered bluff overlooking the track, and some thirty to forty yards from the railway line. It was a fairly light night so siting the Piat would not be difficult.

With regard to the other part of the plan, three men had been detailed to make for the telephone station, place their explosive, hide up until they heard the Piat explosion, then set their part of the caper off and leg it back to the main party.

Next, two men in the train party were sent half a mile up the track, to signal by whacking the rail with a hammer, of a suitable train to bestow the Piat-man's attention upon. They then would rejoin Reuben, and all successfully concluded, make their way back to the bivvy area.

It all went well except for two incidents. Firstly when the train appeared in his sights, the Piat-man fired - and the bomb sailed harmlessly over the top of the engine, hit the ground about forty yards on and exploded with a roar. The number two on the Piat, who loads the bombs, instantly reloaded and the Piat-man saved his face by getting his projectile straight into the boiler of his target, which promptly blew up, causing the following trucks to tumble off the embankment down into the scrubland below.

Hearing this, the telegraph party carried out their part in the proceedings and legged it back to Reuben, with one exception, which brings us to our second incident. As he ran across the railway track, one of the men, one of the replacements in fact, caught his foot under a rail, fell awkwardly and broke his ankle. He called out to his two comrades who were fast disappearing towards the Piat party. They turned back, got him up on to his good leg and with one arm around the shoulders of each man they managed to get him back to the main force.

"What's happened here?" Reuben asked.

"I think he may have broken his ankle," replied the leader of that little section. He with the broken ankle looked up at Reuben in the pale moonlight, his face stricken with fear.

"Have you got to shoot me, captain?"

It was fully understood by all comrades that if one of them was wounded, and that carrying him would endanger the remainder of the party, the officer in charge would have to despatch him. It had only happened once before, during the attack on Kampong Bintang in February 1943. On that occasion, when they had been attacked by aircraft, one man was so badly hit he could not have been moved. Harry had the dreadful task of ending his days.

"We'll get you back to the bivvy area and get a look at you. Stand him up."

As the rest of the party parcelled out the injured man's equipment between them, Reuben crouched down, pulled him on to him piggy-back fashion, and strode off into the darkness. They had only got two or three hundred yards away, when there was an almighty roar from one of the capsized trucks. A balloon of fire went up into the heavens lighting up the country, it seemed, for miles around.

"They must have had petrol or paint in that one," Reuben suggested. Whatever it was, it set fire to two other open trucks with bales of rubber in them. The place was getting as light as day.

"Quick, let's get the hell out of here."

They made their bivvy area some three miles away and having prepared to move off, waited for dawn. In the couple of hours they had remaining there, Reuben examined the fallen man's ankle, splinted it up as best he could and came to the decision he would have to carry the unfortunate man most of the way. They made up a stretcher from bamboo and vines but their route traversed thick jungle, a considerable distance wading in streams, as well as the frequent use of game trails, which by their very nature were only about as wide as a pig. In any open or fairly open country they would give Reuben a break by using the stretcher.

Tommy Isaacs made a very professional job of blowing up the railway workshop and water tank, he too adding a telephone station to his list which he had spotted during his reconnaissance the previous day, and having enough explosive left was able to damage and put out of action a new electricity supply line the Japs had installed.

Harry's job on the face of it was to be the easiest of the four. The approach to the target was well covered, there were no military buildings of any sort within a quarter of a mile of it, or so they had observed on previous visits to the area. They had one main road to traverse but no railway line to cross.

We have stated before that a certain Scottish gentleman has in the past remarked on 'the best laid schemes' etc. etc. Well, when they reached the edge of their cover before having to cross the main K.L. - Ipoh trunk road, what did they see? - lorries stretching in all directions as far as the eye could see, each surrounded by its occupants eating their rice sandwiches, as Harry described it later, and obviously showing no signs whatsoever of moving. This was not a casual relocation of a few dozen squaddies, this had the appearance of a major movement order of a complete division, or more, spaced at intervals between the lorries carrying the troops, a number of them ex-WD, he could spot anti-aircraft trucks carrying the dual barrelled 25mm machine cannons. Harry wondered about this. In a sector where there were no low-flying aircraft, why would they need the protection of anti-aircraft equipment? The guns were no use against the extremely unlikely overflight of Super Fortresses, their projectiles would not reach halfway. Harry made notes of the contents of the convoy to send to Sunrise over the radio. Perhaps they could give a reason for it all. Did the Japs suspect a landing? Were they moving to oppose it?

He came to the conclusion he would have to abort his operation. It would be stupid, even if he could bypass the convoy, to carry out explosions only three or four miles away and then have to get back past all those troops again, assuming they were still there, and there seemed to be no reason to suggest otherwise. Putting a division of troops on alert in your line of retreat would seem to be not exactly the most sensible plan of action.

He told his party he intended to return. There was a certain amount of disappointment, particularly among the three newcomers, who had been looking forward to hitting back at their hated enemy. As a result Harry was back at Camp Four by midday on Monday 19th, waiting for the others to return.

Choon Guan and his men were probably looking forward to their task with greater anticipation than any of the others. They were actually going to have the pleasure of killing Japs. And not only just Japs, but most likely, Jap officers.

Apart from having to cross two tributaries of the Sungai Lipis, fast flowing mountain rivers but not deep, Choon Guan's party had the easiest and shortest distance to travel. They bivvied-up and spent the Saturday observing their target, finding that the Japs had put an extension on one end of the long, single-storied, veranda type bedroom accommodation. Having worked on the information provided by the two brothers who had worked there, when they marked out the plan of this wing on the parade ground back at the camp, Choon Guan had detailed each man to a specific bedroom, ten in all. Now he found he not only had fourteen rooms to contend with, but observing carefully he counted at least ten batmen housed in the servants' wing on the other side of the main reception area, dining room, etc. in the centre of the layout. There was also a police hut some two hundred yards to the front of the Rest House housing some three or four Sikh jaggers. They would be no trouble. One burst above their heads and they would hit the lallang and stay there.

Choon Guan studied the problem long and hard. There were going to be four rooms, each housing an armed Jap, who could not be eliminated at the first assault. He had, of course, to assume all rooms would be occupied, and that all occupants would be armed and well able to use the weapons they carried. He could abort the operation and come back with a larger force. He would lose a lot of face by doing that. He could go in quietly and slit a few throats. That would be a decidedly risky business. As a knowledgeable throat slitter he knew that finding a suitable throat in the dark and incising it accurately without the victim objecting noisily, would be not the easiest of jobs. He had a minimum of four on his shopping list. He ruled the proposition out.

He told himself 'we will just have to go in mob-handed as Captain Chandler would say!'

He called the men up to the observation point one by one and indicated each his target, the more experienced men being given two rooms, the three replacements being allocated only one. These, immediately after killing their man, were to race to the end of the veranda to guard against any incursion from the batmen.

At midnight they moved silently in single file to their target, Choon Guan keeping his fingers crossed that no mangey dog would be on the loose, bark its head off at them, and totally give the game away. Sillier things have happened.

Before they reached the end of the dimly-lit veranda they could hear the noise of laughter, and the music from a wireless or a gramophone coming from number one room. Choon Guan stopped his men against a long thicket of bamboo, twenty or thirty yards away. As he did so a stocky, powerfully built Japanese appeared through the doorway, his shirt unbuttoned, went to the veranda rail and urinated out on to the lallang. As he did so one of the girls they could hear laughing inside came out and joined him, saying "I will give you a hand," vigorously rotated his member until its fluid became exhausted, gave it a thorough shaking and then led him back into the room still holding it, to receive a burst of laughter from the party there as they reappeared.

You may ask, how did I know the girl said, 'I will give you a hand?' The truth is, of course, I don't. But if she did not say that, it would have been something similar. After all, the scope of conversation in that sort of situation is somewhat limited, I imagine.

After an hour or so the party broke up, couples going off along the veranda to their own rooms. There had been three rooms in addition to the party which had had lights on, and which had switched off during the shindig. They were noted as being occupied. Four couples had left the party, those rooms were noted. The last couple to leave were some ten minutes after the others had gone. Choon Guan, watching through his binoculars gave a little gasp of surprise.

"European," he whispered.

The European and his girl walked the length of the veranda to the end room. Choon Guan beckoned to the comrade allocated that task.

"You take my room, number five. I will take the end room," he whispered, "right, let's go."

They went in single file in room number order, and crept along the veranda, halting outside their respective door, or in some cases, doors. At a hand signal from Choon Guan they quietly opened each door, switched on the light, and assassinated each victim quickly, those who awoke not staying awake for very long. Those men allocated two rooms, on two occasions met their targets head on whilst the Japs were heading for the light switch, or searching for their weapons. It was all over in seconds. Quickly they left the screaming girls, shut the doors behind them and took up their positions on the veranda. In a few more seconds they saw the jaggers running over the lallang towards them, and as has already been suspected, one burst over their heads swiftly converted any valorous ambition they may have had to their adopting a prone position, where they remained until they had a pretty good idea the coast was clear.

Strangely enough, a similar situation obtained with regard to the batmen. Given time to wake up, wonder what it was all about, slip some pants on for the sake of decency and get outside, they were faced by the party on the reception end of the veranda. Not only the party, but also facing a number of rounds of .45 ammunition being hose-piped from the barrels of three Thompson sub machine guns. Only one of them was hit, but he yelled loudly enough to be heard in the centre of Frasers Hill, the remainder beating a quick retreat back to their quarters, leaving their unfortunate brother-in-arms to look after himself. The Chinese thought this rather odd. Such experience as they had had before, or heard about before, had led them to believe that if a Jap only had a toothbrush in his hand he would charge into a tommy gun being fired at him. What they didn't know was the batmen were all Formosans, and whilst they might be serving their Japanese Emperor, they certainly had no intention of dying for him if it could be avoided.

Choon Guan burst into the end room, switched on the light to find a European male and Eurasian girl entwined under the sheet beneath the mosquito net.

"Out," he commanded. The girl slid her naked, nubile body under the net and stood in the corner, Choon Guan in the meantime having a number of highly un-party-line thoughts chasing through his mind. The European clambered out after her, the bed being up against the party wall. He was above average height, fair and probably in his mid-fifties.

"Who are you?"

"I am Swiss."

"Papers." As Choon Guan spoke, one of his men joined him.

"All accounted for, Choon Guan."

"Pick that wallet up. Keep this man covered."

Choon Guan very quickly thumbed through the contents of the wallet.

"You are British. Get your clothes and boots on quick or I will shoot you here."

The European moved very slowly to do as he was bid. Choon Guan kicked him hard.

"I will give you one minute or you are dead."

He speedily dressed, pulled his boots on and buckled them, had his hands tied behind his back and was outside on the veranda in only a short while longer than the minute Choon Guan had allowed, leaving a very frightened, very beautiful Eurasian girl standing naked and trembling in the corner as they left - a picture which would return to Choon Guan's dreams many times in the future with predictable results.

Swiftly they moved back to the bivvy point to await the dawn. Hitting railways, electricity sub stations, telegraph posts and so on made the Japanese cross, but killing a dozen of their officers would undoubtedly make them very angry indeed. The quicker they put mileage between Frasers Hill and themselves the better, the minute therefore they saw a glimmer of light in the east they moved out. They were lucky. For two hours before dawn and all the morning the rain came down in torrents. No one, with or without trackers or tracker dogs, would find anything to follow in that weather.

They arrived back at Camp Four about half an hour before dark. Harry came out to meet him, the others not yet having returned.

"What the hell have you got here?"

"He says he's Swiss, sir, but everything in here appears to be in English."

"And he was with the Japs?"

"Yes, sir, they were having a very drunken party, with women." Choon Guan's eyes clouded as his Eurasian girl appeared in his ken.

Harry took the waterproof wallet. "Bring him in."

Seated in Harry's room with Choon Guan, Matthew and Chantek present, Harry asked him, "Who are you? There is no name on any paper in this wallet."

"My name is Schmidt, I am Swiss."

"You speak very good English. Where did you learn it?"

"For many years I was in the Swiss Embassy in London."

"What are you doing here?"

"I am working for the International Red Cross seeking out internees and prisoners of war."

"Why have you no papers to that effect?"

"They were in my suitcase under the bed."

Harry looked at Choon Guan. "Did you see any suitcase?"

"No, sir, but we were not really looking for one, it could have been there."

"Well, look Mr Schmidt, until I can determine who you are, you will be kept under guard. I must warn you if you make any hostile move or attempt to escape you will be shot. Is that clearly understood?"

"Yes, but I protest most strongly."

"Protest noted. Put a bed and net in that empty store-room and mount a guard on him at all times - understood?"

"Yes, sir, I will see to that," Choon Guan replied.

When Tommy and his party arrived, followed a couple of hours later by Reuben, and they had been fed and watered, Harry called an 'O' Group. As they sat down around Harry's bamboo table Reuben asked, "What's all this about a European prisoner?"

"He's Swiss, or says he is," Harry replied, "I've let him sleep for a while; I thought we would all question him together. If he was a Swiss Red Cross representative I would have thought the last thing he would indulge in would be an orgy with the Japs, and according to Choon Guan that's exactly what was in progress."

Reuben looked at Harry. "I spent three winters in Switzerland before the war; can I have a quick word with him? What did he say his name was?"

"Schmidt."

Reuben thought for a moment. "I wonder if he knows how to spell it?"

"Take a couple of minutes, then come straight back."

Reuben left. Harry carried on with de-briefing Tommy.

The sentry unlocked the padlock on the store-room, now a cell, and Reuben entered. He and the prisoner looked at each other.

"I understand you are from the Sudmark," Reuben stated.

"No, I am Swiss," came the reply. Reuben turned and left, leaving the sentry to re-lock the door. He returned to Harry's room.

"He is not Swiss."

"How do you know?"

"He says he is 'Schmidt,' that means he would be German speaking Swiss, they live in the north, generally known as 'the Sudmark.' I stated I understood he came from Sudmark. He replied, 'No, I am Swiss.' He obviously knows little or nothing of Switzerland.

"How the hell did he expect to get away with it?" Tommy asked the party in general.

"Being taken by Chinese he probably thought they would know even less about Switzerland than he did, other than Switzerland was neutral. Perhaps he hoped to bribe them, or his captor's bosses, to let him go," Reuben suggested.

Harry turned to Choon Guan. "You had better make sure you double guard him with your best men. Right now, we will all turn in and question Mr X in the morning."

Harry was a long while getting to sleep. Just as dawn was breaking he sat up with a start.

"Rowlands," he said out loud, "that's bloody Rowlands." He jumped out of bed, slipped on a pair of slacks and his boots and almost ran to the store-room cell. Not only was the cell empty, but also the two guards and their rifles were missing as well.

"Stand-to," he bellowed.

This could be a catastrophe.

* * *

Chapter Eight

Major Dieter von Hassellbek worked hard through the latter months of 1944 to 1945 to make himself indispensable to the Russian War Crimes Court to which he had been seconded after being taken prisoner. His fluent Russian was of considerable help in speeding the trials of the many SS and other concentration camp personnel captured by the swiftly advancing Soviet troops. He had no qualms about acting as prosecuting officer to these evil beasts. As far as he was concerned they had not only committed the most heinous offences against their prisoners for which they should suffer anyway, no matter what their nationality, but they had besmirched the honour of his country for centuries to come.

In January 1945 he had completed his cases at one of the small satellite camps in Poland, and was resting in his room with no papers to prepare for the next day, when a member of the court knocked peremptorily on his door and walked in without being called to enter.

"Major, we are moving very early tomorrow morning. The Red Army has overrun a huge camp at a place called Auschwitz-Birkenau. Be ready at six o'clock to leave."

"I shall be ready, captain."

Three days later they arrived at Birkenau, after innumerable hold ups due to the masses of troops of all descriptions milling around blocking the badly made roads, roads rapidly disintegrating altogether with the passage of tanks over them. On several occasions their American jeeps, part of 'Lease-Lend' to the Soviets, a vehicle which was in the main capable of going anywhere, had to be winched out of holes. It was bitterly cold, Dieter found himself feeling sorry for the Russian infantry plodding along, then telling himself 'I bet the bastards wouldn't feel sorry for me if the boot was on the other foot.'

They arrived at Birkenau and were directed to a factory complex where they were billeted in a flat which had been previously occupied by one of the managers of the IG Farben chemical company. In a few days a lecture room was cleared downstairs to be used as a courtroom.

For a month Dieter worked on the preparation of papers in two languages for the prosecution of those being charged with slave labour, individual acts of cruelty or ill-treatment, even rape and murder by factory bosses and overseers. Whilst working on these cases he got to hear of the appalling findings a few kilometres away at Auschwitz, from which, when the wind was from that direction, one could still smell the aftermath of the ghastly processes which had taken place there.

It was whilst he was working there, on 14th April, a bright sunny spring morning that he opened his window to hear birds singing in full voice, he heard cheers coming from a group of Russian soldiers billeted in an adjacent building. Leaning out of the window he called out, "What's happening?"

"We have captured Vienna," a sergeant called back, "it will all soon be over, Berlin is next." And he was correct, two weeks later the Red Army were fighting in the Berlin suburbs, though not having it all their own way by any means.

This news jolted Dieter into action. He got out the map he had 'found' a month or so after his capture and had kept carefully hidden for the day when he would make a break for it, knowing as he did that if he failed they would have no mercy on him; he would, at the very least, be in a gulag for life - which would not be very long - or even shot.

He studied the map. If he could get to Vienna he had friends there with whom he could hide up. From Birkenau to Cracow it was fifty kilometres. At Cracow there was a railway line direct into Vienna which would almost certainly still be running and used by the Russians to carry troops in and move loot out. There would have been little fighting in that area due to the speed of the Russian advance, therefore little destruction of the infrastructure.

How to accomplish it? - that was the question.

It was three hundred and fifty kilometres from Cracow to Vienna or thereabouts. The more he thought about it the more impossible it appeared. Even if he could, by some magical means, obtain a Russian uniform and try and pass himself off as an officer rejoining his unit he would need papers. With the military police and NKVD people constantly demanding papers at check-points he would be unlikely to get far without being exposed, particularly if he tried to go by train. How about stowing away on a goods train? That would not be difficult, but how the devil would you know where it was going?

He began to get depressed at the difficulties before him. He had to accept the fact that the chances of his covering three hundred and fifty kilometres either walking, by train, or by road were absolutely nil. He would have to stick at his work and hope for a better opportunity.

Meanwhile Rosa had, since receiving the dreadful news that Dieter was 'Missing, believed killed in action' back in August 1944, carried on her work at the Klinik. She worked enormously long hours tending the wounded from France, and later Belgium and Holland, sent to them from an already overwhelmed general hospital at Hannover, a hospital also catering for more and more civilian casualties brought about by the ceaseless day and night bombing by the US air force and the RAF. During this time Frau Doktor Schlenker had dropped all semblance of superiority over Rosa, treating her as an equal, calling her by her Christian name except in front of patients. It was as if she realised the war was as good as over, her Messianic belief in Adolf Hitler having been shattered by what she now knew to be the true state of the National Socialist Party. Of the even more horrific details of the extermination camps, and the nightmare of Belsen only seventy-odd kilometres from the Klinik, she remained in ignorance.

In January, despite the distorted news given out by Goebbels there was no disguising the fact that the Russians had liberated Warsaw, what there was left of it, after their deliberate policy had been put into effect not to press forward to assist in the uprising by the Poles within the city. As a result thousands of Polish men and women lost their lives while the Soviet army stood back and waited. Later in the month Marshal Koniev crossed the River Oder at several points - the only major obstacle before Berlin itself. Refugees were beginning to appear in Bruksheim from the eastern territories with horrendous stories of rape and pillage being carried out by the Russians.

In February came the news that Dresden had been fire-bombed by the RAF and bombed again the following day by US daylight Fortresses. The German News Agency announced openly, in contrast to their usual report that 'slight damage was done,' that 'the allies have reduced Dresden to ashes.' At the same time the agency was boasting that the Fuhrer's secret weapon was 'laying London waste,' in reply to which Frau Doktor Schlenker said to Rosa, "Yes, but how does that stop the Russians?" It was the first occasion upon which Rosa had heard the Frau Doktor query an official news item.

On the 5th of March Cologne was captured by the American army. Cologne was just two hundred and fifty miles from Bruksheim. On that day Frau Doktor Schlenker received an order from the commandant at Ravensbruk concentration camp to return the prisoner von Hassellbek along with the other prisoners who had been with her when she had been sent to the brickworks back in May 1943. An escort would be sent for them on the 12th of March. The Frau Doktor immediately made her way to the Burgemeister's office. Doktor Auerback took one look at the notice and tore it up, dropping it theatrically into his waste-paper basket.

"Frau Doktor, if and when these men arrive please send them on to me. I shall give them a written deposition that all these people were sent to Buchenwald two months ago. By the time they sort that out the war will be over. I only hope and pray that the English or the Americans get here before those evil Russkis. I think they will, there seems little to stop them."

Frau Doktor Schlenker sat on her chair in front of Doktor Auerbach's imposing desk, her face streaming with tears.

"To think of the millions of good German people who will have to suffer the degradation of servitude to those Russian monsters," she cried.

She could not know that, even if one was sickened by the wholesale rape and plundering by the Soviet forces when they at last crossed into the German homeland, it was nothing compared to the murder and brutality inflicted upon the 'untermenschen' by the victorious Wehrmacht and their Einsatzgruppen clearing-up squads when the tide was flowing eastwards.

The Frau Doktor eventually composed herself and returned to the Klinik. She called Rosa in and told her what the Burgemeister had said. Rosa broke down into tears and was held in the comforting arms of the Frau Doktor.

"They are coming on the 12th," she explained to Rosa. "On the 11th you must clear all your papers, any clothing and so on, and take it all to your mother's flat, just in case they decide to disbelieve the Burgemeister and come back here to search for you. I think that is unlikely. After all, if they decide to search for one they have to search for all, and the other women who were with you are spread out all over the countryside around here."

On the 12th two quite elderly auxiliary camp guards appeared at the Klinik. The Frau Doktor was extremely polite to them and examined the list containing the names of all the women who were sent to work at the brickworks, of which Rosa's was one.

"You know that most of these were shot or died on the march, don't you?"

"On the march? What do you mean Frau Doktor, 'on the march'?"

"These women were marched here from Ravensbruk."

"But that is, what? nearly three hundred kilometres! Do you tell me they had to walk all the way?"

"Yes, the Frau Doktor von Hassellbek, who has been working here since, was one of the few survivors."

The two men looked at each other.

"Well, we have to take them back."

"They were rounded up and taken away two months ago. You must go and see the Burgemeister. I will take you."

These two men were ordinary, simple, middle aged fellows, press-ganged into this job, which whilst they had no great love for it, realised that it was better than being drafted into the infantry and being shot at. They therefore followed the order of the Frau Doktor, who of course was way up in the pecking order of things compared to them, and to whom they would defer without question. The same applied, even more so, to Burgemeister Auerbach, an imposing figure at the best of times.

"You have had a wasted journey I am afraid," he told them. "We had orders from Berlin to send them to Buchenwald some while ago. Now look, you go to the Gasthaus across the road with this note from me. They will put you up for a couple of days while Der Anwalt draws up a document, an affidavit which I will swear, for you to take back to Ravensbruk. Now, how did you get here?"

The senior of the two replied,

"We had transport by kuppelwagen into Berlin, then the train from Berlin to Hannover, then changed for Bruksheim." He paused, looked at his comrade, and continued;

"Berlin is in a terrible state from the bombing, and full up with refugees from the east. Our train to Hannover was so crowded with people and their bundles, all they could save from their homes, that we could hardly get on and off our carriage. The people all had that frightened look, even the children were quiet."

"Where is your home?"

"Heinz and I both come from Reinbek, just outside Hamburg. We have heard nothing from our families for several weeks; we don't know whether they are alive or dead. People say that Hamburg is just one heap of rubble. When will all this end, Herr Burgemeister?"

"I don't know my friend, but I have a feeling it will be very soon now. Anyway" .... he wrote a note on his headed pad .... "take this to the landlord, have a few beers and forget your troubles for a day or so, and come back and see me at eight o'clock on Wednesday morning and I will have the sworn document ready for you to take back to Ravensbruk."

"Thank you, Herr Burgemeister," they responded in unison. The Burgemeister rang a small bell on his desk in answer to which his secretary appeared.

"Frau Hiller, will you please show these gentlemen out and point out the direction to the Gasthaus Prinz Albert? Thank you, Frau Hiller."

When they had departed Doktor Auerbach sat back in his chair.

"You realise we could be shot for doing this?"

"Yes. But I think the next month will be so chaotic, everyone, even the SS, will be thinking more of saving his or her own skin than worrying too much about a few concentration camp absentees."

"Let's hope you are right. By doing this I feel we have set to rights, if only in a very small way, a wrong done by our government. How we allowed it to happen in the first place is something, I suspect, most thinking people will agonise over for years to come, to say nothing of the stigma we shall endure in the eyes of the world."

They both sat in silence for a while.

"God bless you, Herr Doktor, God bless you," Frau Doktor stood and shook hands with the Burgemeister then made her way back to the Klinik.

As she returned to her office, Rosa was watching from the window of her step-father's flat overlooking the park entrance. Rosa allowed a few minutes to pass, then telephoned the Klinik. The Frau Doktor was obviously expecting her call, and out of habit of not saying anything on the telephone which could be overheard immediately said,

"Will you come to the Klinik, please, straight away?"

Rosa hurried down the stairs, the lift having one of its awkward days, and swiftly rejoined her chief.

"You had better stay in the flat for a couple of days until the two guards go back to Ravensbruk," Rosa was told. "The Burgemeister is giving them a paper to say you were all sent away. I think it very unlikely they would come here again for any reason, but you never know. Come in again on Wednesday afternoon."

"What will happen when they check up?"

"I don't know, we will cross that bridge when we come to it."

That evening the two guards from Ravensbruk enjoyed a few beers together, decided they would, whilst they had a duty pass to collect camp prisoners, go and see what had happened to their families in Reinbek. It would be just as quick to travel Hannover-Hamburg-Ravensbruk as it would be via Berlin, furthermore they would not have to brave the day and night bombing now being suffered by the capital. In this they were most unfortunate. The Allies that day, the 14th March, began a heavy attack against railway marshalling yards at Hamm, Osnabruck and Hannover in preparation for the invasion of Germany over the Rhine. A new bomb was used containing 22,000 pounds of explosive each, the equivalent force of ten flying bombs or V2s. The guards were three miles north of Hannover city when one of these monsters dropped one hundred yards away and obliterated everything in sight, including their train. Their identification tags were returned to Ravensbruk after a few days, the officials there automatically assuming the prisoners had been killed as well and wrote them all off. Well, what was another thirty names in a book containing thousands, no, tens of thousands?

For the next month Rosa carried on with her work at Bruksheim, the little town itself gradually changing beyond belief with the presence of pitiful numbers of displaced persons flooding in from the east. They had to treat all sorts of conditions in women, children and old people, as well as the continual flow of Wehrmacht casualties. On the 24th of March British and American paratroops jumped the Rhine, swiftly pushing across the North German plain until on Friday 13th April the people of Bruksheim witnessed a handful of German tanks, very few lorries, a string of horse drawn wagons and a bedraggled motley of foot soldiers stream through the little town all day, and then there was silence. During the night, where the huge red and black swastika flags had flown in front of the Rathaus, a white sheet had been suspended, and soon after dawn a trio of armoured cars leap-frogged into and through the town to ensure it was clear, followed by hundreds of weary, tight-lipped Tommies. There was no waving and cheering with the accompanying return waves from the soldiers as there had been in France and Belgium and Holland. Montgomery had given the strictest instructions there was to be absolutely no fraternisation whatsoever. Soldiers were forbidden even to give any sweets or chocolate to children and the Germans were to be ostracised except where it was necessary to maintain civilian organisation.

On Saturday evening Rosa was on duty in the Klinik when a British truck arrived, followed by an army ambulance. A tall captain walked in wearing a Red Cross armband.

"You are?" he asked in a not unfriendly voice.

"I am Frau Doktor Rosa von Hassellbek," she replied. "The Klinik Director is Frau Doktor Schlenker; she is off duty at present."

"You speak very good English."

"I have had little practice these past few years."

"I have two wounded men in the ambulance. I need to operate on them. Will you assist me?"

"Yes of course, but we have no operating theatre as such."

"I have operated on kitchen tables many times, Frau Doktor, in the past four years," he replied cheerfully. He turned to the corporal who had followed him in, "Bring them in," he said.

The two casualties, both sergeants, had bullets lodged in them. The captain and his new assistant, with the aid of the corporal and another orderly who had been driving the ambulance, worked until after midnight until eventually the two wounded, their bullets removed, were put to bed, surrounded, as they told their disbelieving comrades some while afterwards, by women in all the other beds, one of whom was delivered of a baby during the night.

Meanwhile, had Rosa known it, her friend David Chandler was only some thirty miles away from her to the north, but that is another story. Her husband, Dieter, was five hundred miles to the east, but she did not know that either. She did know that for the people of Bruksheim, for her, for her mother, and her stepfather Fritz Strobel, the war was over, though she had few doubts there were to be harsh times to come. At least they would not be at the mercy of the Russian vandals. She offered up a prayer of thanks for their deliverance and a plea for the safety of her husband.

★ ★ ★

Chapter Nine

After David had gone back off leave Margaret and Fred sat in the drawing room at Chandlers Lodge waiting for the nine o'clock news in a little over half an hour's time. Rose had gone out to visit a friend, leaving Jeremy in their care - not an onerous task as he rarely woke up once he had been put to bed. Margaret snuggled up to her husband.

"Fred dear, do you think I could buy a horse?" She added quickly, "with my own money of course."

"As far as I am concerned you can buy a complete herd of horses, if that's what such an accumulation is called, and you, young lady can keep your money in your pocket. However, you've obviously something going on in that pretty head of yours, am I right?"

"Well, I wondered if we could build a stable down in the spinney at the end of the garden, and get a couple of horses so that we can go riding now that you have got more time. I used to love riding when I was in Texas, and you are an excellent horseman."

"Who would look after them? It's very time consuming owning a horse."

"Well, I had a word with Nobby, the gardener. He's an old cavalry man; he said he could do with another hour or so each day to do the mucking out and so on. I would help with the grooming and I guarantee we'll have a waiting list of young ladies in particular, who would like to come in and help."

"Alright, you're on. Go and have a word with Ronnie at the stables. Ask him if he will buy a couple of good tempered nags for us, and will he recommend someone to design and build the stables, tack room, hay and straw storage and so on. An ordinary local builder or joiner wouldn't know the finer points of stable layout, drainage and so on. It will be worthwhile paying a bit more to get it done by a professional."

"You are a lovely man Frederick Chandler."

"Just Fred - for some reason my mother, or perhaps my father, I don't know which, just put 'Fred' on the birth certificate."

"Well, whatever, you're still a lovely man."

"And you, my love, are a very lovely woman." He kissed her gently, then got up to turn on the nine o'clock news, to hear Stuart Hibberd announce:

"This is the news on the twenty fourth of March.

"The Second Army crossed the Rhine into Germany today. The British 6th Airborne Division and the 17th American Airborne Division have landed some miles ahead of the forces crossing the river to protect them in the crossing. Fierce fighting is being experienced but a general advance is being made from the complete bridgehead."

They looked at each other, each having the same unstated fears within them. Margaret closed her eyes, put her hands together and whispered,

"Please God, keep all our boys safe."

"Amen to that," Fred added. They sat in silence whilst the mellifluous tones of Stuart Hibberd gave news of further V2 attacks against London, resulting in casualties and damage, along with sustained V2 attacks against Antwerp, which had caused large scale devastation but had not damaged the port facilities, so necessary to the 21st Army Group. The last rocket bomb would be fired three days later, exploding at Orpington in Kent, and killing one man. In all 2,855 people had been killed in and around London by these monstrous weapons, but it is not generally known that in the attack on Antwerp and other Belgian towns no fewer than 4,483 civilians had been killed, people who had lived through the war under the heel of the Nazis, had experienced the exhilaration of being liberated by the British and Canadian forces, only to die at the hands of their previous conquerors for absolutely no reason whatsoever.

On Monday 26th March Margaret borrowed Rose's bicycle and took herself along to Ronnie Mascall's stables. Ronnie came out to greet her as she pulled up in front of his very spacious premises.

"Margaret, lovely to see you, what can I do for you? You're not dressed for riding, so it can't be a horse you are wanting."

"Well actually it is. Two in fact."

"Two? You going to do a circus act or something?" He took her arm.

"Come in, come in." They went into his comfortably furnished office. "Would you like some tea? Our coffee is pretty abysmal."

"Tea would be fine. Thank you. Fred and I would like your advice on who we could get to build a stable layout for two horses, and for you to buy the horses for us," she then added, "for a fee of course."

"Well, as regards the first item, I know the very man. He can build them, all the groundwork and drainage and so forth, without your having to engage an architect. Oh, and as I have an interest in the firm no fee would be involved." He smiled at her, "I just get Nutty to put it in the price in the first place!"

Margaret laughed. "Nutty, how did he get a name like that?"

"Well, his proper name is Oscar Hazel, but with a surname like that he has been 'Nutty' ever since he was a kid. Having said that there is nothing nutty about Nutty. What he doesn't know about building stables isn't worth knowing. Now, do you want a brick affair, like these here only smaller, or a standard wooden set-up? If you want brick ones you will probably face a considerable delay since bricks have to be issued on a licence basis and that, at this stage of the game, takes time. People do get them on the black market but Nutty wouldn't risk doing that."

"Black market bricks? I didn't know there was such a thing."

"They're mainly second hand ones spirited away from bomb damage sites."

"I think we will go for the timber units."

"Most of that will be second-hand, quite legal second-hand mind, but once it's painted inside and out it will look fine."

They arranged that Nutty would visit the site on Friday, do a 'measure-up,' and give the price, including erection, by Tuesday or Wednesday of next week.

"Good, now what about the horses?" Margaret asked.

"Well, the first question is, what do you want them for? Hunting, hacking, show jumping, dressage, point to point, carriage driving, polo?" He grinned at her. "Most people think of a horse as either being a carthorse or a horse you ride on, but to quote the old adage, horses are for courses. A good hunter would probably be useless for carriage driving."

Margaret thought for a few moments.

"I wonder if I could get Fred to join the hunt?"

"Be great if he would. You get a lot of social life as well as the hunting, once it gets properly under way again, which will not be long now I warrant."

"Well, if he agreed to join we would want a couple of steady mounts that we could use for hacking around at weekends and so on as well."

"Right. Well, you're both of roughly the same height, although he's a bit heavier than you are."

"What a kind man you are - if anything I am a bit heavier than he is."

"Well, we'll let that pass. I reckon a couple of eight- to nine-year-olds; around sixteen hands or sixteen two would fit the bill. Sound of wind and limb of course. I will start looking straight away. By the way, I shall be seeing Fred at Rotary at lunchtime. Is it OK to talk to him about this? I mean it's not a surprise or anything?"

"By all means do and I will look forward to seeing Nutty on Friday - in the morning?"

"Knowing Nutty, it will probably be at about eight o'clock in the morning, so have the tea ready, Nutty likes his tea."

Margaret took her leave, mounted her bike and pedalled back into Sandbury to see Cecely at Country Style. Being Monday morning the shop was not busy. Cecely was just wrapping a garment in very thin brown paper for a customer to take away. The days of expensive, named, carrier-bags were long gone, and would in fact not re-appear for some while yet. Margaret looked at the stock as she waited for Cecely to bid her customer goodbye.

"Yes madam, how can I help you, madam?" she joked as she came over to Margaret.

"Cecely, is it possible to buy riding breeches these days, and a hacking jacket?"

"We have to send away for the breeches, but we have tweed jackets in stock. Mind you, they run away with the coupons."

"Well, being a new civilian I have been allocated my clothing coupon ration, so I think I should be alright there. Oh, and I see you have some very nice roll-neck pullovers there. Can we have a roll-call to see how many coupons I would need for those three items?"

They totted up the requirement, chatted, found that she had coupons enough and some to spare, examined the breeches catalogue, chatted, took the necessary measurements, chatted, selected a pale lemon roll-necked pullover, then decided, as Mrs Draper arrived to take over, they would go over to The Angel for lunch and a chat.

Settled in the conservatory at the rear of The Angel, Cecely asked,

"So you intend patronising our Ronnie, do you?"

"Well no, not exactly, Fred has said we can buy a couple of horses, or rather get Ronnie to buy them for us, and build stables in the spinney. Nobby the gardener will put an hour or so in every day to help look after them. he's an ex-cavalry man and could do with the money. He only does a day a week for us in the garden."

"You realise you will send my Greta green with envy? She will be pestering you to let her help look after them at weekends."

"Perhaps during holidays as well?" Margaret asked artfully, "well, when Fred can't spare the time she could always ride out with me, couldn't she? Do you ride?"

"No, definitely not, horses and Cecely Coates have never hit it off I am pleased to say."

As the two ladies sat talking of the equestrian plans, Fred and Ronnie were only a few yards away, albeit through two or three walls and numerous doors. Across the table Ronnie addressed Fred. The conversation went like this:

"Your very beautiful Margaret came to see me today."

"Yes, I know, were you able to help her?"

"No problem, dear boy. She suggested you might like to join the hunt."

"Do you mean the Hunt from Cuddingham?"

At this there was a roar of laughter from the six Rotarians at the end of that sprig, remembering only too well the occasion when Fred spoke to the local vicar, Canon Rosser, about the 'Hunt from Cuddingham,' but got the 'H' and 'C' the wrong way round, causing them both to realise what he had done, and for them both to collapse against the church railings. Canon Rosser was an ex Great War padre in the Royal West Kents, so knew his way around army language.

As a result of the sudden uproar the sergeant-at-arms rose to his feet.

"Sixpence fine each for unseemly behaviour for those six fellows on sprig two," he announced.

"Why, what have they done?" asked a fellow on sprig one.

"They made raucous laughter."

"About what?" the questions persisted. Ronnie rose to his feet.

"I was talking to fellow Rotarian Fred about the Hunt from Cuddingham," Ronnie explained.

As nearly all the club members were in on the joke there was an instantaneous roar of laughter from the president downwards. The sergeant-at-arms had a field day. Sixpence each from thirty eight members - nearly a pound in the services box. Fred stood up.

"I propose the sergeant-at-arms be fined a shilling. He is the only one who hasn't laughed. That means he is not contributing to Rotary fellowship."

"Order, order," the president intoned. "There are no ordinances which allow the sergeant-at-arms to be fined." Fred was fined a further sixpence for a frivolous demand.

The club settled down to its lunch, leaving the president with the extremely difficult task of explaining what the fuss was all about to the visiting speaker, a Salvation Army officer attending to solicit funds to help build a hostel in Maidstone, the previous one having been destroyed by enemy action.

Back in the conservatory Margaret asked,

"You haven't heard from Charles yet?"

"No, he sent a cable from Cape Town. They were waiting to join a convoy, so could be delayed."

"They are still having to form convoys?"

"Yes, Jack told me that U boat activity in the South Atlantic is still much in evidence, even though we are now sinking more of them than they are of us, particularly in the North Atlantic."

"How terrible it must be to be incarcerated in one of those things under attack," Margaret declared.

"It likewise must be terrible to be in the bowels of a ship when a torpedo from one of them hits you," Cecely replied.

"Let's change the subject," Margaret suggested, "now, how is the new romance coming along?"

Greta's current romantic attachment was discussed, along with David and Paddy being over the Rhine, probably Mark and Charlie waiting to go over, if not already in the bridgehead, how was Gloria getting on as lady of the manor, and a host of small talk until Cecely said she would have to rush, she was late already.

"Isn't the boss allowed to be late?"

"I didn't think of that!"

Friday came and Nutty duly arrived, not at eight o'clock as estimated by Ronnie, but at a quarter to eight, Margaret nevertheless, having seen Fred off to the factory, being ready for him. They walked down to the spinney together.

"Now, which way is south?" it was a dull morning.

"Well the sun comes up from over there so it must be towards the house."

"Which part of the country do you come from, missus? You sound more like a Yank than an Englishwoman."

"I am a Yank, but trying hard to be English."

Nutty didn't quite know what to make of that.

"Well, what I was thinking, if you want to look out of the back of the house to see your horses we'll face the doors that way. Facing south is good for the horses too; they get the sun that way. You got a paddock lined up for them?"

"I hadn't thought of needing a paddock."

Nutty looked through the few silver birch and hazel foliage to the rear of the property.

"I reckon you'd be better off with a paddock. That land behind you would come in handy. There's three or four acres there. Who owns it, and what do they do with it, do you know?"

"I've no idea. I shall have to ask my husband to find out."

"Don't worry. I'll find out for you without anyone twigging somebody wants it. Right, well, I'll have a good measure up, and give you a price. Two boxes 12 x 12, tack room 12 x 6, plus storage area. Separate price for groundwork, including bringing water down from the house. I don't do the electrical work, but I would advise you to run a supply down there. You don't want to be mucking about with lanterns on a cold and frosty night. I'll do a plan for you, won't be up to Christopher Wren standards, but you will get a good idea from it as to what you are getting, and I will come and see you with it and what it's going to cost you on Monday morning."

"Bright and early?"

"Bright and early."

"In that case I will get Mr Chandler to wait for you."

"What time does he usually leave?"

"About seven-thirty."

"Right, I'll be here seven o'clock then it won't mess his day up."

"Thank you, thank you very much, Mr Hazel."

"Nutty, missus, everybody calls me Nutty."

"Seven-thirty it is then, Nutty," she laughed, and shook hands with him.

That evening she asked Fred about the field behind the spinney.

"I don't know whose it is," Fred replied, "every year one of the local farmers makes hay from it; otherwise no-one goes near it. It must be scheduled for agricultural use or someone would have probably bought it for building by now."

As they were talking Jack arrived. He often called in for a chat and a drink, with Moira being away in America. Fred asked him if he knew who owned the paddock.

"I think it's one of those parcels of land that a good many of the livery companies bought after the Great War with the idea of building apartments on them to house war widows of their members, or sons of their members, killed in action. People like the Ironmongers Company and so on did an enormous amount of good work in this respect. I can only imagine, if this was the case, this plot was surplus to their requirements - they've probably even forgotten they own it - or possibly they couldn't get permission to build on it for some reason in the first place."

"Well, Nutty is having a nose round; we'll see what he comes up with."

"If it does turn out to belong to a livery, let me know and I will make some discreet enquiries. I know quite a few of the Masters and Past-Masters. Mind you, knowing them, if it does belong to one of them you won't get it for a knock-down price. They are a crafty lot."

"You should know."

"We Mercers are a race apart."

They then had to explain to a confused Margaret, what livery companies Mercers and Ironmongers were all about.

"What a fascinating place London is," she exclaimed.

"Well, when things get back to normal we will introduce you to it my dear, I promise."

"Have you got a date for that?" asked Fred.

"One year from today," Jack replied, "not fully back to normal, but well on the way."

"Promise?"

"Promise." Fred raised his glass of Whitbreads Light Ale.

"Here's to one year from today." They joined him in the toast.

At seven o'clock 'on the dot,' Nutty arrived on Monday 2nd April.

"Lovely morning, missus, but still very chilly for spring."

"Come in, Nutty, this is my husband." He and Fred shook hands.

"Right, I've got it all laid out." He produced a plan drawn up in a most professional manner.

"You do this drawing?" asked Fred.

"Yes, sir. I've loved drawing ever since I was a kid. I went to evening classes before the war to get a bit of the technical side under my belt. The rest of it, the shading, the trees and so on I've sort of developed as I've gone along."

"Well, I deal with engineering drawings every day. You could earn a living in a drawing office."

"I have thought about it, but I'd rather be outdoors, except during some of the weather we had in February and last month. I make a living, that's the main thing."

"Right, let's have the shock and horror paper."

Margaret looked at Fred quizzically.

"The estimates," Fred enlightened her.

"Here we are, sir."

"Groundwork as per the cut-away there. Levelling, hard core, concrete, drainage channels, concrete hardstanding at the front, concrete pathway here and here. Now, you've got a problem. If lorries deliver hay and straw, or come to collect the manure - you can sell that to a nursery, they'll queue up for it - how are they going to get down to the spinney?"

"We will have to sacrifice a bit of the garden over by the hedge."

"Well you may not have to. If you can get the paddock to the back of the spinney you can get into that from the side road. You don't want lorry loads of muck going through your garden if you can help it."

And so they discussed peripheral items until Fred said, "You trying to delay giving me the price?"

Nutty grinned. "I was a bit."

"Come on, out with it."

"Right. Groundwork, two hundred. Two stables and tack room with common walls, two hundred and ten. Storage. That's only a roof and one rear wall. Seventy pounds. Total, four hundred and eighty. Painting afterwards inside and out sixty pounds, makes it five-forty."

"That sounds alright. Now what have you sussed out about the paddock."

"Belongs to Sir Oliver Routledge. He never uses it except to make hay out of it."

Sir Oliver was the biggest landowner for miles around Sandbury. In addition to having been employed by him it seemed a lifetime ago, Fred was on very good terms with him, having supplied him with tractors and farm machinery before the war and pulled out all the stops during the war in maintaining it for him when he had got into trouble.

"When can you start the groundwork?"

"After Easter."

"Easter's next weekend."

"I could start tomorrow week."

"You're on. I'll give you twenty-five percent to start, fifty per cent when you finish, and the other twenty-five in thirty days from completion. That suit you?"

"That suits me fine, Mr Chandler."

"Right now, all I've got to do is to chat up Sir Oliver - oh, and buy a couple of horses and all the tack that goes with them." He broke into his old familiar habit. "God, I shall have to do a paper-round to get the money for all this."

Nutty and Fred shook hands on the deal, each departing to his place of work. Margaret walked with Fred to the garage to get his bicycle out.

"Fred?"

"Yes, love."

"Suppose I get in touch with Sir Oliver, do you think he would deal with me?"

"Well, I don't see why not. Yes, have a go, although he may put you on to his agent. His number is in our telephone book."

At ten o'clock that morning Margaret took the plunge. Her call was put through to Sir Oliver's secretary.

"Could I speak with Sir Oliver, please?"

"Who is calling?"

"My name is Margaret Chandler. I am Fred Chandler's wife. Mr Chandler, that is, of Sandbury Engineering."

"Oh yes, of course, Mrs Chandler, please hold the line." There was a delay of a minute or so. The secretary was obviously doing what all good secretaries do, namely filling her boss in with the details of the caller, adding 'she sounds very American,' whilst Margaret of course was trying not to sound very American. But then, in the middle of the Kentish countryside the only American sounding voice one heard under normal circumstances was on the silver screen at the 'bug hutch,' or in the Odeon at Maidstone.

"Mrs Chandler, how do you do? I read of your marriage in 'The Messenger,' congratulations, Fred Chandler is one of the finest men I know. Now what can I do for you?"

Margaret explained why she had telephoned. The conversation wandered as to how she came to be in England, how she had met Fred, where she came from in the States until Sir Oliver's secretary clocked up nearly twenty minutes, which compared to her boss's usual terse telephone manner was something of an event. Eventually he said, "Look, Mrs Chandler, I am coming in to Sandbury on Wednesday morning to see Canon Rosser. I'll have a look at that field, I must admit I can't even remember what it looks like which shows how important it must be to me - what?"

"In that case, please come in and have coffee with us."

"I will take you up on that. About eleven be alright?"

"About eleven will be fine."

As she replaced the telephone Rose came into the hallway.

"Newly married ladies making dates already?"

"Yes, and with a baronet too."

"You're joking!"

"No, Sir Oliver Routledge is calling in on Wednesday at eleven o'clock. You will be here, won't you, and I must telephone Fred to ask him to put it in his diary."

"Is it about the field?"

"Yes."

"I would have thought he would have left a minor matter like that to his agent. Perhaps he fancies you."

"He's never seen me, and only spoke to me for a few minutes," Margaret protested.

"Just joking. He's probably just curious. He has known dad for a very long time. In fact he was one of the people who provided a reference to the building society when dad bought Chandlers Lodge."

Rose moved into the kitchen, and Margaret made her call to Fred.

"Sorry love, Wednesday is out. I have two ministry visits that day, one lot I am taking to lunch at The Angel. You can manage him on your own I am sure."

Manage him on her own she did. Well, not exactly on her own. Rose was there, and so was young Jeremy, now four years old. Sir Oliver made a great fuss of him and Jeremy obviously was taken by Sir Oliver. He stayed for nearly an hour, although Margaret was getting somewhat anxious in not being able to raise the question of the field without it looking as though that was the only reason for which she had invited him. Which, really, it was.

Just as he was about to leave he announced, "Oh, by the way, that field. Blackman, my agent, says it's more trouble to us than it's worth being stuck away from our main holdings. Get Fred to contact him and they can argue over the price. We don't want to be bothered with trivialities like money, do we? - what?"

"I must say, Sir Oliver, I have in my not uneventful life so far, not been able to consider money trivial, but thank you very much, you really are most kind."

So Fred agreed the price with Mr Blackman on Thursday. On Good Friday Fred and Margaret, along with Rose and Jeremy, visited Ronnie to see the two horses he had collected for them to view. They fell in love with them on the spot and bought them with a handshake.

On Easter Saturday morning Margaret awoke suffering from what was confirmed by Rose as morning sickness. "How on earth did that happen?" she gasped to Rose.

"Well, if you don't know, I'm sure I don't," a laughing Rose replied. "I suggest you have a large brandy ready for when you tell dad, although where you are going to get it from I'm blessed if I know!"

***

Chapter Ten

On Friday 23rd February, Charles Coates, having had the forethought to purchase a winter-weight suit, pullover and raincoat, took the Qantas flight to Sydney. At Sydney he boarded the train for Melbourne, changed for Adelaide, and then sat back to enjoy(?) the interminable journey across the Nullabar Plain to Perth. He was told that Nullabar was the aborigine name meaning 'No trees,' and how right they were. He had been told many years before by a South African friend, when he had asked him what 'the veldt' was, that it was mile after mile of 'bugger-all.' He included the Nullabar Plain in that category.

After nearly three days, he arrived at Perth, saddle sore and weary. According to his friend Mac's calculations he had a day to spare, the Berentia should be arriving on the morrow. He caught a bus to Fremantle and found his way to the shipping office, shared it seemed with about twenty other lines, since they each only had probably one ship a month coming into Fremantle, not that the port was deserted by any means as the number of RN, US Navy, and other warships gave evidence. There was even an Argentinian destroyer there, Argentina having recently declared war on Germany and Japan, presumably because they now realised which side was going to win. This made it the fifty-third nation to be at war.

Having checked in with the shipping office, and being told the Berentia was on time, he was advised to book in at 'Sadie's' place by the dock gates.

"It's alright for a night - I don't think I'd like to stay any longer," the clerk laughingly told him. He realised why later when at two o'clock in the morning he still had not been able to get to sleep because of the drunken racket downstairs. 'I thought all Australian bars had to shut at six o'clock,' he said to himself. Apparently 'Sadie's' had some special dispensation in that regard.

The next morning he took his small suitcase aboard the Berentia, being met at the top of the gangway by the first officer.

"Mr Coates? I am John Bury, welcome aboard. You were with Captain MacDonald I believe? I sailed with him for a year before the war. Marvellous chap. We thought we'd lost him, it was great to know he has survived."

He led Charles through a veritable maze of corridors and up stairways to the bridge.

"Captain Urquhart, sir, this is Mr Coates."

"Welcome aboard, Mr Coates. I trust you enjoyed your Cook's tour across the green fields of Australia."

"I think the less said about that, Captain, the better. I must say the investment in rolling stock on the Australian railways has been somewhat curtailed over recent years, judging by the state of my backside."

"Well, the first officer here will take you to the cabin deck and introduce you to the other passengers. Is your baggage aboard?"

"I only have this suitcase."

"Well, that makes a change; most people bring everything, including the kitchen sink. Oh, by the way, we already had our full complement of six passengers, so Captain Mac suggested we enrol you on a DBS passage."

"What is a DBS passage for goodness sake?"

"It stands for 'Distressed British Seaman.' We are allowed to carry a seaman who was, say, stranded in hospital somewhere and needs to get to a port to which we are sailing. He is then given a job, put on the manifest, and all is legal."

"So what sort of job do I get?" said Charles with a laugh.

"Well. I don't know if you noticed but there is a little platform at water level at the sharp end of the ship where you go if we hit a minefield. You are provided with a long pole and you push the mines out of the way so that they don't hit the ship. It is, you see, a job that requires little or no training."

Charles laughed heartily. The first officer grinned dutifully. He had heard it all before.

Charles met four of the passengers when John Bury took him to the small cabin he was to occupy for the next few weeks, and then on to the saloon. Here they could sit and read during the voyage. There was, he instantly saw, an enormous number of paperback Penguin type books, shelf after shelf of them into which he could immerse himself. One of the greatest hardships to him during the three years he was in captivity, next only perhaps to his bodily starvation, was the hunger for the written word his mind suffered.

The four men he met did not extend him what might be described as an effusive greeting. They were all younger than he was, he judged in their middle to late thirties, and were British, which led him to wonder why they were not in the forces. They exuded a 'cliqueness' which one can often sense among old boys of the same school, or for that matter old lags from the same slammer. He established later they were junior members of a Ministry of Supply mission visiting Australia for some real or imagined purpose, and like toffee apples, stuck together. Charles wondered who the other two passengers would be. He was to find out at lunch time when the ministry four sat together at one end of the longish dining table totally ignoring the arrival of the fifth passenger, a lady, fortyish, slim, not unattractive, but possessed of totally grey, almost white hair. Charles immediately rose to his feet as she took the chair opposite him, and introduced himself, noting as he did so not only did none of the ministry four stand up as the lady came, neither did they acknowledge her or attempt to introduce her.

She took his outstretched hand and shook it firmly. "I am Jane Robertson," she said. "My husband was an officer on this line but was lost at sea in 1940; because of that connection I've managed a passage back to UK."

"I am so sorry to hear that. You have been in Australia all through the war out here then. Your family will have missed you."

She was obviously very reluctant to reply to that observation. Charles, sensing this, added, "I'm sorry, I should not have made that assumption."

To change the subject he quickly added, "Who is our sixth companion? He will be late for his lunch at this rate." The dining room steward was moving towards them with a small pile of soup plates.

"The sixth passenger is my little girl, Sophia. I give her her midday meal in the cabin. She then has her afternoon sleep."

"Will she join us for dinner?"

"No, I feed her again in the cabin."

Charles mind was racing. This child must be at least five or six years old if Mrs Robertson's husband was lost in 1940. Was the child deformed in some way, or retarded? Without having a father to know and love was she badly behaved? The fact that the other four passengers neither acknowledged her in any way was a bit odd. Common decency would oblige you to say hello, or good evening, or whatever.

"Well, perhaps I shall have the pleasure of saying hello to her later on." There was again a distinct pause before Mrs Robertson replied.

"You will have to know. She is part Japanese, that is why the others ignore me." Charles looked at her and in a low voice asked,

"How old is Sophia?"

"She is two years old."

"Then you were in a camp." He added quickly, "I have just come from a camp."

She waited while the steward served their soup, looked along the table to ensure the other four were engrossed in their somewhat unruly conversation, and said, "I was caught in Manila. The Americans rescued us earlier this year and brought us back to Brisbane. In my first week in the camp I was raped by one of the junior officers. The other women in the camp were so kind. I was not the only one. They looked after us. It was such a shock when I came to Australia and people started to point the finger at me. Not all, you understand, just some, and particularly those four," she nodded towards them without looking in their direction.

"Well, you can rest assured I shall not point the finger. Perhaps later this afternoon I can be introduced to Sophia?"

Jane's eyes misted with tears. "Yes, I will do that. Thank you so much. I was dreading the next few weeks as an outcast. Mr Bury is very kind, but we obviously see little of him because of his duties."

Charles was introduced to Sophia later when her mother carried the little girl, bleary eyed from her afternoon sleep, up on to the deck where Charles was watching the activity involved in loading meat into a refrigerated hold in one section of the ship and huge wooden crates containing he knew not what into another. No time was being lost in getting this vessel on its way.

"So this is Sophia?" Charles exclaimed. "She's very pretty."

"She is named after one of my grandmothers."

"Will she come to me, do you think?" asked Charles. Jane passed her to him, the little girl looking a little apprehensively to her mother at first, and then knuckling her hand, smiled at Charles and rubbed it against his face.

"Now, tell me your name."

"Sophia Robertson, and that is my mummy," she said.

"And do you like being on a ship?" She had to think about that for a moment or two, eventually deciding,

"Sometimes."

"I think you're right, sometimes it's not so nice." His mind flashed back to that hell ship adrift in the South China Sea.

"Now, how old are you?"

"I don't know." She looked at Jane enquiringly. Jane mouthed 'two.'

"I'm two."

"She's gorgeous. Why can't she eat with us?"

"Well, I have to prepare different meals, and the others don't like it. I tried for the first two days but they made it plain the child was not welcome."

"From now on she is, though I suppose her late meal, whatever name you give it, will have to be earlier than ours. I must admit that even with my limited knowledge of young children I seem to recall you cannot feed them at eight o'clock in the evening."

"You have no family?"

And that's how the getting to know each other began. Over the next six weeks, they were badly delayed waiting to join a convoy off Rio de Janeiro, which moved up to the Caribbean and then up to the North Atlantic. Their ship eventually left the convoy north of Ireland and with others headed for Liverpool, where they landed on Friday 20th April.

When Charles asked Jane where she would be staying in England she said she would be going to London in the hope of tracing her only sister, the last address she had of her being in Guildford in Surrey. She had been given travel documents by the shipping line, in view of her being the widow of one of their officers, to take her to that city, along with a generous sum of money to help her until she could get settled. They decided therefore to travel together to London, where he would get a train from Victoria down to Sandbury and she would make for Waterloo. He gave her three telephone numbers where he could be contacted and elicited a promise she would contact him that evening from whichever hotel she was staying.

By now Sophia had got to know Charles very well, running to him when she saw him and being picked up, swung round, and cuddled up. It was therefore, a tearful Sophia who was bade to say 'goodbye to Uncle Charles,' when they arrived at Euston.

"We shall see each other again soon, I promise," he told her. Nearby there was a little kiosk selling small handmade toys for a charity for the homeless. Charles carried her across to it and seeing a small teddy bear, paid five shillings for it and gave it to her, noting as he did so the middle-aged lady manning the stall looking at the little oriental child with considerable interest.

Charles carried Sophia to the taxi rank where they had the usual wait. When their cab arrived he shook hands with Jane, gave Sophia a big kiss, reminded her mother to telephone this evening, even if she had no news, helped them into the cab and they were whisked away, waving until they turned out of sight through the main archway.

Charles suddenly felt very lonely.

He sat in his first class seat at Victoria waiting for the train to leave suddenly apprehensive at this final stage in his long, long journey. He was going to have to meet a sister-in-law who had lost her husband, a niece who had been grief-stricken at the loss of her beloved father, the undoubted questioning he would receive about the lives of the two brothers in the camp, all combined to bring back the horror which had been gradually leaving him over the past few weeks. He stared sightlessly out of the window at the grimy station, feeling depressed, when his common sense told him he should be walking on air at the thought of seeing his loved ones again. That slight self-castigation brightened him a little as the train pulled smoothly out towards Kent.

It was late afternoon when he arrived at Sandbury. He asked the porter - there was only one, Sandbury was not exactly a second Clapham Junction - how far it was to The Angel, and was told 'about ten minutes.' He remembered, afterwards, thinking 'that's a measurement of time, not distance,' realising his old judicial brain was coming to the fore. After all ten minutes to a slow or handicapped walker would be an entirely different distance to a faster walker. Stop being so blasted pedantic, he told himself, by which time in the course of his musings he could see 'The Angel' before him. He walked in and rang the bell on the entry desk.

"Have you a room for a few days?" he asked the well set-up gentleman who had answered his call.

"Yes, sir. Name, sir?"

"Coates. Charles Coates."

"Related to Cecely, sir?"

"I'm her brother-in-law."

"Sit down there, please, Mr Coates. Rosie, phone Mrs Coates at Country Style and tell her Mr Charles is here. We know all about you Mr Coates."

Country Style was three minutes away across the road. Cecely burst in the front doors of The Angel in one minute and twenty seconds, as anyone operating a stop-watch at the time would have been able to register. She threw herself into Charles' arms laughing and crying at the same time, until John Tarrant led them into the small residents' lounge.

"John, dear, could you get Rosie to telephone the Bungalow, Greta should be there by now from Benenden, and ask her to come up here straight away."

"Certainly Cecely, and welcome back to what passes for civilisation, Mr Coates, welcome back." He shook hands with Charles and made his way back to Rosie in the office.

The reunion between Greta and her uncle was predictable, except that Charles, expecting to hug up the schoolgirl he remembered Greta to be, was confronted with a slim, well-proportioned and extremely attractive eighteen year old woman. Like her mother before her, she was laughing and crying at the same time, hugging and kissing this uncle she had always loved so much, had missed so much and who she thought she had lost for ever.

Rosie brought in tea and a tray of Kunzle cakes which settled the three of them down. It is surprising how a state of confusion can be remedied by the simple expedient of having to pour out a cup of tea for those concerned. This having been accomplished Greta asked the question Charles knew would be among the first he would be asked.

"Uncle Charles, can you tell us about Daddy?"

Charles took her hand.

"Your father had contracted beriberi. That is a disease of the nervous system caused by lack of vitamin B, which gradually causes weakness all over the body. He was never in great pain at all, but gradually he slipped away. Many, many people in the camp succumbed to it because of the food, or lack of food, we were given. I have thought many times, why did it not take me, and leave him to come back to you. Being in a camp was one big lottery; no-one knew who would be next. Now, tell me what happened to you, and where and how is Oliver?"

Cecely and Greta told Charles how kind everyone had been, and how deeply grateful they were to the Chandler family, of which they had become an indisputable part, all as a direct result of Nigel meeting Harry at Muar and inviting him to dinner that evening, and to the house-party the following evening.

"Then you loaned him your car – remember, Uncle Charles?"

"Yes, he was a first class chap. I wonder what happened to him?"

"Oh, we know," said Greta excitedly.

And so the bringing-up-to-date went on until it was dinner time. They ate together, at the end of the evening Cecely suggesting he moved down to The Bungalow as soon as he felt he would like to; he could use Oliver's room.

"Yes, I would like that. But I will stay here for a couple of days. I am expecting a telephone call which will come to this number."

The two girls were too polite to ask 'who from,' nevertheless were each agog to know. Their silence after receiving this intelligence brought a smile from Charles, his first real smile of the evening.

"Alright, it will be from a lady I met on the ship." He told them her story and about little Sophia. They were entranced.

The next morning Rose telephoned Cecely before she left The Bungalow. "We have heard that Charles has arrived. Do you think he would like to come here to dinner with us this evening? There will just be the three of us and the three of you, although one or two people will call in afterwards."

"I will telephone him and call you from the shop."

"How is he?"

"He is slimmer, white-haired in place of grey-haired, but otherwise very much like his old self. I think the long sea voyage has probably helped in that respect, particularly since he met a lady on board."

Ever the romantic Rose probed, "Oh, tell me more, please."

"I shall be late for work and will get the sack if I do. I'll tell you later," and with a laugh she replaced the receiver.

The call from Guildford came to The Angel at just after midday. After the usual preliminaries which are the commencement of virtually all telephone conversations - I wonder why it is we can't just come out with the purpose of the call without all the initial shilly-shallying; it must cost a fortune over a lifetime - Jane said she had established her sister was in India. She had already told Charles her sister, Amy, was a nurse, and as far as she knew still unmarried. The almoner's office at Guildford General was able to tell her she had volunteered for the Queen Alexandra Nursing Service and had been posted to Calcutta. The net result of her enquiries was therefore, she had the address to which she could write to her sister, but no sister on the ground, as it were.

"Where are you staying, Jane?"

"At The Angel, in the High Street. I'll stay here for a few days until I can find somewhere more permanent."

"And I am in The Angel at Sandbury. Just proves how our tastes are so identical. Now, can I come over to you, on say, Monday or Tuesday so that we can have a chat?"

Jane thought quickly, 'Get hair done on Monday.'

"Yes, can you make it Tuesday for lunch?"

So it was arranged.

Charles was made very welcome at Chandlers Lodge on Saturday evening. Jack, Anni and Ernie called in after dinner and were introduced, Karl and Rosemary were baby-sitting little Ruth and David.

"And if I may say so, Mr Chandler -"

"Fred, please."

"If I may say so, Fred, if Harry isn't a chip off the old block I don't know who is. I have never seen father and son look so alike."

They dragged every tiny recollection Charles had of Harry from him. Ernie asked him about the car that he had loaned to Harry for his leave and about which Harry had written home in rapture.

"What will have happened to it?" Ernie asked.

"I truly do not know, probably some Jap general is driving around in it. I was taken in Singapore while the car was still at K.L. with John Chea, my syce."

Ernie quickly asked, "What is a syce?"

"Oh, that's what we call a chauffeur in Malaya."

What Charles did not know was that John Chea, as soon as it became obvious the Japs were going to take K.L., decided they would not lay their nasty little hands on his Railton if he could help it. The garage in which it was normally housed was large, thirty feet front to back and twenty-two feet wide. In the days before the occupation he positioned the car sideways on to the front of the garage, and with a trolley-jack, part of his maintenance equipment, he moved the rear of the car a foot or two, then the front, so that it was gradually walking sideways on towards the rear wall. He had little room to spare as the Railton was twenty feet long, but gradually he got it within a foot of the rear wall. He jacked it up on to some baulks of timber and took the wheels off, these latter two tasks not being without some considerable danger to him, but also demanding a bodily flexibility he began to doubt he possessed.

At last it was done. He took the wheels away to hide elsewhere. If they found the car it would be useless, since he even removed the steering wheel and battery along with pieces of electrical equipment. Covering the car carefully with tarpaulins, under which he had spread layer upon layer of old mosquito netting so that the large tarpaulins would not scratch his beloved paint and leather-work, he stood back to survey his handiwork, with tears running down his cheeks at being parted from this machine which he loved next only to his wife and his Tuan, the judge.

To complete the task he boarded the car in, and whitewashed the garage interior. It would take a pretty eagle-eyed Jap to judge the interior front-to-back measurement of the building was seven feet less than the exterior, particularly when he placed a couple of open-topped water tanks strategically on the immediately visible outside wall, and a whole collection of junk inside the garage itself.

And there it stayed all through the war until... but you shall read more of that in due course.

* * *

Chapter Eleven

David arrived back at Bulford late on the 13th March, along with the half of his company which had been on leave at the same time. As they wended their various ways from Bulford sidings back to their barracks there obtained the usual silent progress of men returning from leave. A combination of reliving the pleasures and delights of the past seven days, the thought of that bloody Irish git of a sergeant major who would without doubt be making life unbearable first thing tomorrow, and then the forthcoming drop into Germany, an adventure about which there was absolutely no secrecy whatsoever. The Germans knew they were coming, and had a pretty accurate idea where they would make their presence felt. The Wehrmacht welcome, fighting to defend its own soil, was not going to be of the 'we surrender' variety. They knew it was the beginning of the end, but they would take as many as they could with them before that calamitous day came.

The following weekend the division held a three-day exercise, starting with a parachute descent on the south side of the Humber, having had a four-hour flight to come in from the north. After a twenty-mile forced march David's battalion 'captured' Market Rasen whilst another brigade on their left carried out a similar task to 'take' Louth. They were given a four-hour rest by the roadside then loaded on to TCVs, and ferried to Boston. Arriving at dawn they debussed, to endure another forced march of thirty miles to the outskirts of King's Lynn. Given another four hours to sleep in the hedgerows as before, at nine o'clock that evening they moved off in the dark the twenty-five miles to Watton on the edge of the Thetford training area to carry out a dawn attack with live ammunition and artillery support. At midday the exercise ended, they received their first hot meal for three days, were embussed, arriving back at Bulford in the early hours of Tuesday morning.

Angus shook David violently awake at six thirty.

"'O' Group. CO's office 0800, sir."

What David said in reply as to what should be done to the CO and his 'O' Group would scorch the paper upon which this story is written.

"What time is it?"

"Six-thirty, sir, p'raps a bit after."

"Who the hell woke you up?"

"I get one of the duty cooks to give me a shout. They're always about by four-thirty."

"Bloody hell," was the only comment David's fuddled brain could formulate.

The 'O' Group was short and sweet. Colonel Haimish Gillespie, despite his forty years, looked as sprightly as any of his attendant officers, though to be fair the standard was not exactly all that high on that particular morning.

"We move into Wimbush Transit Camp tomorrow, have a final look at the sand-table, get our final briefing, then off to Germany on Saturday morning. Everything is closed down from now on. No mail out etc - usual programme."

David's company, a well-oiled machine in every department, piled into their transport for the journey to Essex where they arrived late on Thursday afternoon. Each platoon visited the sand-table, each NCO was given an aerial photograph of the 'Drop Zone' or DZ as it will now be called, and then to bed. The next morning they were taken to Boreham airfield to draw parachutes and to get to know the American Dakota crews who were to fly them. They were in bed by seven that evening for reveille at 0100 hours on the morning of Saturday 24th March.

David's Dakota carried twenty men, his company headquarters, less his 2ic. If his plane was shot down there would be a fair chance his 2ic would land and be able to command B Company. The three medics he carried with him were all conscientious objectors but had volunteered as medical parachutists, jumping in on the enemy totally unarmed. David was number one in the stick, Angus number two, Paddy number three, which meant of course that as they emplaned at around seven o'clock they were the last to get on - to get on an aeroplane carrying a huge chalk inscription,

'Chandler's Clowns - Hitler Beware!'

recorded in chalk along the fuselage, a message executed with considerable artistic flair,

Back to army time. At 0730 hours their Dakota rumbled down the runway, took off and in due course settled itself into formation. The weather was good, the estimated air speed at the DZ would be around 5mph - ideal. About half an hour before they were due to jump, the dispatcher, an American air force sergeant, disappeared into the cockpit area. When he re-appeared he produced wide-eyed incredulity from the twenty men, between whom he had to walk, to reach his position at the exit. He looked like a monstrous armadillo. He was a big chap to start with. He was encased in a thick flak-suit which almost doubled his size, but the item which the paras, used as they were to RAF dispatchers being dressed in issue trousers and a roll-neck pullover, found side-splitting was a semi-circular apron on top of the main cladding which covered his Soho operating tackle.

"You don't intend taking any chances do you, sarge?" one wag yelled, above the noise of the engines, pointing to the apron. He grinned back.

"What happens if you get stalky, sarge, you'd never lift that lot." Roars of laughter from the remainder who heard. Keyed up as they were they would have laughed at anything. Funny thing, nerves.

Then came the command "Hook up" from the dispatcher.

They stood down the centre of the aircraft each looking up on the wire running down the roof of the fuselage.

"Check hooks." Each man checked the hook was secure on the man in front of him, the last man turned about and number nineteen checked his hook as well as that of the man in front. They stood waiting for the red light to go on.

"Red light on." They shuffled up so as to be as close to the man in front as it was possible to be. Some men were carrying heavy kit-bags strapped to their legs which they would free once they were airborne and lower them some thirty feet beneath them. They would contain wireless sets, Piats, mortar bombs, machine gun ammunition, medical first aid sets, all sorts of equipment a unit needs when it goes into action.

David stood in the doorway waiting for the green light. Looking down he saw the River Rhine approaching, passed over the river and into enemy territory, the first indication of which was a considerable amount of small arms fire being directed at, he felt, him in particular. He could see the point now of the armadillo suit on the part of the dispatcher. I would rather not be here, he said to himself. They were only seven hundred feet up, and if not sitting ducks they were not far outside that category.

As he was giving thought to these notions there was an almighty bang on the starboard side of the aircraft causing it to lurch over to the left, nearly toppling David out of the door. Fortunately the men were so packed together none fell. Below, David saw that the ground was now becoming covered with a thick mist. In fact what had happened, and could not have been foreseen, was that in addition to there being a heavy mist that morning, the RAF had bombed Wesel to the south of the DZ the previous night. They left large fires in industrial premises, the smoke from which was blowing northwards and combining with the mist to produce, literally, a fog of war.

"Green light on - GO."

David had gone before the dispatcher had shouted 'go' closely followed by the others pushing forward hard so as to land as close together as possible. As number sixteen went there was another almighty bang. This time an ack-ack shell had exploded near the port engine, and in seconds it was on fire. At the same time the aircraft lurched, depositing the last four men on to the side seating. They slowly got to their feet, burdened as they were with their heavy loads, one by one at last making an exit as the pilot valiantly fought to keep the Dakota, fast losing height, level for the men to jump.

The last man left at 300 feet. He barely had time to release his kit bag before he hit the deck, breaking a leg in the process. Number sixteen was another who had an interesting descent. He had no kit bag and had exited at about five hundred feet. As soon as his parachute opened and he was able to look around, not seeing much because of the fog, what he did see was a group of farm buildings on fire, and he was drifting right on to them. Now farms in Germany are often built in a square, with animals and equipment in three of the sides and the farmer and his family occupying the fourth side. In the middle of the square would often be positioned the manure heap, which in a farm of say fifty head of cattle would be of substantial proportions.

Number sixteen tried valiantly to 'spill' his chute so as to miss the fire, but he had so little height to play with in the first place. In the few seconds before he visualised his body adding fuel to the flames as it were, he gave an almighty pull on one side of the chute, felt the flames singeing his legs, their upward draft lifting him a little, and then the chute collapsed to dump him on top of a very smelly, but very soft dung heap. As he said many times afterwards, 'I was never so happy in all my life to be in the shit.'

All the last four dropped in enemy lines and were taken prisoner; but by now, unlike in Normandy, they were treated as prisoners of war and not executed, as Hitler had ordered in the invasion on D-Day.

The aircraft, the captain fighting to keep it level until all had gone, finally crashed, killing all the crew, including the armadillo man.

In the meantime David had landed without mishap to find himself completely alone in the fog and having no idea whatsoever where he was or which way to go. Being the first to jump he should be on the very edge of the DZ. This assumes two things, firstly the pilot had found the DZ and secondly had given the green light at the correct time. Planes were flying in a steady stream above him, he decided therefore to follow their direction, but to find his battalion's RV point in this blasted fog would require a miracle. The strange thing was with all this frenzied activity of aircraft overhead, the incessant booming of eighty-eight millimetre anti-aircraft guns, and the presence of literally thousands of men jumping, he had as yet not seen another soul.

He jogged along for a few minutes during which time he bumped into two Canadians, a captain and a sergeant.

"Know where we are, sir?" to which David replied,

"Haven't a bloody clue."

They came to a small concrete bridge over a deep ditch, obviously put there for the purpose of allowing cattle and farm implements to cross. The captain ran over first, closely followed by David. As he ran over there was a cracking sound as a bullet hit the low side wall and a sliver of concrete embedded itself in David's left hand. He yelled with surprise and pain but immediately the sergeant stumbled and fell having been shot through the heart. The two officers stopped to assure themselves the sergeant was dead and then ran on.

"Where the hell did those shots come from in this light?" David asked the world in general.

"They must have been random ones," the captain replied, "if we couldn't see anybody they could not have seen us."

David's hand was bleeding badly. He pulled out the embedded fragment of concrete and wrapped his handkerchief around the wound to try and contain the bleeding, thinking he would get a field dressing on it as soon as he could.

Gradually the mist was lifting, and the two officers, now having collected a dozen or more soldiers from various battalions came to a bridle path along which was a long line of poplar trees. David stopped and got out his aerial photograph.

"We're here," he pointed to the photo, "and we should be over there." They were in the north western corner of the DZ when they should have been a mile away in the south eastern corner.

And that is what happens when ten thousand-odd men are dropped in fog or in the dark. They land in all sorts of different places, they move off in all sorts of different directions, and if half of them get to the RV in time it is a miracle. David set off at a fast walk, to face another problem. The DZ was covered from about a mile away by a battery of eighty-eights, which, now the fog was lifting in parts, was able to shell the men crossing it, virtually with open sights. To add to the carnage, gliders were beginning to arrive and were being picked off in mid-air or on landing. A Hamilcar carrying two field guns and attendant jeeps and crews was struck at about a hundred feet up, broke up in the middle to jettison guns, jeeps and personnel, followed by the pilot and co-pilot housed on top of the fuselage. The bodies hit the ground about a hundred yards from David and his followers. It was not a pretty sight.

With the continual shelling spurring him on, David's fast walk had broken into a steady trot despite the mass of equipment he was carrying. By the time he reached the RV he was, to put it technically, absolutely knackered. He sank back against a bank to get his breath back when fifteen seconds later there was a whooshing noise, an almighty bang and a shell landed the other side of the bank, half covering him in the fertile soil of the north German plain. He staggered to his feet shaking the earth off his equipment and brushing it from his neck and ears, deciding to move on the last few yards to B Company objective, a large house set in a small copse.

Expecting to find some of his men already there he was surprised to find two glider pilots who had landed their craft successfully, three men from another battalion who had decided to stay put rather than 'roam around with all of them guns goin' off,' and last but not least three Americans from the 17th Airborne who had been dropped in the wrong place.

"Well, that's our objective," David said to his motley crew, "let's go and see what's there."

He led the way cautiously towards the building. A burst of machine gun fire crackled through the branches of the trees above them. As they hit the ground one of the Americans ran forward with his carbine at the ready and put a burst into the open window from which the firing must have come. Under the cover of another burst David then rushed to the front door porch, pushed open the front door, ran into the hallway, put several bursts of fire from his Sten gun up the stairway, yelling,

"Raus, raus, schnell."

He waited a few seconds before repeating his shout, at which four men appeared with their hands up at the top of the stairs. In his fluent German he asked,

"Are there any other men up there?" He was told they were the only ones, and that although they were in the parachute corps they were draftees and had not made any descents. As the leader of the group added to David,

"We have been told you shoot parachute troops."

In the few minutes this little action had taken, a number of David's company had arrived including Paddy and Angus, so he set to to organise his defence of the building and immediate surrounds in preparation for the counter-attack which would almost certainly follow. Except that it didn't.

A number of platoon attacks were made against isolated units housed in farm buildings to their front who were, with their machine guns, causing life to be somewhat uncomfortable for David and the 60% of his company which had now arrived, including all the officers. As a result he sustained some casualties, but by 1600 hours his front was cleared, and they settled in their slit trenches to await either the counter attack or their relief in the form of a famous Scottish Division, the 15th, pressing towards them from the river crossing ten miles away.

Paddy took a roll call. Of the 120 men who jumped they had eighty two, of whom six had been killed in the clearing operations and nine wounded. The rest had either been dropped wide and would eventually turn up, had been killed on the DZ, or had been dropped into enemy lines and been taken prisoner. He only had half a company in the form of effective strength.

In the next eight hours up until midnight men did filter in, a sergeant and a lance corporal bringing a dozen prisoners with them! By midnight fifteen stragglers had arrived, each with a story to tell. As darkness fell there was considerable firing going on to the west, between them and the river. Obviously, retreating Germans had run into the outer perimeter of the airborne division on that side, and were now caught between two fires. Gradually the sounds of battle subsided, and at three o'clock the Jocks made their way through the airborne positions, to take up a defensive position two miles further east along the line of an autobahn. There was the usual banter.

"You took your time, didn't you?"

"We thought we would let you cherry-berries have some fun. You can go home now, leave it to the men."

The next day what is known as 'the administrative tail' caught up, the men got a hot meal, ammunition was made up, and minor things such as torn trousers replaced. It takes a lot of organisation to keep an army in the field.

Most of the men wrote a quick letter home. The dead were buried, the badly wounded quickly despatched back across the river to base hospitals or to Britain, those with lesser wounds treated in field ambulances. Once the chaos of the drop had been overcome the efficiency of the army system was awesome.

However, the Rhine drop would probably have sealed the end of mass parachute daylight assaults. As Hitler discovered at Crete years before, the losses to men and machines were not sustainable. Later when hand-held ground to air missiles were developed this view became even more reinforced. But back to David.

After another day the division, with R Battalion in the lead, commenced the long long journey across the North German Plain. They rode on Churchill tanks crewed by the guards armoured division, in their case the Grenadiers. As soon as they hit a strongpoint, or dug in defences, they were off the tanks and into the attack, with covering fire from the Churchills. Some attacks lasted minutes, others half a day or more, with following up units deployed, artillery support and continual air support from rocket firing Typhoons, flying in under the radio control of an air force officer up with the leading commander.

They had covered 100 miles in four days, had been involved in two major attacks, a night attack, and innumerable minor engagements, and were very tired. At last they were halted, then the orders were changed. They were to advance on Osnabruk. After only a few hours' sleep David found himself the vanguard of the new push. In the next thirty six hours the battalion carried out six major attacks, one against stiff resistance in clearing a village at night, taking four hundred prisoners and a battery of field guns.

Eventually after marching and fighting over thirty-five miles continuously without sleep, with only their emergency rations, carrying their full infantry kit and weapons they found themselves at the gates of Osnabruk. Exhausted beyond measure they were halted and another battalion passed through.

Throughout the march David and Paddy had covered twice the distance, encouraging those at the front, chivvying those at the back. It was an epic action, march and fight, march and fight, give the enemy no rest. Newspaper correspondents trying to keep up with those battling ahead wrote reams of hyperbole with headlines such as:-

THE RED-EYED MEN OF OSNABRUK
PARAS FIGHT THIRTY-SIX HOURS WITHOUT SLEEP
THIRTY FIVE MILES IN THIRTY-SIX HOURS - ON FOOT

Billeted in private houses in Osnabruk, the mail at last caught up with them. David received his fair share, but one in particular from Maria touched him deeply. In it she described how deeply she was missing him after their wonderful leave together. She said she had read a poem written by Joyce Grenfell in The Telegraph. It was entitled 'Seven days' leave - The departure of a soldier.' It ran,

> No pools betray a towel remembered late,
> The bathmat bears no soggy spore.
> No matchstick, spill or stub defiles the grate,
> The passage light burns wastefully no more.
> No smoke, no noise, no mess, no sign of life,
> All's neat and quiet and peaceful,
> At a price,
> For I'm no spinster, dear heart,
> I'm your wife.

Two days hard earned rest at Osnabruk saw them embussed in TCVs to move forward to cross the Weser north of Minden, where once again they were transferred to the vanguard, riding on the Grenadiers' tanks.

After half an hour's steady advance the first tank, carrying no troops, was fired on by bazookas, setting it on fire. The enemy was well dug in and obviously in some strength judging by the fire pattern from their light machine guns. In a matter of minutes smoke was put down and B Company went in under initial cover from the tank's secondary machine guns. The fight was short and brutal, the astounding consequence being that the majority of those killed and captured in the enemy ranks were Hitler Youth - boys of sixteen, led by older men, all of whom were summarily dealt with. There was no mercy afforded those people who inveigled children to take up arms.

David did not come off lightly. He had four men killed and another eight wounded, two seriously. He was the recipient of a piece of grenade in his upper arm, which he insisted on being pulled out by his company medic - one of the Quakers - and having it bound up so that he could carry on.

He and the others had seen some horrific sights since they descended into Germany, but they were nothing compared to what he would experience in a few days' time.

* * *

Chapter Twelve

Harry, sorry, Major Harry, speedily organised a pursuit plan of 'bloody Rowlands,' as he firmly suspected the escaped prisoner of being. They swiftly established the two guards who had gone with him were recent arrivals, who had not been on the raids.

"In that case the only route they would know for certain would be the one they came in on with Sunrise," Harry suggested.

"I think you are right there," his 'O' Group agreed.

"That means they will head north for a while and then when they get to that more open section they will try and get down on to the road/railway area."

"That will take them a good six hours," Tommy suggested.

"Right now. Rowlands cannot be nearly as fit as our people, therefore if we send four men at the double to try and catch them up they should do so. I will take three men and circle west, round to the north, in the hope that if they break off down Lone Gully," as they had christened it in the past, "which they may expect to take them down the mountain, I will head them off. So, Tommy, you get four men and push off. But no firing if you can possibly avoid it. Right, Choon Guan, get two men and come with me."

Harry ran into his room and in addition to his tommy gun picked up his blow pipe and darts sporran. In minutes the pursuit was on. They knew their quarry had something like an hour's start. Harry had taken an educated guess as to the two routes they could take to get down the mountain to the road - their only hope of eluding pursuers who knew the jungle inside out. He knew too, that if he did not catch them he would be faced with having swiftly to vacate Camp Four just when they were beginning to think they would soon be vacating it anyway, but of their own free will.

As the sun appeared on their side of the mountain and it got warmer and warmer they were soon sweating like the proverbial pig. After travelling more or less west for an hour Harry then decided to swing round north to cut off the gully, down which was one of the two places they would be likely to use to get to the main trunk road. There was no doubt in Harry's mind they would not have travelled half as fast as his party had performed, therefore if they came this way they should be in the bag.

Reaching the gully they found the stream was fairly fast flowing and probably a foot or so deep. There was a sizeable game trail running down the south bank of it, with beluka edging up to the other side. They hid in the undergrowth to await, hopefully, their quarry, being bitten in the process by every conceivable blood-hungry insect in the entomological catalogue listed in the Federated States of Malaya.

A thought then struck Harry. This man Rowlands was no idiot. He would know they would be pursued and would be unlikely to be able to outdistance his pursuers. So he could well find a hiding place and sit there for a few hours, then make a break for it, trusting that the hunt would have been called off.

'Well, if he thinks that, he'll find two can play at that game,' Harry told himself, then having to consider that if he sat here all day waiting he was losing camp evacuation time if the bastard really had got away.

There was a 'shush' from the foremost Chinese, to warn Harry someone or something was approaching down the game trail, but hidden at the moment by the beluka. They all froze, and then relaxed as they saw a pair of beautiful deer approaching, sniffing the air suspiciously until they reached the spot where the men were hidden, instinctively then taking to their heels.

A long half hour passed with Harry getting more and more in two minds as to whether he should stay any longer or get back to the camp when the forward look-out gave his very quiet 'shush.' They all froze again. Harry quietly loaded a dart into his blow-pipe. Then suddenly their quarry was there. Harry stepped out on to the game trail and as he did so the Chinese at the back raised his rifle. It was the last activity in which he would indulge in this life, as Harry's dart thudded into his heart. He slumped to the ground, as Harry quickly reloaded, and commanded "Stand still."

The other Chinese was swiftly disarmed. He and the white man were bound by the wrists with vines, turned about and told to move. They removed all signs of identification from the dead man, threw him into the undergrowth and left him for the animals, large and small, winged or perambulant. It became immediately apparent why the trio had taken as long as they had to reach the ambush point. The white man had only ordinary walking shoes, which had rubbed blisters into his heels; as a result he was hobbling along, obviously in some pain. Nevertheless Choon Guan, who had made himself his jailer now, encouraged him to speed up a little with the occasional use of a very pointed cane being jabbed into his not inconsiderable rump.

They got back to camp soon after midday. Tommy, having decided their prey must have slipped down the gully, returned about an hour later. Harry told Choon Guan to bring the Chinese in and to act as interpreter, the Chinese speaking no English.

"Why did you desert?"

"The white man offered us one thousand pounds each in gold sovereigns if we took him to the main road or the railway line."

"He had no money with him, how were you to be paid?"

"We would go with him to Phoenix Mine at Tapah, where he would give it to us."

"How did you know he would keep his side of the bargain and not turn you into the Japs?"

"We were to keep our rifles. Everything would be done at night with no other people around. We would be paid and then slip away, throw our rifles away, and go back to our homes."

Harry looked at Choon Guan. "There's one, in this case two, born every minute." He turned back to the Chinese.

"You will be charged with desertion and other offences when our commanding officer is next here. Take him away."

The Chinese being removed he ordered, "Bring in Mr Schmidt."

An extremely venomous looking 'Mr Schmidt' hobbled into the room. Harry fixed his gaze on the captive's face.

"Mr Schmidt, or should I say Mr Rowlands?" he paused to see what impact this latter name would make on this still arrogant individual slumped in the chair in front of him. There was no doubt by the change of expression on the face of his prisoner that he had hit home.

"My name is Schmidt. I am Swiss."

"So if we brought Mrs Rowlands here to identify you as Rowlands, she would be making a mistake? Secondly, as a Swiss national, how would you have two thousand gold sovereigns tucked away in the Phoenix Mine? Come to that, why should you as a Swiss national, here as you say on Red Cross business, know that Phoenix Mine even existed?" There was no answer from the now not so arrogant captive.

"Frankly, Rowlands, knowing what I know about you I would gladly put a dart into you as you sit there, and get my lads here to bury you. Instead, you will be held captive here until my commanding officer arrives in due course to decide whether we hang you with the other malefactor, or whether our commanding officer decides you will stand trial for war crimes when the Japs have been defeated."

"You will never defeat the Japanese Empire."

"It is already being defeated, day after day, in Burma, at sea, and in the Pacific Islands. Have no doubt, when having defeated Germany the full force of British and American arms, with the possible intervention of the Soviet Union as well, is ranged against them, they will be finished."

He was silent.

"Take him away. Choon Guan, please stay."

Choon Guan knew what he was in for. Two men he had interviewed and passed as being suitable to fight with the guerrillas had not only deserted but in doing so could have jeopardised the lives and further operational effectiveness of the whole of Camp Four. His head would be on the block when the MPAJA commander arrived with Sunrise, as he almost certainly would. Harry addressed him.

"Choon Guan, I know that with all the best people having just returned from ops and being thoroughly exhausted you had little choice of who to choose as guards on Rowlands, nevertheless you will be without doubt called upon to shoulder some of the responsibility for his escape. I am telling you now I will do all I can to speak for you, and tell of your exemplary conduct over the years."

"Thank you, sir." He left, his head sunk on to his chest. Harry composed as concise a message as he could for the radio man to send off to Sunrise, asking if he would visit as a matter of some urgency. A reply came during the next evening.

"ETA seven days Sunrise."

The general comment as first expressed by Reuben was "Christ, he's not wasting any time." The fact was of course that Sunrise knew Harry would only use the term 'urgent' if it really was so. The problem must be way out of his authority to deal with to get Sunrise involved with it. He puzzled as to what it could be.

In the meantime Choon Guan, without Harry's knowledge of course, had indulged in a little chat with the prisoner.

"Mr Rowlands, I want you to know that if you attempt to bribe my soldiers again, or if you try to escape, we shall kill you very slowly, very very slowly. I personally will remove your ears, your eyelids and your lips; others will remove your genitals. You will still be alive after that, but praying for death. We shall then tie you down on the ant hill on the east side of the parade ground and pour honey on you. The ants will clean your bones. Do you understand, prisoner Rowlands?"

A little of the old arrogance returned.

"Your officers would never allow such barbarity."

"It would be done at night. No-one would know until it was over. Do you understand prisoner Rowlands? We are prepared to pay any penalties to kill you."

Rowlands knew that his escape and the desertion of the two Chinese had caused Choon Guan a loss of face that nothing could restore, not only with Force 136 and his immediate commanders, but even more importantly with the MPAJA. In most organisations one default was excusable, in the communist world there was no tolerance of failure of any kind or at any time.

On Wednesday 28th March Sunrise arrived accompanied as always with Bam and Boo, and a studious looking young Chinese of about thirty years of age, who was introduced as Lee Tong Lim, deputy to the MPAJA commandant and authorised to make decisions on his behalf. They rested that evening and the next morning sat down to discuss what the procedure was to be regarding the two prisoners. Sunrise, having heard the full story, immediately ordered a court-martial with regard to the soldier, but found himself at a loss as to what could be done with Rowlands.

"I know what I would like to do, but he is not a soldier under our jurisdiction therefore we cannot try him. And if he were, what could we try him with? We know that he has colluded with the enemy, but we are in no position to obtain evidence to substantiate that fact. Secondly, we ourselves may for all I know be liable to prosecution for holding him against his will. It is what our friend Mr Gilbert might suggest as a paradox, a paradox, a most ingenious paradox, don't you think?"

His audience looked at one another. Harry asked,

"You're not going to sing it to us I suppose, sir?"

"I would if I knew all the words. The bit I know goes like this 'A paradox, a paradox, a most ingenious paradox,' but then I run out of words, and most of the tune, come to that."

"The last time you were here you had a Gilbert and Sullivan ditty about 'The Plan'."

"Did I? Oh yes, I remember."

"Bam and Boo enjoyed it. Do you often sing to them, Colonel?" asked Reuben.

"I have a shrewd suspicion that someone is starting to extract the urine," the colonel replied, laughingly. "Now what are our combined brains going to do about Rowlands?"

"We have no alternative but to keep him here, as I see it," Harry suggested, "and hope the war is not going to last much longer. Mind you, if we shot him no-one would be any the wiser, would they?"

"A tempting thought, a tempting thought," Sunrise replied. "Well, alright, I'll leave him in your hands. In the meantime I will endeavour to get guidance from Colombo. Now, this court-martial. When, members, prosecuting officer, defending officer?" This latter sentence put as a question. "I will determine the members. Myself - president, members Major Chandler, comrade Lee Tong Lim. This leaves Captains Ault and Isaacs to toss who is going to defend and prosecute, and remember gentlemen, this trial will be recorded to both me and comrade Lee, so it has got to be done according to the book."

It was on Saturday 31st March 1945, whilst David was resting his and his men's weary bodies on the outskirts of Osnabruk, the folks at Chandlers Lodge and in South Eastern England in general having seen the last of the rocket bombs, that the court martial to try comrade Lo Tong Yu was convened. The preliminary swearing in of the court members, Sunrise and Harry, and the affirmation by comrade Lee having been carried out, the prisoner was brought in. The prisoner pleaded 'Not Guilty'.

Tommy Isaacs had, by the toss of a coin, become the prosecuting officer. He gave a concise outline of the case against the prisoner, called his witnesses, namely Choon Guan and Choong Hong, established the prisoner had been given a direct order to guard prisoner Schmidt, and then deserted his post, carrying his weapon, having released the prisoner from custody. Choon Guan then described how with Major Chandler and Choong Hong they set out to recapture the two sentries and the prisoner which they did, one of the sentries attempting to shoot at them in the process but being killed by the major.

Comrade Lo had no defence other than to state he did not want to take part in this plan, comrade Yuen, the man who died, being the ringleader and forcing him into it.

A question from the president.

"But were you prepared to go to Phoenix Mine to get your pay-off?"

Comrade Lo did not answer.

The court withdrew to consider its verdict, which could be only, 'Guilty.'

"Bring in the prisoner." The president paused whilst comrade Lo was hustled in.

"Comrade Lo Tong Yu, you have been found guilty of desertion, for which the only sentence is death by firing squad. In consultation with the MPAJA commandant, as authorised by comrade Lee Tong Lim, his deputy, knowing that a firing squad cannot be provided under the circumstances obtaining here, should you have been found guilty, the sentence would be amended to death by hanging. There is no appeal against the sentence in the case of desertion. The sentence will be carried out at dawn tomorrow 1st April. Take the prisoner away."

After the sentence became known Matthew Lee asked to be allowed to approach Sunrise.

"Sir, I know this man committed a grievous offence, but could you not spare his life? Surely it does us a greater good to show clemency than summarily end the life of another?"

"Matthew, I have the highest regard for you, the very highest, but you have to know that that man could have caused the deaths of not only the men in this camp, but of you yourself as well. There is no way I would allow that to go unpunished. As it is, I have to conform to the law, and the law admits to only one sentence for the crime of desertion, that of death within forty-eight hours of sentence."

"I shall pray for you all."

"Thank you, Matthew."

Harry and his colleagues, along with comrade Lee and Choon Guan, rejoined the colonel.

"We now have to build a gallows and provide a burial party. When he is taken down he will be placed in the grave the burial party have excavated. There will be no ceremony. Now we have to discuss the mechanics of carrying out this ghastly business. Any ideas?"

Tommy Isaacs answered.

"I have seen several executions at Outram Road jail before the war, of men of roughly his size and weight. They required a drop of around four and a half to five feet. The platform therefore would need to be some six feet off the ground. I suggest we fabricate a pyramid structure with say four lengths of male bamboo, each around fifteen feet long, joined together with nylon cord at the apex. At six feet from floor level we provide a divided platform one half fixed, the other half able to be tilted or pulled away from beneath the condemned. The rope must be of a reasonable thickness. We can't use parachute cord as that would ... well, for obvious reasons. The body should be left for twenty-five minutes before Matthew certifies him dead."

There was a long silence.

"I think Tommy has said it all. I will leave you Harry to decide where to position the gallows and where the burial plot will be, away of course from the main war graves. In the meantime, Tommy, will you get on with getting the bamboo and getting the thing fabricated. The sooner this is over the better we all shall be pleased."

Tommy and his selected gang worked through the afternoon and by sunset the structure was finished, tucked away in the corner of the camp site, the grave having been dug literally on the edge of the jungle. At dawn Tommy and two men, accompanied by Matthew, fetched the bound prisoner from the guard hut. Matthew approached him.

"Is there anything I can do before you depart this life?" he asked.

The prisoner looked at him with a mixture of fear and hatred showing on his face.

"Go to hell with your religious clap trap."

"I will pray for you, brother Tong Yu."

After that there was no delay. The prisoner was hustled to the scaffold where the officers and the two Chinese representatives awaited them. He was pushed up the steps on to the platform.

Tommy put a hood over his head, the noose around his neck, with the knot just beneath his right ear, gave the signal to Reuben to dislodge the prisoners' section of the platform and Lo Tong Yu paid for the crime of deserting his comrades. Half an hour later he was taken down and buried.

Matthew had the last word.

"Oh Lord, accept this unbeliever's soul into your Kingdom, for the sake of Jesus Christ our Lord. Amen."

* * *

Chapter Thirteen

It was Saturday 21st April at the small party at Chandlers Lodge, which had been organised to welcome Judge Charles, that Fred made the announcement of the increase in the Chandler family to be expected around Christmas time. He had been suffering collywobbles all the evening at the prospect of carrying out this task. Had he been twenty-four instead of sixty-four it would have been an announcement made with pride, excitement and a feeling of accomplishment. Now he had this sense of embarrassment almost at the thought that, as he put it to himself, 'at sixty-four he was still at it!' It seemed almost improper for some convoluted reason!

He left it until nine o'clock, by which time most of the people had been fairly well oiled with that superb lubricant, Whitbreads Light Ale, when Fred took the plunge.

"Ladies and gentlemen, I wonder if I might have your attention for a moment or two." There was silence and a general air of curiosity at Fred taking the floor. His face was untroubled, so it couldn't be bad news. On the other hand it was not exactly beaming so it hardly looked like good news. Perhaps it was just news.

"Ladies and gentlemen." He stood with his arm around Margaret's waist. He repeated himself - "Ladies and gentlemen, Margaret and I are very thrilled to tell you we are expecting a little Chandler at the end of this year."

He was not allowed to say any more due to the hubbub which ensued, all pressing towards them both, congratulations filling the air, genuine good wishes from each and every person present and the thought in Charles Coates' mind that 'perhaps I haven't left it too late after all!' As the clamour subsided Jack took the floor.

"Ladies and gentlemen, may I take it upon myself to congratulate these two happy people on your behalf. Since Margaret has come into our little community she has endeared herself to us all. I give you a toast - Margaret and Fred, and the little Chandler to be!" The toast was drunk enthusiastically by all present. Jack continued,

"It is certain that he, or she, will be born into a peaceful Europe. Let us hope and pray it will be into a peaceful world, a world in which all our wide family, and I count us all as one big family, will be reunited with those now carrying the fight to vanquish our enemies."

There was a resounding chorus of 'Hear hears' followed by prolonged applause. There was no doubt that with the cessation of the shelling, buzz-bombs, and V2s delivery, along with the continued good news from Germany - the Russians were at the gates of Berlin - people's expectations were high for permanent peace. Several among those present in Chandlers Lodge that evening however, despite their euphoria regarding peace in Europe, had serious misgivings about those future battles which would need to take place against the fanatical Japanese. There was still an awful lot to do, although news had arrived only that day that the attack was building up. The Royal Navy had bombarded Sabang, the most northerly port in Sumatra, and Padang, the largest town and port on the west coast was bombed by naval aircraft. The Japanese no longer had mastery of the seas.

To counteract the exhilaration regarding these events there was however a sadness abroad, particularly with Margaret. President Roosevelt, our great benefactor from the early days of the war, without whose help from an otherwise hostile and isolationist American government we would not have survived, had died that day. He was succeeded by an unknown senator, Harry Truman, who became arguably one of the greatest presidents the United States ever had.

On Tuesday 24th April Charles made his way to Guildford, arriving in good time for lunch, to be greeted with ecstasy by little Sophia, who had been primed by her mother that 'Uncle Charles' was coming to see her. It must be added here that he also received a very pleasant and far from unwelcome kiss and a hug from the mother.

They had a pleasant lunch, after which Jane said she would take Sophia up for her afternoon sleep for an hour. She had a room with a small sitting room next to it, perhaps he would care to join her there, they could talk whilst Sophia took her nap.

"What will the staff think?" he asked jocularly. She smiled but made no answer.

Jane put Sophia down for her sleep.
"Night night Uncle Charles."
"Night night my love," Charles replied.

Those simple words produced an overflow of emotion in Jane. She turned away into the sitting room in tears, closely followed by Charles closing the communicating door then taking her in his arms and holding her tight.

"There, there dear, everything is alright now."

He had sensed immediately the cause of the distress. When a person has been in the brutal confines of a camp, treated like an animal, raped like an animal in Jane's case, a few kind loving words can bring about a reaction which can only be assuaged with tears.

She quickly quietened.

"I'm sorry about that."

Charles smiled at her.

"It will be a long time before you get over the horror of the camp, but with good friends around you it will happen."

"But I'm here with no friends."

"You have me, and I am going to suggest you come to live at Sandbury where you will swiftly be surrounded by dozens of friends, as I have been."

"Charles, you are so kind to me and to Sophia, I don't know what I would have done without your help and friendship."

"Jane, I hope I am not going to spoil it all now, but I have known you and been in close contact with you every day for weeks on end until recently. To put it plainly I have fallen in love with you. I don't know how you feel toward me of course, but I would be very honoured if you will consider marrying me - sounds a bit stilted I know, but will you?"

She looked up at him, still in his arms.

"I would like nothing more."

They stood silent in each other's arms for several long seconds until Charles said,

"When can you leave here?"

She smiled up at him.

"When I've paid my bill, I suppose."

"Well, let's book you out now and you come back with me. John Tarrant has some rooms, he's not busy at the moment, and then we can find you an apartment, or lodgings or something until we can arrange our wedding. I will, with your agreement, go down to the reception now and get it organised, while you pack. By the time all that is done, Sophia will be awake and we can wend our way back to Sandbury."

Arriving at The Angel at Sandbury Charles put in a call to Country Style, answered by Cecely.

"Cecely, dear, when you leave the shop could you call in before you go to The Bungalow. I have something important to discuss with you."

"Yes, of course, Charles, I'll be there just after five thirty," and with the thought to herself, 'I wonder what that's all about,' went forward to serve her last customer of the day.

Charles met her at the reception and led her into the small residents' room, where a smiling lady stood waiting for her with a beautiful two-year-old in her arms. She at once knew what Charles had to say.

"Cecely, dear, this is Jane Robertson and her daughter Sophia, whose story I have told you."

The ladies shook hands warmly, followed by Cecely holding Sophia's hand and giving her a little kiss on the cheek.

"I'll come straight to the point," Charles continued, "Jane and I are to marry as soon as we can arrange it. We will find her lodgings tomorrow and then search for a place to live after the wedding."

"How marvellous, I'm so happy for you both. But you don't have to search for lodgings. Jane and Sophia can stay at The Bungalow now that Oliver isn't here - provided they can share a room of course."

Charles looked at Jane enquiringly.

"We would be most grateful - but would it be alright with Greta?" Jane asked.

"She will love having her new auntie and cousin with her, you can be sure of that!"

Jane was almost in tears again at that reply. It really is difficult for people who have had no serious adversity or tragedy in their lives to understand how comparatively easy it is for those who have, to become emotional over a seemingly ordinary, innocent utterance.

"Well, we've booked Jane in here for tonight, so perhaps we can join you tomorrow," Charles suggested.

"Look. Tomorrow is early closing day. Suppose I come here and we lunch together then we take your luggage down to The Bungalow and get you settled in during the afternoon."

"All my luggage?" Jane laughed. "One very battered old suitcase and a couple of linen shopping bags I'm afraid."

While this conversation was taking place, Sophia was regarding Cecely with some interest. 'I wonder who she is. She seems friendly with Uncle Charles? In that case she is probably a nice person. I hope she's not taking Uncle Charles away. I don't think so, but you never know. I wouldn't want to be without Uncle Charles.'

Now, they may not have been the exact thoughts running through Sophia's mind, but I hazard a guess that similar feelings, if not thoughts, were possessing her at that moment. She clung more tightly to her mother.

"Will Sophia come to me?" Cecely asked, holding her hands out to take the little girl.

Sophia thought for a moment as her mother queried, "Would you like to go to Auntie Cecely?"

She went, and as Cecely cuddled her up, she decided that this auntie was not going to take Uncle Charles away. How she decided this is anyone's guess, but decide it she did. She smiled.

"Do you like pussycats?" Cecely asked.

"I don't know," she replied.

"She hasn't come into close contact with animals," Jane explained. "There were no cats or any other animals, except rats of course, in the camp. There was a cat on the ship, but it was very unfriendly."

"Well, we have a lovely big tortoiseshell pussycat. Her name is Susie. You will be able to play with her."

"Will Uncle Charles come?"

"Yes, of course, all the time."

"When will I see Susie?"

"Tomorrow."

"With Uncle Charles?"

Cecely looked across laughingly to her brother-in-law.

"You've certainly made a hit here."

Jane took his hand. "And here as well," she affirmed.

When she arrived home at The Bungalow Cecely made two telephone calls, the first to Benenden to ask the secretary to pass a message to Greta asking her to telephone home - "no cause for panic, just routine," she had added. Secondly she telephoned Rose to give her all the news of Charles and Jane. Then she decided she ought to tell Gloria. Then she ought to tell Maria - it was seven thirty before an irate Greta managed to get through saying "I'm told to telephone urgently and all I get is 'line engaged'." As soon as she heard the news she calmed down to become as excited as her mother.

With the announcement of Margaret's pregnancy at the back of Fred's mind was the fact they had just bought two horses and had stables built - when were they going to be able to put them to use? Nutty had made a first class job of the layout, Fred's works electrician had, in his own time, organised the lighting, and installed a couple of access lights along the pathway from the house to the spinney. Water had been laid on at a good depth so that it did not freeze in winter. All in all everything had been carried out efficiently and professionally. The horses were delivered on Saturday 28th April, to a great welcome by Margaret and Greta, Fred of course being at the factory. They were named Lady Jane, Janie for short, and Dylan.

That evening Margaret suggested to Fred they take the horses out tomorrow, just a short outing to familiarise them with any little foibles their equestrian companions might choose to indulge in. Fred's immediate reply was, "Should you be riding, love?"

"Do you mean because of my delicate condition?" Margaret teased.

"Well, yes."

"Ladies have been known to ride, to feel the birth-pangs, get off, have the baby and then remount - didn't you know that?"

"Well, that's not going to happen to you I can assure you."

"Don't worry my love. I'm seeing John Power next week; I'll ask him how long I can go before I should stop. After all I'm not doing point-to-point or steeple-chasing, am I? I'm sure he will say 'stop at six months,' or something like that."

On Sunday therefore they saddled up at around ten o'clock on a beautiful sunny morning and made their way at a gentle pace towards Offham and Mereworth Woods. As they approached the forest area they spotted a caravan tucked away behind a thicket of young hazel saplings.

"That looks like Ephraim Lee's caravan," Fred suggested. They turned their horses towards the gaily painted carriage, a fire burning at the front, Ephraim's readily distinguishable skewbald tethered at the rear. They had met Ephraim the previous year when, returning from a visit to Lorna and Harry Digby at the Whitbread Hop Farm, their afternoon had been interrupted by the unwelcome visit of a buzz-bomb. They had dismounted and were taking cover in a ditch when the ghastly thing landed in a nearby field and exploded, the horses taking off in fright, to be stopped by Ephraim a few hundred yards down the road.

As they approached, three of Ephraim's five children ran out to meet them, their shouts bringing Ephraim around to meet them from a chore he was carrying out at the back of the caravan.

"Mr Lee, good morning, how are you and the family?"

It was then that Fred noticed Ephraim was wearing a black cap and a wide black armband over his left sleeve.

"Mr Lee - you had a sadness?" Fred enquired.

"Yes guvnor. My eldest boy was killed on a raid on Germany; he was a rear gunner in a Lancaster."

The two riders expressed their joint commiserations.

"How old was he, Mr Lee?" Margaret asked.

"He was eighteen. He joined up at sixteen telling them he was eighteen; they took his word 'cos he had no birth certificate. Anyways, he was such a good shot on the rifle range – well, he would be, wouldn't he? - they suggested he went for air gunner. He passed out top of his course; they made him a sergeant like they do all air gunners. He was on his last raid of the tour and they was shot down."

"Oh how sad." They were each silent for a short while until Fred asked,

"Could he be a prisoner?"

"No, guvnor. Only one got out - he was blown out and lost a leg."

"We are very sorry for you and your family, Mr Lee. This war is a terrible thing." Margaret was close to tears. "If there is anything we can do ....." She didn't quite know how to finish the sentence.

"There is one thing, guvnor, you might be able to help with."

"Name it, Mr Lee."

"We don't live anywhere in particular. After the war they'll put the names of the killed on the village war memorials. No-one will know about our Morgan. Do you think you could get 'em to put Sergeant Morgan Lee on the Sandbury one?"

"I'll make sure of that, Mr Lee, I promise."

"Thank 'ee, guvnor."

"Mr Lee," Margaret added, "we now have a paddock behind Chandlers Lodge - you know Chandlers Lodge?"

"Oh, yes, missus, I knows it well."

"Suppose you find a sturdy oak sapling in the woods and plant it in the paddock in memory of Morgan. We would put a fence around it until it was well grown, and get a cast iron plaque made with 'Morgan's Oak' on it, or any other words you might like. That would keep his memory alive for three hundred years or more."

"Could all the family come and see it planted, missus?"

"Yes, of course."

"There might be thirty or more wagons there."

"There would be plenty of room in the paddock."

"We'd stay overnight, leave everything neat and tidy, I promise."

"That's settled then, let us know when you plan to come."

"Would Whit weekend do?"

Margaret looked to Fred, noting he was smiling quizzically. He nodded his head in agreement.

"Missus - one thing more - when we plants the tree will you put the first shovelful of earth in? We'll do it Whit Sunday morning."

"I would be very honoured, Mr Lee."

They shook hands and rode off leaving a much beholden Ephraim Lee to get the news to his clan scattered all over the south of England. Margaret's thoughtfulness would serve the Chandlers well one day.

Once they were clear of Ephraim's caravan Margaret said, "Fred dear, you didn't mind my suggesting the tree?"

"Not at all, not at all. It was a marvellous thought on your part."

"Well, you looked a little unsure."

"Not about the tree; about the thirty caravans. You see, my love, the sight of one gypsy caravan going through a country village is enough for the inhabitants to lock everything lockable, turn the children's faces to the wall to prevent them receiving the evil eye, and to produce a sigh of relief once they're gone. We now have thirty odd descending on Sandbury all at once; the townsfolk won't know what has hit them!"

"Will there be any trouble?"

"Oh no. Ephraim will see to that, you can be sure."

"Perhaps it wasn't such a good idea."

"It was a marvellous idea. We'll take all the family out into the paddock to meet the Lee's. It will be a great experience for them all."

They made their steady way back through Mereworth village and on past Sandbury airfield back to Chandlers Lodge. Waiting for them, sitting on the fence in front of the stables, they were surprised to see Greta and her Polish airman boyfriend, Stanley.

"Hallo Stanley, back again to Sandbury?"

"Yes, Mr Chandler, only for a couple of weeks, then I go on leave."

"Uncle Fred, can we rub the horses down for you and Auntie Margaret?" Fred and Margaret looked at each other, smiling broadly.

"You're sure you know which end to start?"

"Of course, when we have been riding at school we always have to do it."

It was then she realised what a clanger she had dropped! Up until now since she had met Stanley at the beginning of March, she had not told him she was still at school! In the sixth form, and eighteen years of age, it is true, but still at school. He was three years and a bit older than her, those three years and a bit making all the difference between being seriously a grown-up and seriously a schoolgirl. Stanley seemed not to have noticed as Fred continued,

"Right, I'll leave you to it. When you've finished let them out into the paddock, will you please? Then come into the house and I'll find you both a drink."

As the two would-be grooms started work Stanley asked, "Where are you at school?"

"At Benenden. I leave this summer."

"My sister was at Benenden before the war. I don't think she liked it very much. Do you like it?"

"Yes, I do, very much. But it does depend on what sort of friends you make, doesn't it? Some people you can get on with, others you can't, that, I suppose, is the same everywhere."

"How do you get on with that fellow Stanislaus Rakowski?"

"He's not bad when you get to know him," she ribbed, "mind you, I don't know what he kisses like, that would give me a clearer indication if I knew that."

There was a clatter as a curry comb fell on to the concrete, a fellow in corduroy trousers, surmounted by a regulation RAF

141

pullover, appeared at the rear end of Lady Jane, put his arms around the lady groom (why not a groomess?) and proceeded to demonstrate his ability in the kissing stakes. As Stanley enfolded her in his arms, Greta noticed Janie's tail being elevated. Realising what was going to happen she pushed the ardent suitor away, took a rapid pace backward herself, and yelled, "Man the lifeboats." Janie, having been saving that mini deluge up a long time, gave a little whinny of satisfaction and looked round to see what was delaying her beauty treatment. She observed two young people standing on either side of a rivulet of a somewhat pungent liquid running to the drain and then the soak-away, laughing their heads off. Funny creatures, humans, she said to herself. Well, she had no means that we know of for telling anyone else.

When the laughing ceased and the flow had taken its course, Stanley held Greta again and kissed her firmly, but not crushingly, and at some length.

"How do you get on with Stanislaus Rakowski now?" he asked.

"I think with a little more practice I could get on with him very well. Practice makes perfect, you know."

He gave her another, shorter kiss. "I shall remember that little aphorism every day."

"What's aphorism?"

"I don't know, but it sounds intelligent."

It was a happy couple that finished their chores, turned the horses out into the paddock, knocked on the back door of The Chandlers, were bellowed 'come in' and refreshed with the inevitable Whitbreads Light Ale, although Fred first asked Greta whether she would prefer an orange squash or something - swiftly declined!

* * *

Chapter Fourteen

David and Paddy were sitting in comfortable armchairs in a small farmhouse on the eastern side of the River Leine after further engagements subsequent to their leaving Minden. There had been no fixed defences to overcome, it was a question of one long succession of smaller actions where they were fired on, jumped off the tanks, smoke down if necessary, and straight into the attack. These were the sorts of actions where he had to leave it to his platoon commanders to control the battle, and they didn't let him down. Nevertheless each platoon was being reduced in ones and twos until the brigadier called a halt, another brigade passed through, and 'R' Battalion found themselves on a three day rest just north of Celle.

Their host – well, that is a very apposite description. The definition of 'host' is one who entertains another as his guest. A secondary definition is 'an animal having a parasite.' Since the 'guests' were forced upon the owner of the property the first description cannot logically apply, which leaves definition number two, which if taken literally means we must describe David and Paddy as parasites. Since that would not be fair we shall get on with our story.

Their host was a very large, extremely polite, well educated ex-major of the panzer grenadiers, who had lost a leg in the hell of Stalingrad and had been one of the last to be flown out of that carnage by JU 52 air ambulance.

As David and Paddy were lounging in their armchairs each drinking a reasonable measure of Steinhager and feeling clean all over as a result of having indulged in a bath for the first time for lord knows how long, a knock came on the door. Being bade to enter, the door opened and their host appeared. David had explained to him when they had been indicated their billet that he was not allowed to fraternise with the major or his family except in matters relating to accommodation or behaviour of the men occupying his house and farm buildings.

"Yes, major, how can I help you?" David asked in his faultless German.

"I have been told that your soldiers have discovered a concentration camp some twenty-five kilometres north from here on the Soltau road."

"When you say 'discovered,' did you not know it was there?"

"There have always been rumours, but the whole area has always been an exclusion zone."

"What you are saying is that the people around here didn't want to know it was there."

"I'm afraid that is the case or you would probably end up in there yourself. But that will be nothing compared to what they did in Russia and Poland. They executed millions, special squads were formed out of the scum of the earth to annihilate men, women and children, all of them almost without exception not guilty of any crime whatsoever." He paused, overcome, with the despair as to what the Nazis had reduced his country to in the eyes of the rest of the world.

"Thank you for telling us major, we will see if we can find the camp in the morning."

The major left and David explained to Paddy the substance of their conversation.

"Shall we have a shufti then tomorrow, sir? I'll have a word with the RSM and get him to lend us his jeep."

Paddy hoisted his bulk out of his armchair and made his way to battalion HQ, found RSM Forster and made the necessary arrangements for the morning, with a small alteration to the plan, namely the RSM would go with them along with his driver.

At eight o'clock they left Celle on the Soltau road and in ten kilometres met a military police road block, who on seeing the jeep was occupied by an RSM a CSM and a major thought it prudent not to ask where they were going, the fact they were paras also having something to do with their just waving them through. After another ten kilometres David said, "God, what on earth is that smell?" As they got nearer to the source of the sickening odour they came to a village name-plate:-

BERGEN - BELSEN

They motored over a slight rise, joined a more major road upon which there was a certain amount of traffic, and literally followed their noses, coming to a wired enclosure with a double gate, over which was the iniquitous lie 'Arbeit macht frei' - 'work and you will be free' being a rough translation. At the gate there was a military police post, all occupants wearing masks, an incongruous sight when set against the heavily blancoed webbing and gaiters which always seem to adorn British army police wherever they may be carrying out their overzealous duties throughout the world.

A sergeant came forward to the jeep and saluted David.

"I'm afraid you can't come in, sir," he said.

"My general says we may be taking the camp over and I am to get a first impression as to what would be required."

"Which general would that be, sir?"

"General Bols, commander of 6th Airborne. He was with General Montgomery yesterday."

That last sentence was true; as a result David was able to uncross his fingers.

"Well, alright, sir, but only go as far as the pits, don't go anywhere near the accommodation blocks. We have typhus here, and I don't think you would want to take that back to your general."

"What did he mean by 'the pits?'" Paddy asked. They soon found out. As they breasted a rise they looked down on two excavated trenches each some fifty yards long, ten feet wide and six to eight feet deep. One was already half full of grotesque naked bodies, thrown in one on top of the other, a large proportion of them in various stages of decomposition. Alongside the second pit more bodies had been piled, thousands upon thousands of them. They were being brought from the barrack blocks by the Hungarian army troops, who had been the previous camp guards, and thrown on to one long pile of skeletal objects which had once been laughing, happy, human beings.

RSM Forster broke the silence.

"Jesus Christ."

At the far end of the burial pits there was a large Royal Engineers bulldozer. Up until now the only noise was the idling motor of their jeep, no birds were singing, the RSM's enunciation was the only statement made, the men carrying out this gruesome work did it in absolute silence. Suddenly the quiet was shattered by a roar from the bulldozer as it was started up, and a lance corporal from the Royal Engineers was seen lighting a cigarette as he attended to his first task, that of covering the first pit with the soil he had previously removed. This took about twenty minutes, maybe a little longer.

He then stopped, came round to the second pit and calmly and efficiently bulldozed the bodies of the long pile the guards had completed into the pit. Halfway through he stopped to light another cigarette. He had just buried some five thousand human beings. Before he was finished he would bury <u>thirty-five thousand</u>, for that was the number of corpses found when the British troops arrived. One of them was Anne Frank, another her sister Margot.

The little group watched in silence as the Hungarians pulled small handcarts of bodies and commenced another line, beside which the engineer lance corporal started to excavate a third pit. There were not enough of these carts for all to have them, as a result the majority of the guards were either carrying or dragging their loads. In this case the word 'load,' usually indicating a weighty object, was a misnomer as the poor wretches, starved to death or typhus victims, weighed nothing. One guard appeared dragging four corpses, each of his hands encompassing a pair of ankles. Paddy exclaimed, "Holy Mary, look at that," as the bodies were whirled around in pairs and deposited on top of the rapidly growing pile. But the final horror was to come. Two guards presented a cart to the line, starting a new pile by tipping it sideways and depositing the shrunken bodies of some six or seven babies. He was followed by another guard with the shrivelled form of two young children under each arm which he casually dropped on to those from the cart.

"Let's get the hell out of here," David muttered.

When the British arrived, in addition to the thirty-five thousand corpses, there were thirty thousand living dead who despite medical help and food died at the rate of one hundred a day for the next two weeks and thereafter at some sixty a day for several weeks. As the inmates were gradually dispersed the army moved in with flame-throwers and burnt down this evil place. The Commandant of Belsen, Josef Kramer, was sentenced to death by the British, and hanged.

The four soldiers drove back to Celle, each consumed with his own feelings of shock, horror and an intense anger that a civilised nation could have sunk to such depths as they had witnessed today. As they drove up to the farmhouse, the owner appeared.

"Good day, major, did you find the place?" he asked with a pleasant smile. There was no pleasant smile on the four faces that confronted him. Sensing their hostility he asked,

"Was it an unpleasant visit?"

David replied in his fluent German.

"Major, the sight that we experienced at Bergen-Belsen will go down in history as one of the greatest evils inflicted by man on innocent men, women, children and babies. You have seen many dead in Russia and Poland, but I will tell you we have seen thousands of bodies obviously starved to death and left to rot in a camp run by a so-called civilised nation. I have to tell you, major, that if all the other camps we know about are like the one we saw today the name of Germany will take centuries to recover from the degradation and shame these Nazis have brought upon your nation. Good-day, major."

With that he pushed past the major, closely followed by the RSM and Paddy, while the driver revved up and drove off, leaving their German host meditating the depth of depravity these professional soldiers had seen which had obviously affected them so much. He had not long to wait; the pictures were flashed on to the cinema screens in the next few days. He was sick to his very soul.

The next morning an 'O' Group was called by the CO. Haimish told them that they were to stay at Celle and prepare for an airborne operation to jump the River Elbe. Three days later it was cancelled, for two reasons. Firstly their old friends, the 15th Scottish Division had fought their way through Uelzen which opened up the way to Luneburg and thence on to the river, and secondly there were no airplanes and no airfields in their immediate location to mount such an operation anyway. 'R' Battalion's description of the 6th Airborne planners, and those above them, both physical and mental, would be too indecent to be repeated. As Haimish explained, "Even 'R' Battalion cannot jump without aircraft!"

On the 25th therefore the battalion embussed and were driven the sixty miles towards Luneburg where they encamped in the forest. They were still thirty five miles from Lauenburg, where the commando's had engaged in a boat assault and captured the town on the east bank, after which the Royal Engineers had thrown a pontoon bridge across for the paras. But no paras arrived. As a result of one of those GMFUs of which we have seen a number of examples in these chronicles over the years, an order had been despatched to the RASC troop carrying vehicles to return to their base. Haimish Gillespie added a few more words to his junior officer's vocabulary when this news was brought to him.

"We shall just have to foot it then," he bellowed, "move off at 0600 hours, stop at twenty minutes to adjust equipment, then march three hours at a time with fifteen minute breaks. All water bottles to be filled, no one to drink without permission. Issue iron rations, we have got to cross the Eibe for reasons I will tell you tomorrow evening. Right - MOVE."

And that was how 'R' Battalion and the other para battalions carried out the crossing of the Elbe. They set off at six o'clock in the morning, they marched and they marched and they marched, until by eight o'clock that evening they had covered thirty-five miles and were on the eastern bank of the Elbe. They had covered the thirty-five miles in twelve hours of actual marching, laden with all the war gear a paratrooper has to carry. In 'B' Company the platoon commanders worked wonders keeping up the men's spirits, helping those in difficulties where they could, and leaving the odd one or two who had to fall out to be collected by the battalion QM three-tonners and in one or two cases the battalion blood-wagon. All the time David and Paddy moved up and down the company ranks, particularly in the later stages, encouraging and occasionally chivvying the men on. When they bivvied in the woods overlooking Lauenburg that night, having crossed the Elbe, had had the inevitable foot inspection, they were proud to be told that once again they were the foremost unit in the whole British Army.

On Sunday 29th April the TCVs caught up with them again. Haimish had been to brigade HQ to receive his orders and had returned to meet his senior officers.

"Gentlemen," he began, "this first announcement is for your ears only, that is, not to be divulged to your junior officers and men until further word is given. We, that is 6th Airborne, are to make a dash for the Baltic coast. The Russians, having captured Rostock on the Baltic, are moving fast towards Lubeck with the intention of getting into Denmark. We are the spearhead to stop their so doing. This therefore means, assuming we get to the Baltic at a place called Wismar first, the Russians will either halt, or they will try and push us aside. We may therefore be fighting Russians in a few days' time.

We shall, therefore, embus at 0600 tomorrow now that the TCVs have caught up. We shall have tanks from The Scots Greys in the lead. Third brigade will be on the left to get to Wismar itself, we are on the right to get to Mecklenburgdorf about seven miles south of Wismar. We dig in and wait to see what the Russians will get up to. The general feeling at staff HQ is that they are so drunk with all their successes and the booze they are looting they will not stop. We shall see. That is all, gentlemen, I will update you as we get near to the objective."

Even Haimish was unaware that this order had come from Prime Minister Churchill himself, to General Montgomery. "The Russians must not get into Denmark," he had told Monty. "Denmark is a monarchy and must stay that way." There was no way a communist satellite could be countenanced with direct access to the North Sea.

It was fifty miles to Mecklenburgdorf. They met several pockets of resistance on the way which slowed the advance a little, but these were swiftly and ruthlessly dealt with so that by four o'clock that afternoon they had reached their objective. 'B' and 'C' Companies to dig in facing the direction in which the Russians would come, and everybody put on full alert until otherwise informed.

David and Paddy stood watching their three platoons digging their defences. No wire was to be put out. If the Russians did not attempt to continue their advance, the wire would be considered an unfriendly gesture, and 'nothing must be done to upset our gallant allies.'

"You realise, sir, World War Three could start here in the next couple of days or so?"

"Paddy, I was just thinking exactly the same thought. What's more, I was thinking we would have the privilege of being the first poor sods to be hit."

"We, sir? I'll be back in Luneburg by then, and run all the way."

"I can just imagine that happening," said David with a grin. He looked around to see RSM Forster coming up to them. The RSM saluted punctiliously, the salute returned with equal correctness.

"Sir, I wondered how much extra ammunition you will need up here. I've got three three-tonner loads ready. I'm told the Russkis have got ten million men in their army and they are all coming this way."

"Do you think he is trying to put the wind up us, Mr O'Riordan?"

"I don't know about us, sir, but he's putting the shits up me, even worse than I had before, so he is."

"Well, all I can tell you is that every available anti tank gun is being brought from the 2nd Army and being positioned about a mile back. The Russian tanks won't know what hit them once they overrun you lot up here."

David, at that evening's 'O' Group found out that what the RSM had said, as he had thought in jest, was in fact true. Whilst the folks back home were singing the praises of our heroic Soviet allies, and rightly so, the men in Mecklenburg and all down the line to the Swiss border were standing to.

On the 2nd of May Major General Bols, commander of the 6th Airborne went forward to a meeting with Marshall Rokossovsky, who said he had orders to take Lubeck and proceed into Denmark. General Bols told him the British had orders to stay at Wismar. The Marshall was very angry, saying he must insist on being allowed to proceed or he would have to take matters into his own hands. General Bols called the Russians bluff by telling him he had a division of artillery lined up behind his troops and would not hesitate to use it. The Russians backed down.

Meanwhile on David's front, early on the morning of 1st May, a runner came from Roger Hammick's platoon saying that they could see a long column of German soldiers, led by an officer on horseback, coming towards them about a mile away, the Russians presumably pushing hard on their heels.

David and Paddy collected their weapons and hurried up to Roger's platoon position where they could confirm that what would appear to be a complete battalion marching in good order, fully armed, was approaching them. As the three officers stood there, David and Paddy wearing their red berets, they saw the officer on the horse looking towards them through his binoculars, give an order, at which the first men in the column produced a large white flag and held it up above them on rifles.

"Keep them covered," David ordered, and moved out some fifty yards left of the platoon position, indicating to the horseman to bring his column to that point so that they could be covered by 6 platoon's Bren guns. When they arrived the officer saluted David saying, "I wish to surrender my battalion to the British forces." His

German sounded as though he was from Munich or thereabouts, David judged. David replied in German.

"In the first place you will get down off that horse. I will not have someone surrendering to me literally talking down to me."

The major, as he turned out to be, stiffly lowered his somewhat podgy carcase to the ground.

"You may take your panniers off the horse."

Turning to Roger he asked, "That jockey in your platoon?"

"You mean Porteous?"

"Yes, that is he. Is he here?"

Roger yelled across the intervening space between them and the platoon position.

"Porteous - over here at the double." As the tallish lad ran towards him David said,

"He's a bit tall for a jockey, isn't he?"

"He's a steeplechaser."

Porteous joined them. David gave him his instructions.

"Take this horse to company HQ in the farm buildings and ask Captain Patterson to see that it is rubbed down, fed and watered."

"Right, sir. I'll see to it myself." He paused for a moment. "Is it finder's keepers, sir?" David grinned.

"If you know a way of getting it in your pack when you go home I don't see why not."

The German interrupted.

"Why are you taking my horse?"

"For two reasons, major. One, you won't need it where you are going, and two, I'm damned if I will let you ride into captivity as if you were a conquering hero. The Wehrmacht is finished. For the second time in twenty-five-years you have started a war and been beaten, so you will walk into captivity, and thank your lucky stars we don't turn you around and send you back to the Russians. Now, tell your men to lay down their arms here, and hand me your Luger."

This being carried out David turned to Roger.

"Detail me a sergeant and four men to escort this lot to the battalion cage, will you, Roger?"

Paddy made a quick count as the troops passed him on their way into captivity.

"Three officers and four hundred and fifty odd men, sir, not bad for a morning's work."

But they had not finished. All day Germans staggered in having kept a day, or even a few hours, ahead of the Russians, all without exception petrified at the thought of being a prisoner of war in some hell-hole in Siberia, and not knowing of the hell-holes that had existed for others in their own country. In this they had good cause for fear. The Russian troops had been spurred on by radio broadcasts from Moscow, now that they were on German soil. Ilya Ehrenburg, one of the most notorious writers and broadcasters, openly told Russian troops to loot, and to rape the arrogant German women. In the final Russian occupied zone it was later calculated that no female between twelve years of age up to, and including, pensioners escaped the clutches of the Soviet troops, to which their officers not only turned a blind eye, but almost universally took part.

Perhaps the most cruel, most wicked episode, was when the Russian troops liberated the women's concentration camp at Ravensbruk. Since a large proportion of the inmates were German they too suffered unspeakable multi-rape, despite their skeletal condition and the fact they were almost certainly anti-Nazi to have been incarcerated in the camp in the first place.

On the 2nd of May David's forward troops reported that Russians had occupied the village opposite them, some three quarters of a mile away. The next day a Kuppelwagen with a driver and three Russian officers was seen driving towards their positions. They were met by Andy Gilchrist, who saluted smartly, although he had no idea what their ranks might be, since they were each wearing different types of leather jerkins, obviously looted from German civilians, over their uniforms, again which seemed far from uniform. They spoke no English, but pointed towards where they assumed battalion headquarters were established. Andy waved them on, saluted again, and they drove down into David's company headquarters area, where David came out to meet them. Again there was the language problem except that one of them, a man of some forty five years David assessed, spoke some basic German, which David was able to understand meant they would like to see the commanding officer. David pointed out the building to him, they motored off and David got on the land-line which had been laid to his HQ to tell the adjutant to expect visitors. Paddy joined him.

"Doesn't look as though World War Three is on then, sir, does it?"

"If you hear any big bangs in the night don't put it down to thunder," was David's reply, "they are probably sussing us out."

As a footnote to this little episode, three hours later the Kuppelwagen returned, with three very inebriated Russian officers in it, leaving a still standing Haimish Gillespie - but only just - and half a dozen more or less empty bottles of John Haig from the mess stock. They had drunk together for three hours without understanding a word each said to his opposite number, but then I suggest that some of you have experienced that sort of situation in the past!

The war in Europe ended on the 8th of May That night the battalion built a huge bonfire, fired off Very lights and in general enjoyed themselves. Not to be outdone, the next day the Russians in the next village scavenged for every bit of burnable material, piled it in the space between two haystacks and when it was dark, set the lot alight to produce a tremendous bonfire, infinitely superior to that of their inferior allies. Still, we thought of it first, didn't we?

A week later the news trickled down to the squaddies - 'we're going home.' However, that was the good news. Up until now they had been part of the BLA - British Liberation Army. Of recent weeks BLA had been interpreted as designating 'Burma Looms Ahead.' And so it was to be. 'R' Battalion would go back to Bulford, would go on leave, would go to India, would then go to fight the Japs. But then, they were soldiers, were they not? and soldiers were there to fight, not sit around in comfortable barracks. There was a degree of disagreement in respect of that latter statement, many asking, "Why can't some other buggers have a go?"

* * *

Chapter Fifteen

On Tuesday 3rd April Sunrise left Camp Four having suggested to Harry 'keep 'em busy now, a hanging might make them a bit morbid!' It was Harry's considered opinion that not one of them would have objected to dislodging that platform himself, knowing what could have happened had the escape been successful. Nevertheless, Rowlands was a problem. If he was to be a captive for say, another year until the war ended, he would be more than a problem; he would become a bloody nuisance. When he had recovered from his badly blistered feet, there would be no doubt he might try another escape. He had to have exercise, therefore had as a regular routine to be released from his confinement, under guard it is true, but one day they might be somewhat careless and he would give them the slip. Come to that the quarters in which he was confined were far from being escape proof. Richard Lovelace wrote, two hundred years before,

> 'Stone walls do not a prison make
> Nor iron bars a cage'

He was the chap who told his sweetheart, when he had decided to go off to the wars,

> 'I could not love thee dear so much
> Loved I not honour more'

Bit of a back handed compliment I would suggest, but that is entirely irrelevant. As far as Harry was concerned he would have much preferred to have a stone built prison with iron bars at the window and on the door than the wooden shed his captive at present occupied, this covered by an atap roof which one could put a fist through without difficulty. He would be guarded of course, but how do you make that foolproof without having at least two sentries on duty twenty four hours a day, a terribly boring monotonous job designed to lower morale as few things would.

Reuben's solution was for the camp blacksmith to make some shackles and chain him down. Tommy suggested finding a way to entice him to decamp then put a dart into him as he went. Whilst Harry was tempted to this latter course, he much preferred the trial and hanging formula decided for ridding the world of this traitorous scum. In the end they just had to rely on keeping him guarded, taking his shoes away at all times unless he was exercising, and keeping particularly close watch on him when he visited the shower or the latrines. An item in their favour was the fact that Rowlands knew that every man in the camp would like him to make a false move so that they could have the pleasure of shooting him.

Sunrise had asked Harry to make one of his sorties another visit to the airfield at Kuala Lipis. Last summer, 1944, they had made a raid on this target, a pre-war RAF aerodrome which was being up-graded to take heavier aircraft, bombers and large transport planes. Harry had been shot in a most inconvenient part of his anatomy, namely his bum, as the raiders made their getaway after having blown up a number of parked aircraft. This however was to be a reconnaissance mission. Should the target now be suitable, it would be passed on to Colombo and would receive the attention of Super Fortresses in due course.

Harry decided to send Tommy on this operation along with six men, not to cause any havoc, just go to the airfield, note what was on it, and come home. At the same time to note any unusual traffic on the narrow gauge railway which ran past the airfield, and which started at the Siam border, running down the centre of Malaya to join the wide gauge railway inland from Malacca thence on to Singapore.

"Oh well, it will make a nice stroll," Tommy commented. They would be away about six days, perhaps a week.

They set off on Monday 9th April, Tommy, his six armed men, and two camp men who would man the bivvy area, make the meals and so on. Getting there they encountered no problems other than the, to be expected, periodic soakings. To counter these they now had large waterproof cape-like garments sent in recent air drops. They were called 'ponchos,' had the minor disadvantage of making a man sweat even more than he would normally, but at least kept his top half dry, feet and legs still getting wet through. They bivvied up in the lower jungle some two miles from the target, Tommy planning to go forward with three of the men the next morning. They moved out an hour after dawn proceeding cautiously along a game trail until they reached a bluff overlooking this air field some half a mile away. By now it was nearly eight o'clock in the morning. Tommy began to sweep the airfield and its surrounds systematically through his binoculars.

"Holy shit," he exclaimed, as his eyepieces settled on the far side of the 'drome.'

"What is it, sir?" the man on his immediate right asked. Tommy handed him the glasses, which he pointed in the direction Tommy had been making his observation.

They were looking at three large, semi-circular, corrugated iron, open ended structures. Nothing extraordinary about that you might say and you would be right. It was the contents that had produced Tommy's somewhat irreverent expletive. Inside he could see row upon row upon row of bombs, piled up four or five high, and ranging, he guessed, as well as he could from this distance, from fifty to two hundred and fifty kilos. Next to the metal structures there were some twenty, eight-man tents, in front of which there was a scattering of Japanese soldiers. A distance away to his right there was a long, low barrack-like structure, with an atap roof, around which he could see other men. But - they were not soldiers, they were white, or at least had been white until they had been forced to work twelve hour days in the sun for their masters. Tommy looked closely at his map.

"I would like to get round to the other side for a closer look at that set-up," he said to Choong Hong, his second in command, "but we obviously cannot move in the open country in daylight. We will take all the details we can and get it down on paper, sleep this afternoon, get round over the railway line during the night and find a place to observe from."

"Won't that add a day or so to our patrol, sir?"

"Yes, but we've got enough food, and judging by those clouds over to the east we're not going to be short of water."

The progress around the northern perimeter of the airfield that night was accomplished without incident, apart from a brush with some particularly vicious wild pigs they bumped into on one of the game trails they followed. Following game trails, whilst it made the going easier, could be hazardous if something large was making use of it, as the jungle or beluka on either side was frequently almost impenetrable. In this instance it was sparse, the three-man patrol was able to take to the country, as you might say, and the pigs careered past.

More by luck than judgement they found a small hill covered with scrub from which when daylight came, they could see quite clearly what had been the far side from their previous observation point. Railway sidings had been built here. Soon after dawn a train arrived from Siam in the north and was diverted into one of the sidings to be met by around a hundred or so of the white men captives. Tommy studied them carefully. It was difficult to tell whether they were POWs or civilians. They could have been either.

The train had a series of flat bed trucks each covered in a tarpaulin. The labour gang, driven by much shouting and the occasional kick from the guards, took the tarpaulins off to reveal a further delivery of bombs, which were then put singly on a made up stretcher and carried by four men to the bomb dumps. They watched until the sun was high in the sky then Tommy, feeling they had seen enough, retreated into the jungle proper, where they remained for the rest of the day until it was nearly dark. They then made their move back to the bivvy area without incident.

They arrived back at camp on Sunday night 15th April to an enthusiastic welcome from all, especially Harry. Two of Tommy's patrol had developed a temperature on the second to last day and struggled hard to finally make it. They were whisked away by Matthew who quickly diagnosed malaria, his and his assistants' ministrations over the next few days returning them to health in due course.

Tommy had a long session with Harry, Reuben and Choon Guan the next morning, producing all the drawings he had made of the layout of the new bomb dump. They came to the conclusion that since Kuala Lipis was in the centre of the Malay Peninsular it was going to be used as a base from which the Japanese air force could operate against an invasion force from the British or Americans wherever they were going to choose to make their assault, or assaults.

"Even if we joined up with another camp we couldn't carry out an operation against a target like this," Harry stated, a belief readily agreed by the others. "On the other hand, if we could get word of the map reference of the site to Sunrise, he might be able to organise the Yanks to bomb it, which would do more damage in half an hour than we could in a week."

"And what happens to the POWs?" asked Tommy.

"This is why I'm glad I'm not a general," Harry replied, "knowing I have fifteen thousand men for an attack and five thousand of them will be killed." They were all silent. Harry continued, "If we can get those bombs disposed of, they will not be able to be used against our people when they invade, or against our ships and landing craft bringing them in."

"The POWs have got to be sacrificed - that's what you're saying?" This put by Reuben more as a question than a statement.

"If I don't report this to Sunrise then they live, and we then have to live with our consciences if our landing craft are blown out of the water and their occupants die. As I said before, I'm glad I'm not a general."

"You have no choice," Reuben resolved, "Sunrise must be told."

"And you all agree?" asked Harry.

"Yes," was the unanimous but reluctant reply.

"Now, what about the aircraft there?"

"There were nine Mitsubishi medium bombers, three in front of the main buildings and the others in pairs on dispersal points around the perimeter."

"Any civilian dwellings nearby?"

"A handful around the station, otherwise no."

"Anti-aircraft? Not that they would have anything to reach strato-cruisers in a place like that."

"They had weapon points at the places I have marked but they weren't manned. They would only be any use against low flying attackers, and they are unlikely to get any of those at present."

"Right, we'll leave it at that. I will get the message off to Sunrise. When, and if, the bombing takes place, will you go back and have a shufti to see what success they had?"

"Gladly."

Harry prepared as concise a message as possible to describe the target and location, had it coded and sent that night. It was acknowledged within an hour.

Two weeks later a message arrived, was decoded, and taken to Harry.

'Our friends will be dropping on May 6 or 7, depending on weather, Sunrise.'

"That's next Sunday or Monday," Harry said. "Crikey, I would love to watch it."

"And supposing they dropped a few wide, say on your hidey-hole?" Reuben replied, "you know how good the Yanks are at that."

"And not only the Yanks," Harry suggested, "the RAF put the wind up me a few times in France."

They decided to stick to an after-strike visit as previously planned. In the event the strato-cruisers flew over it on the 6th, could not see the target because of heavy rain at the time, and flew on to bomb their secondary target at Singapore navy base.

The disappointment engendered by this non-event was completely forgotten by the news over their short wave radio on the 9th of May of 'Victory in Europe.' This, added to the news that Rangoon had been recaptured from the Japanese, produced euphoria.

On the 10th May Camp Four received another coded message. 'Repeat party by our friends on 15th May. Please report result.'

"That's tomorrow week. Tommy, get ready to move out on the 14th." It would of course take two days to get to the target.

At midday on the 15th, it was a beautiful, bright, clear day; Chantek was seated beside Harry as he sat at his table cleaning his tommy gun. Several times she pricked up her ears and looked towards the west. Harry took little notice. She could hear thunder, of which she was very afraid, long before he could hear it. He assumed there was a storm brewing out towards the Straits of Malacca - 'as long as it doesn't come this way,' he said to himself, 'and blot the bloody target out again it can do what it likes.' But it wasn't thunder; it was the Royal Navy's big guns making the noise, in a pitched battle with Japanese warships ending in a Jap cruiser being sunk, with no losses to our ships. Britannia was again beginning to rule the waves in the Far East.

He smoothed her head. "Don't worry, my love; no-one is going to hurt you."

Two minutes later, she nearly jumped out of her skin and looking almost in the opposite direction to her previous viewing, she rose to her feet and pressed herself hard against Harry's leg, pushing her head into his lap.

"What can you hear then?" Chantek started making that little sawing noise in the back of her throat showing she was really scared, still Harry could not hear anything unusual over the customary noises of the jungle in daytime. After some ten minutes she settled down. Harry looked at the clock, it was 12.15. He received a message that night 'Target successfully struck 12 noon Sunrise.'

Impatiently they awaited the return of Tommy and his party. As they marched into camp on the late afternoon of Friday 18th, they were surrounded by an excited company, all eager to know what a bombing looked like, particularly since their force had been the instigators of the action. After Tommy had carried out the usual weapon and foot inspections he joined Harry, Reuben and Choon Guan in Harry's room.

"We made very good time, as we were lightly laden," Tommy commenced telling them, "as a result we were only some seven miles from the airfield when the planes came over. We could actually see the bombs falling although we couldn't see the target of course. It was almost exactly midday."

"A minute or two after I believe," Harry interjected.

"Yes, that's right. How did you know?"

"Chantek told me."

"I didn't know she could talk."

"Only to me, she's very fussy who she has conversations with."

The others looked at each other with eyebrows raised.

"Well, to continue my story, when we reached the obbo we had about half an hour of daylight. The Japs were running around like blue-arsed flies, the main building was still burning, six of the nine bombers were more or less in pieces, the other three furthest away from the HQ seemed untouched. The station was just one big hole, railway lines sticking twenty to thirty feet up into the air. We counted twenty three bomb craters across the airfield, and last but not least, one bomb had made a direct hit on the centre of the three semi-circular structures, or to put it more correctly, where the centre one had been, since not only was there nothing of it left now, but the resultant explosion had set off a number of the bombs which in turn had blown the neighbouring structures into shreds. Along with that, dozens of bombs in the sheds which had not exploded had been spread over a considerable area. The place was wrecked, and will take several weeks to become operational again."

"So it was pretty accurate bombing then?" asked Harry.

"I would say they were the good ones, or perhaps the lucky ones. There were craters as far in the distance as we could see, so a lot were off target. Still, they did a marvellous job. What I find even more marvellous is that we can spot the target, we can send a message, someone else passes the message on, some high-up air force wallah gets it, gets a few planes into the air and blows the target to bits. The Duke of Wellington couldn't have done that," Tommy replied.

Reuben looked across at him.

"Getting quite philosophical in our old age, are we not?"

"I shall be quite happy if I reach an old age," Tommy replied quite seriously.

"Now you haven't mentioned the POWs," Harry reminded him.

"Well their quarters were flattened, obviously by blast as there were no craters where they had stood, and a few were being worked by the Japs on the clearing up operation. Some of them must have bought it, there were fewer there than before the raid."

"Poor sods," Reuben sighed. The deaths of those unaccounted for would come back into the three officers' thoughts and dreams for years to come. There seemed something terribly unjust in a man suffering over three years of slavery only to be killed by his own allies. But it happened time and again, being torpedoed when being shipped between islands or to the Japanese mainland, being bombed when in slave camps and dockyards in Japan, and when building those bridges on the Burma-Siam railway. As fast as a bridge was built, Liberators from Burma would come and blow it up, or attempt to. Many POWs died with their Japanese captors.

They were quiet for a few moments.

"It had to be done," Harry decided. "Now, we have to get a message off to Sunrise to tell him all that has happened."

This was done and on Saturday night, or to be more exact Sunday morning 20th May a message came through which, when decoded, read,

'SACSEA congratulates you on successful conclusion operation Bulldog.'

Reuben's first questions were "Who the hell's SACSEA and what is Bulldog?"

"SACSEA would be Supreme Allied Commander South East Asia, and Bulldog the code name for the bombing."

"And who the devil would the SACSEA bloke be then?" Reuben asked.

"Haven't a clue," Harry replied, "we'll ask Sunrise the next time he is here. I don't suppose they would tell us over the radio, even in code."

They were most surprised to find out shortly afterwards, when the copies of The Times of India were included in their next drop, he was openly referred to in every other page. It was Lord Mountbatten.

"Isn't he the chap they sent out here so that he didn't bugger up D-Day after the mess he made of the Dieppe lark?" Reuben asked.

"The very chap," was Harry's reply, "or so my brother wrote and told me."

"Well, let's hope he's learnt a thing or two before he invades Malaya."

* * *

Chapter Sixteen

It was the 1st of June 1945. major Dieter von Hassellbek had been at Auschwitz for a month when the Russian head of his Legal Unit sent for him. The colonel had taken a firm liking for the major, despite the fact Dieter had been his former enemy and had in fact been highly decorated for 'bravery in knocking out Russian tanks.'

"Major, we are being moved to Berlin to carry on our work there. I have thought long and hard about retaining your services, since you will be very tempted to slip away. My superiors have told me that if I take you, I have explained how very essential you are to this unit, I shall have to stand security for you. You will of course be in the Russian Zone, so it would not be easy to abscond but Berlin itself is being divided into four parts, we to take the largest section, the British, Americans and French to also have a section. What I am saying is that I can only take you if you give me your word of honour you will not try to escape my custody."

Dieter thought hard for a few minutes before replying.

"Sir, as a prisoner of war it is my duty to try and escape, that is a known and accepted military principle. However I would be prepared to give you my word of honour not to try to escape all the time I am in your custody. I would not under any circumstances do anything to jeopardize your position after the very courteous manner in which you have treated me."

"Very good, be ready to move out in the morning. We drive north to Poznan then entrain for Berlin. Have you ever been to Berlin?"

"Yes, sir, I was at cadet school at Potsdam."

"I am given to understand you will find it has altered somewhat."

That could well have qualified as the understatement of the age, Dieter considered, when they received their first sighting of the eastern suburbs. The buildings the RAF had left standing had been battered by the assault of the Red Army, with only a handful of dwellings here and there habitable, with strangely enough, the odd factory or office block virtually unscathed apart from its total loss of window glass.

They were met in Berlin and taken to their new headquarters in a hastily repaired and refurbished office block. By the end of the month they had started work, mainly on those accused of lesser crimes, very few being found 'not guilty,' the guilty ones, stealing from Soviet billets and so on, being despatched to the gulags for fifteen or twenty-years. Prostitutes who attempted to steal from their drunken customers, knowing they would not be paid anyway, similarly faced twenty year sentences. Trials of that nature took ten minutes, more complex ones rarely longer than half an hour. They nearly all ended up in the gulags.

In July there was to be a big trial of some of the officials from Sachsenhausen and Ravensbruk camps which had housed a number of Russian slave workers incarcerated there for various civil offences against the Third Reich. They had been brutally treated and a number executed at the whim of those accused.

"I want you to act as interpreter to the proceedings," the colonel told Dieter. There are going to be observers from England, America, and France. You are the only person I have been able to find who can speak Russian, English and French. It will be time-consuming repeating everything in the four languages but we have no sophisticated translation system, so you will have to do it."

"Very good, sir."

That night, as Dieter lay on his mattress, he tried to form a plan whereby he could get one of the visitors to get a message to Rosa that he was still alive. The obvious way would be to write two letters in English and one in French to give to the visitors. That would not be as straightforward as it sounds. It could well be he would never be close enough to them to be able to give the messages to them. It could well be that they would not want to do anything for a German anyway, particularly if they were legal people, and particularly in the case of the Frenchman. He decided he would write notes to the American and the Englishman, he wouldn't risk the Frenchman. If he was unable to pass the letter, but able to speak to the two English speaking people, he would say, 'I am a German officer. My wife has been told I am dead. Will you please contact her and tell her you have seen me and I am well?'

He struggled in his mind how to cut that long-winded statement down, and how the devil to add Rosa's address. Giving a telephone number would be useless; the whole system was probably so disrupted as to be quite unusable. It was a long time before he got to sleep.

A week later the trials began, more professionally carried out than the previous charades. On the other hand, since some of the alleged crimes had been carried out by three or four of the accused, they were all bundled into the dock together. Dieter made an excellent and extremely quick multi-translation, which at the end of the day brought praise from the American representative - a colonel, but with only a very few medal ribbons, indicating he probably held only a courtesy rank in the military legal system. An American colonel at that stage of the war would normally have probably four rows of ribbons, whether he had fired a shot or not.

In any event Dieter had to translate the complimentary statement to the court president, again a colonel, plastered with so many medals it was a wonder he could stand up. The Russians loved their medals.

On the second morning Dieter and his colonel arrived early, to find there was no-one in the courtroom as yet. His colonel said, "I must find a lavatory, something I ate upset me last night." He rushed off, with Dieter thinking, 'I hope he makes it.' Laughing to himself he turned to be confronted by the three visitors. They had allowed good time to get through the control point into the Russian Zone, only to be waved through without the usual palaver of scrutinising documents, passes, vehicle details and contents of the boot, so beloved of the Russian border guards. Dieter saluted, which the American and British officer returned. 'I was right about the Frenchman,' Dieter concluded.

The American came over to him.

"I must congratulate you on your languages, sir" he stated. Americans call everybody they think a bit posh 'Sir.'

Dieter saw his colonel returning, looking a little less alarmed than when he went. Before he could cross the room to where they were standing he turned his back on his colonel, took a small envelope from his pocket, gave it quickly to the American, and said,

"Will you take this please, sir, it explains itself."

The American immediately placed it in his pocket without saying another word. Dieter had no further opportunity to speak to, or be near, his message-bearer, who obviously read it during the morning, since, when the afternoon session began, he looked across to Dieter, and catching his eye, slowly nodded his head.

The next evening, the visitors' three-day visit over, General Gargarov, now himself in Berlin, was to give a reception for them.

At the end of the second day Dieter's colonel told him to make himself available to act as interpreter for the general.

"The general may invite you to drink during the evening when he usually gets a little relaxed." He looked at Dieter meaningfully. In other words when he is well sloshed, Dieter construed the statement. "It is not allowed, you must make some excuse."

If a general orders you to drink, surely to God you drink? was his first thought. I don't want to end up in a gulag just because I refused to drink with a blasted general. As if I didn't have enough complications in my life without this one being added. I am not much of a drinker anyway; two of their measures of 'a drink' would put me on my back.

The dinner passed without incident. At the reception Dieter had been told to stay at the general's right elbow as he was deaf in his left ear. When seated he was to sit immediately behind him as the American was on Gargarov's right, whilst the English and French guests were on his left. Course after course was brought to the table, each with copious quantities of wine. Dieter noticed the American and the French officers were knocking it back without any visual effects, but the Englishman was already visibly wilting. The meal ending, the toasts began. Three nations' armies, three nations' heads of state, three nations victory, followed by return toasts to the Red Army, Party Secretary Stalin, and the victory of the Soviet Union, each in the equivalent of a double measure of vodka, soon sorted the men from the boys. The first to go, slumped back in his chair, was the English lieutenant colonel. The second was a trio of Russians on a side sprig. The American and the Frenchman upheld the honour of the Allies when at eleven o'clock they had run out of toasts and the only three standing were the two visitors and the general. It must be added that when I say 'standing' it goes without saying each of them could have been blown over by the slightest puff of wind.

Dieter managed to stay out of trouble by constantly keeping himself behind, and therefore out of the direct line of the general's vision, who as he became more and more inebriated forgot his interpreter was there anyway, despite the continual translations. As the guests left and were helped to their staff car, the American managed to say to Dieter, "Will contact Rosa," and then as Dieter's colonel made his extremely unsteady way towards them raised his voice, "and many thanks for all your help. Hello, colonel, you have a very professional aide here, congratulations."

Dieter translated, the colonel replying with a simple "danke schon, danke schon." He was at the stage of his thought processes being well and truly liquefied in alcohol.

Two days later Dieter's colonel received a letter from Gargarov saying that he was to comment favourably to Major von Hassellbek for his excellent work at the reception. He had arranged, in view of the previous excellent service he had given, that the major would be released in three years' from this date provided he continued to carry out his duties as assigned to him.

The colonel carried out his general's instructions to the letter. Dieter was silent for a few moments.

"Sir, is there anyone who can countermand this decision, about the three years, I mean?"

"Very few people would dare to countermand Gargarov. He has the ear of Comrade Stalin."

"Thank you, colonel. Will you please thank the general for me?"

"Yes, I will. He is my father-in-law - but that is not generally known - you understand?"

"Perfectly, sir."

When Dieter got back to his quarters that night, he mulled over the events of the day. At least he knew he would be free in three years' time. He would still be only twenty-six years of age. On the other hand, could he trust their word? Should he risk trying to escape for the sake of three years? If he was caught he would probably never survive a Russian work camp. It all boiled down to the one factor. Could he trust the bastards? He came to the conclusion he would be a fool to do so, and from now on would look for a way to get to one of the other zones. There he would be put in a POW camp, probably for some time, but certainly not for three years.

He finally decided he would keep his word to the colonel. If that meant for three years so be it. Otherwise he would play it by ear. At least Rosa and his family would now, hopefully, know he was still alive.

Three days after the reception, at least the American colonel was given to understand it was three days, having no knowledge of at least one and half of them, he flew from Tempelhof back to his base at Kassel. There he was told to stand by to return to the States thence to proceed to Pacific Command. 'In which case,' he said to himself, 'I have got to find out where this Bruksheim is and get there p.d.q.'

He found a map and discovered there was a direct train service Kassel-Bruksheim-Hannover, decided he would travel the next day, by which time he would hopefully have fully regained his sight and his sense of smell, and lost that awful taste in his mouth, to say nothing of those two drummers tattooing away in his cranium. It would be a seventy-mile journey; he would need to be fit!

It was Monday 16th July therefore; he set off on his errand of mercy. On the way he saw at every small town dozens of barrack-like structures being hurriedly thrown up to accept the millions of displaced persons from the east who had fled before the Russians. They were people who no longer had homes, few possessions, and were lost and bemused after the fear of rape and possible death at the hands of their conquerors. It is estimated that over ten million Germans flooded westward, to say nothing of a million Poles, Czechs and others. The country was awash with refugees, all to be housed in a bomb-blasted country before the continental winter set in.

He arrived at Bruksheim, asked for the address he had been given and eventually found himself at Major Strobel's apartment. The lift was having one of its off days; as a result he had to climb the stairway, realising by the time he reached the Strobel landing that a) he was not as young as he used to be, b) that bloody drummer was still at it, c) if he didn't get to a can soon there would be an accident. He rang the bell, to have it answered by a trim lady, late forties, who smilingly asked in, just, passable English,

"Good morning, are you looking for Major Strobel?"

"Well, no, ma'am, not exactly. I am Colonel Reilly, US Army. I was hoping to find Mrs von Hassellbek."

"Oh, I see, it's about the Klinik, please come in. She is in bed; she has been working on the night shift."

Despite her unsure, ungrammatical English the colonel gathered the gist of her information.

"No ma'am, nothing to do with the Klinik. I have recently come from Berlin where I met her husband, the major."

Gita uttered a little scream as Fritz, wondering what was happening, joined her in the hallway.

"Dieter is alive, this gentleman has met him. Oh, please, please, please do come in. I will wake Rosa up." She ran to Rosa's room leaving Fritz to lead the colonel to the sitting room. In seconds Rosa ran in, tying up her dressing gown as she came.

"You have seen Dieter?" she cried out, her English not forgotten in the ferment of the moment.

"Yes ma'am. He is alive and well and having to work for the Russian war crimes people as an interpreter. I guess his ability to speak Russian, French and English as well as his native German, has saved him from being sent to a prisoner of war camp."

"But was he hurt or disabled in any way?"

"No, he was as fit as a flea."

"Wait a minute, please." She ran off to her room returning with a large photograph of Dieter taken on his last leave when he came to Bruksheim.

"Please, colonel, was that him? You have not made a mistake?"

"Oh, that's him OK. Anyway, he wrote this note - you are bound to recognise the handwriting."

Rosa took the hastily scribbled letter on the scrappy piece of paper.

"Oh, yes, that's his writing." She showed the note to Gita and Fritz, and turning to the colonel took his hand and covered it with a combination of tears and kisses.

"Thank you, thank you so much. We and his parents will never forget you for what you have done for us, never, never."

The two women having broken off to discuss how they could let the von Hassellbeks know the good news, the colonel asked Fritz,

"Can I use your bathroom please?"

With the drummer taking time off it seemed, as he returned to the trio, he was now back to normal. They ate a light lunch together, obtained Colonel Reilly's home address so as to keep in touch with him, although as he said, "I've to go off to the Japan war now, so I don't know when I will be back home."

"With the might of the United States and the British Empire the Japanese cannot last long now," Fritz suggested.

"I hope you are right, I hope you are right," the colonel replied. "Well, I must take my leave of you. You are going to have to face difficult times, particularly through the next winter. I wish you all the best of luck, and I trust Dieter will soon be back with you."

'But it won't be in the next five minutes if I know the Russians,' he said to himself. Nor was it. Germany and its allies had devastated Mother Russia, now they were to pay for so doing. Of the ninety-one thousand German soldiers captured after the battle of Stalingrad, kept in captivity as they were for fifteen years, only five thousand survived the gulags to return home. There were over four million taken prisoner. Estimates vary between five to ten per cent of survivors.

After Colonel Reilly had left they tried again to telephone to Ulm and surprisingly got through almost immediately. The von Hasselbeks were thrilled with the news, but had bad news as well to tell. When the war ended, Inge, their daughter, had gone into hiding in the American zone, with friends in Munich. As an official in the concentration camp system she was on the secondary list, that is, not for murder or organised cruelty, but for being a major part of the organisation of the evil system in the domestic camps, particularly Ravensbruk. Someone had given her away; as a result she had been arrested by the American Nazi-hunters.

"At least she will be better treated by her American jailers than you were by your Ravensbruk ones," Fritz remarked. Rosa thought for a while.

"Yes, no doubt about that. But despite her politics she was a loving, caring girl. Dieter and I were devoted to her; we pretended not to notice her infatuation with the Nazis hoping she would grow out of it."

"Well, she will have plenty of time to ponder whether she was right or wrong now, I imagine. The camp people will be made to pay for the iniquities they made others suffer. I don't think she will ever be able to look you in the face again."

Nor could she.

* * *

Chapter Seventeen

Sandbury, at the end of April, was agog with excitement. The war in Europe was as good as over. The American and Soviet troops had met up at Torgau. Since it was expected that the Nazis would make a last stand in their 'Southern Redoubt,' that is the mountain area around Berchtesgaden, Hitler's home, three hundred and fifty Lancasters were despatched to bomb the main buildings and SS barracks which they did to great effect.

On the black side, the US forces liberated Dachau, the news of which again brought back the horror of Anni's mother's death to her and her father. When the troops arrived at the camp they found thirty nine locked railway trucks in the sidings filled with corpses of prisoners, left to starve, who had been moved from Buchenwald to Dachau before the arrival of the US Army. The American soldiers, discovering this, ran amok and killed some three hundred SS guards before their divisional commander was informed of what was happening and sent in another battalion to stop the killings. The slaughter did not cease immediately, as when prisoners saw the guards being killed they took up the weapons from the dead men and joined in the hunt for those SS trying to hide from the vengeance seeking them out. With order finally restored, thirty-two thousand prisoners were released, thirty-two thousand!! How do you feed thirty-two thousand starving people at a moment's notice? How do you treat a large proportion of them who are chronically ill? How do you then despatch thirty-two thousand people to all the ends of Europe to their homes? And when you have a hundred of these camps, perhaps two hundred, plus all the prisoner of war camps - there were two million French prisoners of war alone - one begins to wonder at the miracles the liberating powers had to perform.

But back to Sandbury.

Charles and Jane lost no time in contacting Canon Rosser with regard to putting up their banns, and in having Sophia christened. It was decided that the little girl would be baptised on Sunday 27th May. The godparents would be Cecely of course and Fred and Margaret had been asked. Discussing the actual ritual Canon Rosser explained,

"We have a different procedure in one respect. A child of this age is too heavy to cradle in one's arms. Therefore we have a chair upon which she will stand, put her hands on the font, and bow her head over the edge. I then take the shell, scoop up the water and pour it on her head three times, mark her with the sign of the cross, and then pat her dry. If you tell her, or even rehearse her in what is going to happen it will not take her by surprise. I then light a candle for her, but will hand it to one of the godparents - you can let me know which one - it would be a trifle unsafe in the hands of a two-year-old! The duties of the godparents are established in the service, so it is all quite straightforward. So we shall see you after matins on the 6th."

The wedding posed problems. Charles would have liked Oliver to have been his best man but Oliver was in an armoured unit some miles from the Russian Zone border, the unit still being on full alert since relations with the Soviets were souring day by day. However, he had now applied for a commission. He and his friend Fotheringham had decided to defer their applications to become officers, after they were posted to their service units on completion of their training, in case they 'missed the war.' They didn't miss the war; in fact once or twice they saw more of it than they had bargained for, both having been 'brewed-up' on two occasions. Charles therefore was going to have to find a substitute.

May 8th 1945 - V.E. day! Victory in Europe. The town went wild – well, as wild as a small town such as Sandbury could go wild. People not 'on the town' were glued to their wireless sets listening to almost hysterical descriptions by B.B.C. commentators telling the world, and Britain in particular, of the celebrations in Piccadilly, the Mall, and in front of Buckingham Palace, where the King and Queen, and the two princesses came out on to the famous balcony, battered a little as it was like so many of dwellings of the cheering crowds below. And then there was a doubling of the cheering as Winston Churchill appeared with Their Majesties. It was a great night, pictures of which will remain for all time in the annals of British history.

At nine o'clock the telephone rang at The Bungalow.

"Who can that be?" asked Cecely of Jane and Charles, as if they were likely to know.

"Cecely Coates."

"Cecely, dear, it's me, or should I say 'tis I? I am never really sure."

"Oh Hugh, how lovely to hear from you. Where have you been? Where have you been? I've missed you so much."

"Well, they sent me to Italy a month or so ago, to assist in the German surrender to General Alexander of last Wednesday. Alex didn't want me any more so I cadged a lift home this afternoon and here I am making my first, and most important, telephone call."

"Hugh, Charles is here with a lady and her daughter, who he is going to marry, isn't it exciting?"

"I am puzzled. Is he marrying the lady or the daughter?"

"Since the daughter is only two years old - I presume that answers your question? Now, when shall I see you?"

"Would tomorrow be convenient?"

"Oh yes, yes, yes."

"Can you book me in at John Tarrant's?"

"How long for?"

"Say two weeks in the first instance. You see I have all sorts of things to arrange, and I only have a month's leave."

"I'll do that straight away. Goodnight, darling Hugh."

"Goodnight, my love."

Cecely returned to the sitting room, her face flushed and excited, a detail immediately noticed by both Charles and Jane who looked at each other with slightly raised eyebrows. Charles greeted her with, "Someone interesting, dear?"

"Very interesting, very interesting indeed, someone I must tell you all about." The slightly raised eyebrows expression repeated itself on her listeners. She continued,

"That was Hugh Ramsford. I have known him since the end of 1942, that's nearly three years. He was David's commanding officer when David did his operations behind enemy lines - we still don't know where David went or what he did. Anyway, Hugh was very kind to me, and always I hasten to add a complete gentleman, respecting the fact I was married and my husband was in a camp."

Charles interrupted.

"Now this Hugh Ramsford, is he the Lord Ramsford I have heard mentioned?"

"Yes, that's right."

"So what you are telling us is that you will soon be Lady Ramsford?"

Cecely looked at him, and started gently to cry. Quickly Jane went to her and held her close.

"I'm sorry, my dear," he said, "I didn't mean to upset you."

Charles knew exactly why she was upset. She was in love with Hugh, she knew now she was free to marry him if he proposed to her, yet she still had this guilt of betraying her beloved Nigel. Cecely composed herself.

"I'm sorry. Hugh is coming down to stay for a couple of weeks at The Angel. I think he may ask me to marry him and I shall say 'yes' if he does. You don't disapprove, dear Charles, do you?"

"Disapprove? Good God, no. I think it's wonderful that you should have found happiness again. Don't you dear?"

Despite the circumstances Cecely could not help but note these two lovely people had already begun to act as one.

"What's more important," Charles continued, "Nigel himself would give you his full and unbridled blessing if he were able. I'm his brother; I know that for a fact."

The three of them sat down as Cecely composed herself again.

"Well, we shall see. I will go and book Hugh in at John's."

When John Tarrant answered the telephone Cecely could hardly make herself heard. The centuries-old coaching inn had never, ever, contained such a volume of clamour and tumult as it did that night, and probably never would again. Eventually through the pandemonium, after a number of 'what did you say,' 'what was that,' and similar expressions, she managed to relay Hugh's message, going back to the others secure in their blessing, and deliriously happy in the knowledge there was nothing now to prevent her from becoming his wife. She then brought herself up with a jolt - 'yes, but he has to ask you first!'

Next day was early closing day - not that a lot of places even bothered to open. Those that did had staff who were devoid of thought, and in some cases movement, their only saving grace being that the majority of the very few customers who had surfaced, through necessity, to visit them, were in a similar state. John Tarrant found three airmen from RAF Sandbury fast asleep on some hay in one of his outhouses. He offered them breakfast, which, for some unknown reason, they refused, before going off to attend company orders for being absent, or whatever it is they call it in the RAF

Hugh arrived at midday, and having booked in, decided to stroll over to Country Style. It was deserted, other than for a lonesome Cecely seated at the end of the showroom. Seeing him coming through the open doorway - it's a funny thing about shops in those days, probably the same nowadays for all I know, that it was considered a closed door presented a barrier to a prospective customer entering a shop. A psychological barrier, that is. The fact the door was not open indicated a lack of welcome, therefore the shopper's instinct told her, or him, to try somewhere else. As a result, except on exceptionally cold days the front door was always open. I suspect that did not necessarily apply to funeral parlours.

Now, where were we? Oh! yes.

Seeing him coming through the open doorway Cecely leapt to her feet and almost flew down the carpeted showroom to greet him, a greeting which took some little while to complete, and which fairly took her breath away.

"Now let me look at you," he said, holding her at arm's length. "Yes, you are very very lovely, dear Cecely. I have missed you so much."

"And I too you, dearest Hugh. Let me close the shop, nobody has been in this morning anyway, then we can have some lunch at John Tarrant's. I can tell you all the news and you can tell me where you have been and what you have been doing. Oh! I am so thrilled to see you."

Hugh kissed her lightly, smiling at her excitement at seeing him, and feeling, deep down inside, as happy as he had ever felt in his whole life.

The dining room at The Angel was almost empty, another indicator of the probable pursuits of its regular customers the previous evening. Their order taken by the somewhat unsteady hand of John's venerable head waiter, Hugh reached across the table and took Cecely's hands in his.

"Cecely, dear Cecely, this is not the most romantic of places, despite that, will you marry me?"

"Yes."

There was silence as Hugh assimilated this answer, given most emphatically almost before he had finished the question. Then a huge smile spread over his face, as he reached into the voluminous pocket of his sports jacket to bring out a burgundy coloured box with gold edges, which he opened to display a magnificent solitaire diamond ring. He indicated to Cecely to give him her hand, slid the ring on, gently pulled her to her feet and leaning over the table, kissed her lightly. As he did so John Tarrant walked into the dining room to welcome them, having been told by Henry, the waiter, 'His Lordship and Mrs Coates are in the restaurant.' Cecely held her left hand out to John, knuckles uppermost.

"Oh, congratulations Cecely, and to you, my lord. This calls for a celebration, if my head will stand it after last night." He went away to return with a dusty bottle of Moet et Chandon, along with three fluted glasses. With a soft 'pop' he professionally opened the bottle, poured the amber fluid, handed them a glass each and taking a glass himself toasted the elated couple.

"May you have a long and happy life together."

Having sampled their wine, Cecely thanked John, then added,

"John, not a word outside until we have told everybody, please."

"My lips are sealed. Hoteliers and landlords see and hear a myriad of things which they keep to themselves, and this will head the list until you tell me otherwise. Ah, here's Henry with your soup."

After lunch Cecely suggested they should go and tell Charles and Jane, their story having been imparted to Hugh over the meal. They strolled the mile or so to The Bungalow to find Charles sitting on the sun lounger by himself.

"Charles dear, this is Hugh Ramsford." The two men shook hands warmly, and as they did so Jane appeared, carrying a sleepy-eyed, rosy-cheeked Sophia, these two followed by a gorgeous tortoiseshell cat which moved silently to rub itself around Cecely's legs.

"And this is Jane, this is Sophia - and last of all, Susie."

As a silence followed the 'how do you do's,' Cecely held out her knuckled hand again, to the squeals of delight from Jane, congratulations to you both, and a sense of bewilderment from Sophia, who was wondering what all the fuss was about - I wonder who he is - must be important - got that look about him - they seem to like him - must be alright. She smiled at Hugh. He smiled back.

They had tea after which Cecely said, "I must telephone Rose, Maria and your stepmother" she suggested to Hugh.

"I have already told Gloria," Hugh replied.

"When was that?" asked Cecely, and added, laughingly, "it must have been before you saw me. How did you know I would say yes?"

"I didn't. I left a caveat - 'if she is barmy enough to have me.' "

"In that case I have no need to telephone. She knows there is no-one else in the world I would rather have."

The calls to Rose and Maria were predictable. Much questioning about when and where the wedding will be etcetera, etcetera, what would she wear, etcetera, etcetera. At length Rose asked, "Why don't you all come here for a drink? Say seven o'clock? Dad will run you home afterwards and Sophia can have a nap upstairs. Did you know the petrol ration has increased to five gallons a month from today? I think the news has gone to Dad's head. He and Margaret are talking of visiting all the cathedral towns in the south of England, but on five gallons a month they won't get far."

It was therefore agreed they would assemble at Chandlers Lodge, Rose immediately warning Fred to be home, contacting Anni, she to get in touch with Karl and Rosemary, and most importantly making sure Jack would be home in time for the occasion. After all, it is not every day that one celebrates the betrothal of a friend to a peer of the realm.

It was at this point that Jane asked Cecely,

"What did Greta say when you told her?"

To which Cecely put her hand to her mouth and almost shrieked "Greta! Oh my goodness, I've forgotten Greta. I've been so busy being excited and wanting to tell everybody and I have forgotten to tell my own daughter. Oh! How could I?" She literally ran out to the telephone in the hallway, only to be informed by the bursar's clerk at Benenden that the sixth form were attending a function at Tonbridge School and would not be back until late in the evening.

"Will you ask her to telephone me at Chandlers Lodge when she comes in. It is important, but not..." she tried to find a word suggesting there was no panic involved, "... not alarming." It was the best she could do.

Returning to the patio, Hugh asked Charles whether he and Jane had settled on a date yet for their wedding. Charles replied that they had been discussing it just before their arrival and had decided to make it the 16th June. Having telephoned Canon Rosser to establish that would be suitable date, and that 2.30pm would be a suitable time, they had then considered who the attendants would be. As best man Charles had determined to ask Fred Chandler.

Without the Chandlers, Cecely would not have had a firm base at which to settle and a second family to which to belong. In fact the roof over her head had been provided by David Chandler! He would ask him this evening. Jane was going to ask Megan and Rose if they would act as matrons of honour.

"We seem to be on the same tack," Hugh replied. "I could not think of anyone I would like more to stand for me. He and Ruth, who so sadly died on New Year's Eve 1942 - God, was it all that while ago? - were like a second family to young Charlie, and through them my father met Gloria. So we all owe the Chandlers so much - and when you meet the Schultz's, if you haven't already done so, you will find they would give the freedom of the city to everybody named Chandler in the whole blessed country!"

That evening, an hour or so after the party assembled, Charles nodded to Hugh and indicated Fred's direction. They moved purposefully towards him until they were almost upon him, when he turned and found himself hemmed in. He immediately put his hands up in the air.

"I give in," he laughed.

"That solves those two problems then Charles, wouldn't you say?"

"Indubitably."

"May I ask what you two gentlemen are up to?" Fred enquired.

"We each would like you stand as best man at our respective weddings. Charles, as you know, has settled, along with Jane, on the sixteenth of June, Cecely and I have not as yet settled on a date, but I imagine it will be around the end of August, at Ramsford."

Fred looked at them both, literally open-mouthed.

"But why me? You must know many people much higher in the social strata than I am who would be more suitable," he protested.

"We both," Hugh replied, "came to the same conclusion; there would be no person we would like more to stand for us than you. So - how about it?"

"Well, yes, and I can assure you I feel very honoured to be asked."

"Asked about what?" Jack, seeing Fred being 'quizzed,' as he told himself, joined them.

"These two gentlemen have asked me to stand as best man for them."

"Well, they couldn't have made a better choice as far as I am concerned. Mind you," he continued, putting his arm around his great friend's shoulders, "you will have to make sure he stays sober at least until after the service. We all know what he's like when he's had one or two."

They all laughed at the sally.

The telephone rang at a little after nine thirty. Rose answered it - it was Greta.

"What's all the panic, Rose? Mummy left a message for me to telephone Chandlers Lodge this evening when I got back."

"Got back? Have you been out on the razzle again? I've heard what you sixth form Benendeners get up to in the fleshpots of Tenterden or wherever it is you descend upon."

"We have been attending a social evening at Tonbridge school."

"But that's a boy's school."

"Yes, we go to enable the sixth formers to develop their social graces in the company of elegant young ladies from Benenden."

"A Tonbridge sixth former I knew was a real randy blighter."

"Most of them are I'm pleased to say."

"You're incorrigible."

"C of E actually. Anyhow, what does this mother of mine want, do you know?"

"Oh, I don't think it's anything important. I'll get her for you." She made her way to find Cecely, chuckling as she went.

"Greta, dear, are you sitting comfortably?"

"Well, I'm not actually. This blasted phone is in the draftiest passageway in the building. Anyway, what's up?"

"Hugh and I are to be married."

SHRIEK.

"Oh, I am pleased for you, really I am, please tell His Lordship that won't you? Do I now have to call you 'Your Ladyship?' and 'Your Grace' one day. And is Charlie now my step-brother? Since he's an 'Hon', am I an 'Hon'? You are making life very complicated for me, but I really am so happy for you - tell everybody that won't you?"

"I will dear, I will. Hugh will be here when you come home on Friday, so you can have a good chat then. Goodnight now dear, goodnight."

Cecely rejoined the gathering, her face being intensely studied by Hugh as she crossed the room to be at his side. He looked at her, his raised eyebrows asking the inevitable question.

"She is screamingly happy for us both."

"I've never come across that phrase before. How does one become screamingly happy? But then I know so little of real life."

"I think, my darling Hugh, that you know so much of real life that you must have an inner courage most of us in this room cannot even begin to fathom."

He looked at her intently, put his arm around her and held her very close.

"You really meant that didn't you." A statement rather than a question.

"Yes, and everybody else who knows you, especially these people here, think the same."

He kissed her lightly on the forehead, an action noted by Rose on the other side of the room. Not for nothing had David, many years ago, re-christened her 'Hawkeye.'

The next morning Rose telephoned all the gossip to Maria, and invited her to come for the Whit weekend, and her parents as well, to witness the planting of Morgan's oak, to put Sophia's christening in her diary for the following Sunday, Charles and Jane's wedding on the sixteenth of June and Cecely and Hugh sometime in August.

On Monday the 14th of May the postman made his usual clattering delivery through the Schultz's letter box.

"I've never known a postman make so much noise putting as little as a postcard through the letter box, as that one does," had been Henry Schultz's oft repeated comment upon the delivery of His Majesty's mail by that particular servant of the G.P.O. However, hearing the clatter, Maria came down the stairs two at a time in the hope she would be rewarded with an envelope with no stamp on it, just the heading 'On Active Service.' She gave a little squeal of delight when she espied beneath the telephone bill and three somewhat bulky envelopes of different sizes obviously for her father, no fewer than three rather battered looking envelopes with that magical O.A.S. on them. She was then faced with an awful quandary, a dilemma of considerable proportions. Which one to open first? They had no legible date stamp on them. She could well open one only to find it referred to things contained in another. Well, 'faute de mieux' she told herself, remembering a fraction of her school French. She opened all three at once, to find David had dated them as always, thus solving the problem.

The first one was mainly luvvy-duvvy as brother Harry would have described it. The second one was in the same mould, but the third one, although mainly a variation of the other two, only put in somewhat more lustful terms, had a P.S. scribbled on it, written in different ink.

P.S. we are coming home in a few days, or so we are told.

She did a little jig, watched by her mother who had appeared from the kitchen.

"Good news?"

"David is coming home in a few days' time."

"What on leave? For good?"

"He doesn't say, it's just a little P.S. on the end of the letter. I suppose he was in a hurry to get it in to the post corporal. Perhaps we shall know more during the week.

Susan Schultz turned away. She had a dreadful premonition that David and his men were being rushed home to be refitted and made up to strength, to be sent to fight those other evil people in the Far East. They would not let a crack unit like the 6th Airborne Division sit around on garrison duty in Germany. Susan Schultz had already lost her only son, she so feared the loss of David who she had grown to love as if he were her own.

Maria ate a hurried breakfast and then booked a call to Rose, which came through in under half an hour. As the bell rang at Chandlers Lodge Rose said to the world in general, "Who the devil's that at 8.15 in the morning?" and having punished Henry Schultz's telephone bill to a considerable degree, finally hung up, with the first problem, who to tell the great news to first. The second problem in her highly intelligent and very army-orientated mind was, 'why are they bringing them home so quickly?' She too had a feeling of fear in common with Susan Schultz.

Chapter Eighteen

At Mecklenburgdorf David's company, along with the others, were still on full alert. Guards and outlying pickets were doubled at night, to the confused acceptance of the rank and file who, having been fed on the story line of the gallant Red Army, our 'Glorious Allies,' were now having to accept they could be attacked by them at any moment. As news began to filter in of the appalling behaviour of the Russian troops, apparently out of control of, or with the tacit approval of their officers, in the rape and pillage of the civilians in adjacent villages, the attitude of the average squaddie noticeably changed. Night after night civilians, and soldiers who had not as yet been captured, approached the British, and further south, the American lines, many at their last gasp, and were given sanctuary. They brought with them stories of wanton killings, of fit, able men and women being whisked away to, presumably, labour camps in Siberia. Of wholesale plunder of machinery, farm equipment, vehicles and livestock, all being sent east. It was no more than the Germans had inflicted upon the Russian Motherland, but the average squaddie knew little or nothing of that. From admiring the Red Army the allied soldier began to despise his former comrade in arms, particularly those from the far eastern republics who behaved particularly atrociously.

The hand over to the Ox and Bucks all went smoothly. Their forward units doubled up with David's company for three nights in order to get the feel of what to expect. Then on Saturday 19th May, the move back to Luneberg airfield began, where they were piled into every shape and size of airplane that would fly in order to get them back to Upavon and from there in a matter of a few minutes to their barracks at Bulford. David and Paddy found themselves in a stripped-out Halifax along with, it seemed, half their company seated on the floor. The normal bomb load of a Halifax would be around 13-15000 pounds, so it could comfortably carry forty men, except it would appear, on take off. As a result everyone had to pile up the front end in indecent closeness, resulting in such cries as:-

"Sir, Corporal Harris is feeling my chopper."

"Oh, that's the loveliest little bum I've felt in months."

"If that's not your rifle sticking in my back you can call me 'darling.' "

"You'll have to marry me after this," along with other such witticisms far too lewd to put in a respectable account of this nature.

During the flight David and Paddy were invited up to the flight deck, where David at one stage sat in the co-pilot's seat and took over the controls. The young pilot giving him instruction asked,

"Been in one of these before, sir?"

"Yes, Paddy and I," indicating his companion, "dropped into Yugoslavia from one many moons ago."

"How did you get back?"

"In a submarine, an experience I can tell you I hope never to have to repeat."

"Hear bloody hear," commented Paddy.

"Have you always flown the Halifax?" David asked.

"No, Mick and I," indicating his sergeant co-pilot, "did a tour in Lancs after our first Halifax tour."

"You have done two tours?"

"Two and a bit."

"Bloody hell," came Paddy's inevitable reply.

"You are telling me you have both been on over sixty bombing raids on Germany? May I ask how old you both are?"

"He's twenty-two; I'll be twenty two next month."

We all can guess Paddy's comment which followed.

Eventually the giant aircraft circled Upavon, where requiring its passengers to again carry out indecent assaults on one another, it landed safely. Having shaken the hands of his two pilots, David found himself with Paddy in a Dodge being whisked back to dear old Bulford. Dear old Bulford? That is not exactly what they had named it on many occasions before, having returned from the pleasures of connubial bliss to its somewhat spartan environment.

It seemed impossible that in the space of a few hours they had left a land of rape and pillage for the green and pleasant Wiltshire countryside, a land lit with street lamps, and cars fitted with headlamps you could now see from more than fifty yards away.

They also discovered they had been awarded a service medal for France and Germany. Even if you had fought in Normandy, the Ardennes, Holland and Germany as they had, one medal covered the lot. They were highly amused to discover the Yanks got one for each country, including Luxembourg if they happened to go there. Drive a truck through five different countries - five medals!!

It was very late when David at last reached his quarters, having seen his company had been fed and bedded down. He ate a welcome supper in the mess before deciding he was too tired to have a bath before getting to bed, despite the fact he had not experienced such enjoyment for at least a month. To his surprise, Angus, having anticipated the approximate time of his return, had drawn him a bath and had laid out pyjamas for him drawn from the locker he had left before they jumped the Rhine.

"Angus, you are an absolute blooming gem, you really are. Now, buzz off, and get to bed. Have you eaten?"

"Yes, sir, the officer's mess cook gave me some supper while you were seeing the company in."

"Right. Off you go then."

Then followed the inevitable, "What time tea in the morning, sir, and what will you be wearing?"

The transition of a fighting soldier, bodyguard, messenger under fire, to valet and personal servant had all occurred within twenty-four hours. It's a funny business at times, being a soldier.

At nine o'clock, as instructed, Angus woke his officer. It was Whit Sunday. After a leisurely late breakfast, David queued for a while for one of the three telephones in the mess annex. Having been told of a delay of thirty minutes to Chingford he spent a little time catching up on the world news from a copy of Reynolds News, the only paper not to have been snaffled up by others before him. Nevertheless, Reynolds was a good, liberal newspaper, well written and presented, only to disappear in the years to come like The News Chronicle, Daily Herald, and others.

He read of increasing air attacks on the Japanese in Malaya - that will cheer our Harry up he considered. He read the final tally of civilian casualties in Britain. 60585 killed of which 50% were in the London area. There had been 1050 V2 rockets landed, again mainly in the London area in the six months from September 1944 killing a further 2754 people, the worst incident being the direct hit on New Cross Woolworth's, where 160 were killed.

"Thank God," he said to himself, "that horror is now over."

The mess orderly appeared at his elbow.

"Your call to Chingford came through, sir, but there was no reply."

"Bugger."

"It's Sunday, sir," grinned his informant.

"In that case, dash it, mustn't swear on Sundays!"

He tried to get Chandlers Lodge, and although he got through almost immediately the blasted thing just rang and rang.

"I suppose they have all gone to salvage their consciences in church," he told himself. But they had not. The Schultz's, the Hoopers, the Reisners, the Boltons with all the remainder of the Chandler clan had congregated in what was to be known as 'Morgan's Field' from that day on.

Since Friday, when Ephraim Lee and his family arrived, a steady stream of gaily painted vehicles had gathered. Fred had told Ephraim they could draw water from the stable tap, Jack remarking that he had better lock up his hay and other fodder, to say nothing of the saddles and equipment in the tack room.

"Mr Lee promised nothing would be touched without permission," Fred replied. "I don't think we will have a problem. He is the head of the clan and from what I know his word is law."

Ephraim marshalled his vans around the perimeter of the paddock, all facing inwards, and with sufficient space at the rear of each for the horse, or in some cases horses, to be tethered. Several of the mares had young foals who ran free, but were rarely far from their mothers' sides. Every family had its cluster of dogs, especially lurchers, a dog cross-bred between a collie, or a sheep dog, with a greyhound. These were much prized by professional poachers. Gypsies of course did not consider themselves poachers in the eyes of the law. The animals and birds were wild, they themselves were free spirits to come and go as they please, therefore they were free to live from nature's goodness.

The gaily painted homes, never before seen in such numbers in Sandbury, provoked keen interest in the local population, many families strolling out of the town to Fred's paddock. Margaret had had thoughts about the Romas' horses eating the paddock bare, but Fred assured her that if they fed on it for a week, in a couple of days after they had gone Janie and Dylan would have plenty. And so it proved.

On Saturday Ephraim consulted with Fred where the tree was to go and it was decided it would be planted in as near the centre as could be established since the field itself was far from being a perfect square or rectangle. On Saturday morning early, half a dozen men, armed with pick-axes and shovels and a pile of sacks, rode off on a flat-bed cart, normally used for collecting scrap metal, legally or otherwise. In time they came to a wood a couple of miles out of Sandbury where, after much searching, Ephraim had found a suitable oak sapling. All the morning they dug carefully around it so as not to damage the roots, then finally, securing it with light ropes to neighbouring trees to keep it upright, they carefully excavated beneath it so as to retrieve the taproot growing vertically downwards. That part of the operation successfully accomplished, they gradually eased Morgan's Oak out of its birthplace, soaked the sacking they had brought with them in a nearby ditch and wrapped the roots and as much soil as they could salvage in the wet sacking, the whole tied firmly, but not too tightly, for it to be carried back to Sandbury.

They arrived back at Morgan's Field a little after eleven o'clock to find several more arrivals, and a half dozen other men digging a circular hole some six feet in diameter, and by now some three feet deep. When Fred came home from the factory, now resplendent in its new sign 'SANDBURY ENGINEERING LIMITED' after years of being, as Harry had put it, 'Blank, Blank Ltd' - all road signs and name signs had been removed in 1940 because of the invasion scare - he strolled over to the paddock. He was instantly surrounded by a gang of excited children who had followed Ephraim coming to meet him.

"All going alright, Mr Lee?"

"Yes, guv'nor, come and look at the tree, see what you think."

As he spoke a Sandbury Engineering truck drove into the open gateway, stopped by the tree, the driver let the tailboard down and dragged out two semi-circular frameworks, which when stood upright would bolt together around the fledgling trunk.

"That will stop the horses rubbing against it," Fred suggested. "We've got your nameplate that will screw on to it. We'll bring that tomorrow."

"What do I owe you, guv'nor?"

"You don't owe us anything. We owe you. You gave us your son."

Ephraim wiped his eyes with the back of his land. After a few moments he asked,

"When you brings the family out tomorrer, guv'nor, can you bring some chairs for the ladies to sit down on. Don't tell them beforehand. We're going to sing you all some Roma songs and the children are going to dance. Morgan would've liked us to do that for 'ee all."

"That's very kind of you, Mr Lee. I shan't say a word; they will have a lovely surprise. Let's hope it doesn't rain."

Ephraim turned to the south and peered into the sky.

"We shall 'ave a drop or two tonight I reckon, but it'll be dry tomorrer."

And it was.

Soon after ten on Whit Sunday morning the extended Chandler family arrived to take part in an experience not one of them would ever participate in again. Megan's twins Mark and Elizabeth, along with young John Hooper, these three now getting on for eight years of age, and when together, which seemed to be most of the time, constantly getting into trouble, were so excited they could burst. To a lesser degree all the grown-ups were looking forward with keen anticipation to being in the company of Ephraim and his clan, an opportunity not to be wasted, since the Roma generally speaking kept themselves strictly to themselves. In view of the persecution and harassment they had suffered over the centuries throughout Europe this could be understood. The first Roma reached England in the 1500s. One wonders why they decided to cross the water, whether they came with their vans and horses, how they paid for their passage. There are so many things to know. But I digress.

The chairs were carried out by the men, the ladies duly sat some fifteen yards from the hole in the ground with the men standing behind them. At eleven o'clock, just as David was trying again to reach them by telephone, Ephraim came forward, followed by his family who took up station on the wings of the Chandler group. Each wore a black armband - 'perhaps we should have thought of that' ran through several minds in Fred's party. Although not a big man, Ephraim started the proceedings in a clear, resonant voice, speaking in the Romani dialect he and his family and forbears had used for hundreds of years. The Chandlers heard 'Morgan' mentioned twice during this address, but otherwise of course understood nothing, until Ephraim turned to them and announced,

"I have told my family of the great kindness you have done for us. You have give us this place where Morgan's spirit can live with the seasons. We will never forget what you have done. If you need anything - anything - we can do or give, in all your days, you ask and it will be done."

There was silence for a moment, when Jack started to applaud, swiftly joined by the remainder. Fred walked forward and shook hands with Ephraim.

"Thank you, Mr Lee, thank you," and to his family, "thank you all."

Ephraim turned. "We shall now plant the oak."

The sapling was lifted carefully by four of the Roma and held over the hole. Two others lay on the ground, gently removed the sacking, then teased the roots out taking care not to fracture them. Gradually the tree was lowered into the hole so that the tap root slid down into the tubular opening in the base. The men then tied four pieces of cord so that they could hold the tree in a vertical position whilst it was embedded.

This part of the proceedings being accomplished successfully, Ephraim walked to where Margaret was seated, and handed her a spade.

"Will you put the first shovelful in, missus, please?" he asked.

Margaret took the spade from him. He turned to his clan and in their dialect told them it was this lady who had offered to have Morgan remembered in this way, and to be beholden to her all their days. As Margaret shovelled the first spadeful in so the Roma began to sing a low-keyed song, led by two of the family playing violins and two others with octagonal shaped squeeze-boxes. It was a sad song, reflecting the sadness the Roma had had to endure over the centuries, because they were different.

"Thank you, missus," Ephraim murmured as he took the spade from her. There were tears in his eyes as he said it, which led Margaret to be somewhat emotionally upset. As she sat down again Fred, seeing she was a little distressed, surreptitiously passed her a handkerchief. It is often the little things, the noticing things, that seal a good marriage.

Gradually the hole was filled, the earth being tamped down from time to time, carefully, so as not to damage those precious roots, but firmly enough to keep it secure in the ground until it regained its own natural strength, to take on everything that nature would throw at it over the next two hundred years or more. With a stout pole on either side to help it through the next couple of years or so it should thrive.

Finally the galvanised steel railing enclosure was put around it and bolted together. Fred handed Ephraim the cast iron plate with 'Morgan's Oak' on it, which was screwed into place.

These activities had taken a little over an hour, towards the end of which time Mark and John, followed at a short distance by Elizabeth, had decided they would try and get a look into one of the caravans. So that they would not be spotted by interfering grown-ups they chose one which faced the back of the seated party. The shafts of the van, sloping down to the ground, seemed as good a way as any of getting up on to the front so as to look inside. However, they had not counted on one problem. Dogs. All dogs had been tied up whilst the caravans had been harboured. The owners might be family but the dogs, particularly when their owners were <u>not</u> in attendance, were most certainly not. To prevent constant fights to establish who was the 'top dog,' as you might describe it, they were put on leads secured to one of the wheels which allowed them a certain amount of moving around space without infringing others' territory.

Mark and John decided to link hands and each walk up a shaft. Having tried two or three times and overbalanced they finally got the hang of it. It was then that a cross-bred bull mastiff, a little upset at having its midday siesta disturbed by unknown kids, hurled itself from under the caravan at the two boys. They, seeing this fiendish animal flying at them, promptly fell off the shafts on to the grass, to look up and see 'ferocious teeth' and 'slobbering jaws' trying to get at them. Fortunately for them the rope holding the animal was two feet shorter than the distance to its quarry. Try as it might, and it tried very hard indeed, it couldn't quite reach them. They rolled over, stood up and ran for it, preceded by Elizabeth who had felt sure they would be eaten at any minute.

The strange thing was, nobody had missed them, and nobody took any notice of a dog barking. After all, with around thirty caravans and probably double that number of dogs, or more, one of them was bound to bark every now and then out of sheer boredom.

With the tree now standing proudly within its protective metalwork Ephraim gave a signal, at which some twenty young girls, the oldest probably around ten or eleven years of age, lined up in front of their guests. The orchestra, now augmented by a couple more fiddlers and another concertina player, started slowly with the children carrying out graceful, interweaving movements, then moving into pairs and whirling around faster and faster, their voluminous skirts flying out emphasising the speed of the dance. Margaret and several of the other ladies remarked afterwards that, considering all the children so rarely were altogether in one place at any one time, their dancing was so in concert as to be almost professional.

The proceedings ended with some Roma songs from some twenty of the men present. It was all very pleasant and unique.

The visitors moving away, the men collecting their chairs, Ephraim approached Margaret and Fred.

"Missus, my daughter you saw when the horses was frightened that day, her name's Rhona, is getting wed tonight. We wondered if just you and the guv'nor would like to come. As a rule we..." he hesitated as to how to tell them that normally gorgas, as the gypsies called the natives of the country they were in, would not be permitted to take part in such a ceremony.

"We shall be delighted to come," Fred swiftly replied, realising the cause of Ephraim's confusion.

"And we feel very highly honoured to be asked," added Margaret, "but, Mr Lee, we have no present to give. One always takes a present for the couple being married."

"That's no trouble, missus. In our tribe we 'ave a custom. A cottage loaf is baked, and then hollowed out. It is then passed around and people put money in it to give the young 'uns a start. Nothing too great, mind, we Roma don't never have a lot of money, we lives on what the good earth gives us."

Fred grinned.

"I always understood the floors of Romani caravans were lined with gold bars, or so I've been told."

Ephraim laughed. He rarely laughed, Fred thought. Perhaps their continual rejection wherever they went plucked out the mirth from them.

"Well, I grant you there are some 'omes that are worth a lot more than you'd give them credit for by just looking at 'em, but they be few and far between."

"Like yours, you mean?" Ephraim laughed again.

"I'm not lettin' on."

"How did the youngsters meet, Mr Lee?" Margaret asked - ever the romantic.

"Well, missus, it was like this."

Ephraim then described how, since they usually travel singly the only time they meet up is in the picking seasons, peas, strawberries and other soft fruit, apples and pears in the autumn, and of course hop-picking. If then a lad likes the look of a girl he eyes her up and if she fancies him she doesn't turn away, but smiles back.

"You have to remember," Ephraim pointed out, "he's only got two or three weeks at the most to get his card marked before they both move on."

He continued by saying if the lad doesn't get turned down he will then give the girl his dicklo, which is the scarf all Roma men wear with the ends fastened to their braces. If the next time he sees her she is wearing the scarf on her head, that means they are walking out, and they approach both sets of parents to settle the wedding.

The wedding ceremony itself varies considerably from country to country and for that matter from tribe to tribe.

"He's a Smith, so they are more or less the same as us," Ephraim pointed out. "Some tribes go in for a 'mingling of the blood' marriage. A little cut is made in the wrists which they hold together. We don't do that. You come over at about half past nine and we will all make you welcome."

It was nearly two o'clock before Fred led the party in through the back door of The Chandlers to a buffet lunch they proposed giving to those who had attended the tree-planting ceremony. As he opened the door he heard the telephone shrilling out.

"Chandlers Lodge."

"Dad, it's David. I've been trying to get you, Maria, Ernie or somebody all the morning. I even thought of telephoning the local police to see whether Sandbury had suffered an earthquake or something."

"Well, now you've got a somebody, where are you?"

"We are back at Bulford. I should be coming on leave at the end of the week."

"Then where are you going?"

David paused for a moment.

"Doesn't take a lot of guessing does it? But mum's the word for now, O.K.?"

"O.K." Fred thought, 'everybody's saying bloody O.K. these days.' He called out to Maria, just arriving.

"I'll pass you over to your infinitely better half, hang on."

There then followed the inevitable, 'David darling, where are you? Why haven't you phoned? When will I see you? Are you alright, not wounded or anything?' Etcetera, etcetera, until,

"Now, let me get a word in edgeways. I am at Bulford, I expect to be on leave at the end of the week, and most importantly you haven't been seeing that seventeen-stone stoker again, which would explain why my telephone calls all have gone unanswered, I suppose?"

"Only on Wednesdays. I keep my weekends free."

It was a standing joke between them that, when Maria was in the Wrens, she had the company of a heavyweight stoker while David was away. At least, David always thought it was a joke, Maria assured her friends.

"And my baby?"

"He's just going to have his feed."

"Save some for me. When are you going home?"

"Mummy and daddy are here. I will tell you all about it later. We are going back this evening. We came in daddy's Lanchester as we had to bring the carrycot and so on. We've been here since Friday night. There's so much to tell you, I'm so excited. How long a leave will you get?"

"At least twenty-one days, perhaps a bit more."

"That's a long time. Darling, you are not going away again?"

David delayed his reply for a short while. He had hoped to be able to break this news face to face. He decided he had to be frank.

"I'm afraid so, my love. We are being sent out to the Far East. I am to help get my brother back." He could sense the shock this knowledge had brought about to his darling Maria, "but we shall have a lovely leave together, go away for some of the time, and with all the strength of the armies here, and perhaps Russia joining in we shall soon finish the war for good."

"Will you telephone me at Chingford tomorrow evening?"

"Yes, my darling, I shall know more by then."

A disconsolate Maria joined the party, her downcast demeanour immediately noticed by Rose, and Susan and Henry Schultz.

"Anything wrong, dear?" Susan asked.

"David is being sent to the Japanese war after his leave." Rose put her hand to her mouth.

"Oh no! Oh, hasn't he done enough?"

"He said, 'I am going to get my brother back.' "

Henry broke in, "That's the sort of brave thing David would say."

But they all knew that defeating the Japs would be no walkover.

Margaret and Fred arrived back in Morgan's Field at exactly nine-thirty and were seated on folding chairs in front of the standing throng of friends and relatives of the two young people to be wed. In a few minutes Ephraim and another man, presumably the father of the groom, appeared. Under normal circumstances the ceremony would be conducted by the groom's father, but as Ephraim was the senior elder of his clan, therefore a man of importance, he would preside over the ritual. Finally Rhona and her husband-to-be, Rudi, came hand in hand to stand before Ephraim.

On Ephraim's left hand a young girl stood holding a bunch of twigs which had been broken from seven different types of trees. The proceedings commenced with a rendering of ancient lore in a language totally incomprehensible to Fred and Margaret. As Ephraim intoned so he broke the sticks one by one and threw them to all different points of the compass. This completed he stressed to Rhona and Rudi how sacred was the marriage bond and that to break their pledge to each other until death would be most wicked. They had to share life's pleasures together, life's sadnesses together and to work together for the benefit of their family and their clan. This homily completed he indicated to a young woman on his right to come forward, taking from her a loaf and some salt. They each then ate a little of the bread sprinkled with the salt. Now Rudi took a small cup from his pocket, which the young lady attendant filled with water.

The young couple now drank from the cup in turn, after which Rudi smashed it to the ground. The tradition had it that never again would the couple drink from the same cup, and whenever a drink was poured Rudi would be the one to drink first.

Ephraim now stood aside. Behind him lying on the grass was a besom, a broom made from flowering gorse. A pace or two beyond that was a violin and beyond that fortune-telling cards were laid out. The two young people joined hands, leapt over the broom, the violin and the cards, and they were wed. There was loud applause along with the instant disappearance of the newly married couple to Rudi's caravan given him by his family. In less well-off clans it would be to a 'bender', or tent, the husband would have made.

The drink and food was then provided in abundance. All manner of homemade wines, elderberry, parsnip, rhubarb; they seemed to be able to make wine from anything. Cowslip, dandelion, even pansies, though since the latter did not grow wild one wonders whose gardens had suffered, all were pressed into service. During the eating and drinking the hollowed-out cottage loaf was passed around, arriving at Fred and Margaret fairly late on. It was overflowing with ten shilling and one pound notes, with here and there the white of the big fiver showing in the firelight. Fred added another fiver, pushing it down into the bulge of the base of the loaf. As he did so Ephraim appeared at his elbow.

"You was a guest, guv'nor, you didn't have to do that." Margaret answered.

"Mr Lee, you have given us an insight into your world which makes us feel very, very, privileged people. That is the least we can do for your young people. Does this mean you have now lost Rhona?"

"Yes, missus. She's a Smith now, but he's a good lad, he'll treat her well I reckon. We shall meet up from time to time at the pickings." He sounded very sad; he loved his pretty, boisterous little Rhona very much.

"But that's the way of the world, missus, ain't it?"

* * *

Chapter Nineteen

As Fred sat in his office on Tuesday 22nd May, the day before being Whit Monday was again a Bank Holiday, his secretary telephoned him.

"There's a Mr Stevens from the Ministry wishes to speak to you, Mr Chandler."

"Righto, Miss Russell, put him through."

"Good morning, Mr Chandler. I wonder if I can come down to see you at a time to suit you?"

"Certainly. When would you like to make it?"

"Would tomorrow morning be alright, say ten o'clock?"

"Yes, that would be O.K." Then thought, bloody O.K. again. "Do you require any special figures prepared or anything of that nature?"

"No, thank you. I will see you then. Good morning, Mr Chandler."

Fred sat back. What the hell does he want, I wonder? He decided to telephone Jack at Shorts in Rochester.

"I'm glad you have phoned, Fred, I have just had some news."

"Me too."

"Right, you go first then."

"I've got a Ministry wallah coming to see me tomorrow morning. I have a funny feeling in my water it's not going to be good news. I wondered if you could spare an hour to be in in the meeting, along with Ernie."

"Yes, I can manage that; in fact my news might cast the cat among the pigeons. You know when I was made chairman and M.D. here two years ago, the M.D. bit was to be phased out after six months, but I was to carry on as chairman. Well, the powers that be kept on putting off the phasing out bit. Now, I am being required to find a new M.D. by the end of the year, someone with a background in civilian plane making, and I shall then be relieved of the chairmanship at the end of June '46. So, if you've got an office boy's job going next summer will you think of me for it?"

"I take it you can now come back on to our board again in that case?"

"Yes, but not in any executive capacity. I want a few years to enjoy my wife and family."

"I thought you always enjoyed your wife very much? She was always boasting about it."

"We will let that pass, however now that the war is on its last legs it's time she gave up her job. She comes back from Nevada in three weeks and I'm going to get her to call it a day. She has done more than her fair share. Most of what she has done we know nothing about, but it has been a great strain on her over the past couple of years as you know only too well."

"Right. Well, we'll see what the ministry man wants tomorrow and then go to The Angel for lunch if you can spare the time."

"Good idea. See you before ten then. Cheerio now."

The Ministry Man arrived the next morning in a chauffeur-driven Humber - 'Must be top brass' was Fred's immediate appreciation of the situation. Being installed at Fred's boardroom table, and with Jack and Ernie in attendance, Fred introduced his colleagues.

"Mr Stevens, this is Sir Jack Hooper, who will be rejoining our board in the near future, and Mr Bolton who is our senior director."

Mr Stevens considered the youthful Ernie to be anything but senior, but shook hands just the same.

"I'll come to the point, Mr Chandler. You have government contracts for various items which are now to be scaled down."

"You think we're going to win then?" asked Fred with tongue in cheek.

The peculiar simper which passes across Ministry Men's faces in place of a full blown smile evidenced itself in Mr Stevens rather po-faced visage, as Charlie Crew would have described it.

"I think we can assume that, don't you?"

Fred, thinking of David, Harry and all the others who were going to have to bring about this bland assumption replied,

"Well, it's not over yet, not by a bloody long chalk. Anyway, what is it you have to tell us?"

"We shall be phasing out your Mosquito contract over the next six months. You will be required to provide only one more Hamilcar after the one you are at present building, and the smaller contracts for radio vans and so on are to stop immediately.

There was a silence around the table, broken by Fred saying,

"What is the position regarding the cancellations? Do I take it we receive some compensation for materials bought in and other expenses, the cost of discharging part of the workforce and so on?"

"Oh yes, of course. Your accountants will prepare a final schedule, including loss of profits of course, which he will agree with us." There was a further silence.

"Well, I suppose we've known this would happen sooner or later," Fred reflected, "at least we have six months to phase things out."

"What will you do now, Mr Chandler, may I ask - if it is not a board secret of course?"

"We have our agricultural machinery market of course. We have just got to get our thinking caps on."

"Export, Mr Chandler. Export. That's what we and the country needs. The government is coming out with a slogan "Export or die." Rather over the top in my opinion, but then civil servants are not allowed opinions are they?"

It was not only a momentous day for Sandbury Engineering; it was also a momentous day for the country as a whole. It was the day, 23rd of May 1945, when the war-time coalition government, which had worked so wonderfully for over five years, was ended. Winston Churchill went to see the King, dissolved the coalition and formed a new government until dissolution on the 15th June with new elections to take place on the 25th of July. With his personal popularity there was no doubt he would sweep the country.

We shall see.

After the 'Ministry Man' had left the three directors sat in silence for a short while, a silence eventually broken by Fred saying,

"I think we had better have a session, including Ray Osbourne, to try and determine an outline plan of what we can do or can't do. If each of us brings ideas, no matter how fanciful, we can pick them about and arrive at the way ahead. I have already had some ideas, I know Ernie and Ray have, and I would be surprised indeed if you haven't," looking pointedly at Jack.

"Particularly the plastics side," Ernie suggested.

"And we have to try and establish where Harry and David will fit in," Jack reminded them. "They will be among the first out when the war finishes."

Fred considered Jack's last remark.

"They are going to have to learn a new trade after six or more years of war. They can't be expected to settle into civilian life in five minutes after all they have been through, and we don't know a tenth of what that was anyway."

There was no doubt there was to be an awful lot of soul-searching in the transition of war to peace. To some it provided few problems, to others it came in due course, to some on the other hand, particularly ex POWs, it would leave scars which would never heal, despite the care of loving families.

David came on leave on Friday 25th May to the welcoming arms of his Maria and her parents, and was surprised to see how his son Henry had grown. Now ten months old he was fast becoming a 'chip off the old block,' as Ernie Bolton had described him the previous weekend. As the Schultz's had been invited to Sophia's baptism on Sunday along with Maria and David, they decided they would travel on Sunday morning, the Schultz's would come back on Sunday evening and Maria and David would stay on at Chandlers Lodge for a few days, making plans for the rest of the leave.

When Jane carried Sophia into the church on Sunday afternoon she was again distressed when she saw the numbers of people who had gathered there to see her little daughter baptised. Only such a short while ago she had been alone and treated with disdain at having an Eurasian child, now they had become part of a family, something she had not been able to visualise in her wildest dreams. Charles, knowing how sensitive she was to these displays of friendship and support kept a tight hold on her elbow. She looked up at him, the love in her eyes thanking him for his understanding.

Sophia in the meantime looked around with interest at all the people gathered there. Her mother had explained what was to happen, to the extent of standing her on a chair by the kitchen sink, pouring three saucers of water on her head, then drying her off. She found it rather fun. She had also been told that when they got to the church her mother would not pour the water on, but a friend of Charles would do it, a very nice man, so she had no unease about that. After all, if he was a friend of Charles he must be a very nice man.

On the strike of four o'clock Canon Rosser approached the font.

"Hath this child already been baptised, or no?"

Jane and the Godparents, Cecely, Fred and Margaret, answered,

"No."

The Canon continued,

"Dearly beloved... " until he came to the part of the service when he spoke to the Godparents.

"Ye have brought this child to be baptised ... to give her the kingdom of heaven, and everlasting life ... you that are her sureties give that she will renounce the devil and all his works ... and obediently keep God's commandments."

And so the solemn promises and assurances were given until the Canon indicated to Jane to stand Sophia on the chair against the font. Sophia at this point began to be a little apprehensive. 'This is going on a long time - looks as though he is going to splash me now - why is he wearing that nightdress I wonder - I hope that water in there is not too cold - I don't like cold water.'

"Name this child."

"Sophia."

"Sophia, I baptise thee in the name of the Father," a shell of water was poured over her head, "and of the Son," another shellful, "and of the Holy Ghost. Amen," a third shellful. The man in the nightdress then made the sign of The Cross upon her forehead before patting her damp head dry with a small hand-towel from the edge of the font.

"We receive this Child into the congregation of Christ's flock."

After further exhortations to the Godparents as to their duties, in particular to teach her her Catechism, the service ended, with Sophia saying to herself, 'well, I don't know what the fuss was all about." She could not know, and would not know for many years, how she was considered to have been born in the deepest of sins, which her baptism had wiped away.

The christening over they all made their ways to The Angel, where Charles had organised John Tarrant to provide a tea, as he and Jane had no home of their own to which they could invite guests as would normally be the case. Fred and Jack, standing together, were vaguely amused at the sight of Hugh Ramsford assisting Cecely in replenishing other guest's tea cups.

"I bet that's the first time he's done that," Jack jested.

"Perhaps he and Cecely will turn Ramsford Grange into a hotel when he's demobbed," laughed Fred. "Mind you, having said that, I wonder what will happen to a whacking great place like that? I mean, the days of house parties with fifty guests and all their servants are long gone, I should think, unless you are an Indian nabob or something."

"Well, pulling them down started in the thirties, if my memory serves me right," Jack continued. "I seem to remember the Barings virtually demolishing The Grange down in Hampshire because of the exorbitant taxes put on it. That was sheer vandalism in my opinion."

"What are you two hatching up?" It was David at their elbows.

"We were just watching Charlie's father practising as a waiter for when he gets demobbed," Jack replied. "He's not bad at it actually." He turned to David.

"Now, tell us what you think of our gallant Russian allies."

"Well, since I believe there were some twenty millions of them I suppose it would be difficult to be specific. In general, those I saw were coarse, brutal and uncivilised. Furthermore, despite the fear you would have considered they would have of the ferocious punishments they could receive, they seemed to be totally undisciplined in respect of their treatment of civilians and prisoners of war. I don't think somehow they are going to remain our allies for long. I can't see them joining with us against the Japanese for a start."

"They may do what the Americans did in the last lot," Jack suggested, "stay out until it is nearly all over, then come in so as to get a share of the spoils." He didn't realise how prophetic he was being. That is exactly what they did do.

The nine o'clock news that evening when they returned to Chandlers Lodge contained a good deal of what we were doing to the Japanese. A few weeks earlier a thirty minute news contained twenty minutes about the B.L.A. and the bombing offensive, five minutes of home news and five minutes of news about the Far East, tacked on to the end. No wonder the people in Burma called themselves 'The Forgotten Army.'

That evening in addition to the grim news that 105,000 Japanese bodies had been counted in the recent advance on Rangoon, they were told Tokyo had been heavily bombed by 500 Superfortresses dropping 4000 tons of incendiaries. The Imperial Palace and two other palaces had been burned down and fifty-one square miles of the city had been completely destroyed, leaving five million of its seven million inhabitants homeless. They too were reaping the whirlwind; Japanese towns were good burning material.

So that euphoria engendered by news such as that above should not give the public in Britain, America, and in the United States in particular, a false sense of over-optimism, General Marshall, the American overall allied commander, issued a warning. Japan conquered three million square miles of territory in their original assaults, of which only seven per cent had been recaptured. They held vast stocks of oil, two million tons of shipping, huge stocks of war materials from Korean, Manchurian and Chinese sources, along with large chemical, shipbuilding and munitions industries. Far from being on their knees, despite their losses, they were still a formidable, fanatical foe.

After the news, people drifted away. Henry pointed the Lanchester towards Blackwall Tunnel, Charles and Hugh walked Cecely and Jane back to The Bungalow, Charles carrying Sophia seated up on his shoulders in which position she felt very important since she was looking down on everybody else.

"Uncle Hugh," - a questioning announcement.

Hugh looked up at her in the pale moonlight.

"Yes, dear?"

"Do you love Auntie Cecely like Charles loves mummy?"

The three adults looked at each other in amusement.

"Why do you want to know?"

"I think it would be nice if you did."

"Well I do, so what have you got to say about that?"

They could see Sophia thinking this question over.

"I think you are lucky. Auntie Cecely is ever so kind and pretty."

"And I think you are very clever." They walked on, this colloquy bringing even greater perfection to the end of a perfect day.

At Chandlers Lodge the family sat in the kitchen, each asking the other news of those not present. 'Have you heard from Harry lately?' to Megan. 'What did you think of the Russians?' from those, other than Fred, anxious to get every grain of knowledge about our valiant allies, 'Where is Charlie now?' 'Any news of when Mark will be on leave?' and so on, the sort of disjointed conversation which inevitably occurs within a family which has not been together for some time. Margaret listened to the exchange closely, not in any sense feeling out of it, but gradually absorbing snippets of information which bound her closer to those present. Family, after all, is not just being a relative, it is a fundamental knowledge of one another unknown to those not part of it that binds it together. It must be one of life's saddest circumstances not to be part of an inseparable family. On the other hand I suppose some families can't stand one another. We are a funny lot.

They drifted off to bed, Rose and Megan each secretly envying Maria and Margaret who would have the strong arms of their husbands to enfold them. Again that night David and Maria made passionate love to each other without taking precautions. They had not discussed this; it was as if they both had an inner feeling that David was facing a danger even greater than those he had thus encountered, and they had been grave enough. The two lovers therefore would hope for a tangible reminder of their last great unions together should he not return, without either of them having put the thought into words.

Whilst they were at Sandbury, David and Maria spent as much time as they could with Megan, taking her and the children to London on two occasions. With a map of Malaya they endeavoured to work out the most likely place Harry would be. They had little to go on as he had, because of the censorship problem, been able to say little of what he was doing in the few letters he had been able to despatch. They were, incidentally, fascinated by the drawings of him with Chantek. However, since the few pointers they got from Megan - "I am certainly not going to let you read the letters," she had told them, "you are much too young" - indicated he was in the high jungle (cold at night), that they crossed a railway line after a day, ("I don't know how that slipped through the censor," David remarked) it would seem likely he would be somewhere from Cameron Highlands southwards towards Frasers Hill. North of that the railway is much further away than one day; southwards the jungle is on much lower mountains. His final pronouncement was,

"Since that covers over a thousand square miles of jungle or more, it's no wonder the Japs can't find them. No, when I get there, I am afraid we shall have to wait for them to come out. Just think of it, Harry would need to ask the way to get to Sevenoaks when he lived here, now I bet he knows every track, every stream, like the back of his hand, for anything up to a hundred miles from wherever his camp is. God, if anyone deserves Victoria Crosses those blokes do, and no matter how brave those Japs are reputed as being, I bet they still look over their shoulders every time they move out of their cosy little billets to make sure the men from the jungle are not upon them."

And he was not far wrong in this viewpoint.

On Friday 4th June they returned to Chingford. Rose, Anni and Megan tried hard not to be more upset than they were normally when one of their soldiers was returning to the war. Harry, David, Mark, Charlie, Oliver, The Canadians, Tim, Alec and Jim. Their extended family, Paddy, Kenny Barclay and the two marine majors, Ivan and Ken. They had not been quite so close with the two Welsh Guards majors; nevertheless they were often in the thoughts of those left behind. Today it was different. There was an underlying feeling present in all of them, Fred and Jack included, that David was to face the greatest peril of his life. Paratroops inevitably faced great unknown dangers in being dropped into defended positions; positions in this case defended by the fanatical Japanese would be doubly fearsome. More than one of that family group saying goodbye wondered if it would be the last time they would see their David, then, guiltily, brushed the thought aside.

At Chingford they gave further thought as to where they should spend their week away. Susan had insisted they leave the baby with her. He was now on the bottle so would be 'no problem,' they would then be free to 'hit the town,' as Susan described it.

"I wonder what Bangor is like at this time of the year?" Maria mused.

"Knowing Paddy, he has probably already got it booked," David replied. It was a stock joke that in his honeymoon cottage in Bangor Paddy and Mary had only ventured out twice in the week to buy bread and milk from the corner shop.

"Will Paddy be going with you?"

"I doubt it. He's already time expired although as Mr Kipling said, 'there's no discharge in the war.' They will probably leave this last clearing up to we younger ones." He tried to make it as flippant as possible, but in no way did he fool his Maria.

Eventually they decided on Torquay and with the aid of a 1939 AA directory provided by Henry Schultz decided to push the boat out and stay at The Grand on the seafront. They were not disappointed in any respect whatsoever. The service was almost pre-war, the food excellent, the weather great, the pubs welcoming, the bed - well, it would be difficult to describe the bed should one need to rely on the evidence of Major and Mrs David Chandler. The problem to be overcome here would be to get a balanced account of its opulence, luxury, comfort or whatever, from a series of nightly hyper-activity followed by insensate exhaustion until being roused with morning tea by the delightful young chambermaid. Despite all that activity they still managed to be late for breakfast on at least two occasions - we shall not delve into the reasons for that. You can appreciate therefore; an opinion of the bed would be like asking a drunk if he enjoyed the party.

They had such a carefree, happy week, that for most of the time the sick feeling Maria felt at the coming separation was forgotten. But all things come to an end. As they settled into their first class seats back to Paddington it returned with a vengeance. She looked silently out of the window at the gorgeous countryside struggling hard to say something, anything, with a voice that would not betray her inner feelings. She was glad when they reached London.

"Shall we go and see Mr Stratton before we go home?"

"Yes, let's."

They left their suitcases in the left-luggage department and got a cab to the Corner House. Now that most of the Yanks had left London it was much easier to get a taxi.

Mr Stratton was delighted to see them, seating them at his own table tucked away out of sight of the hoi polloi, and joining them for a somewhat belated lunch. Naturally he was shown the photograph of the infant Chandler at which he was delighted.

"Just to think it is over three years since you were one of us," he said to Maria, "so much has happened in that time."

He then, unknowingly, said the wrong thing.

"I take it you are now posted home, Major?"

Maria's face fell.

"No, I'm afraid not, Mr Stratton. They have decided I should be one of those who will have the pleasure of showing Hirohito and company the error of their ways."

Mr Stratton's hand went out to be placed on David's arm.

"I would have thought you have done more than enough already."

"That is exactly what I said," Maria agreed.

David shrugged, grinned and replied, "It can't last long now, they are now surrounded and on the run. Japan itself is being battered day by day when they thought they were secure against air attack. It would not surprise me if it wasn't all over long before I get there."

'And, by God,' he said to himself, 'if that doesn't search the depths of wishful thinking nothing ever will.'

"I would like to telephone you from time to time if I may, Maria, to hear how the major is getting on. Would you mind if I did so?"

"Not at all, I shall be most pleased to hear from you."

Having said goodbye to Mr Stratton they made their way back to Chingford, being picked up at the station by Henry Schultz, along with Susan and the baby. There was the usual 'Have you been a good boy?' 'Did you have a nice time?' from Susan with marginally raised eyebrows so as to make the question not too obvious. 'How was the hotel?' as if the Grand Hotel would be anything but grand.

"Oh David, a telegram came for you today. I haven't opened it as I knew you would soon be home." Henry handed over the buff envelope. Maria looked anxious. Everybody looks anxious when a telegram appears on the scene. David slit the envelope open. It read,

"Leave extended six days. Lucky sod. Haimish."

The three people watched his face for an indication of its expression to give them the knowledge, good news, or bad news?

David smiled. They relaxed. "I have six more days' leave," he told them in some jubilation.

"Oh, lovely, lovely, now you can come to Jane and Charles' wedding with us."

David was originally to go back to Bulford on the Friday before the wedding on the 16th of June.

"They will all be fed up with seeing me again having already said goodbye," he quipped.

"Ah, but Rose telephoned and said Mark and Charlie and Emma are all going to be there, and the Earl and Gloria too are coming."

"What's the dress?"

"Morning suit or uniform," Henry replied, "you will be lucky to get a morning suit in time, it's only three days away, so uniform it is."

"I badly need a haircut."

"It won't take two days to get a haircut, who is going to look at you anyway?" was Maria's comment upon this statement.

"I shall get rude remarks from Charlie and Mark if I go like this. Have you bought a violin, David? Is Friday night Amami night David? Are you thinking of having plaits, David?"

The others stood laughing at him.

"And to think he believes only women are vain," quipped Maria.

Nevertheless he did get his hair cut. He was taking no chances.

* * *

Chapter Twenty

The Schultz family arrived at Chandlers Lodge soon after lunch on Friday 15th June to be met with much hugging and kissing from the Chandlers, the Laurensons, and the Crews, who were also staying at Chandlers Lodge. However I would like to make it clear that whilst there was a certain amount of hugging between David, Mark and Charlie, the kissing bit was confined to welcoming the female members of the gathering. I like to be clear about matters of this nature.

Well, where to start? So much had happened since they had all met. We shall start with Charlie, he being the youngest of our three warriors. He was still not A1 but was in a home service battalion and was now a captain. Mark had survived many battles as part of an armoured division and had collected an MC to prove it. On the downside, of the one hundred and twenty-odd of his company he took to France he now only had twenty-two of the originals. In addition, his platoon commanders, all lieutenants, had twice been replaced through becoming casualties. At least now they were settled in Osnabruk so would not be going to the Far East. "Not that there is much need for an armoured division of our type in the jungle," he had added, thinking, 'but might yet be useful against the Russkis.'

The wedding, and the reception laid on by John Tarrant, went well, Charles and Jane electing to honeymoon in Eastbourne where many hotels now had managed to throw off the dilapidated appearance they had acquired as being the homes of hobnail booted members of His Majesty's Forces, to regain if not their original pristine condition, at least approaching that appearance.

Inevitably, Sophia raised curiosity. In 1945, outside the dock areas of, say, London, Liverpool, Glasgow, the sight of any black or oriental person was a rarity. Jane and Charles had discussed whether they should get Sophia to call him 'Daddy,' finding it extremely difficult to arrive at a decision. Calling him 'Charles' now would excite no curiosity, but what would it sound like in a few years time?

"I think we must grasp the bull by the horns," he suggested to Jane. "When I legally adopt Sophia she will be my daughter with my name. She can then call me 'Daddy.' If people think that's a bit odd, hard luck. Any very close people will know the story anyway and they are the only ones who count." It was decided therefore that as soon as they returned from Eastbourne they would put the wheels in motion to have Sophia legally adopted. In the meantime Jane asked the little girl,

"Now mummy and Charles are married would you like to call him 'daddy,' instead of Charles?"

Sophia thought about this change for a while.

"Do you mean like John calls Uncle Jack?"

"That's right, dear."

"Why haven't Mark and Elizabeth got a daddy? I like them - and John."

"Mark and Elizabeth have got a daddy but he is a soldier fighting a long way away."

"I think I would like to have a daddy. Why haven't I got a daddy?"

Jane had not expected to be faced with that question for a few years yet and was thrown on to the backfoot. After a moment's hesitation she replied,

"We are waiting for Charles to be your daddy."

This answer seemed utterly logical to Sophia. She smiled; as she did so Charles came out into the sun lounge where they were seated, to be greeted,

"Hello daddy."

Jane had a little weep. Charles was not far from it. Sophia smiled again. She rather liked the sound of 'daddy,' and used it quite a lot from then on; sometimes it must be said to the puzzlement of others overhearing her.

Back at Sandbury they all went to church on Sunday morning, then back to Chandlers Lodge. It was the first occasion upon which Charlie had an opportunity to talk to his father, and to congratulate him on a 'very wise choice.' "There is another reason to congratulate you," he added. Hugh's eyebrows raised enquiringly.

"We think you will be a grandfather in the not too distant future."

"How do you mean - think? Don't you know?"

"We shall very shortly now. But nobody knows yet but you, so please keep stumm until we're sure."

Hugh was delighted.

"It's all bloody happening, isn't it? Your grandfather enjoying the comfort of a very attractive older lady down at Ramsford in his declining years, my marrying someone I fell in love with literally at first sight, and your producing an heir for the Otbourne's."

"Might be an heiress - you never know. Anyway, pater, what will you do with Ramsford Grange when grandfather passes on? It really is so huge."

"I'm afraid a great many people are, or will be faced with that problem over the next few years," his father replied. "We are fortunate in that our land income will more than pay for its upkeep; on the other hand, keeping it up to scratch is money down the drain if it is not used. The days of big entertaining I am certain will not obtain in a post-war Britain. We will leave the problem until your grandfather passes on, then we will get some land and property consultants in to come up with ideas. They will probably say pull the bloody place down and live in the gardener's cottage or over the stables."

"Well, in that case let's hope grandfather lives to a hundred or more."

But the long weekend and David's extra six days were soon over, with tearful goodbyes from Maria, Rose, and Emma to prove it. David bumped into Roger Hammick on Waterloo station so they travelled back to Bulford together.

"David, we know nothing about jungle fighting. Do you think we shall get some training before we are let loose on our oriental friends? And another thing, how can you drop a battalion in trees or blooming paddy fields? As far as my limited knowledge goes it's either one thing or the other out in the Far East."

"I know as much about it as you do, my son, but since the overall commander is a gentleman I shall not name, I fear that a G.M.F.U. is inevitable. Having said that, the landing at Elephant Point of 152nd Para was 'successful in the capture of Rangoon,' so perhaps he has learnt something since Dieppe."

Nevertheless David had an uneasy feeling that paras trained for a European war were going to be thrown into jungle fighting without having a clue as to the tricks of the trade.

When they had got bodies and souls together on Friday 22nd June, Haimish called an 'O' Group of company commanders, but first he saw David in his office.

"David, a number of the longer serving people of all ranks will not be going to the Far East. That includes RSM Forster and Tony Bellows." Tony was second-in-command of the battalion. He continued, "I am therefore making you 2ic and promoting O'Riordan to RSM - provided he wants to go, otherwise he can see the rest of his service out back here. Will you have a word with him?"

David did just that, in the following manner, when he returned to his company office, by asking his company clerk to find the sergeant major at the double.

"What's up, sir?"

"Because of your advanced years they say they are leaving you behind." He failed to say who 'they' were.

"They can't do that, sir, how would you manage?"

"I've got a new job, second-in-command. Still a major of course."

"Have you, sir? Congratulations. Christ Almighty, you'll be the youngest bloody colonel in the regiment before we know it. But you were pulling my pisser about not going weren't you, sir?"

"Well, there is a way we can get round it."

"I'll revert to rifleman, so I will, if I must."

"The colonel says that if you will take on the thankless task of RSM since Mr Forster will not be going, then you can come with us."

Paddy looked at David in total disbelief.

"You're pulling my pisser again, sir, aren't you?"

"No. Cross my heart." David knew what Paddy's next pronouncement would be.

"Bloody hell," followed by, "me, an RSM What will Mary say about that? And it's all down to you. It was the best day of my life when I got you at Winchester."

"You mean the second best."

Paddy thought for a moment. "No, equal best. If I hadn't got you to look after at the depot I would haven't have met Mary anyway. Jesus wept; we've seen some sights in the last five years. And now, with the RSM and the 2ic, working together we'll see some more, even if it's not up at the sharp end."

"I think it's all one big sharp end in the jungle. Anyway I must be off to the 'O' Group."

For the next few days the battalion worked day and night to get ready for the move. They only had two weeks to lose the old sweats, induct the new, including officers, organise tropical gear which the troops would need to replace their serge uniforms once they reached Suez. David had to say farewell to Sandy Patterson, as the Canadians were now bowing out of the war, they were not to be involved with the Japs.

"You'll come to Canada to see us after the war, won't you?"

"Try and stop me. Now give Amanda One our love, Paddy and me, and keep in touch."

"You bet."

Unlike many agreements of that nature by bosom pals that fell by the wayside, that one did in fact survive.

On the 6th July therefore R Battalion boarded its special train in the sidings they knew so well and left Bulford for the last time on the long journey to Greenock on the River Clyde where they were to board the Corfu, a P and O liner, now a trooper, for Bombay.

As they approached the Mediterranean RSM O'Riordan M.C. got all the W.O.s and sergeants together and read the riot act about the men getting sunburnt. Paddy was an old India hand and knew what rookies would do once they hit the hot weather.

"Any man who gets burnt so that he has to be treated for it has caused himself to have a self-inflicted wound, and will be charged. In addition every section sergeant will be charged with neglect of duty if he allows it to happen to the men under his command."

One sergeant, new to the battalion, was heard to say as they left the meeting, "Forster was bad enough they tell me, but that Irish git would take some beating." Overhearing this, another sergeant who had been with the battalion since its formation, told him. "Yes, but where will you find another RSM with an M.C.? He's seen more fighting than the rest of us put together."

It was all new to the vast majority of the battalion. Scraping through the canal, finding the Red Sea was not red, then emerging into the Gulf of Aden and the Indian Ocean, where once again they were on a war footing. Every man to carry his life jacket at all times, the ship blacked out at night, lifeboat assembly drill every day. Japanese submarines would be doing their best to find a single ship of this size, unaccompanied as it was by an escort, relying on its speed for safety.

If being on a ship in tropical waters was new to the squaddies, the culture shock when they eventually landed at Bombay was an even greater assault on their senses. The smells, the begging, the poverty, above all the sheer numbers of people especially children, the police method of crowd control, namely a whack across the shoulders with a lathi, a long cane, liberally applied. All these things, but especially the people - thousands of them, with the general question in every newly-arrived mind, what the hell do they all do for a living?

They reached their barracks on the edge of the Western Ghats late on the afternoon of 26th July, at a place called Kalyan. It rained and it rained. The camp was new, the thoroughfares between the blocks of huts were as yet unpaved, and provided with ditches on either side designed to take the water away. Which they didn't. Gradually the sides of the ditches caved in, the roadways then becoming a sea of mud. The first task to which the battalion was put therefore, immediately on arrival, was digging ditches, not an occupation designed to sustain morale nor to prepare 550 men for war with the Japanese enemy.

The next day, the 27th of July, they heard the astounding news that Winston Churchill had been overwhelmingly defeated in the general election. Labour with 392 seats, had taken 179 Conservative seats, the Liberals had been totally eclipsed with only 12 seats remaining to them. In Kent David read that the solidly Conservative constituencies at Chislehurst, Dover, Faversham and Gravesend had all, with others, been lost to Labour. The reason for this landslide was generally attributed to the forces. For the first time all members of the three services had been allowed to vote for their home member. There was no doubt that the average squaddie considered the officers to be Conservative, therefore on the basis of the 'us and them' factor they voted Labour. In addition the prospect of the new National Health service, children's allowances and so on, dangled a desirable carrot before them, just as buying a council house would do for Margaret Thatcher years later.

In the meantime Italy, aligning herself, as she stated, more closely with the United Nations, declared war on Japan.

"That will have the Japs quaking in their boots," was David's view to Haimish, which opinion had been echoed almost exactly by his father to Jack Hooper the day before when it was announced on the English wireless.

With the rain ceasing, the ditches dug, although how long they would last in the next deluge was anyone's guess, the battalion started training, firstly to get fit after the voyage and the particularly good food they had received on the Corfu which had added a few pounds to a number of waistlines.

On the 5th of August they heard that the battering of Japanese cities was being kept up with thirty-one towns being told to evacuate with a leaflet drop. The next day they heard that a place called Hiroshima had been bombed with a new bomb, to be known as the atom bomb, a missile two thousand times as powerful as the greatest bomb in the RAF's arsenal. The whole city had been obliterated.

The next day Russia declared war on Japan. Sir Jack's prophesy had come true. Something like six hundred thousand Japanese prisoners were taken in Manchuria to eventually feed the gulags.

There was total mystification in all ranks as to how one bomb could blast a city. On the 9th of August a second such bomb was dropped on Nagasaki; in addition the normal air offensive with fire bombs continued on other cities. Eight hundred Superforts attacked the mainland after the dropping of the second atom bomb. On the night of the 14th/15th August Japan surrendered unconditionally.

When David awoke in the morning, shaken into wakefulness by an Angus more excited than he had ever known him, he was greeted by the news,

"The war's over, sir, the war is over."

David sat up, pushed his mosquito net aside and said one of the most fatuous things he had ever uttered, as he readily admitted to many times later,

"Which war?"

"Our war, sir, our war, our bloody war, the Jap bloody war."

David had never heard Angus say a word out of place before in the years they had been together, least of all swear.

To compound his fatuity David added,

"How could it be? We're not there yet."

"It's those bombs, sir, those bombs."

"Look, we had thousands of bombs dropped on us in Britain during the war. They did nothing to stop us. How could a couple of bombs stop the Japs?"

"I don't know, sir; they must have been bloody big bombs, that's all I can say."

David hurriedly washed and shaved and hurried to the somewhat spartan mess they had inherited. It was true, it was over. Even at that time of the morning there was a palpable sense of relief followed by wild exhilaration, such as a condemned man might experience having received a reprieve at the last minute. Not one of those thinking officers there ever expected to see England again, or in Haimish's case Scotland. Now with a bit of luck they would soon be on their way home again. And all because of some magic bomb that made the unyielding Jap throw in the towel.

They had the mother and father of all parties that night. So did the sergeant's mess, so did the Naafi canteen. By morning there was not a single drop of alcoholic liquid still in existence in the camp at Kalyan. Even Haimish had to be poured into his bed, and that state of affairs was a rarity among rarities. We shall make no comment on the condition of one major David Chandler M.C., D.C.M. not that he would be able to argue about it if we did so.

Nevertheless, although 'the war' may have been over, another one was beginning to surface elsewhere in the east. R Battalion of The Parachute Regiment were not finished with fighting by a long chalk.

* * *

Chapter Twenty-One

Chantek was now a little over eighteen months old and almost fully grown. She was still playful from time to time, which when you compare her in weight to a large Alsatian, will give some idea of the effect on Harry when she took it upon herself to jump on him as he lay on his charpoy having his afternoon kip. She rarely bared her claws however, which was a good thing! Matthew and Harry clipped them periodically, to which she submitted with good grace having been brought up to it from a cub; still they were very powerful and her legs incredibly strong. Leopards, having made a kill, invariably have to drag a carcase weighing as much as themselves, up into a tree for safety. For this they need strong legs and ultra-strong jaws.

On Friday night 1st June Harry was awakened by his pet banging against the access door to his room.

"Go away, let me get some sleep," he called out, which request was answered by an even more violent banging and scratching from the other side of the wall.

"Oh, you are a pest," he told her, lifting his mosquito net and flashing his torch on the floor to make sure he had no unwelcome visitors. He then slipped on his plimsolls, first shaking them out, an automatic precaution and a habit which followed him for years after he left the jungle. He lifted the flap, Chantek hurtling in and jumping up on to the charpoy. She seemed quite distressed, which Harry immediately assumed was caused by a storm somewhere very distant which the human ear could not catch, but which was loud and clear to a leopard. As he was considering this they were subjected to the most deafening clap of thunder anyone in the camp had ever heard. It went on and on, seeming to be immediately above them. The camp was alight with the continual lightning; everyone was awake, some thinking their last hour had come. After some thirty seconds there was a tremendous noise like a piece of heavy artillery being fired, followed by a series of smaller explosions ending in a crash of monumental proportions. One of the giant forest trees had ended its days, fortunately not falling on any part of the camp. This latter hazard had always been of concern to Harry, but in his usual positive-thinking manner he had considered the trees had been there a hundred or more years so would probably be safe for a few more.

Chantek huddled in fear against the wall. Harry went over to her as the big bangs started and cuddled her head against him.

"There, there, baby, it will be alright," he told her. She understood perfectly. As they sat there together on the bed, there was a knock on the door, followed by the entry of Matthew and Tommy.

"Is she alright, sir?" Matthew asked, followed by Tommy saying,

"It put the bloody wind up me, so it must have frightened her to death."

Not one of those three extremely intelligent men thought it odd that they should have left their beds solely to enquire after the health and well-being of a leopard!

When the storm had passed Harry let his silky companion stay with him, having to nudge her from time to time when she snored, and on one occasion when she opened and closed her claws against his back.

On Sunday night a message arrived on the wireless from Sunrise. During his recent visit Harry had approached him regarding awards for Matthew, Tommy and Reuben. Without Matthew they would have lost half the company through disease and injury. Reuben and Tommy had led successful patrols and operations time and again and had gained the respect of even the most indoctrinated of the communist force. Harry had even mentioned Choon Guan, but Sunrise ventured the opinion that the M.P.A.J.A. big-wigs would hardly accept honours or awards from an imperial power. He could not have been more wrong. Their leader, the top communist in Malaya, was offered the O.B.E. and accepted it, wearing it on the eventual victory parade - but that's another story.

The message, when decoded, read,

Awards. Lee, Isaacs, Ault, Choon Guan. Each will receive M.B.E. Acknowledgement of acceptance required by return. Major Chandler M.B.E. to be raised to O.B.E. Congratulations Sunrise.

"Keep this under your hat until tomorrow," Harry told the operator.

The next morning Harry called an 'O' group.

"I'll not keep you long," he announced. "We had a message from Sunrise last night. You four have each been awarded the

M.B.E. I have to acknowledge immediately whether you accept or not."

There was an immediate hubbub, everyone talking at once, everyone that is except Choon Guan. Harry looked at him.

"Having problems?"

"I would like to accept but I do not know the position with regard to my general secretary."

"He has been awarded the O.B.E. and has accepted."

"Then I accept."

Reuben was quite unable to resist pulling the leg of this po-faced communist, as he frequently described him.

"You realise, Choon Guan, taking this award makes you an imperialist, a Member of the Order of the British Empire. That, by definition, makes you a capitalist, since the empire was built on sound capitalist principals which as a Member of the Order you are bound to uphold. How are you going to balance it out? Monday to Friday, communist, weekends capitalist or vice versa?"

As po-faced as ever Choon Guan replied he would remain a communist but accept the award as an appreciation of the service he had performed for the British Empire against their enemies.

"They were your enemies as well, you know. In which case your communist party should give us all a medal for fighting your enemies. Wouldn't that be right and proper, sir?" addressing a grinning Harry.

"Not only that," Reuben continued, "your communist party ought to pay half towards the cost of our ammunition and the air-drops. Think how much petrol they must use. It's well known that the communist international is rolling in money, I reckon they ought to dip into their kitty and help out."

"The colonial powers have been living on the labour of the coolie for generations, it is time they gave something back," Choon Guan flashed back. Harry, sensing this could develop from a jocular repartee among friends to an unnecessary argument, quickly stepped in.

"Right, no politics, you know the rules. 'O' group over."

The four new Members of the Order of the British Empire rose, Choon Guan the only one a little apprehensive as to what his proletarian comrades were going to make of his accepting an honour from the King to whom they were bitterly opposed, in principle if not in fact.

.

In the middle of June they heard on their radio, new batteries for which had been sent in the last drop, that four hundred and fifty Super Fortresses had bombed Japan, and that Okinawa, the first of the islands south of the Japanese mainland, had now been captured, and at the beginning of July the Philippines had been totally liberated, four hundred thousand Japanese having been annihilated in the process.

"So, any minute now," Harry suggested to his officers as they sat eating their evening meal. "The point is, what will they want us to do to help?"

Reuben had the answer.

"Most of the sods don't know we're here. Those that do will want us to keep out of the way. Ninety-nine per cent of British and Indian forces don't know the difference between a Chinese and a Japanese. If they see a company of fully-armed oriental-looking bods through their gunsights or whatever, they will automatically assume they are enemy. I reckon our best bet is to lie very low until it's all over."

On the ninth of July they heard on the news that our aircraft carriers Indefatigable and Victorious had been damaged by Kamikaze planes, which took the smile off their faces for a while until they heard an announcement from Tokyo that thirty-nine cities had been laid waste, with severe damage to twenty-seven others.

"They won't be able to take that for long, I shouldn't think," Tommy declared.

"Don't you believe it," Reuben asserted. "You've seen them; they will fight through the ruins with only kitchen knives rather than give in. We, that is the allied armies, have got to land in Japan and kill every bloody Japanese before we win this war. People don't realise how many hundreds of thousands of people will die in the assault on Japan."

He was right, but as we shall see, he was wrong.

On Sunday, 8th of July, they had another air drop, and on the following Sunday received orders to cause as much damage as possible to both the west coast and centre small gauge railways. Harry discussed this with his officers and decided on a four prong attack in sequence. They only had one Piat, but had received further supplies of projectiles. He therefore made up raiding parties of eight men, led by an officer, to hit a train in either a deep cutting or on a bridge, where the blockage would cause the most mayhem. One party would raid east, return with the Piat, which would immediately be taken by raiding party two to the west, and so on. With other camps probably doing the same or similar things, the Jap communications system would be in chaos. It was pretty clear to them all that this was to be a prelude for the invasion causing considerable excitement and anticipation within the camp, so much so that Harry had to issue a firm admonishment.

"When this invasion comes, as it surely will in the very near future, the Japanese will fight for every inch of Malaya. If they are driven back from the coast, they will fight in this jungle. The possibility of the British and Indian armies invading and recapturing your homeland in the course of a few days is out of the question. We must now do all we can, as ordered by our commanders, to harass the enemy as often and as expertly as possible."

Choon Guan translated all this for the benefit of the majority of Chinese, whose knowledge of English was limited, or nil. However, he got stuck at 'harass,' but sensing the meaning inserted the word 'kick.'

Harry took the first patrol out. On their map a ferry was marked on the upper reaches of the Pahang river, where the river ran fairly near the narrow gauge railway and the only metalled road running through the centre of the country at that point. He planned to sink the ferry at night, provided it was tied up on his side of the river of course, pull back to the railway by dawn and blow up a train as it passed over the bridge spanning the road, then disappear into the jungle on the slopes of the seven thousand feet Mount Benom. They knew the country well; it could be done in six to seven days, or less with a bit of luck. With four porters, two men in the Piat team, and three riflemen they set off.

They made good time, crossed the railway and the metalled road without incident and by an hour before darkness fell came to a slight bluff from which they could see the ferry some quarter of a mile away. Harry had been concerned as to what sort of a vessel the ferry might be. His main experience of such animals was of riding on the Woolwich Ferry, which in itself consisted of a whacking great steel ship, or ships, since there were more than one of them. The one he now observed could not have been more different. It was a large wooden flat bottomed barge, with on one side a covered section containing a long wooden bench, on the other side a railed-in section obviously provided to house goats and other animals, and the centre large enough to take two vehicles. There appeared to be no motive power whatsoever, until studying the fore and aft closely, Harry spied chains falling into the water. The river here was only some forty to fifty yards across, the motive power therefore was probably a couple of coolies winding the chain round a windlass. Harry had once been up to Norfolk Broads on a trip before the war and remembered such a system, smaller it was true, at Horning Ferry. He smiled at the remembrance, particularly at the recollection of the girl he met on that holiday. Holy mackerel, she was a goer. What was her name now? Can't remember.' Then added to himself - 'before I was married of course!' That made it alright, but he couldn't help having second thoughts about her. 'Wonder where she is now?' His Piat man broke into his reverie.

"Seems a shame to waste a bomb on that, sir, couldn't we set it on fire?"

"That, my son, is the cleverest thing I've heard today."

"Well, we brought those incendiary grenades with us, might as well use them."

Harry took another long look at the ferry.

"It's all wood, but I bet it's bloody hard wood. Might find it a problem to get a fire started. Pity we've got no petrol."

"I wonder what's in that shed at the load point, sir?"

"I expect..." he stopped, "hang on, there's a lorry arriving."

They watched the little pantomime which then ensued. The driver of the lorry obviously wanted to get across. He might have been on to a promise further down the road for all we know, but he urgently wanted to get across. The ferryman had finished for the day, furthermore his winders were nowhere to be seen, so they had probably disappeared to take advantage of any promise they might be on. The driver waved his arms about, eventually pulled some notes out of his back pocket and offered them to the ferryman, all to no avail. Eventually, the ferryman must have told him to put his lorry on the ferry and he would take it over first thing in the morning, at which the driver did just that, dismounted from the cab and walked off to the nearby Kampong, either in the hope of another promise or to get a bed for the night, or both, not that it's any business of ours.

With the rear of the vehicle now visible they could see what it was carrying - rubber!

"Manna from heaven," Harry exclaimed.

There they were. Beautiful big eighteen-inch cubes of rubber sheets, piled up in regular lines with little gaps between the rows. The rubber itself would not ignite easily, but with a starter of three or four phosphorous grenades it would be as good a bonfire as the River Pahang had housed for a good many years, if ever.

They waited until ten o'clock when everything was quiet with the exception of an occasional dog sounding off in the nearby Kampong. Then, swiftly, they moved on to their target, cut the canvas cover at four points, and waited for Harry's order. It was essential they all dropped their grenades at the same time and made a quick retirement before it had time to be activated. Phosphorous grenades tend to spit like mad; hanging about close to one about to ignite was, at the least, undesirable. They each found a gap between the cubes, by feel, since it was dark inside the canvas enclosed load. In a low voice Harry called,

"Everyone ready?"

Three 'yes's' answered.

"Right, prime grenades."

This was duly carried out.

"Release and walk away."

This they did, although it must be said that their individual perambulations varied from a steady walk by Harry to a very fast trot by the most inexperienced of the four. After seven seconds they heard the four, almost synchronised, cracks of the grenades exploding, although there was little indication of a flame at this stage.

"Don't stand about. Get moving," Harry ordered.

They made their way back to the bluff. When they reached it, flattened themselves on the skyline, and looked back to the ferry, a huge flame roared upwards followed by a thick cloud of smoke billowing into the calm night air. Swiftly the fire took hold, lighting up the surrounding sheds and riverside. They then had a bonus. The petrol in its tank underneath the lorry's body exploded, sending masses of blazing liquid all over the ferry, setting fire to the shed which itself must have had some highly combustible materials in it, since it too blazed like a torch. The ferry now was burning from end to end, people running from the Kampong totally unable to do anything about it as one eruption of flame followed another into the night air, completely unsuspecting that sabotage had any part in the conflagration.

"Right. Move back to the railway," Harry ordered. They had three hours before dawn during which they catnapped in turn. As dawn broke, a train appeared on the down trip. It was a small passenger train. Harry decided to let it go; there was no way he wanted to kill or risk the lives of innocent Malays. Forty minutes later a goods train, puffing hard on the upward gradient, appeared from the south.

"This one will do," he primed the Piat man.

They moved into a position some forty to fifty yards from the bridge. The number two loaded the Piat bomb. As the engine rolled on to the bridge number one fired. It was a beautiful shot. The engine virtually blew itself in half, sliding over the parapet on to the road below and taking a good section of the bridge with it. Quickly number two loaded another bomb. Number one lined himself up on a small tanker, and fired again. The tanker must have had tar in it, since, as it split open, it sprayed all over the road below, then flooded down where it was set alight by burning coals from the engine. Finally he put a third bomb into an enclosed wagon, which apart from blowing it into smithereens, provided little entertainment.

"Right, move back into cover, quick," Harry bellowed. He had no intention of stopping a stray bullet from an over-enthusiastic escort picket who might possibly have been in the guards van. His concern was well founded. They had not quite reached the beluka when a shot ran out, hitting the last man low down in his spine. He fell to the ground screaming with pain. With the exception of the Piat man, the other four men in the patrol dropped to the ground in cover, to see a pair of Japanese running towards them.

"Hold your fire," Harry ordered in a low voice. No others appeared to be following the two train guards. As they closed in on the fallen Chinese, Harry ordered,

"Fire." They both fell instantly.

"Keep me covered." Harry moved forward to the stricken man.

"Can you stand?" He put his arms under his soldier's armpits and heaved him up. His legs gave way and he immediately slumped back to the ground, looking at Harry with a dreadful fear in his eyes.

"I know what you have to do, sir," he said as he drifted into unconsciousness. Harry took his revolver and shot him through the temple, tears streaming down his face as he did so, and thinking that the only time he had used that revolver before that day was to carry out a similar task during their attack at Kampong Bintang back in February 43. There was no way they could carry a paralysed man.

He quickly went through the man's pockets. There was a strict requirement that nothing other than military equipment was to be carried on operations. This man had complied, except that he had a small locket in his breast pocket, which Harry took and put in his bush jacket. He picked up the soldiers' rifle and bandolier, and hurried back to the silent group of men who had been watching the grim proceeding. The Piat man held out his hand and shook hands with Harry.

"You had to do it, sir, we are all very sorry for you." They could see the tracks his tears had made down his grimy face.

They pushed on back to the camp, not stopping to bivvy up, just taking two hour breaks when they needed to. As a result their return was unexpected, the camp turning out to welcome them, then realising there was one short, which immediately put a dampener on the welcome.

After the usual weapon and foot inspections, as a result of which one man was admitted to hospital with a very deep scratch from some unfriendly foliage, which had turned septic, Harry joined the other officers to fill them in on the results of the patrol. It was an occasion which should have been an exuberant affair, but was now blighted by the loss of a man and the hideous manner of his destruction.

With the results coded and dispatched they put in motion Reuben's proposed attack on the west coast line. He and his party went off on the 29th July and returned on the following Saturday well pleased with themselves having hit a train of fuel tankers, but not only that, having seen a flight of British aircraft attacking an airfield. They must have been despatched from an aircraft carrier in the Straits of Malacca, this knowledge therefore providing as much excitement as the success of the raid. To add to the euphoria they heard on the radio that evening that the Americans had sunk five Japanese ships off the coast of Japan, one an aircraft carrier, Amagi, and another the heavy cruiser Tone. The significance of this particular action was that both these ships had been involved in the original attack on Pearl Harbour. Apart from the destroyer Ushio, every one of the twenty-five ships involved in that infamy had now been sent to the bottom.

Tommy's expedition, planned to hit the telegraph station and electricity main grid east of Frasers Hill for the eighth of August had to be delayed. On the sixth a message came in clear Morse to the effect that all operations were to cease. On the radio that evening they learnt a bomb had been dropped on Hiroshima which had obliterated the city. As millions throughout the world remarked on that fateful day, Harry exclaimed,

"How can one bomb wipe out a city?"

Three days later they heard that a second bomb had been dropped on Nagasaki and that massive fleets of Super Fortresses were maintaining the offensive on other cities and on Korea. Japan was being called upon to surrender, and on the 15th of August they did so, unconditionally. Two hundred and sixty thousand Japanese civilians, and thousands of POWs and internees had been killed, with over nine million made homeless.

With the announcement that the war was over there was great jubilation in the camp among the Chinese Christians and the officers. The Chinese communists knew it was only an interlude between the war they had just fought and the one they would now fight to drive the imperialists out of Malaya.

Harry called the officers, with Matthew, together.

"We don't know what Choon Guan and his men have been instructed to do in the event of the war ending. In the extreme we have got to be on our guard they have not had instructions to eliminate us and take over this camp. I am seeking urgent advice from Sunrise as to what now to do."

That advice arrived uncoded that night.

'All forces to remain on maximum alert. Count Terauchi, commander of Japanese forces in Malaya, has stated he will not observe the unconditional surrender but will continue the fight.'

"Just our bloody luck," was Reuben's immediate comment.

Pressure was placed on Terauchi, finally by the Emperor himself with a direct order to observe the cease fire, whereupon the commander of the M.P.A.J.A. called upon all his troops to immediately converge on his headquarters in Kuala Lumpur with their arms. Choon Guan marshalled his fifty men, watched by Harry and his party. He called them to attention, saluted Harry and said,

"Goodbye, sir."

And that was all before they disappeared into the jungle.

They were followed by the inevitable remark from Reuben.

"Thank Christ for that. I had a funny feeling I was going to have my bloody throat cut at any moment."

And it could easily have happened, but the commander of M.P.A.J.A. knew he was not strong enough to attempt a coup yet, particularly since a complete army was ready to invade Malaya. He would wait until they had all been sent home and then strike. Which is what he did.

* * *

Chapter Twenty-Two

On the 11th of July the Inter-Allied Military Komendatura assumed official control of the City of Berlin comprising Soviet, American and British zones. Dieter's base was in the Lichtenberg area. He studied the layout of the zones with a view to evolving an escape plan, and decided, when the time came, to get into the British zone.

Churchill, Truman and Stalin met at Potsdam where they held a number of sessions. On July 25th Churchill returned to London for the results of the general election only to find he had been overwhelmingly defeated by Clement Attlee, whose less forcible presence took its place at the conference table, to the astonishment of Stalin and his Foreign Secretary Molotov who firmly expected Churchill to have rigged the election in his own favour.

When the conference resumed, the entrance from the gateway on the road to the building itself was lined by a guard of honour of the Scots Guards. As Stalin arrived lorry loads of NKVD guards surrounded the guard of honour and the building itself and packed themselves around the Soviet leader, which did not please His Majesty's guardsmen at all.

Next, Mr Truman arrived in a bullet proof car preceded by armoured jeeps and a mass of FBI agents who jumped out and took station whenever the car stopped, and eventually at the conference centre repeated the Soviet agents' antics.

Mr Attlee then arrived in a Humber staff car and walked up the pathway accompanied by one plain-clothed detective.

On the 1st of August the Potsdam agreement was signed. In the meantime the British had given up part of their zone to the French, this section, bordering on the Soviet zone in the north of the city being exactly where Dieter had planned to make his crossing when the time came. No way would he risk giving himself up to the French - they would probably hand him straight back to the Russians was his considered view. It was back to the drawing board.

In August he learnt of the Japanese surrender; the war was truly over. Through September he worked conscientiously with his colonel, being accepted more and more by the Russian officers on the war crimes circuit, to the extent that he was much less restricted in his movements. He wore civilian clothes now, hand-me-downs it is true, but reasonably presentable. There was no Berlin Wall yet, nevertheless the divisions between the Western zones and the Soviet zone were thickly wired and guarded, both in the city itself and around the outer borders of the western perimeters. The Russians did not intend the East Germans should escape, although many tried and many hundreds were shot and killed attempting it.

Gradually news of these shootings reached Dieter, usually in the form of boasting by young Russian officers, along the lines, 'I see we shot six more escapees yesterday.' He realised he was going to take his life in his hands when he did decide to go, and wondered whether his promise of release in three years would be a better bet. Still in the back of his mind, however, was the thought 'can you trust the bastards?'

On Sunday the 9th of September he was in his room when his colonel knocked and came in.

"Dieter, I have to tell you that I shall be leaving at the end of the week. I am being transferred to Moscow, which means I shall see my wife and family again after two and a half years." He paused. "That is if she has not run off with someone else of course," he joked. He continued,

"I asked to take you with me, but as I shall not require an interpreter it was naturally refused. Colonel Kruglor is taking over. He is a fair man, I think you will find. If I do not see you again before I go I wish you well." He paused and with considerable gravity issued a warning. "I know it is difficult to be so near and yet so far from your loved ones. Do not, however, even think of going to them until you are released. It would be a very dangerous thing to contemplate."

"I understand, sir."

They shook hands, never expecting to meet again. They did, many years later, under the most exceptional circumstances - but that is another story.

Dieter kept his head down working with his new colonel, a youngish chap who would, in later years, have been described as a 'high flyer,' and who made a habit of 'bumping into' more senior officers armed with knowledge or statistics he had obtained previously from underlings, then declaring them as his own. He took on work which strictly speaking was not connected with his department, farmed it out to his subordinates, with given time limits for action, and then again presenting it to his superiors. This of course meant extra work for his staff, which did not endear him to them, particularly since, as Dieter had already found out on many occasions, Russian men, generally speaking, did not consider the work ethic to be of high importance or for that matter at all to be encouraged.

In an old desk in the offices which had been commandeered Dieter had found a town plan of Berlin and its environs. From a map in the general office of the zones now established he was able to mark on his street plan the boundaries of the American and British zones. In his civilian suit he would be able to move about freely, except that he had no identity documents of any kind and given the present situation of men in the east trying to escape to the west people were being required to show their papers at frequent intervals in the streets of the city.

He therefore concluded that he could find his way round the city boundary, moving only at night, and attempt to get into the American sector in the Potsdam district, an area he knew very well from his cadet days. Secondly he could attempt to cover the one hundred miles from Potsdam due west to the border of the British zone, again moving by night in country he knew fairly well. The third option would be the quickest method, but probably the most dangerous. The River Spree flows through the city of Berlin, and quite near to Dieter's base in Lichtenburg. At this point the Landwahr Canal connects with it, running almost due west into the American zone south of the Tempelhof airfield. From the River Spree to the American zone it was a little over a mile and a half according to his calculations.

Dieter was a first class swimmer to whom before the war a little over a mile and a half, or say three kilometres in his terms, would not have been beyond his capabilities. Far from it in fact. However, six years of war had brought few opportunities for serious swimming; he was therefore so out of practice, the thought of covering three kilometres in the cold unpleasant waters of a canal into which all sorts of effluent was being discharged was to say the least, off-putting. 'Think positive,' he told himself. If the undertaking was that impossible the Russians would almost certainly not give it a high priority in the escape prospect.

The more he thought of it the less appealing it became. It would have to be at night, but as the canal passed under several roads there would always be the chance of being spotted, and at one point it ran along parallel with the border only a couple of dozen yards away.

He began going back to plan two, walking west to the British border. Even on this journey he would have to swim the River Elbe, a fast flowing, wide river, but infinitely cleaner than the Landwahr canal. As he pondered these problems, arriving at and then discounting the solutions, he had a stroke of luck. Sent to translate at an army ordnance depot a mile or so away he was given a pass to carry for that purpose as he was to proceed there on his own. He presented himself to the officer in charge who told him in no uncertain terms that he had not asked for an interpreter, furthermore he wouldn't deal with an arse-crawler like Kruglor if he was the last man on earth, 'and you can tell him that,' he added. Dieter considered what his chances would be against his ending up in a gulag if he did just that.

He took a wrong turning out of the commanding officer's block, to find himself in a large bay stacked high with salvaged German army equipment of every description. There was nobody about as Dieter had a quick look in some of the big boxes he passed. In one he spied wire cutters. Quickly he put a pair into his inside pocket. At the end of the row along which he was walking there was a stack of waterproof groundsheets. He quickly took one, rolled it up, and tucked it under his arm. These two pieces of equipment were making his escape attempt all the more possible whichever plan he adopted, added to which he still had his pass, which with a little careful doctoring he would be able to use again. His spirits rose accordingly.

Now, why did he seize on wire cutters and a waterproof groundsheet? Taking the latter first, like all cadets he had been taught how to swim across rivers and have your clothes and equipment dry when you reached the other side. You made them up into a parcel by laying them on to a groundsheet, stiffening the base with a weapon and equipment, or in this case an odd length of timber of some sort. The groundsheet then was folded upwards and secured at the top. It would then float. The last item that went in would be a towel so that when you reached the other side of the water obstacle you had a brisk rub down, dressed, re-armed and you were once more a fighting soldier. So, into this parcel would go his suit, underclothes and boots and he would push it along as he swam, and attach a length of rope to it to pull it if necessary.

Now the wire cutters. At the point where he would leave the Soviet zone, near Karl Marx Strasse, the Russians would without doubt have put barbed wire into the canal. Canals he knew were only some two metres deep as a rule, sometimes less, therefore the possibility of swimming under a barbed wire obstacle would be remote. He would therefore have to cut his way through. Hence the cutters.

The more he thought about this escapade the less he liked it. Suppose he got a mouthful or more of the foul water. He had a road and a railway to swim under before he reached the boundary. Suppose he was spotted there, the Russians would have no second thoughts about shooting him in the water. Suppose when he reached the boundary, the wire was so thick it would take hours to cut through it, what would he do, swim back again?

His mind finally was made up for him. On the morning of 26th September Kruglor called him in.

"We shall no longer require your services, von Hassellbek. You will report to me a week today to be transferred elsewhere. Be here at eight o'clock."

"May I ask the colonel where this is likely to be?" Dieter asked politely.

"You are being passed to the Main Camp Administration." In Russian this is 'Glavno upravlenie lagerei,' the acronym for which is GULAG.

Dieter looked hard at the colonel. He could see nothing but malice in those pale blue, icy-cold eyes. Dieter clicked his heels.

"Thank you, sir." He was not going to let the bastard think he had scored over him if he could help it.

He looked at a calendar in the main office and found that Friday, Saturday and Sunday nights were moonless. He decided he would go on Friday. Friday was pay day for the troops. Those who were not on duty would be out getting drunk; those on duty would most likely have a bottle tucked away. Russian soldiers, come to that Russian civilians as well, were, and are, great drinkers. After finishing his duty on Friday therefore he slipped his cutters into an inside pocket, tucked his rolled groundsheet under his arm, and armed with his doctored pass, made his way to a partially demolished building, a warehouse at some time, on the banks of the River Spree, a quarter of a mile from the Landwahr canal junction. He was unsure as to whether there were lock gates at this point, assumed there must be, but since these were well away from the border guards he should be able to negotiate them without being seen.

He reached his jumping off point in daylight - there was a curfew at that time for civilians after dark - and hid in a blocked off corner near the wharf side. He waited. His stomach played all sorts of tunes. This could be his last night on earth. If it was, none of his nearest and dearest would ever know what had happened to him. From being delighted to hear he was alive they would be left in an empty void for months, even years, before they would have to conclude he was dead. He almost gave up then, but decided he was between the devil and the deep blue sea - in a gulag he would not be able to contact them; his death would almost certainly be inevitable, after perhaps years of hardship and brutality. He steeled himself to face his only chance, but if he had reconciled his spirit to action, his stomach certainly had not.

At eleven o'clock it was fairly dark. He stripped off and made up his clothing bundle. There was an abundant supply of loose pieces of timber lying around with which to stiffen the parcel and make it float well; the groundsheet was black, which would help to some extent to camouflage it in the water. At midnight he took the first few dangerous steps, stark naked, his white body feeling very noticeable during the crossing of the twenty odd metres of the wharf side, before he lowered himself and his bundle carefully into the slowly flowing River Spree.

The river here is not very wide. He decided to keep to the centre as there had appeared, in his first couple of hundred metres, many obstructions close to the bank, where cranes and parts of buildings had collapsed into it during the fighting. He was swimming with the current, such as it was, but even so had to stop for a breather every now and then, holding lightly to his float, which to his surprise was much more buoyant than he had expected it would be.

Eventually he came to the point where the river ran parallel to a main road, which being elevated compared to him he could see very well on the skyline. He knew that at this point he had to look for lock gates, if any, therefore swam over to the right hand side of the river. There they were, and to his surprise both sets were partially open.

Now he knew he would soon be facing the most dangerous part of his journey. He decided to rest for a short while on one of the immensely thick wooden cross beams on the second gate, but it was very cold out of the water, which itself was far from being a warm bath, so he decided to push on.

After another hours' steady swimming he arrived at the start of the border defences running parallel with the canal. There seemed to be no military presence, although since the wire defences were some distance from the canal, it was probably patrolled by prowler guards.

The canal was not as dirty as he had expected, for which he was grateful, neither was it polluted to any extent, in that with the destruction of the factories on its banks few noxious substances were being discharged into it, neither were there boats using it.

It was, he judged, about two o'clock in the morning when, thirty or forty yards ahead, he saw the archway over the canal where the boundary of the Russian zone swung south. On the other side of that archway he would be in American territory, and it was here that he had no doubt the water would be full of barbed wire. Slowly, keeping in the lee of the canal bank which was concreted along this stretch - perhaps being close to the main road, sometimes the boats tied up there for the night - he approached this last hurdle. To his surprise, there was barbed wire, but not in the density he had expected. It was very dark and he could see little but by feeling his way bit by bit he could tell it would present little difficulty in cutting a way through.

He held on to a projection from the concrete wall for a few minutes to gather his strength, then moving forward very gently he brushed against a horizontal strand of thin wire. As a soldier he knew straight away what it was. The Russians had not relied on just barbed wire, they had booby-trapped the surface, for all he knew below the surface as well, with trip wires running to grenades or other such explosive devices fixed to the walls or arch above, the arch being no more than eight feet or so off the water level. He was in a quandary. Trip wires come in two categories, those that when brushed against cause the explosive device to operate, or those that when cut do the same thing by releasing the activating mechanism.

'It's a fifty fifty chance' he told himself. He had no option but to find the wires and cut them. If the first one was a release type, even if he wasn't killed by the explosion, it would rapidly bring the border guards racing to find out what was going on.

He lifted the cutters from the piece of rope around his neck and snipped the wire. There was no explosion; they were obviously trip wires, not release wires. Working along the concrete edge he slowly cut enough wire away to allow his body through, at the same time searching very diligently for more trip wires, finding the Russians had not only installed them horizontally, but vertically as well. He cut six altogether, the 'click' of the cutters sounding like thunderclaps inside that covered area, particularly so when cutting the thick barbed wire strands.

Cutting his last strand of the barrier he heard shouts from the Soviet side. He quickly pulled his floating bundle to him by its short tow rope and started to swim out of the cover of the archway. He was now technically in American territory but this did not stop the Russian guards firing at him in the water. The shooting in the darkness was very wild, nevertheless one bullet hit his left shoulder and another took a chunk out of his left thigh. He yelled with pain. A few seconds later a burst of tommy gun fire came from in front of him, the American guards firing into the air to warn the Russians off.

"I'm over here," Dieter yelled in his perfect English.

"Jesus, it's a bloody limey," one of his rescuers called out.

They came to the edge of the canal and dragged him out. Dieter was not only thoroughly exhausted from his long swim, but was by now in considerable pain from his two wounds, both of which the Americans bound up with their own field dressings, which all soldiers carry. With one carrying his bundle, two others supporting him, they hurried to their guard post, where a young lieutenant was standing and waiting.

"We got a limey here, lootenant," said the sergeant in charge, "though how the hell he got through the wire and booby traps under that bridge ..." he left the rest of the sentence unsaid.

"Right, put some blankets round him and take him to the hospital. I will instruct the military police to meet you there."

At the hospital they pumped him full of anti-tetanus drugs, washed him, dressed his wounds and put him to bed, the MPs standing by until he was settled. They then opened his bundle. It had obviously been, not only well packed, but also carefully handled in the water, since everything was still dry. Carefully the MPs went through the jacket to find in the inside breast pocket Dieter's pass, typed in both Russian and German, and with his name 'Major von Hassellbek' clearly written across the top.

"Are you Major von Hassellbek?"

"Yes, sergeant."

"They told us you was English."

"That is because I spoke to them in English, so they assumed I was, what I believe they describe an English person, a limey."

"So what were you doing escaping from the Soviets?"

Dieter started to tell his story, but because so exhausted he dozed off. A young doctor then said, "No more now, sergeant, come back again later today."

The sergeant left an MP at Dieter's bed and went back to his HQ where, having told his superiors about the incident, they decided to contact intelligence and hand the case over to them. A male colonel, aided by a particularly attractive female captain, came to visit him that evening. They stayed some two hours, saying they would be back again in the morning. This they did, and after a further two hours told him he was to be taken, as soon as his wounds allowed, to the intelligence headquarters at Kassel, the doctors having said this could be effected in two days. In two days, namely the 5th of October, Dieter found himself on a Dakota aircraft, escorted by two lieutenants and the female captain, taking off from Tempelhof airfield for Kassel.

He would be only one hundred kilometres from his darling Rosa.

* * *

Chapter Twenty-Three

The stentorian voice of Canon Rosser gave forth on Sunday the 5th of August. "I publish the Banns of Marriage between Hugh Beresford Crew, Lord Ramsford, bachelor of the parish of St Swithins, Ramsford, in Worcestershire and Cecely Jean Coates, widow of this parish," followed by the names of two other couples and ending with "If any of you know any cause or just impediment why these persons may not be joined together in Holy Matrimony ye are to declare it."

The Chandler clan gathered together at matins smiled at each other at this announcement. Cecely and Hugh had decided on the date, the 1st of September, but had had difficulty in settling on the place. They had three choices it would appear. St Margaret's, Westminster, the parish church at Ramsford, or St John's at Sandbury.

"I am going to leave it entirely to you," Hugh had told Cecely, who without hesitation asked if it could be Sandbury.

"Sandbury it is then," had been his immediate response. And the honeymoon? The Carlton at Cannes, now back almost to peacetime affluence. The best man? As previously decided - Fred Chandler. Matrons of honour? Just Greta. Reception? Now, there they were stumped. There would be, they estimated some two hundred people invited to the great occasion. The Angel could only cater for around half that number. The lawns at either Jack's 'Hollies' or Chandlers Lodge would not be large enough to accept marquees to seat and entertain two hundred people. Fred tentatively suggested putting them on the paddock. There would be access direct from the road, ample room for parking for those people who came by car, the field was level and the contractors would provide wooden floors and a very ample supply of toilet facilities, albeit if the latter were of the same standard as those seen at point to points and other such events they would definitely lower the tone of the proceedings!

The problem was solved by Cecely and Hugh bumping into Dr Carew and his wife in the dining room at The Angel. Hugh immediately suggested they join them for lunch. The ordering phase completed, the inevitable small talk began by the doctor asking,

"Everything organised then, my lord?"

"Well, virtually everything. We decided as you know for the wedding to be here in Sandbury without realising there would be a problem regarding the reception. In other words, there is no place large enough to accommodate some two hundred people. Fred Chandler has offered us the use of a field in which to erect marquees, but this offer, kind though it is, presents all sorts of problems, doubly so if it were to rain."

Dr Carew thought for a moment.

"We have a dining hall at Cantelbury which seats four hundred boys. It is only four miles away; you are welcome to use that if you would care to. The school of course is on holiday, as too are the catering people, but all the equipment is there should your caterers require to use it. There would be no problem in getting Luke Kelsey's charabanc people to ferry those guests in and out who do not have their own transport. He does all our school functions so would be very accommodating in that respect."

Hugh looked at Cecely.

"What do you think, dear?"

Mrs Carew, noting this very short and seemingly insignificant question, registered at once that it might well be a peer of the realm who has to make the decision, but that he is getting the advice of his wife-to-be before so doing. An awful lot of people she knew in much lower stations rarely did that!

"I think it's a wonderful idea, and the dining hall at Cantelbury is a beautiful room," Cecely replied.

"With an elevated platform where the masters normally are served, upon which you could place your top table," added Mrs Carew, "and look down upon us lesser mortals."

"I am afraid that will not be possible," Hugh replied in a pseudo-serious tone, "since of course you will be on the top table with us. Now, we shall have to sort out the cost."

"There will be no charge; you may accept it as our wedding present to you. We would have no idea what to buy you both anyway, so that solves a problem."

"Well, thank you very much, doctor, thank you very much. As it is I take your point. I fancy we shall be knee-deep in toast-racks by the time the day is out. However, I do insist on making some sort of payment, it is only fair."

"Well in that case, a small, and I emphasise small, donation to the school library fund would be very acceptable."

"Library fund it is, and again thank you."

They enjoyed the rest of their meal together.

The day after their lunch the incredible news came of the bomb on Hiroshima, and three days later the second bomb on Nagasaki. The town again went wild. The war was really and truly over. When the results of the atom bombs became known, many people were aghast at their use. The alternative however would have been the invasion of mainland Japan, where hard-line militarists intended to conduct a suicidal defence of the country. They could put into the field over two million troops, four million army and navy staff and a twenty-eight million home guard organisation. They had nearly ten thousand aircraft still flying, though most of those would be useless against the US and British aircraft. Each and every one of those would be willing to die for their Emperor. He, however, gave a direct order for the surrender.

On Friday 17th August the verger at St John's came to lock up at six o'clock, saw a lady praying in the side chapel, and without disturbing her wandered off to complete another task. At six-thirty he came back to find her still there upon her knees. He decided to tell Canon Rosser, who took the verger's keys telling him he would wait for the lady to leave and then lock up. By ten minutes to seven, the lady having still not left, the canon decided he had better make sure she was not in distress. He walked over to the chapel. Quietly approaching the supplicant he recognised her immediately as Jack's wife, Moira Hooper. She raised a distraught face to the canon.

"I'm sorry, Canon Rosser, are you waiting to close the church?"

"It will stay open as long as you need it my dear, you may be sure of that." He paused for a while, then continued, "Is there anything I can help with? You are obviously very troubled about something when everyone else is so deliriously happy at the ending of the war."

"I have been working on this atom bomb project for five years. At no time did we know whether we were behind the Germans or the Russians in its perfection. When the bombs dropped on those two cities I had a great surge of relief, we had mastered it first. Then after a day and a night and today again, I realised I had helped to incinerate probably a quarter of a million people, old folks, mothers, children and babies. I heard descriptions on the wireless of the utter devastation, of seven square miles of Hiroshima turned into a wasteland along with everything and everyone in it, and one commentator was almost screaming with delight. Delight, I ask you, how could anyone express delight at such a horrendous disaster?" She sobbed quietly for a few minutes.

"And I helped to bring it about. God will never forgive me."

"Lady Moira, you did only your duty, that must be clear. Many things have to be done in war which seem wicked, heinous even, if only to prevent even greater wickedness being perpetrated. The innocent suffer, as they did in the blitz or in the Japanese camps. I have no answer as to how to prevent it happening in the first place, but this I do know; we have a loving and compassionate Father who will know there was no wickedness in you, that you did your duty, and that there is nothing in what you have done which needs absolution of any kind. That I can solemnly assure you." He paused again.

"Can we say a short prayer together and then go to the Rectory for a cup of tea, when I will telephone sir Jack to come and pick you up - he will wonder where you are."

"Thank you, Canon Rosser, thank you so much."

The priest knelt beside her.

"O God, the Creator and Preserver of all mankind, we commend to thy fatherly goodness all those who are any ways afflicted in mind or body, but especially for our sister Moira. May it please thee to comfort and relieve her, give her patience under her sufferings and a happy issue out of her afflictions. This we beg for Jesus Christ, his sake. Amen."

"Amen," Moira echoed.

They knelt quietly for a few moments; the canon then taking her elbow assisted her to rise. He locked the church and they walked slowly back to the Rectory. The canon having telephoned Sir Jack, Mrs Rosser, well used to sorrow and suffering after thirty years as a parson's wife, brought in a tray of tea to a Moira now beginning to be a little more like her normal self.

"Does Sir Jack know what your task has been?" asked the canon.

"No, I haven't been able to talk about it until the evil thing was dropped. Even now I can only say I was involved; under the Official Secrets Act I obviously cannot go into detail in any way."

"Five years. Five years you and others have had to keep a secret of this enormity. I have known many brave people, but none braver than you, having to go about your daily life, mixing with the ones you love day by day, week by week, year by year, knowing of this sword of Damocles hanging above all our heads and yet still doing your duty for your country."

As he spoke, Sir Jack arrived and hurried towards his beloved Moira.

"What is the matter my love?" he asked, holding her close. Moira could no find the words to tell him. The canon spoke for her.

"Your wife has been guarding the terrible secret for five years that she was involved in the atom bomb project. She could tell no one, not even yourself. Now she is distressed at the suffering it has brought upon the people of Hiroshima and Nagasaki, and felt she was part of the cause of the tragedy inflicted upon them."

Jack was far-sighted enough not to rush immediately into disputing this belief, he just quietly affirmed, "The bomb saved millions of lives, be sure of that, including almost certainly David's and Paddy's." She clung to him, after a while turning to the Canon.

"Thank you Canon Rosser, and you, Mrs Rosser, for your help and kindness. I feel so much better now."

They said their goodbyes. Arriving at The Hollies Jack wondered whether to call Dr Power. Moira smiled a faint smile and said,

"I have you, why should I need a doctor?"

In Sandbury in the meantime there was a considerable flurry being experienced by each and every female guest to what was, after all, a society wedding. Clothing coupons provided only sufficient garments to cover oneself to ensure basic decency. There was no margin for luxury apparel, and since this state of affairs had continued for some six years, any such glad rags bought in the heady days of peace by now were looking somewhat jaded. Furthermore since there was little demand for such splendiferous garments, few were made. It was, however, provided one had coupons to spare, possible to buy cloth and have something made by a 'Court Dressmaker' as most of these ladies carrying out this business described their trade. Since these skilled tradespeople were not exactly thick on the ground, it followed that it was 'first come - first served,' and with the lead-time to the wedding being fairly short many were disappointed or had to go far afield.

The Sandbury Moss Bros agent, it follows, did a roaring trade in morning suit hire, the difference between the men folk and the female side being the former didn't give a damn about all looking the same.

Charlie and Mark obtained leave for the wedding. After all, if you mention the wedding is that of your father, in Charlie's case - and of a friend who is a lord, and a brigadier to boot, in Mark's case, leave could hardly be refused.

As Fred lay in the bed early that morning determined not to disturb Margaret so that she lost her beauty sleep, his mind dwelt on all the things that had happened to him, particularly over the past ten years. Before that, the heat and danger of the war in South Africa, the hell of the trenches in the Great War, being a farm worker with the prospect of remaining one until the end of his working days, now in a few hours' time, to be the best man to a peer of the realm and to give a speech to a large proportion of the Kentish nobility and gentry and from further afield to say nothing of family, friends - 'stop worrying' he told himself, 'it can't last for ever.' It was funny about that 'can't last forever' tag. He and his comrades often used to say it when they were almost on their uppers with fatigue, or when it seemed the shelling would never stop. Sadly, time and again, one or another of them would never know how long it would be before the torment ended. Fred gave an involuntary shrug, which awakened Margaret, who turned towards him, put her free arm around him and lightly kissed him.

"Looking forward to your big day?"

"I'm scared witless."

"My Fred would be scared of nothing, that I am sure," she replied gently caressing his back and squeezing herself closer to him. He held her tight and marvelled at the fact that when he lost his darling Ruth he thought his life was to all intents and purposes at an end, only to experience a further miracle in being blessed with another love in his life when he met Margaret.

"How is our little one?"

"Behaving himself."

"How do you know it's a 'him'?"

"I don't. Neither do I know it's a 'her' and I positively refuse to call my baby an 'it.' I think what I shall do is to call our little one 'him' on the odd dates, and 'her' on the even. Do you think that would be a good idea? Then the little mite would not be put out at being wrongly described."

Fred chuckled. "Well, whatever 'it' might turn out to be 'it' is going to be a very lucky baby to have such a beautiful and intelligent mum."

"You called it 'it.'"

"What is the date today?" Fred asked.

"First of September."

"Then you should have called him 'him' not 'it.'" Fred reasoned.

When you think of it, it is surprising how much real pleasure can be obtained from a little word like 'it,' isn't it?

A wedding with some two hundred guests can result in chaos if not suitably managed. Since Ernie Bolton was on the spot and was at the right hand of Fred, he was given the job of chief usher, to be assisted by Mark, Charlie and Ray Osbourne on the day, along with an unexpected Oliver who arrived on Friday evening from his unit in Germany, being forced to sleep on the sofa in The Bungalow as every other bed was taken, not only there, but also in Chandlers Lodge, The Hollies, and The Angel. When asked on Saturday morning whether he had been comfortable or not he replied, "It's a damned sight more comfortable than kipping in a tank."

"That didn't come into your English vocabulary at Sevenoaks, I'll be bound," his mother replied.

"Nor did a lot of other phrases we use," laughed Oliver. Cecely's schoolboy son had grown to a man in the past year; there was no doubt about that.

The great and the good had either converged, or were converging, on the pleasant little market town of Sandbury. The weather was fine, the church bells rang their clarion changes as well as they had ever been mandated so to do, as they invited the ushers, the guests, the bridegroom and best man, the matron of honour, and finally the bride herself on the arm of her brother-in-law, Charles. Ernie welcomed them,

"All ready?" He thought afterwards, 'what a bloody silly question,' but then what else could he have said? He moved inside the church to give Canon Rosser and the organist their cue. As Cecely and Charles moved forward Richard Wagner's wedding march boomed out, making Cecely jump momentarily. Charles held her arm tight and looked down at her, smiling.

"As I once heard Harry joke to Greta back in Muar, ''ere we go as the earwig said.'"

Cecely smiled back. "Dear Harry," was all she replied.

They moved in a calm, easy manner up the aisle toward a beaming Canon Rosser. Cecely wore a pale green suit, beautifully cut by the same lady who had made Rose's wedding dress when she was first married to Jeremy, and then her suit when she became Mark's wife after Jeremy was killed. The pale green was decorated with small touches of a darker green, with dark green covered buttons. She wore a small, off the face beige hat, trimmed again with the same colour green, and carried a small bouquet of chrysanthemums. She presented an extremely elegant picture as she made her way to her new husband-to-be.

Greta, keeping pace behind, was dressed in a three quarter length apricot coloured frock fitted with a belt of darker shade, the belt emphasising her shapely figure. She had a small wreath of flowers in her hair and carried a small posy of autumn flowers. Flight Lieutenant Stanislaus Rakowsky, watching her from halfway along pew eight, resolved, 'I am going to marry that girl,' and then added a codicil to that design 'if she will have me.'

Things like that happen at weddings.

The ceremony took its standard course, but meanwhile something else was happening in Sandbury, which created far more excitement in part of the extended family of the Chandlers than even a wedding.

Nanny had volunteered to look after all the children for the day. Most people will agree that children at a wedding are a pain in the neck, not only for the grown ups, but for the children as well in most cases. Harold, her husband, had elected to take the older ones, Mark, Elizabeth and John to the Sandbury afternoon pictures, in what, as we have heard, was named 'The Palace,' but which was generally referred to as the 'bug hutch.' On that day the cinema had received a new Pathe newsreel, the projectionist deciding to try it out on the kids' afternoon programme before putting it in with the evening performance.

The first two items were of little interest to the children being concerned with the Potsdam conference and the state of the refugees still arriving in West Germany from the east. Item three was then shown:-

VICTORY PARADE IN SINGAPORE

The march past by the newly arrived troops was thrown up on the screen, and then a close up of a group of green uniformed soldiers, led by a man holding a leopard on a harness. Mark jumped to his feet and screamed at the top of his voice,

"There's daddy, with Chantek, there's daddy with Chantek. Look Uncle Harold, there's daddy."

By now the man and the leopard had been faded out, but the tremendous uproar engendered by Mark's extraordinary lung power had reached the manager in his office. Now there is nothing to be astonished at in that. The manager's office was barely six feet from the auditorium. It was also in fact coincidentally, only six feet from the front doors, it was that sort of a cinema. On a wet night with a good film being shown you had to put up with queuing in the rain to get your ticket. But I digress.

Harold and party were in the best seats, third row from the back. The decibel rating of Mark's shrieks immediately led the manager to believe that rape, or at least indecent assault, was being perpetrated against an innocent young lass in the back row. He switched all the lights on in the house and rushed in, in his Sir Galahad mode, intent on saving a maiden in distress, only to find an eight-year-old boy standing on his seat, in imminent danger of falling off, the seats in the bug hutch being a bit wobbly, screaming "It was my daddy and Chantek on the news."

Patiently, Harold explained to the manager what had happened. The manager, who at first had been irate, since stopping his presentation without cause was, in his mind, the same as some idiot holding up the 'Flying Scotsman' on a record breaking run. He gradually cooled down.

"Perhaps you could re-run that stretch," Harold suggested, "so that the children can see it again. If you explain to the audience what is happening they will all be part of the excitement, most people in Sandbury know of the Chandlers. May I suggest too, that you get the local paper in to photograph it. Major Harry Chandler M.B.E. M.C. with his leopard would make a great story, give you lots of publicity, and provide some good stills for the family to have. As it is, the word will go around the town from the people here over the weekend. The major was so popular folks will be flocking in next week just to see the newsreel."

Harold should have been a salesman, not a chauffeur.

The manager immediately seized upon the idea, climbed on to the small stage in front of the silver screen, well, stage, more like a shelf really, and told the audience what was happening. They all settled down for another viewing of the Pathe Gazette, they now being all part and parcel of the proceedings.

We shall, as you have already indubitably hazarded a guess, be reading more of the actual parade later in the narrative.

When Harold left with the children, the manager button-holed him, saying he had arranged for the projectionist to come in early at four o'clock on Sunday afternoon and for the reporter and photographer from the Sandbury Times to be there. All the Chandler family would be welcome to the showing and there would be no charge.

The wedding reception had been a great success, the bride and groom having been driven off to the White Cliffs Hotel in Dover, to catch the ferry on Sunday and thence for two glorious weeks at The Carlton in Cannes, probably the hotel most people in the world, and that means most people in the world, would like to stay at but would never be able to afford. Never mind, money isn't everything - I wonder what idiot made that observation?

As soon as Jack arrived, Harold told him of the afternoon's events. Jack immediately telephoned Fred and the midnight chain of telephone calls was put into motion, every single recipient, without exception, upon hearing its summons expressing the query, 'who on earth can that be at this time of night?' As a result every member of the family, however connected, including the earl and Gloria, down to the postman who called on Megan and the Chandlers, workers at the factory who had known or vaguely heard of Harry, all lined up to get in the bug hutch for nothing.

"I should have charged!" wailed the manager to himself.

Canon Rosser and his good lady were there. They thoroughly disbelieved in Sunday cinemas but this was not to be missed. Even people from Mountfield, Harry's old stomping ground four miles away, came over to see a presentation which, though shown twice, only lasted two or three minutes. The children were allowed to go again, this time with Nanny while Harold held the fort with the young ones back at The Hollies.

Altogether it was a very exciting weekend. It did not end with the weekend. The Sandbury Times man also acted as a stringer for the Daily Express. As a result a picture and brief write up appeared in that newspaper on Tuesday, mainly of course because of the leopard - you rarely see soldiers walking along holding leopards in England. Some regiments have goats, some ponies, but leopards? - most unlikely.

Two weeks later, September 15th, was designated Battle of Britain day. RAF Sandbury put on the sort of show one would come to expect from the RAF, and the forces generally for that matter. There were fly-pasts, lots of games for the Sandbury children, a demonstration of aerodrome defence and counter-attack by the RAF Regiment, accompanied by the furious firing of thousands of blanks and discharging of hundreds of thunder flashes and anti-personnel grenades. It was all great fun. In the evening the officers held a reception and dance to which they could invite three guests. Stanley had asked Greta if she would be his guest, her reply being, "Try leaving me out!"

Knowing he could invite three people, she wondered whether his mother and father would be there. Her intuition was well founded. His father was a tall, distinguished looking man around the fifty mark she conjectured, his mother petite and extremely elegant. Well, being a diplomat I suppose you would expect him to be distinguished looking and have an elegant looking wife, would you not? Not that he was going to be a diplomat for very long now, with Poland having two governments still, one in Warsaw, one in London.

"So you are the young lady we hear nothing else about. I must say I can quite understand why," was Stanley's father's opening gambit, as he shook hands with her. His mother took her hand, kissed her lightly on the cheek, telling her how pleased they were to meet her. The station commander, having been warned there was diplomatic brass around, came across to meet them, which interruption gave Greta the opportunity to ask Stanley what he had been telling his parents about her.

"Nothing much really, just that I am besotted with you, cannot sleep because of you, have had your photo blown up by the photo-reconnaissance lab to life size and placed it on the wall of my quarters, have had a floodlight fixed to shine on it at all times so that if I wake up in the night I can see you."

"You just said you can't sleep at night, and then contradicted yourself by saying you wake up in the night."

"So I did. I'll have another think about that."

"You don't need to worry; I'm in the same boat."

It took a moment or two for the significance of that remark to sink in, before he took her hands in his and asked, "Are you really, darling Greta, are you really?"

"Yes, though I haven't been able to go to the lengths of having a full sized picture in my study at Benenden, the postcard-sized one you gave me has to suffice. Come to that, I can't muck about with the electrics either."

They looked into each other's eyes and laughed and laughed in the pure joy of being in love. They never forgot that moment.

* * *

Chapter Twenty-Four

David was suffering from prickly heat, a ghastly skin disorder, from mild dysentery, necessitating Olympic style dashes to the karzi at frequent intervals, and toothache. David was not a happy little major. The Army Dental Corps had no surgery at Kalyan, the nearest being at Bombay. Given the state of his intestines a journey of that measure was quite out of the question, so he had to take handfuls of aspirin for the toothache, which seemed to make all three afflictions worse instead of better, bucketfuls of sulpha tablets to combat the dysentery and coat himself from top to toe with calamine lotion in a vain attempt to alleviate the incredible itch that goes with prickly heat, the best relief from which he found was standing naked in the monsoon rain to the great amusement of the Indian bearers.

Paddy came to his room to see how he was. Arriving at the doorway he was almost bowled over by meeting David in flight for the fourth time that afternoon, and it was still only a little after four o'clock.

When David returned and had settled himself back on his bed Paddy commented,

"You know, sir, if we have a sports day you would be a cert for the hundred yards."

"Ha bloody ha."

Paddy grinned amiably and continued, "I hear we have an 'O' Group in the morning. The CO went to Brigade this afternoon, there's a rumour we're off again."

"Off again? Where the hell to? And where do these rumours surface from?"

"Usually from some orderly room clerk trying to make himself sound important, starting with division, then brigade, then the battalion; it soon finds its way down."

"So I say again, where are we going?"

"I reckon Singapore, seems the only logical place."

"Then I stand a good chance of seeing my brother if he is not repatriated by then."

"Wouldn't it be great if we did, sir, and Chantek as well. By all the saints, I'd love to see that leopard, so I would."

"It might snarl at you."

"I'd snarl back - we'd get on alright, you'll see."

The 'O' Group the next morning provided the confirmation they had only got a week to prepare the complete brigade for re-embarkation in Bombay to follow 2 Div into Singapore. With his trots easing off, David was able to get into Bombay to have his tooth fixed - an experience he trusted he would never have to have repeated. The dentist operated in a caravan in the grounds of the British consulate. David needed a particularly difficult filling, about which he was far from happy. He was even more unhappy when he found that far from being operated from the electricity supply, the motive power to the drill was a foot pump; moreover his unhappiness descended into sheer terror when he realised the dentist not only did the drilling, but also did the pumping! He had a mental image of the confounded persecutor having his foot slip off the pump, causing his body to stumble and the drill to penetrate anything other than the cavity it was designed to explore. It was not just the Bombay weather causing him to sweat and his stomach to practise the tango once more. The dentist, however, seemed quite unperturbed about it all.

"Open wide, shall we? Oh yes, well now, have you had trouble with this before?"

'With half his bloody fist three parts of the way down my throat how does he expect me to answer for Christ's sake?' David thought, but replied,

"Gug gug."

"Thought so. Apart from that you have a good set of gnashers, major. Now, we shall have to do a little bit of drilling and you will be as good as new."

He picked up the drill and placed his foot on the pump. David, telling the tale afterwards to Paddy, swore that when the swine smiled into his victim's face there was a demoniacal look about his eyes, saliva dripped from his lips, and his knuckles were white with the intensity of grip on that instrument of torture he waved in front of his captive. Furthermore, David swore he could count the revolutions per minute as the blasted thing rotated, to say nothing of the hand holding it being far from stationary due to the movement of the other part of the body providing the basic energy. David closed his eyes, told himself it couldn't last for ever, hoped against hope his innards would hold out and prepared himself for the assault. When it came it felt, and sounded, like someone bashing away with a road drill. He could feel bits of his molar being bludgeoned off...

"This one's being a bit stubborn..."

...a piercing pain as the foul instrument touched the nerve, and even more pain as the silly sod kept it there. After what seemed like an hour and a half, but was in fact a little over a minute, the professionally saccharine voice said, "Shall we have a little rinse?"

'Thank God that's over,' David thought.

But it wasn't.

"I've a little more to do yet, major. Open wide."

David was fast coming to the conclusion that this bastard just hated majors, dentists being ranked lieutenant, and was beginning to wonder what would happen if he got out of his chair and walked off, correction, ran off, when once again the drill was waved in front of him. More burr-burr-burr, David revising his belief that 'it couldn't last for ever' to that it bloody well was lasting for what seemed like for ever.

"Another little rinse, major? There, that wasn't so bad was it? I've to put the filling in now, that shouldn't take long."

'Wasn't so bad? I've killed people for less than he has done to me,' flashed through his mind.

Eventually he climbed out of his tormentors' chair, and with the final instruction 'don't eat on that side for a couple of days major,' ringing in his ears, he swayed out to his jeep, to be greeted by the cheerful voice of Lance-Corporal Angus – note the promotion since he was now the batman to the second-in-command of the battalion.

"Everything go alright, sir?"

"When I regain the use of my jaw I will let you know," he replied to a grinning comrade, for though there were nine degrees of rank between them, that's what they were.

Three days later they were aboard the Chitral, another P and O liner converted to a trooper, for the three thousand mile journey to Singapore. At the northern mouth of the Malacca straits they were met by a pair of minesweepers which preceded them without incident down to the same Keppel Harbour where Harry had come ashore four long years ago.

'R' Battalion assembled on the quayside while Haimish held a hurried 'O' Group.

"These people have never seen paras before. I know the men are carrying half a ton of kit each, but I want them to march like guardsmen only more so. Mr O'Riordan will be keeping a very close eye on any sloppiness. If, when you pass unit guard posts they turn out the guard, you will return the compliment by platoons, so make sure your platoon commanders are in good voice. Any questions?" There were none, the company commanders returned to their respective companies and passed on the C.O.'s orders - swank orders!

They were to march some two miles to their billets in the old officers' married quarters at Alexandra Barracks, the scene of the dreadful massacre of the hospital patients, and appalling crimes of rape and murder of the nurses by the Japanese when they took the island, back in 1942. On the way they passed half a dozen units, mainly Indian Army, billeted in various buildings, each having a quarter guard at the entrance, and each turning out at the 'present' as the paras passed, receiving an 'eyes right,' or 'eyes left' by platoons in returning the courtesy. Paddy in the meantime was covering ground to make sure there was no sloppiness.

"Mr Harvey, sir, your men are very sloppy at the rear."

"Sergeant James, see to it."

"Yes, sir."

Sergeant James detaches himself and bawls out the men at the rear of his platoon. They brighten themselves up, swearing under their breaths. 'Bloody ninety degrees in the sodding shade and carrying sixty pounds of army rubbish, what does he expect?'

It's a soldier's privilege to moan, even paras.

They settled in to their billets, David and Paddy now being in the battalion headquarters. When the dust had settled after a couple of days, and the various units had been allocated their tasks, David went to the adjutant's office.

"Bryan, how would you find out where or if another unit was here on the island?"

"I would have a word with the brigade major, he would have access to SACSEA as we are an independent brigade and do not have to go through a divisional HQ"

"SACSEA being?"

"Supreme Allied Commander South East Asia. Who do you want to find?"

"My brother. He has been in Force 136 here all through the war."

"Name, rank, number?" David gave it to him. "Leave it with me. I'll have a word with brigade as soon as we get a line through."

He was in luck. Because no land-lines were yet through the brigade major visited them late that afternoon. As a result the adjutant was able to pass on David's query. Later that evening the land lines were connected, and on Tuesday 11th Bryan was able to tell David that the Force 136 people were billeted in a large mansion out on the lower Bukit Timah Road, waiting for repatriation in due course. David went to see Haimish.

"Sir, do you mind if I try and see my brother this afternoon? Bryan has found out where he is."

"Of course not. Why not bring him back for dinner. I'd like to meet him."

Mess dinners were still fairly spartan, but were gradually getting more organised. Tonight was to be the first actual 'dinner night,' that is when all the officers not on duty somewhere would eat together.

Angus picked David up at two o'clock and they made a somewhat hesitant way out to the Bukit Timah Road. The problem was they had no actual address. Premises taken over by the military had, as a rule, a board placed at the entrance with the name of the unit on it, which meant cruising along until you found the one you were looking for. Suddenly Angus pointed to a building.

"Look, sir, there's the Dental Corps place; we'd better keep that in mind."

David glowered, "Don't remind me. I can still feel that five rpm drill when I wake up in panic at night."

"There it is, sir." Angus pointed to a sign '136 Mess.'

"They don't mean to advertise themselves do they?" David remarked, "that board must be all of two feet square.

They pulled into a short driveway which ended in a circle in front of a traditional colonial style house. In its day, before the war, it had been the home, obviously, of a wealthy merchant of some standing. Now it showed evidence of having been damaged during the Japanese bombing, in that one wing was in rubble. However, the main pillared entrance portico was still intact - an essential part of a Singapore building allowing the 'tuan bezar' and his family and visitors to alight from their carriages away from the torrential downpours which suddenly deluge this fascinating city.

David climbed out of the jeep telling Angus he would let him know what his future movements would be, and walked into the main entrance hall. A Malay servant, immaculately dressed in white drill, came forward to meet him.

"Good afternoon, tuan, can I help you?"

"I am trying to find major Chandler."

"He is in his room, tuan, shall I fetch him for you?"

"No thank you, which room is it?"

"The third door along the front veranda tuan."

David climbed up to the front veranda. One, two, three. He knocked.

"Who is it?"

David put on his best attempt at the high-pitched voice of a Chinese laundryman.

"Major's laundry, sir."

"Hang on." David heard him say something like 'come here baby,' and wondered for a moment if he had interrupted something, realising immediately after having had that thought, that his brother could have Chantek in with him.

"Right, come in."

David opened the door, walked into the room and said,

"Doctor Livingstone, I presume."

"Holy bloody smoke. Where did you spring from?"

And that is how the two brothers, who had not seen each other for four years, greeted one another!

Harry sprang from his bed and hugged David excitedly. Chantek in the meantime had leapt to the floor and seeing another man wrestling with her master would have been expected to attack his attacker, as it were. Quite the contrary. She almost danced around the two men, going first one way then the other, at times with all four feet off the floor, as if she knew of their excitement and wished to be part of it, which as we know perfectly well, having watched her grow up from a cub no larger than a bag of sugar were undoubtedly her feelings! Am I not right?

David held Harry at arm's length.

"You haven't changed much."

"What? I'm as white-haired as a ninety-year-old."

"Well you are approaching that aren't you? I tell you what; we'll call it ash-blonde, how's that?"

And so they joshed each other, as our American cousins would say, until Harry said,

"Now fill me in on all the people in Sandbury, starting with Megan and the kids."

An hour later, with occasional interruptions from Chantek rubbing against them in turn, Harry said,

"Let's go down to the garden and meet the others. We usually have tea at this time."

"Right, now what are you doing tonight. My CO said to bring you to our mess for dinner."

"Well, I was going out with Reuben and Tommy, my two captains."

"Bring them as well. Haimish will be delighted to meet you all, particularly since I've been bullshitting you up like mad, slaughtered Japs by the score and so on."

"What about your driver? I take it you didn't walk here?"

"It's against my religion to walk anywhere, you know that. No, he's alright. He will have a book with him."

"I'll get Osman to give him some tea."

Harry slipped the harness on Chantek and they walked down to where Angus was seated in the jeep, as David had predicted. Seeing them approach he jumped out and saluted smartly.

"Angus, this is my brother Harry."

Harry held out his hand, which was taken by the lance-corporal with the thought, 'they've got at least two gentlemen in the family.' Harry called the Malay who had met David when they first arrived.

"Oh, Osman, will you please find some tea and some of those sweet biscuits you hide away, for our friend Corporal Angus here?"

"Yes, major, certainly, sir."

The brothers walked back through the house. As they emerged on to the patio at the back Harry suddenly stopped. From where they were standing David could see a little cluster of men sitting on rattan chairs accompanied by a solitary lady, probably fiftyish.

"Come back inside for a moment. There is something I must tell you."

David, his mind racing in all directions, wondered what on earth his brother had to tell him. Whatever it was, it was to do with that lady in the white dress sitting with his colleagues. 'Don't tell me...' his thoughts raced.

"I should have told you about the lady out there. I've not mentioned her in many of my letters home so you won't know about her."

David's mind went into overdrive, except I can't remember there was such a thing as overdrive in 1945.

"She is Pat's mother."

"What???"

"You know she came out here with a bastard called Rowlands. I will tell you all about him later. He is going to hang and she is going to help in achieving that end. She has bitterly repented the wickedness she committed in leaving Jack and her tiny daughter. She has been in the jungle with us for nearly four years, not with me, but at another camp. She has carried out soul destroying work, year after year, and in my view, although when I first met her in Muar before the war here started I despised her for what she had done, she has more than made up, in my eyes, for her previous wrong doings."

David was silent. Harry continued.

"I don't expect you to think like that. Would you prefer not to meet her?"

A combination of curiosity, a lessening of the ill-feeling as a result of the passing years. The fact the woman had served the cause under appallingly uncivilised conditions for so long, induced David to say, especially since she was now Harry's friend,

"Yes. I will meet her."

They approached the group, who, with the exception of Marian Rowlands, stood up to meet the officer with Harry. Harry went first to Marian.

"Marian, this is my brother David."

The shock, registered immediately on her face, was noticed by Reuben and Tommy. She tried to get up from her chair, but the strength in her legs deserted her. David sat on Reuben's vacated seat beside her, and put his hand on her arm. Marian started to cry quietly, but fiercely, whilst the others remained silent, Tommy and Reuben mystified as to why the arrival of Harry's brother should produce such a sudden change in Marian's previously cheerful demeanour. Harry explained to his two colleagues.

"David was married to Marian's daughter Pat. Pat was killed in an air raid in 1940." He made no mention of Marian's desertion, the other two assuming the first marriage to Pat's father had not been a success and she had remarried Rowlands.

Marian quietened. David spoke to her quietly.

"It is all in the past now, Marian - may I call you Marian?"

"Please do, David, please do."

"It is all in the past. I will tell you all about Pat when we have time to get together. I have married again and have a year old son, but I shall never forget the love Pat and I shared."

There was what is sometimes described as a pregnant pause, nobody saying anything as nobody knew what to say. It was broken by Harry announcing, "Ah, here's the tea," remarking to himself as he said it 'that was a bloody obvious statement.'

They all sat down to drink excellent tea and to eat very thinly cut sandwiches, so thinly cut in fact that the weevils baked in with the flour could be clearly distinguished.

"Sorry about the weevils," Harry apologised to his guest, "all good protein, we shall miss them when we get back to eating English bread, or Australian bread in Reuben's case. Have you made your mind up yet, Reuben, with which country you are going to grace your presence?" He turned to David.

"You see, when we started getting mail after about eighteen months Reuben here received piles of different coloured envelopes, all with different pungent smells, indicating he not only had friends, but expensively perfumed ones at that. Now we never ever found out where they all came from, although on the rare occasions we caught a glimpse of them as the mail was sorted out, there was a wide variety of handwriting indicating he was profligate in his circle of female attachments."

Entering into the sort of leg-pull that he enjoyed so much with his own circle, David asked,

"But doesn't profligate mean dissolute or licentious?"

"Of course, that's why he kept getting the letters. So where will you be making for, Reuben?"

Even Marian was beginning to smile again in anticipation of Reuben's reply.

"Well, I've seriously thought of a monastery I once saw up in Northern Greece. You could only get to it by climbing up a sheer rock face, so you never got any visitors. I thought that might do for a start. Then I changed my mind and remembered a little place I knew quite well in Kings Cross, Sydney, Australia, provided Sadie was still there. Sadie? I believe her name was Sadie, we didn't get round to names much in those days."

"Well, what will you do?" asked Tommy, "I mean you've got to earn a living, haven't you?"

Reuben thought for a moment or two.

"Well no, I don't as it happens, have to earn a living. I'm what they used to call a remittance man. My family own great swathes of Warwickshire and they pay me to stay away."

"But you have never told us this before," Tommy challenged.

"If I had, you would have wanted to know all the whys and wherefores, you're a nosey lot. Anyway, you're too young."

"I'm not," Harry maintained.

"Ah, but your brother is."

"I just look young," David observed.

"Well, if you must know, my elder brother inherits the estates and the mines beneath. He married a beautiful girl somewhat younger than he in 1930. She in turn fell in love with me, as I did with her. He couldn't give me a thrashing as I could have bashed his brains in, such as they were, with one hand behind my back. In the meantime she became pregnant, his I emphasise, not mine, so my father said, either you get out and leave them to get on with their lives or I shall have you dealt with. He would have done too; he didn't get where he was by pussyfooting around as many of his enemies, and for that matter a number of his friends, had reason to find out. For that reason, and for the sake of the child, I upped sticks and buggered off to Australia and then here, where before the war started I joined the Singapore Volunteer Corps for a bit of fun." He paused for a moment.

"... and look where it landed me."

"In a glorious holiday camp in the jungle. Will you go back to Warwickshire?" asked Marian.

"Yes, just a visit. I don't even know if my father is still alive."

"What about your mother?"

"She died having me. My father always hated me for that. Apparently he was devoted to her; in fact she was the only person he ever had any feeling for." He was quiet for a moment or two.

"Fancy going through a large part of your life not caring about anyone at all." He hesitated again. "I couldn't be like that. Do you know" - he turned to David - "after a few months I began to like those two, after another few months I began to think they were jolly good fellows, a few months later I even began to think they were quite pretty. It's a damned good job the war ended when it did."

His audience roared with laughter.

Marian stood up and begged to be excused. She made a fuss of Chantek stretched out in the shade, who accepted her light touch with the appreciation indicated by the opening and closing of her claws. David was entranced.

"You know, you take all this for granted, having a pet which could tear you to pieces if it wanted to."

"Shush," replied Harry, "she understands every word you say, so don't give her ideas, you lummock."

To confirm this Chantek rolled over towards them and gave a huge yawn showing rows of incredibly menacing teeth.

"He's as daft as ever," David grinned at the two captains. "Now," he continued, "what happened to the camp?" Tommy replied.

"Well, after the Chinese left we had a message from Sunrise, our CO up in Cameron Highlands, to destroy every single piece of equipment and burn down every building. Nothing was to be left which would be of use to the communists should they decide to attempt a take-over. It was the last thing we did before we marched out."

"How did you feel when you did that? After all, you had been there a long time."

Harry answered. "It had given us shelter, saved us suffering the evil of being a POW and gave us the opportunity to hit back at the bastards from a firm base. Because of that we were grateful to it. On the other hand we were in a kind of open prison, surrounded by all sorts of very nasty reptiles and insects waging a constant war against us, from which we all suffered from time to time. For that reason it was like hitting your head with a hammer - lovely when it stopped. When I made that last journey down the game trails to the roadway at Slim, twenty-five miles away, I sang all the way."

"Not out loud, thank God," Reuben stressed, "there were few things which could have caused mutiny, but that would have been one of them."

It was approaching five o'clock. David queried, "Are you gentlemen doing anything this evening? If not, my colonel has asked me to invite you to our mess. It's a bit spartan but we seem to have engaged a couple of good cooks who worked for one of the messes before the war, so you won't starve."

They looked at each other, agreed between themselves and answered, almost in unison, "Thank you very much."

"What about transport?" David asked.

"We have nothing here," Harry replied.

"Right. I'll send a jeep for you at say 6.30 - that suit you? How about bringing Chantek, would she be alright in a noisy crowd?"

"No, I don't think I had better risk that yet. She was as good as gold on the Victory Parade, strutting along and showing off, but at one point where the road narrowed and she was near the crowd she wasn't very happy."

"You had a Victory Parade?"

"Yes, last Saturday."

"I wonder if it's on the newsreel back home."

"Could be, I suppose, there were quite a few cameras of all sizes about."

David took his leave and made his way back to the mess to let the mess sergeant know there would be three extra that evening.

"Who might they be, sir?"

"My brother and two of his captains. They have been in the jungle all through the war raiding the Japanese."

"They've lived in the jungle for three and half years?" the sergeant asked incredulously.

"That's right."

"Well, if anyone deserves a decent dinner by God, they do," he exclaimed. "One night there would frighten the life out of me. You leave it to me, sir."

It was only then as he walked back to his room to get showered and changed that it suddenly occurred to him that one of their guests was black. He stopped in his tracks. 'I'd better have a word with Haimish,' he thought to himself. He was almost at the CO's door. He knocked.

"Come in - oh, hello, David, how did you get on?"

"Very well, sir, I've invited Harry and his two captains to dinner this evening. I've seen the mess sergeant about the extra numbers, now I've realised I might have dropped a clanger."

"How do you mean?"

"Well, it has only just occurred to me that one of Harry's captains, Tommy Isaacs, is black."

"Well, what's that got to do with it?"

"We've one or two old regulars, India hands, who might well object to having a black officer in the mess."

"Well, I'm an old regular and an old India hand and I don't object, so bugger them, that's what I say.

But there was more than one or two among the twenty-four officers who sat down that evening whose eyebrows were raised at the sight of a black man, officer or not, being so warmly welcomed by their commanding officer, and not only among the 'old India hands'; several of the new young subalterns were not exactly pleased at the turn of events.

* * *

Chapter Twenty-Five

After the excitement of the cinema showing, life for the Chandlers, and Megan in particular, was a blend of elation that Harry was coming home, impatience that he had not even left Singapore yet and conjecture as to whether he would be bringing Chantek with him and if he did, where he would keep her. Megan had butterflies about this latter situation, having the opinion that a leopard was a 'bit like a tiger, perhaps not quite so big, but just as ferocious.'

On the 18th of September she had a cable from Harry 'Have met with David. Going to Muar weekend. Will report after visit. Love Harry.'

She was delighted to receive the cable, but disappointed in its contents in that it did not tell her what she most wanted to know - when she would be safely wrapped in his arms again. She telephoned Maria and Fred and the rest of the family the news that the brothers had met up, and to Charles they were to visit Muar.

"It would be nice if they could travel back together," Margaret reflected, when discussing the news that evening.

"I don't think that will happen," Fred replied, "this bloke Soekarno, who has set up a provisional Indonesian Republican Government in Java, means business. He doesn't intend to let the Dutch back in. They have no forces there as yet to combat him, and he in turn has thousands of troops, all conscripts, called Heiho, armed and trained originally by the Japanese. I can see us having to intervene on behalf of the Dutch."

As he spoke, Moira and Jack arrived.

"Who's intervening on behalf of who - or should it be whom - I never know?" Jack asked.

"This Java business - that could blow up into something nasty," Fred replied, "we have got thousands of our POW's there, along with all the Dutch civilian internees and POW's and the Indonesians have already attacked one camp killing two Dutchmen before the Jap guards drove them off. Talk about poacher turned gamekeeper, Japs having to defend the prisoners now! The problem will be, when the internees have to move to the ports on the coast, they will be very vulnerable if the Indonesians continue their rebellion."

Jack mused, "I don't know, we get over one war and before we know it we are faced with the prospect of another. Well there's nothing we can do about it. I am afraid that the big empires, French, Dutch and British, will all have their problems over the next few years with wars of independence. I just hope our government will have the sense to talk to our territories. I think this Labour Government will be more prudent than Churchill would have been, although to be fair he did promise India its independence when they raised the biggest volunteer army the world has ever seen - two million men - to help in the fight both in Europe and in Burma. Anyway, enough about war, the good news is the petrol price has gone down to just under two shillings a gallon. All we need now is the rationing to cease and I really shall believe we have won the war."

"Enough of war," Moira sighed. "Who can we talk about? Is Cecely back yet? And what about young Greta? She seems very struck on that rather nice Polish boy."

It transpired that Hugh and Cecely had decided to stay at Cannes for a further week. Greta, having left Benenden, was trying to decide what to do, but putting off the decision until her mother returned.

"What will happen to The Bungalow now, Fred?" Jack asked.

"Search me," was Fred's answer. "Charles and Jane are staying there at present but are actively looking around for a place of their own. Obviously it will not be any use to Lord and Lady Ramsford. When Harry gets home he will be looking for a bigger place; their cottage by the river, lovely though it is, will not be big enough for a growing family, and then of course David will be home in a few months and we don't know what he's going to do, or where he will decide to live. So everything is up in the air at the moment."

"What about you, Rose?" Moira asked.

"Well, my husband is a career officer, so I suppose I shall be required to follow the drum when army service settles down to normal." She paused for a moment. "But you know, I can't imagine living anywhere else but at The Chandlers."

"You will do when we start charging you rent," Fred joked.

"It's a very itinerant life, or at least it was before the war," Jack observed "I remember our dear Lady Halton telling me once that in the years 1919 up to 1939, say twenty years, they had lived at eighteen different places. No sooner had she got the curtains right for one set of windows than she had to alter them or get new for a different set. Mind you, travel will be easier now as airlines spring up all over the place."

"You think that will happen soon then, Jack?" Fred asked.

"Definitely."

"I'll believe it when it does," Fred replied, "that is, at reasonable enough prices for ordinary people like me to be able to afford it."

"Ordinary people? Like you? I understood you are known as the only multi-millionaire in Sandbury," Jack declared.

"No, you've got the wrong end of the stick there, that's you."

Jack laughed. "I suppose we've both got to admit to having a bob or two if the truth was known."

They broke up, Fred reminding Jack of the Sandbury Engineering board meeting on Friday next 21st September. This would determine the company's fortunes for many years to come.

When Greta had broken up for the last time at Benenden she had decided, in view of her mother and Hugh's imminent wedding, to leave all thoughts of what she was going to do until they returned from Cannes. She would be seeing little of Stanley for a while as he was being posted to Northumberland, although no doubt he would be demobbed sometime in the not too distant future. On the Saturday evening, walking back to The Bungalow, having visited the bug hutch to witness Errol Flynn winning the war for the British in Burma, Greta asked him,

"Have you decided what you are going to do when you are demobbed?"

"I'm going to find a rich widow with a pub."

"You rotter."

"Then I am going to employ you as a barmaid."

"I would be useless as a barmaid."

"That wouldn't matter; it would not be your barmaiding I would be employing you for."

"Then what would you be employing me for?" She paused for a moment. "We each ended those sentences with a preposition. That's not allowed. So, for what would you be employing me?"

"Oh, orgies and things like that."

"Sounds interesting. What would the pay be?"

"Oh, you don't get paid; you just have a good time and all found."

"Well, I must say it's an interesting prospect, now, can I get some sense out of you. What, repeat what, are you thinking of doing when you leave His Majesty's Royal Air Force?"

He did not reply for a minute or so, then he halted, turned towards her and very seriously said,

"I would like to marry you if you will have me."

Greta was not exactly taken aback, but was, I suppose you might say, caught on the wrong foot. Only seconds before she had been taking part in the sort of earthy discourse young people who know each other well enjoy together, suddenly to be confronted with probably the most important request a woman is likely to receive in her whole life. She hesitated, not because she had any doubt about her answer, but purely because the change of tenor had momentarily thrown her off-balance.

"Will you marry me then, darling Greta?"

"Yes, of course I will, oh I do love you so much Stanley."

"Well, before you decide absolutely I had better tell you what I propose doing when I get into civvy street. My father knows that his days as an ambassador are over now that the communists have taken over Poland, which means they have taken over our family estates as well. We, that is mother, father and I will stay here. They will become naturalised. I am already British by birth. Knowing what was certain to happen when the Russians occupied Eastern Europe he put feelers out to do something he had always wanted to do. He bought a farm in Sussex where they breed beef cattle. I have decided to go in with him to help run it. If you decide to marry me..."

"I have already decided."

"... if you decide to marry me you will be a farmer's wife. We would have our own house about a mile from my parents. If you decide to marry me..."

"I have already decided."

"... if you decide to marry me I will take you to see the house and the land. The countryside is quite beautiful; it's about seven miles this side of Lewes."

"Stanislaus Rakowsky, will you please stop talking."

They stood in silence for a moment.

"Yes. Yes. Yes. Now, is that definite enough?"

They walked on air for the few hundred yards left to reach The Bungalow.

"When can I ask your mother?"

"They will be home tomorrow but will only be here a few hours before they go off to Hugh's flat in town."

"What time will they be here?"

"Midday or thereabouts until early evening."

"I will come at two o'clock."

"In which case I shall say nothing to anyone until you have seen them."

They said their fond goodnights after which Stanley pedalled off into the darkness.

But Greta could not keep it to herself. Bubbling over with excitement she told Jane and Charles. Rose happened to telephone Jane the next morning to establish when Cecely would be back so, naturally, Jane told Rose in confidence. Rose immediately told Moira, in confidence, who happened to be at The Chandlers at the time, and then told Megan, Karl and Rosemary, Ray and June Osbourne, all of whom she met at church, in confidence of course. By the time Cecely arrived at The Bungalow everyone who was anyone in Sandbury knew her daughter was going to be married except her.

Things like that happen before weddings.

It was a shy young flight lieutenant who arrived at The Bungalow on a borrowed bicycle the next afternoon. Led into the sitting room by Greta, Jane and Charles having diplomatically disappeared into the conservatory, he approached Cecely.

"Mrs Coates." Immediately realising his error he became somewhat embarrassed.

"Oh, I do apologise, Lady Ramsford."

"No need for apologies Stanley, I get mixed up myself at times, even now. What can I do for you?"

"Lady Ramsford, I have asked Greta to marry me. We would like your permission to wed."

"What do your parents think about it?"

"They think I'm the luckiest blighter under the sun. My father has bought a farm in Sussex. When I am demobbed the intention is for me to go and help run it. There is a nice house there for us."

"Stanley, you not only have my permission, you have my blessing, and my thanks for all the brave things you have done for us in this war. David told me all about what you were involved in."

"Thank you, Lady Ramsford."

He turned to Greta and they hugged each other. Greta asked, "So what about that rich widow with the pub?"

"I've decided against that project."

Cecely looked mystified at Hugh, who thus far had said nothing.

"It's alright my dear, all servicemen say that when they leave they are going to marry a rich widow with a pub. It's a sort of ambition which as far as I know has never yet been fulfilled."

With hugs all round, including Jane and Charles called from the conservatory, Stanley told the assembly he was to be posted to a place called Brunton in Northumberland on Wednesday, so he would take Greta into Maidstone on Monday to buy an engagement ring. Perhaps they could all discuss the wedding details on his next long leave in November.

"Are you saying I shall not see you again until November?" Greta lamented.

"Poor Megan hasn't seen Harry for over three years," Cecely reminded her daughter.

"I know, but we all saw him and Chantek on the Pathe newsreel," Greta said excitedly, "it was absolutely ripping, everyone, even Canon Rosser and Mrs Rosser in front of us were clapping and cheering. So too were the earl and Gloria. Oh I do hope he can bring Chantek home, she looked so proud and beautiful marching along with Harry and his men. Do you know what the regulations are regarding the keeping of animals like Chantek, Lord Ramsford?"

There was a complete silence, Greta immediately realising the cause of it and that she had precipitated it. Hugh answered with a smile.

"Now young Greta, you have not had much time to assimilate our new relationship, particularly since you have probably been somewhat absorbed by influences from other quarters. However, as I now hold the extremely privileged position of being your stepfather, and since that is such a mouthful, may I suggest that you and Oliver address me as Hugh? What do you think? I am not very well up in these things but, I would think, that would be the modern thing to do. After all, it is 1945 now, not 1895. Do you know," he continued, addressing the whole company, "I was in America a while ago and men there call each other by their Christian names even when they have only just been introduced, for example - I'm

Harry Bernstein, oh, hi, Harry - and they've never seen each other before in all their lives! They looked at me in a very old fashioned way when I kept addressing them as 'Mister.'"

"How did they cope with your being Lord Ramsford?" asked Charles.

"No problem there. I was just addressed as 'Brigadier,' they probably thought 'Lord' was my Christian name, in fact one chap did come up to me and ask, 'Lord, can you make this point clear?' Earl is quite common as a Christian name, so is Duke. I didn't come across any Kings or Queens, but I wouldn't mind betting they exist. Anyway, my gracious step-daughter, is it Hugh?"

Greta held his arm and kissed his cheek "Hugh it is. Thank you very much for looking after my mother."

"That has been, and will be, the greatest privilege of my life, I assure you. Now, back to the original question, Chantek in England. I have to admit I haven't a clue. I would think she would have to go into quarantine, but where Heaven only knows, nor for how long. However, I will find out, then you can send Harry a cable to put him in the picture. How's that?"

"Marvellous. Won't it be exciting to see him again and to hear of everything he has done while he has been in the jungle?"

Hugh pursed his lips before replying.

"I doubt very much if you will hear a great deal. From what I know of all the Chandlers, and I know quite a bit, they tend to keep their cards very close to their chests regarding their active service, and by God! between them they've seen more or less everything there is to see, on land in any event."

"Well now, let's have some tea," Jane suggested. With general assent she and Charles moved off towards the kitchen.

"Do you know how to make tea then, Charles?" Cecely teased.

"I am taking evening classes in Maidstone," he replied, "along with the study of the art of making cucumber sandwiches." He disappeared from view.

"How is the shop managing without you, mummy?" Greta asked.

"Well, Mrs Draper's sister has been staying with her for a little while; she's just lost her husband. She knows the trade well so she has been helping out. The problem is, she is going back to Cambridge at the end of next week, so I shall have to get something organised pretty soon now."

"Couldn't I help out?"

"A Benenden girl in a shop?"

"You helped out in the shop. It could be fun until I become Mrs Rakowsky. As I see it Harry and David saved our bacon; it's the least I can do in return."

"What do you think, dear?" Cecely asked Hugh.

"Jolly good idea I would say. One thing puzzles me though, Greta. You said, and I repeat, 'it could be fun until I become Mrs Rakowsky.' Are we to assume from that remark that when you become Mrs Rakowsky your fun will cease?"

Greta was immediately cognizant of the fact that, underlying that quip, Hugh was treating her as a grown up woman. He would not have made a sally of that nature to a schoolgirl - even if she were a sixth former. She held Stanley's arm tight to her.

"Definitely not. Fun, fun and more fun, and then even more fun." She looked laughingly up into Stanley's face. "Don't you agree?"

"Ab-so-lute-ly," he replied, hugging her up.

Cecely laughed. "Very well then. When I come down on Tuesday we'll see Mrs Draper together and if she has no objections we will sort something out, although I give you warning. When you have been on your feet for eight hours on a busy day you will most certainly have forgotten the 'fun' bit."

Before Cecely and Hugh went back that evening they called in at Chandlers Lodge where they were warmly welcomed by Margaret and Rose, and joined shortly afterwards by Fred having an 'early night' from the factory. The truth of the matter was, he was taking an increasing number of early nights these days; he wished to spend all the time he could with his Margaret. At sixty-four, he told himself, he had to make good use of every minute, three score years and ten not being all that far away.

"Have you heard about that Black List they have found in the Gestapo headquarters in Berlin, Lord Ramsford?"

"Look here Fred. We've known each other long enough, why don't you call me Hugh?"

"Thank you for the privilege. Hugh it is. This Black List, people due for the chop when they had succeeded in their invasion of Britain. All the top brass were on it, Churchill, Attlee, Bevin, Bevan and so on."

"I understand both I and my father are on it too," Hugh replied, "me for obvious reasons, my father because of his outspoken opposition to Chamberlain just before the war in a speech in the Upper House and his far from complimentary remarks about the Hitler, Goering gang, as he called them."

Having sampled a tankard of Whitbreads and Cecely having downed a rather nice sherry, supplies of which were now beginning to arrive from Spain, the Ramsfords were driven to the station by Fred. On the way he asked the Brigadier whether he had any news of the situation in Java. They at Sandbury were all concerned that it might blow up into a minor war, and as David's parachute brigade was close to hand it seemed logical they might be used.

"All I can tell you, though I shall find out more during this week, is that Lord Mountbatten has given orders to the Japanese forces on the island to maintain law and order until occupation troops arrive. I cannot see Dutch forces getting there for months; it seems logical therefore that we shall have to step in. After all, we have a large number of POW's there in danger if hostilities do commence. I will telephone you later in the week when I have found out more, Fred."

"Thank you very much. It would be an absolute disaster after all he and Paddy and the others have gone through if David should come to harm at this late stage."

But there was no good news. British and Indian troops were going to be involved, and the paras would be among the first to go.

* * *

Chapter Twenty-Six

The evening was a great success. Each of the three 136 men was seated between two of the paras, Harry between David and Haimish, the latter pumping his guest unceasingly about their way of life in such a hostile environment as the high jungle. Tommy was seated next to Roger Hammick, now a captain, who during his relentless pursuit of detail from his guest elicited the gem of information that Harry had not only mastered the art of the blowpipe but also had sent a number of Japanese to an early grave with it. During the course of the meal, since it wasn't a formal dinner night, he stood up, looked toward the colonel and asked,

"Sir, may I have permission to make a short announcement?"

"Carry on, Roger."

"Sir, would it be in order for us to ask our principal guest, one, how as a land soldier he was able to sink a Japanese gunboat, and two, how did he put his proficiency with an aborigine blowpipe to good use with his poisoned arrows?"

Haimish turned to Harry.

"Somebody's been telling tales out of school."

"Yes, sir, and I'll break his bloody neck when we get back to Bukit Timah road."

"Yes, do leave it until then, we are very sensitive people here. Nevertheless, how about telling us about it, I'm absolutely intrigued."

"If I may be allowed to say, sir, it's all bullshit compared to what you and your people have done. Even the Times of India gave you a write-up and they only have a vague idea of where Europe is normally."

"On the other hand I would rather spend a week in action in Europe than one night in the jungle, and I speak as one who has been in the jungle in India just for the experience, never wanting to repeat it, certainly not to fight in it. So, come on, have a bash, as your brother would undoubtedly say."

Harry rose to address a silent, intensely interested group of highly professional soldiers. He said very little about himself. It was all, 'we moved to so and so, we attacked this place, with regard to the boat incident, we approached the moorings which were not visible to us over a brow in the hill to see this gunboat tied up. We rushed it, dropped grenades down the chimney and into the hatchway and got off it on to the landing stage quickly. One of the grenades must have struck lucky because suddenly the whole blooming vessel exploded into two and sank into the river, one or two of us being injured in the process. That's all there was to it!'

He then went on to explain how he mastered the art of the blowpipe, and of his two friends, Bam and Boo. He concluded, "Their instruction was put to good use on a number of occasions."

Several of the officers stood up to ask questions, Haimish stating,

"No more tonight, gentlemen, we did not ask these three very brave men to come here to sing for their supper, much as I would like to hear everything there is to hear." He nodded to the mess president, who in turn stood up.

"Mr Vice, the King."

The vice president stood, the others following.

"The King."

The toast was drunk, the dinner night was over.

During the course of the conversation at the bar afterwards Harry mentioned he wanted to go up to Muar at the weekend to find Ah Chin, 'without whom I would not be alive today' he added.

"What's stopping you?"

"Transport. We have been promised a jeep and driver, but nothing has arrived. I'm afraid I might get repatriated before I get an opportunity to go up there."

"Go up where?" Haimish at their elbow had caught the end of the statement.

"Up to Muar, sir, at the weekend. I want to thank Ah Chin, who saved my life, and to establish what has happened to the property our friends the Coates owned there."

"You got anything on at the weekend, David?"

"No, sir, nothing at all."

"Well, why don't you take my staff car and go with him. My driver is in the sick bay but Corporal Angus can drive it. How far is it?"

"About a hundred miles, sir."

"Well, go up on Friday and come back on Monday; you deserve a couple of days off."

"Thank you very much, sir, I'll do that."

"Now Harry, tell me all about this leopard of yours."

On Friday 16th of September David arrived at eight a.m. to pick Harry up, driven by Lance-Corporal Angus. They were not alone. On the day after the dinner described above Paddy came into David's office, saluted precisely and stood before his desk.

"What can I do for you, Mr O'Riordan?" he answered precisely, as befits a reply to a precisely given salute.

"I hear on the grapevine, sir, that you and your brother are going to Muar at the weekend and it occurred to me you should have a bodyguard, so it did, and as I'm having a couple of days off I thought you might take me along in that capacity."

"You realise we shall be taking the leopard?"

"She can sit on my lap, sir."

"Right, 7.45 outside the mess here. I don't know, when we first met at Winchester who the devil would have thought we would one day be swanning around Malaya together cuddling a leopard?"

"Well, I think we'd better make the most of the weekend, sir. My spies at SACSEA tell me we shall be back on board ship again before many days are out."

They picked Harry up as arranged, David suggesting he ride up front with Angus as he knew the way, which left David and Paddy on the rear seats, and a leopard called Chantek free to roam in the luggage space behind them. Since the seats did not go up to the roof of the Humber staff car it necessarily follows there was an opening of some two feet or more adjoining Chantek's compartment, the full width of the car.

As they drove away, Chantek, who had stretched out on the floor when Harry put her in the vehicle, decided to see what was beyond her present home, raised herself slightly, put her paws up on the back of the bench seat and thrust her head between a startled David and Paddy. Now, looking at a leopard's jaws at a distance of a few yards, or even a few feet may not be too frightening, having them less than a foot from one's throat was distinctly off-putting. Strangely enough they both instinctively put up a hand to stroke the beautiful creature, who, suspended as she was over the back of the seat, lapped up the attention she was getting until her supportive rear legs became uncomfortable when she withdrew her presence, stretched out on the floor and went to sleep.

Paddy looked at David.

"Bloody hell," was all he said; it inferred volumes.

They reached the outskirts of Muar soon after eleven o'clock. Prior to that as they left Sulong Harry pointed out the little path he had taken to reach the Force 136 communists.

"To think that was there three and a half years ago," he mused.

They headed into Muar until they reached the padang.

"Now I know where I am," Harry announced, giving instructions to Angus where to go. As they swung around a bend to where the Coates' house once stood, they saw the row of outhouses where Ah Chin and his family had lived. As they approached they saw a number of Chinese men, women and children, obviously in a serious altercation with two very large white men, one of whom was pushing a Chinese man violently in the chest.

"That's Ah Chin," Harry exclaimed.

Angus drove the Humber up close to the group. Harry jumped out, closely followed by Paddy and David, and ran to the white man mishandling Ah Chin.

"What the hell are you doing?" he shouted.

Ah Chin spun round. "Mr Chandler," he shrieked, "you alive, you alive."

He threw his arms around Harry, calling, "Anna, May, Mr Chandler here, Mr Chandler here."

To the astonishment of David and Paddy two extremely pretty Chinese women ran forward, hugged Harry and kissed him again and again. This was remarkable, as that sort of comportment was as foreign to their traditions as rubbing noses would be to ours. Harry put his arm around Ah Chin's shoulders.

"What's going on?"

"These men say they now own this plot and tell us get out."

Harry turned to them.

"Who are you and what right have you to disturb these people?"

The two men rapidly recovered their first attitude of aggression, one replying,

"This has nothing to do with military matters, so kindly mind your own business."

"We have just seen you committing an assault against this gentleman, and unless you start talking I shall send my driver for the police and charge you."

"We have bought these premises."

"Who from?"

"The government."

"The government does not own them."

"Sir," it was Angus. "Sir, I've heard that certain people are establishing themselves in premises trusting the original owners have died in the camps. If no-one returns to claim them they can claim them for nothing after seven years. If the original owners or solicitors turn up they just vacate and move on. If they put a stake on half a dozen properties or more, they may end up with half of them."

"So that's it," said Harry. "I suggest you get out of here before you end up in the River Muar, and I can tell you from my own experience that is a very, very nasty place to end up."

As Harry was addressing the pair Paddy had moved close to the man who had been pushing Ah Chin around so violently, a man half his size. When they turned to leave, he confronted Paddy. None saw what happened. Paddy's fist travelled no more than six inches but it hit Ah Chin's assailant right in the solar plexus with such force that he dropped to the ground moaning and gasping for breath, his arms and legs threshing around as he fought to get his nervous system working again.

"Looks as though your mate is having a fit, so it does," Paddy observed.

"You did that, you bastard," the other said.

"You shouldn't have said that, sir, that was very offensive, particularly to my mother and father."

Paddy moved with the speed of a feather-weight and put a second blow in the identical place on number two's carcase, the effect duplicating that exhibited by number one, who was still unable to get up. Paddy pulled them both up by the collars of their expensive alpaca jackets, turned them towards the town centre, and with a friendly 'now piss off,' in their ears pushed them off the premises. A burst of cheering and clapping came from Ah Chin and his assembled family who rushed to surround Paddy, shake his hands and pat his back. Harry looked at David.

"That's what I call a very useful RSM to have around."

"You should see him when he gets annoyed."

"You stay have tiffin with us, Mr Chandler?"

"First I must introduce these gentlemen to you Ah Chin. This is my brother David, who is a great friend of Mrs Coates, that is Regimental sergeant major O'Riordan..."

"Call me Paddy."

..."and this is Corporal Angus, who is Scottish."

"Mrs Coates' father in Scottish regiment," Ah Chin informed Angus as they shook hands. Ah Chin repeated his invitation.

"You stay have tiffin - yes? We plenty of food now Japs gone."

The two girls were still each holding Harry's arms.

"Thank you, Ah Chin, we will be very pleased to stay." He turned to his companions.

"I will tell you, Ah Chin is the finest cook in the whole Federated States of Malaya."

Ah Chin's eyes literally disappeared as his smile indicated his pleasure at the compliment.

"I want to show my friends the river," said Harry.

"You go see river, you luckiest man on earth. I do cooking, take half hour."

"I'll take Chantek, give her some exercise," Harry announced, went to the back of the staff car, unfastened the leash within the vehicle and let her drop down on to the ground. Immediately there were gasps of surprise from the younger members of the family and a general retreat to behind the older ones as Harry brought Chantek bouncing towards them. The Chinese chattered among themselves about this ferocious animal, now sitting on its haunches a few yards from them. One of the children, bolder than the rest, stepped forward, asked a question in Chinese, holding out his hand at the same time. Ah Chin translated.

"He say can he stroke animal."

"Yes, but move slowly."

The youngster walked slowly forward with his hand out, holding it close to Chantek's head. He then stroked her head, then her back, then her head again, all of which Chantek accepted. Gradually the others came forward, Ah Chin, his daughters and their husbands as they later turned out to be, watching with intense interest. Harry kept a very tight rein on the animal. Up until now she had not been in the presence of small children. It occurred to him that her instinct might consider them prey, prey the size of which she could readily drag up a tree. On the other hand she had never hunted or been taught by her mother how to hunt, least of all had she climbed trees. Nevertheless, it was as well to be careful.

The youngsters made such a fuss of her. Again this indicated to Harry how she might behave when she got to Sandbury and was confronted by his own children and young John and Jeremy. He felt much happier at that prospect now he had seen how she behaved with Ah Chin's grandchildren.

"Right, that's all. We will go to see the river."

Ah Chin gave a sharp word of command to rejoin the grown-ups which the children obeyed instantly and Harry led the way to the river wall, some one hundred yards away. His three companions stood looking at the menacing flow passing through. Since it was low tide, black mud banks were constantly erupting with the foul gases contained in them.

"You swam that, wounded, sir?" asked Angus.

"Yes, and in the dark. That's why Ah Chin says I was very lucky. Firstly there are very venomous sea snakes in there, this being tidal, then it contains giant leeches they call horse leeches. Half a dozen of those on you for more than a few minutes would see you off, and last but by no means least there are crocodiles, particularly further along where the mangrove starts, big ones, like the Australian ones. I have nightmares even now when I think about it. I came out up that slipway up there." He pointed to a gap in the wall some seventy to eighty yards away. "The slipway was rightly named, it was covered in slippery mud, it took all the strength I had left to get up to the wall. When I got my breath back I crawled across the road to those casuarina trees. I couldn't stand because of my wound, so I managed to make a crutch out of timber which had been blasted out of the trees during the Jap shelling. I managed to get myself up, made my way to Ah Chin's quarters and collapsed there. They took me in, and the rest you know."

Paddy answered, "Bloody hell," and continued, "but I bet we don't know a quarter, sir, but we'll get it out of you one day, that we will."

Harry thought deeply for a moment.

"Ah Chin and the two girls saved my life. We were surrounded by Japs. If they had decided to search the cellar I was in and found me, not only would I have been bayoneted, but they would have killed them as well. They knew that but still they took me in."

David put his arm around his brother's shoulders.

"How do you repay people who have done that for you?"

"I'm blessed if I know. I've dreamt about it many times up in the jungle, I've not been able to think of a way."

"I think, sir," Paddy suggested, "they may think that your coming to see them and sorting out these, what did they call them in 'Gone With The Wind,' oh, I know, carpetbaggers, sorting out these carpetbaggers, that would go a long way towards it."

Harry laughed. "Well, as I recall, you did the sorting out, and lovely it was to see. As and when I get back to Sandbury I shall tell Mrs Coates exactly what happened - blow by blow, you might say."

They laughed together as they moved back to Ah Chin's headquarters, where under an awning a table had been laid for them. As they passed the Humber, Angus said to David,

"Shall I have mine in here, sir?"

"Good lord, no; they've laid a place for you. How many times have we eaten together in the bottom of a slit trench? Dozens, so come and sit down."

"I know how you feel, son," Paddy added. "When I first went to Chandlers Lodge, the major's mother said, 'come and sit down Paddy,' and I remember saying to the dear lady - God rest her soul - we don't normally sit down with the officers ma'am.' She said, 'You do in this house, Paddy.' Do you remember, sir?"

"I remember it well," David replied, "what's more he ate us out of house and home in the process."

With Ah Chin's superb cooking, the constant replacement of dishes by Anna and May, the meal lasted for two hours, during the course of which Harry learnt that the Judge's quarters at K.L. had, throughout the war, been requisitioned by a Japanese staff officer and his comfort girl, or girls, according to Ah Chin. He had however, kept Mark Chea and his wife, housekeeper and manservant to the Judge, on to look after him, so they were still there.

"I have some news for you," David revealed to Ah Chin, "the Judge has just got married."

"Sir," replied Ah Chin excitedly, "we know. He told us he wed soon when he cable bad news of Mr Coates and send us money."

"What happened to John, his syce?"

"He sent to work on railway in Siam. He die we think, he not come back yet."

"Well, it will take a long while to get them all back again, so don't give up hope."

But John Chea never did come back. Somewhere alongside that infamous Siam-Burma railway lie his remains and those of a hundred thousand others, one body for every sleeper, many of them British and Australian, the vast majority of them Chinese and Indian.

"And what happened to the Railton?"

"It disappeared. John hid it. We don't known where. He not let Japs get it."

Harry explained how Judge Charles Coates had loaned him his magnificent Railton motor, complete with chauffeur, for a long weekend leave, back in 1941, and how proud John Chea was of it. It was an experience he would never forget.

It was getting on towards five o'clock when Harry said they must get on to the Rest House for the night.

"We will run up to K.L. tomorrow and see Mark while we are there."

"Mister Chandler, can you come and take food to them? Food short in K.L."

"Yes of course. 7.30 tomorrow, OK?"

"OK Mister Chandler."

They said their goodbyes, Paddy giving Ah Chin such a hug he almost disappeared from view. In the morning they collected a sack containing two chickens, newly departed this earthly creation, mangoes, tapioca, and several other indeterminate objects. No rice, rice was desperately short everywhere, except on the black market, an enterprise growing rapidly throughout the peninsula, especially in K.L. and Singapore. It was sad they would never see Ah Chin and his family again, but they would never forget them.

* * *

Chapter Twenty-Seven

The board meetings called for Friday 21st September commenced at 10.30am. The schedule was arranged that the directors of Sandbury Engineering Ltd would meet first; the directors of Sandbury Properties would meet at a convenient time after the first board meeting had concluded its business. Jack would have a watching brief.

The main matter under discussion of the engineering board, was the planning of future operations when, as we have already been made aware, the government contracts ran out. As soon as the purely financial items had been dealt with, it was proposed that Ray Osbourne be invited to join the discussions on 'future operations.'

The first item on their agenda was to discuss the possible future diversification of Sandbury Engineering Ltd. After considerable deliberation in which all four put forward views, it was decided that Sandbury Engineering Ltd would revert to its pre-war role of agricultural engineers and suppliers. A second company would be formed to be known as Sandbury Plastics Ltd. With regard to the directors of these companies Ernie Bolton would be the managing director of Sandbury Engineering, to recruit a marketing director. Similarly Ray Osbourne to be M.D. of the plastics company, again to recruit, in due course, a sales director.

"That leaves the problem of what to do with the huge Hamilcar bay."

"I've had some thoughts on that guvnor," Ernie replied.

"Fire away."

"Caravans. We know all about fabricating wooden structures. Caravans are wooden and aluminium structures with furnishings inside. From now on when people are able to drive cars again, which will not be long, they will buy caravans. We would need to do some work on designing towing attachments and so forth, but the rest of it we could do standing on our heads. What's more, it would save those jobs."

"Yes, but who's going to run it?"

"Arthur Tregorran, the existing shop foreman, could run the manufacturing side. He's only in his thirties, very intelligent, and a good company man."

Jack asked, "In his thirties? Why wasn't he called up?"

"He had a reserved occupation here. He was more use building Hamilcars than firing a rifle. Anyway, he would have been graded with having flat feet."

Fred reasoned, "You would need a lot of space for caravans, and we are going to need all our forecourt hardstanding for farm machinery once we get under way."

"Caravans can be parked on grass," Ernie suggested, "we've still got a couple of acres on the side of the Hamilcar shop."

"Look. Horry Digby over at the Hop Farm has got a caravan, let's go and have a look at it over the weekend. We can pick up some hints from Horry and Lorna as users. The more I think of it the more I like it, I must say. The demand will only grow slowly and we can grow with it. We have the advantage of having all the equipment needed so there should be little capital expenditure on tools. We will need to buy stocks of fittings, decide on what size or sizes we are going to make and so on. Yes, could be very interesting."

And that's how the Sandbury Group began to be formed. Sandbury Holdings Ltd was the majority shareholder in Engineering, Plastics, Caravans, and Properties. It was resolved to despatch Ray to America to find out all there was to know about plastics, to return and recommend which product would be the best prospect for the facilities and investment capability of Sandbury Holdings.

They were on their way.

Later that afternoon Fred phoned Horry at Beltring.

"Horry, am I correct in believing you have a caravan."

"Yes, don't tell me you are thinking of getting one?"

Fred did not answer the question directly.

"I wondered if we, that is Jack, Ernie and I could come and have a look at it?"

"Why, are you thinking of making them?"

"You're not as daft as you look, are you? The answer is yes and we want to pick your brains as a 'user.'"

"Well, we haven't used it since the first year of the war, but it's been kept under a lean-to so it's in good condition, that is if the mice haven't found a way in. I haven't looked in it for years."

"How about if we bring our better halves and we take you and Lorna to lunch at Paddock Wood."

"What do you mean, instead of a consultancy payment?"

"Something like that."

"You're on."

"Right, eleven tomorrow then. Cheerio now."

'Now I've got to see if that fits in with everybody else' he told himself. In the event they all fitted in with it; as a result Ernie and Anni went with Jack and Moira in their car and Fred and Margaret took the opportunity to ride over, their horses being looked after by Sandy, the Land Army girl who had taken care of them on their first visit. Sandy, however, was now not wearing her Land Army gear; she was now demobbed, but had elected to stay on to look after the 'beautiful shires.'

They were warmly welcomed by Lorna and Horry when they arrived almost simultaneously, Jack overtaking the riders in the last quarter mile.

"Come in, come in, the coffee's ready," Lorna told them, "and I'm showing off, I've got some real coffee at long last."

"That must be a sure sign the war is over and that we won," boomed Jack.

"I'll believe that when I can get as much petrol as I need," Fred responded.

But it was going to be a long time in the austere period after the war ended before butter, bacon, even bread which was now rationed, could be bought in abundance.

They settled around Lorna's big kitchen table to sample this real coffee. After nearly six years of coffee out of a bottle it tasted, as Jack pronounced, "Nectar of the gods."

When the men stood to go and inspect the caravan, Margaret asked, "Lorna, dear, while they are planning to keep the wheels of British industry turning, do you think we could see the shires?"

"Oh yes, please," Anni echoed, "I have never seen them."

"Right, off we go then."

They met Sandy as they approached the stables who took them to each box in turn, giving a run-down on its occupant and its foibles - they each seemed to possess their own individual little eccentricities and mannerisms.

"Just like people I suppose, when you come to think of it," Moira observed.

"You mean just like other people," Anni suggested, with the accent on 'other.'

Meanwhile the men examined the caravan. Steel base frame and towing attachment, wooden frame, aluminium sheeting exterior, and so on.

"I think we've got to start from basics," Fred suggested, "we need to get a design out, something a bit more streamlined than the pre-war ones, and perhaps in three sizes, a small one for two people, a medium-sized one for four and a larger one for six. As I see it the ends would all the be the same, we would just stretch the middle."

"Well, one thing you've got to give thought to is the lavatory. On this one it's just a bucket under a seat in the corner, concealed by a curtain."

"Perhaps we can design a sort of chemically charged container removable from outside," Ernie suggested, and continued, "what about washing?"

"You wash in the kitchen sink. In a caravan all sorts of things double up, beds become settees and so on."

Fred was looking at the towing mechanism.

"Ernie, do you reckon we could make that?"

"We could make it alright, but with the comparatively small quantities we would want it might be cheaper to buy it in. Who made this one?"

They could just make out the name 'Fryers of Cambridge.'

"They may not be around any more. Hundreds of firms went bust in the first months of the war," Fred suggested.

And so the discussion went on. It seems difficult to understand that there was so much to know about making a simple object like a caravan.

"It's a damned good job we didn't decide to go into making aeroplanes," Fred remarked, as they made their way back to join their respective spouses, the latter still marvelling at the power and beauty of those magnificent creatures.

Over lunch, during which the men studiously avoided talking shop, Lorna raised the question as to where they would recruit the senior people, managing director and marketing director or manager.

"We haven't got round to that yet," Fred replied. "I doubt if there are any ready-made people in those categories. We shall probably have to train them up."

"You know," said Horry, "you could do worse than contact The Officers Association. That was formed after the Great War to assist ex-service officers get jobs. That's how I came to join Whitbreads."

"Crikey, there must have been a queue a mile long for your job," Jack joked.

"Well, I had an appraisal at The Officers Association. They card-indexed me and sent me for an interview to the brewery. They must have taken a liking to me, since I knew little about farming and nothing at all about hops, but they must have thought I was a good organiser so they gave me the job on a six-month trial. I've been here ever since," he added.

"Actually," said Lorna, "they asked him if he had a photograph of his wife. He produced one and got the job. That's how it happened."

"You know, there's a good deal of truth in that," Horry continued, following the laughter from their guests. "We have to attend all sorts of functions at the brewery, visit places where the shires are on show, as well as look after overseas visitors here. I presume that will all start again in the near future. It's essential therefore that the manager here has a presentable better half."

"Or in your case, infinitely better half," Fred jested.

"What would have happened if you had been a teetotaller like the guvnor here?" asked Ernie.

"I doubt if they would consider anybody in that category. As for the guvnor, as you call him, being a teetotaller, that, I imagine, would have got him drummed out of the regiment - at least in his day when the Crimea was on."

"That's one I owe you, Horry Digby."

The party broke up. Fred and Margaret rode slowly home. When they reached the stables Margaret descended from her saddle on to the mounting block instead of sliding off to the ground as she usually did, and walked round to fold Lady Jane's muzzle in her arms.

"We shall not be going out together for a few months, my darling," she said. "I shall miss you very much."

Janey understood perfectly, and whinnied in reply. She was pleased she had been told; she would have worried otherwise. Horses are incredibly intelligent.

Fred, unsaddling Dylan nearby, heard this exchange.

"So you have made the big decision then?"

"Yes, my love, I am going to do everything according to Dr Power's orders, the right sort of food, right sort of exercise and not more than a bottle of Whitbreads per day."

"Pint or quart?"

"I think I had better stick to Wincarnis don't you?"

"If it does all it says it does." They laughed together. "You go on in; I will rub them down and turn them out."

Margaret made her way into the house. She was feeling rather more tired than she had expected to feel. The Hop Farm was not a tremendous distance away and they had not hurried. Admittedly she had had a larger lunch than she normally gave herself, that might be the cause of the lethargy she was experiencing. She sank into an armchair deciding to wait for Fred to come and pull off her riding boots, and almost immediately fell sound asleep. When Fred came in he met Rose at the bottom of the stairway. They both looked into the kitchen, expecting to find Margaret there, but failing to find her went across the hall to the sitting room. Fred was just about to speak when Rose took his arm and held her finger to her lips. She took a rug off the nearby sofa and gently placed it over her stepmother. With Fred she then retreated to the kitchen.

"Margaret has just told Janey she won't be riding her for a while," Fred imparted to Rose. "She probably realised she had overdone it a little, going over to Beltring. Do you think she's alright? Should we get John Power?"

"Good Lord, no. I will keep an eye on her, but she will be as right as rain in a couple of hours. I'm pleased she's given up the riding though. With a first baby at her age you can't be too careful."

"Right, I'll get myself a bath."

Rose's estimation was almost spot on. Margaret awoke just before seven o'clock, found the rug on her and realised she must have been very sound asleep not to have heard who it was had covered her up. As she stretched her arms Rose poked her head round the doorway.

"How do you feel?"

"I suddenly came over very tired. I think that was a warning shot not to overdo things, don't you?" She was obviously going to be a sensible mum-to-be, if you follow me.

On Monday Ray got down to finding a passage to New York, pumped old ministry contacts to organise him visits to plastics firms on the eastern seaboard through the commercial attaché in

Washington, and was lucky to get a berth on a White Star ship scheduled to leave on the 5th of October. He would be away for a month or perhaps a little more, depending on the return passage availability.

So that was one project under way.

Jack had a bright idea regarding the interior design of the caravan, the chassis and exterior providing no problems.

"We at Shorts have to put quarts into pint pots inside the flying boats you know. There are one or two people at Rochester who worked on the design of the pre-war ones. There could be somebody there who could put his mind to fitting up a caravan. I'm thinking in particular of several people of different disciplines who will be pensioned off shortly, but could still take on a temporary job. I'll put my ear to the ground tomorrow."

"These are utility jobs compared to aircraft fittings, I should think," Fred replied.

"Oh, war time fittings were pretty basic. Anyway, I'll see what I can find out. Now I have the new MD starting on the 1st of October I shall have a bit more time to myself."

Jack mentioned to the Chief Design Engineer the type of chap he was looking for on behalf of a friend.

"Richard Coombs might fill the bill," he was told. "He's two years overdue for retirement, but as fit as a flea; he even still referees under fifteen's football on Saturday's. I understand he's on the new release list."

"Where does he live?"

"Snodland."

"That's only just up the road from where my friend has his plant. Ask him if he will come along to my office during his dinner hour for five minutes, will you?"

"Certainly, sir."

Richard Coombs came along to see Jack, confirmed he would be delighted to talk to Mr Chandler at the weekend or any evening, and that he was scheduled for retirement at the end of the year. This he did. Fred was impressed with his knowledge and above all his lively mind as exemplified by his saying, "There will be new materials available soon, sir, better wearing, brighter colours and so on, as soon as this nylon becomes available, and the mixture cloths, too."

So it was arranged he would come in on Saturday mornings, when being 'staff' at Shorts, he did not work, and get the feel of Sandbury Engineering.

So that was another project under way.

The unknowns of course which exercised all their minds at one time or another was how Harry and David would be fitted in, even whether they would want to be fitted in. For six long years they had exercised the skills of killing other people without getting killed themselves. There would be little call for those talents back at Sandbury. It would be true they had learnt man-management skills in as tough an environment as could be conceived, but on the other hand they had doubtless lost any technological skills they might have possessed, in David's case at considerable expense. As Jack said, "They can soon learn the technology side of things. We have just got to see whether they can settle or not after all they have been through."

And this was a problem hundreds of thousands of men now had to face. Only recently facing the terror of eight-hour night flights in bombers over Germany, weeks of filth and rain in the jungle, the merciless pounding of Atlantic gales or the nerve-racking incarceration in submarines, they would now have to be ordinary instead of extraordinary, for that was what they had been.

Fred summed it up as it could only be summed up, "Well, we shall just have to wait and see."

On Tuesday 25th of September Cecely took an early train down to Sandbury and was met at the station at 9.26 by Greta proudly wearing her new engagement ring. Together they walked to Country Style where Mrs Draper and her sister awaited them. There were already two prospective customers in the shop. Cecely and Greta therefore waited until the sales, or possibly 'swops' as people who didn't buy were known in the trade, were registered.

With a break in the flow of customers - it must be said that usually on Tuesday mornings the flow was more of a trickle - the four ladies discussed the arrival of a rather posh speaking 'junior sales.' It was decided that Greta would come in the following day, Wednesday, for the rest of the week to understudy Mrs Draper and her sister, and then take 'second sales' on the following Monday. She soon got used to calling people 'madam' as her mother had before her, and enjoyed working in an atmosphere of quality goods. On her first Saturday they were busy, and she found herself serving two customers at the same time on several occasions, a taxing task for a skilled sales lady, but with a minor panic here and there she managed quite well. When she arrived back at The Bungalow that evening though at a little after six o'clock, the reply she gave to Jane when she was asked, mischievously,

"Going to the dance tonight dear?"

was strictly Benenden sixth form.

***

Chapter Twenty-Eight

Dieter's wounds were very painful as he sat on the hard seats of the Dakota and was bumped about, not only on takeoff, but also on the flight, the weather being very stormy. Seated either side of him were the two lieutenants, neither of them making any conversation with him.

'Rather unusual,' Dieter thought, 'I always understood Americans never stop talking.'

However, without letting it appear on the surface, he was ecstatic at the fact he had saved himself from the gulag, from torture, degradation and almost certain death, and that soon he would be back in his home country, a prisoner, true, but at least a prisoner of civilised people. As he sat congratulating himself on his good fortune, and how excited Rosa and his parents would be to know he was no longer a Russian captive, the American female captain made her way down the aircraft to him.

"How are your wounds, major?"

"Not too bad," he answered, with his best attempt at a smile, "the bumping about doesn't help."

"Oh well, it won't be long now." She turned and left. As she did so the lieutenants each turned towards him.

"You English, bud?" asked one, "We were told you were a German. We weren't told you were an English major."

"I'm sorry to have to disillusion you, gentlemen, but I am, or was, a German major."

"Waal, I never heard a German talking English like you do. How did you get wounded, the war being over now five months, and all?"

"I was shot escaping from the Russians."

"Hey, tell us all about it. We guessed you must be valuable for two of us to be detailed for escort, so how come you're so highly prized?"

"I didn't know I was. I've been working on the Russian war crimes organisation as an interpreter and as a prosecutor."

"You mean you been prosecuting other Germans?"

"All sorts, Germans, Austrians, Hungarians, every eastern bloc nationality you can think of was pressed into working as guards on the concentration camps."

"Did you get any from Auschwitz?"

"Yes, I was stationed there for a while."

"And those that were condemned by the Russian court, were they allowed to appeal?"

"Definitely not. Depending on where the court was they were shot within minutes sometimes."

"Gee, major, I sure would like to talk to you. When I get home I'm going to write a book on what I've seen and heard over here, not the fighting scene you understand, I'm not a front line man. Would you be prepared to talk with me if I can fix it?"

Dieter thought quickly. 'If I do him a good turn, he will do me one and contact Rosa if they lock me up.'

"Yes, of course," he replied. The other lieutenant joined in.

"What did you think of the Russians, major."

"Whatever may be thought of the Russians, you have to consider the starting point to be the iniquitous treatment to which they were subjected in the first place. Having said that, with one or two very notable exceptions, I found them to be coarse and brutal. Again you have to appreciate they are not one people. The soldiers from, say, Ukraine or White Russia are as different again to those from Kazahkstan or beyond the Urals."

So they talked on until they heard the engines throttling back indicating they would land shortly.

And land they did, with a bump which made Dieter barely suppress crying out.

"You OK, major?"

"Yes, thank you very much." But he wasn't 'OK.' That last bump had opened up the thigh wound which became immediately obvious as the blood saturated the fatigue trousers he had been given to travel in. As the aircraft came to a halt one of the lieutenants called the captain.

"The major's wounds opened up, captain."

Other people on the aircraft were all then looking towards Dieter wondering what the devil a wounded major was doing flying out of Berlin.

The two lieutenants and the captain clustered around Dieter.

"Slip your pants down," she asked.

"I haven't been asked to do that lately," he replied, to roars of laughter from the lieutenants and a tight-lipped response from the captain. In the meantime the aircraft had come to a halt, its passengers standing ready to depart, those having to pass the wounded major looking curiously to see what was going on.

"Ask the co-pilot for the medical box," she ordered one of her young officers. When he returned with the co-pilot, another lieutenant, his old dressing was removed and he was tightly re-bandaged.

"Personally I would let you bleed to death," was the co-pilot's parting shot as he returned to the cockpit.

Dieter kept silent as he pulled his pants up. That chap could have been witness to any of a myriad of evil episodes perpetrated by the Nazis, which would leave a scar on the face of Germany for all time.

They were the last off the plane, to be met by a sergeant with a staff car. He saluted the captain, rather sloppily Dieter considered, wondering whether it was because he was saluting a female officer, or whether he was generally sloppy anyway, or whether all Americans were sloppy full stop.

They travelled into Kassel but before reaching the city centre turned off into a leafy suburb, not as leafy as it would have been since a number of the trees had been blown to bits by the bombing. At length they reached a large house standing in its own grounds, but as Dieter immediately noticed provided with a substantial barbed wire fence all around it, and a military police post at the entrance. An MP came out to check their car, giving another sloppy salute to the captain sitting in the front passenger seat, waving them through with the other hand. The general air of unmilitary, offhand conduct offended Dieter's soldierly upbringing until he told himself, 'what have we got to be so proud about.'

The lieutenant, the one who was intending to write the book, was detailed to take Dieter to his room, which he found was plainly furnished with just a bed, small table and chair, wash-stand and mirror. Being October already, the weather was becoming quite cold, so he was pleased to note a double radiator had produced a welcoming warmth to otherwise spartan accommodation.

"I'm Lieutenant Parry, major; I will come and collect you at six o'clock for dinner."

"I won't know when it is six o'clock," Dieter smiled. "The Russians almost fought among themselves over my service watch when I was captured."

"I'll find you a clock. Anyway it's only a half hour wait."

"May I ask what is to happen to me?"

"The colonel will tell you all that in the morning. You must be fairly important to be here."

Dieter decided not to question his guard (?) escort (?) - he would doubtless be put in the picture in due course. One thing was certain - it was a thousand per cent better than being in the gulag. His bowels turned over at the thought.

"Where is the lavatory?" he asked his warder.

"Just at the end of the corridor. You are free to go about on this landing, but please do not wander elsewhere until you have been assessed tomorrow. After dinner you are to see the medical officer, purely to check on your wounds. He's not on the permanent staff here, but visits most evenings. I will be back in a half hour then," and with that he left, leaving Dieter to think what a civilised form of incarceration he apparently was to enjoy.

Dieter's thoughts after the meal were, that, firstly, the Yanks knew how to look after themselves, secondly, why did they all take such large portions and then leave at least a quarter of what they had on their plates? He felt a bit of a pig having scoffed everything he was given, but being the good solider he was he justified this by considering he knew not what he would receive tomorrow, so stoke up now!

Despite being tired he slept fitfully, his newly dressed wounds still giving him trouble, particularly the shoulder wound which, healing rapidly, itched like hell.

Lieutenant Parry, now known as Marvin after having a few beers over dinner, but still respectfully calling Dieter 'major,' collected his charge for breakfast, and at nine o'clock took him to the colonel's office. The colonel was of a professorial appearance rather than that of a warrior, in that he badly needed a haircut as compared to the usual almost shaven headed appearance of the American field officers.

"Major von Hassellbek, please sit down."

'Somewhat different to the Russians' was Dieter's immediate thought, but he then had to admit to himself he had not after all, been slaughtering Americans, as he had Russians.

"I have, major, your papers here in respect of certain trials in which you were involved with our Russian allies. You seemed to have no compunction in sending men from your own army found guilty of war crimes, for execution."

He looked over the top of his half-glasses with piercing blue eyes.

"Sir, had those men carried out those crimes, and had they been in my own regiment, or even my own family, I would have had them shot."

"Do you know the extent of the atrocities committed by the Nazis?"

"No, sir, I don't. All I know is what I have seen in Poland, and what my wife told me who was in Ravensbruk."

"Yes, we were told about that. You mention family. What would you have done if your sister had appeared before you?"

"It would depend on the gravity of the charges and whether they were proven. She would have received, if found guilty, the sentence prescribed by the law, less a reduction for mitigating circumstances, if any. In the case of the Russian trials there was no question whatsoever of the existence of mitigating circumstances."

"Yes, we have noticed that. Well now, down to what we require of you. Firstly, I require you to undergo in-depth questioning of all you know about the Russians, not only their legal system, but everything you have learnt from being with them all these months. You may not know this, but we and the British are still in a state of 'alert' regarding the Red Army, having considered it likely they would try and at least push us out of Germany, despite the agreement reached at Yalta and elsewhere. It is considered that hostility between our two blocs will increase from now on; the only reason they don't make a move now is because we have the atom bomb."

Dieter listened attentively.

"We are commencing the trials of the senior war criminals in Nuremberg shortly. At present you have prisoner of war status. We will release you from that if you are prepared to join our interpreter team there, purely to check on whether the Russian interpreters are putting the true meaning of the evidence to their judges. As you will probably have guessed, the judges will come from all three allies, possibly four if the French stick their noses in."

'He doesn't like the French either,' Dieter concluded. The colonel continued.

"You will not be part of the court; you will sit in a back room monitoring the Russian translation of the evidence which could be given in English, German, French or Russian. We shall have to employ others for Polish etc. That's all for now. You will spend the next three days with our intelligence people, at the end of which I shall require you to give me an answer regarding Nuremberg. Any questions?"

"How long will the Nuremberg trial last, sir?"

"God knows, could be months, could be over in a few weeks. Anything else?"

"Could I contact my wife in Bruksheim to let her know I am safe from the Russians?"

"That has already been done."

Dieter was struck dumb at this statement. At length he said in little more than a whisper.

"Thank you, sir, thank you very much."

The colonel said no more, but called out,

"Marvin." The young lieutenant bustled in.

"Take the major to Room Twelve."

"Yes, sir."

Dieter arose, clicked his heels, turned and followed Marvin to a room where three civilians were seated, one who looked as though he would be useful in a bar brawl, the other two fortyish, nondescript, one of whom rose to his feet, shook hands with Dieter and introduced him to the other two.

"What's your given name, major?"

"Dieter, sir."

"No Sirs here. We are officers of the Central Intelligence Agency. Our job is to find out from you absolutely everything you know about the Russians right down to what sort of toilet roll they use if any - get me?"

So for almost three days they extracted every bit of, what in many cases Dieter felt was totally useless information, all of which was recorded on a machine, presumably to be typed and filed elsewhere.

In the meantime Rosa was living on a cloud having been given the news about Dieter. The information had arrived by letter; the post was nearly back to normal now after five months of peace. It was from US Interrogation Centre, Kassel, and true presumably to their normal predilection for secrecy was not signed, only initialled. It read,

'Madam,
We have your husband Major Dieter von Hassellbek with us here. He will be contacting you in a few days.
Signed
JCH

The letter had been delivered long after she had left for work that morning. She could not get back to the flat at lunch time. When she eventually left the Klinik at eight o'clock on a dark cold blustery night and arrived home, she poked her head in the sitting room doorway in passing, called out, "I'm going to shower," and before her mother could tell her there was a letter for her, she had disappeared into the bathroom.

Returning from her shower, dressed in a big white towelling robe, too long, too much wrap-around, sleeves turned up halfway up the arms - it had belonged to Fritz before she took possession of it - and drying her hair vigorously, she spotted the letter on the sideboard.

"This for me?" she enquired.

"Well, there is only one von Hassellbek in this flat, but what she is doing receiving mail from someone in the American army I don't know."

Rosa looked at the postmark.

"Kassel," she noted, "perhaps it's from that nice American who met Dieter in the Russian Zone." She eagerly opened the envelope, read its contents and promptly shrieked with excitement.

"Dieter is here, look, Dieter is here. He must have escaped, he's with the Americans."

Her hand trembling with excitement, tears beginning to flow down her cheeks, she handed the all-important piece of paper to her mother whilst she in turn held the letter so that both she and Fritz could read it together. After a short while Fritz digested its contents and came to the conclusion that it did not mean Dieter was free. It stated 'will contact you,' that did not necessarily mean in person, he was still a prisoner of war.

"I don't care as long as he is not with the Russians. At least I know I shall see him again now. Now I must telephone to Ulm."

The von Hassellbek house was in the south west of Germany in the French Zone, telephone communications to which were unreliable to say the least. However, at midnight a sleepy voice answered, "von Hassellbek."

"Uncle Konrad. Dieter has escaped from the Russians and is with the Americans."

There was a heartfelt "thank God" in reply, followed by "How do you know?"

Rosa told him all she knew, and that as soon as she had more news she would telephone again. "How are things with you?" she asked.

"We live on a knife edge here," was the reply. "Most of the troops in this vicinity are French colonial men, Senegalese, North African and so on. They steal and rape, brutalise old people, it is appalling. Their officers either have no control over them, or more likely encourage them in their evil behaviour. I have heard of what certain of our troops did in Poland and Russia, as well as their behaviour to you and your poor fellow prisoners on the march from Ravensbruk. The French troops are doing the same here. But I must not depress you in your hour of great joy. Please do let me know future developments, and give our kindest regards to your mother and step-father. Goodnight, my dear."

Rosa passed the information on to her parents sad that, despite the relief the conflict was ending, they were having to suffer new tribulation at the hands of their conquerors, seemingly totally out of control.

On Wednesday the 10th Dieter was again called to the colonel's office. The latter wasted no time.

"Have you decided about Nuremberg, major?"

"Yes, sir, I shall be pleased to help."

"Right. Your discharge papers from prisoner of war status have been gotten ready. You will be paid as from today at the standard translator's rate. You will be given a return rail pass to Bruksheim. You will return here on Sunday evening for our flight to Nuremberg at 0700 Monday 15th, returning each weekend, flying conditions permitting. If you visit our commissariat with this requisition, they will fit you out with civilian clothing. I think that's all. Any questions?"

"I don't think so, sir. Thank you for giving me my life back."

"Well, I warn you, there will be many who will be far from well-intentioned towards you, especially when some of the evidence is produced."

"I understand, sir."

"Marvin." The young lieutenant appeared at the double.

"Take Herr von Hassellbek to the commissariat please with this requisition."

"Yes, sir."

Dieter noted - he was no longer a major. He shrugged and told himself he was lucky to be alive, millions of his former comrades were not and another million were suffering a living death.

Fitted out now as a civilian, Dieter made his way to the station and an hour later was speeding towards Bruksheim and the Strobel flat.

Arriving at five o'clock in the afternoon when it was nearly dark produced a total anti-climax. No one answered the door. He decided he would walk to the Klinik. He pressed the lift button but it was engaged and he therefore decided to walk down. As he walked down, the lift came up past him, but as the back of the lift was towards him on this landing he was unable to see it contained not only Mr and Mrs Fritz Strobel, but Mrs Rosa von Hassellbek as well. He walked to the Klinik only five minutes away, asked for Frau Doktor von Hassellbek, was told that she was not on duty until eight o'clock that evening, turned and made his way back to the flat.

The lift had malfunctioned again. He climbed the stairs, knocked again on the Strobel door to be welcomed by a laughing, crying, almost inarticulate Rosa.

And that is all we shall read about Dieter in these chronicles.

Or is it?

We shall see.

* * *

Chapter Twenty-Nine

With Ah Chin and the whole family waving them goodbye, and the children running behind them as far as the padang, Harry and party drove off into Muar for a good night's sleep. There was a certain amount of concern by the staff at the sight of a fully grown leopard being led in, along with very considerable interest from the guests, but the qualms of the extremely pretty Chinese receptionist and the Malay under-manager were soon put at rest.

The next morning they had a six o'clock breakfast and were on their way by six thirty, arriving in Charles Coates' former apartment at ten thirty or thereabouts. On the way they passed the spot where Harry, his Australian friends, the young English lieutenant and his company of Rajputs had battled with the Japanese.

"The three Australians were beheaded just there," he told them, "I was lying up there with two dead Rajputs covering most of me." He stopped briefly, then pointing to Paddy's badge of rank on his wrist, he continued, "I was wearing one of those then, and just as the Jap was about to bayonet me - he'd already bayonetted the Rajputs even though they were dead - he spotted my wrist-strap, stuck his bayonet in the ground and tried to get it off me. He had trouble with the buckles on the strap, was yelled at by the officer, so he dropped my arm, pulled his rifle out of the ground and ran back to the main party. That's how close I came to not being here."

And Paddy's inevitable comment? - "Bloody hell."

They were welcomed with tears of joy by Mark Chea and his wife. They had heard from the judge and been sent money to continue to look after the property.

"Now, what happened to the Railton?" Harry asked.

"Come with me, sir," Mark replied. He led them to the garage, opened the doors, to show one large open empty space. He paced deliberately from the doorway to the rear wall, twelve paces. He led them outside. He then paced from the front of the building to the back wall, fifteen paces and a bit. All four immediately cottoned on to what he was demonstrating.

"A false wall," Harry exclaimed, "the Railton has been behind that false wall all through the war and the Japs didn't realise it."

"Well, sir, they didn't know it was there in the first place, and the officers we had here were senior ones. The strange thing was their drivers used to park the staff car in there, and it never occurred to them the outside was longer than the inside."

"That would be because it's a big garage to start with," David suggested.

"Well, you see, sir, it was also John's workshop, although the Japanese stole all the tools as soon as they arrived."

"I will talk to the judge when I get to England, and see whether he would like it shipped back to him there," Harry told Mark. "In any event you know he will look after you both."

"Yes, sir. Judge very honourable man."

They said their goodbyes to the Cheas and started on their way back to Singapore, Harry pointing out two places they blew up in the early days before they were driven north of Frasers Hill.

On the 17th of September they returned via the main trunk road to Singapore, dropping Harry and Chantek off first. As they arrived Reuben came out to meet them.

"You've a passage home, Harry. I went to see the ship's colonel this morning to ask about Chantek. I had to wait around an hour or so while he went to see the captain I imagine. I told him there was no way you would go without her even if you had to swim, and piled on the agony about your heroic deeds in the jungle and so on."

"Silly sod," Harry interjected.

"As I was saying until I was so rudely interrupted, I piled on the agony; he in turn must have been caught up with my rhetoric, because he returned, all smiles, saying they would be delighted to have such a beautiful passenger. Oh, and they said they would take the leopard as well."

Harry turned to David.

"You see what I've had to put up with all these years?"

"Now the really good news."

There was a brief pause.

"I'm coming with you."

"And you call that good news?" Harry exclaimed in mock exasperation. "Now tell me the really good news - when?"

"On board Friday night, sail Saturday morning. Arrive Liverpool 29th October, provided we don't hit a stray mine on the way."

"Is he always as cheerful as this?" David asked.

"He's having one of his happy days today," Harry replied. "Reuben, my old son, if we get a couple of oars out to help with the rowing do you think that would get us there any quicker?"

"You would be catching crabs all the time I shouldn't wonder."

"Well, I must get back. I'll come and see you during the week. Good luck to you both in the meantime." David and Paddy drove off.

As we have seen so many times in the course of these narratives, things do not necessarily always go according to plan. When David and Paddy were driven up to battalion HQ they were met by the adjutant.

"We're off to Java day after tomorrow. Will you both go and see the CO straight away?"

They hastened to the CO's office, knocked, entered, saluted and were faced with a map of Java in general and Batavia in particular, on the CO's wall at the side of his desk.

"Things are turning nasty with the Indonesians," Haimish told them without preamble. "They have started killing POW's and preventing their movement to ports from which they can be evacuated. Our brigade is to be part of a small force, along with a handful of Dutch troops, to go to Tanjong Priok and into Batavia, the capital. The Japs have been ordered to maintain law and order until we arrive. What the hell is going to happen in the rest of the country, God only knows."

At 0400 hours on the 19th of September 'R' Battalion was rudely awakened, breakfasted and at 0600 was on the march to Keppel Harbour to board 'The City of Canterbury' for Batavia, not knowing from Adam what to expect when they arrived.

Would they march in? Have to fight their way in? And once in a town like that would they be at the mercy of snipers? Haimish had to prepare for all eventualities. He knew the Heihos were well armed, they knew the territory, and if they were fighting for their independence they could not afford to lose. Brigade intelligence had allocated the three battalion positions in major office buildings, planned from pre-war streets maps from the Dutch consulate in Singapore. Having reached and occupied them they were on their own.

The landing was unopposed, unopposed that is by the Indonesians, but met with a full company of Japanese troops lined up on the quayside, all fully armed, who, as the brigadier, Haimish, and the brigade major came ashore presented arms. The brigadier saluted in return, the Japanese major in command gave the 'order arms,' or the Japanese equivalent, then screamed in the guttural manner of the race a welcome to the British soldiers, or at least that was what the trio assumed he was stating. Their assumptions were correct, in that a studious young man with thick glasses, an example of what all the Japanese soldiers looked like if you believed the propaganda dished out to the allied soldiery before you met them, translated,

"Major Sasaki welcomes you to Java, sir."

"Ask the major to march your men off, and for him to come and see me in this building at six o'clock this evening."

An intelligence officer produced a street plan and indicated what was to be brigade HQ.

The interpreter passed on the message, the major saluted and bowed, gave his orders to a sergeant major - a very important rank in the Japanese army - and they marched off quite silently in their canvas and rubber boots.

It took the rest of the day to get everybody off the ship, less a platoon left behind to guard the ship overnight.

'R' Battalion found itself in a bank building, sleeping on concrete floors until a supply ship with Ordnance Corps troops aboard brought them charpoys and other necessaries. In the meantime they had used Japanese labour to assist in wiring a perimeter around their building. It was unlikely the Indonesians would attack in any strength in the centre of Batavia, but it made good military sense to be prepared, if only to indicate to the troops they were now in a war situation.

After a week, Haimish decided it was time to start patrols out of the city, 'just,' as he put it 'to show the flag.' The problem was they had no flags to show, the Heihos neither knew nor cared whether the Europeans were Dutch or not, as a result there were several minor fire fights, with few casualties. As these were pretty inconclusive Paddy said to David,

"Sir, couldn't we try what we did in Palestine before the war?"

"Well, as I was not in Palestine before the war - I presume you mean this war, I knew you were probably there before the Boer War - perhaps you could enlighten me."

"If the intelligence people there had an idea the terrorists blowing up the pipe lines lived in a certain village, or had information from paid informers, the powers that be would get us out and surround it before dawn. If we had gone during the day the people we were after would have seen us coming and vanished into the hills. So we would surround the village, all men would be screened by the informers from the inside of a truck through a spy hole, any known or suspicious looking ones were taken in for questioning."

"What do you mean by questioning?"

"Well, sir, I wouldn't know. I was only a buckshee rifleman, but I daresay a little gentle persuasion could have been dished out."

David thought for a moment.

"Good idea," he said, "these people have got to come back to their kampongs at night to feed."

"And have a bit of the other," Paddy added.

"Yes, that as well. You can't live on bread alone, or rice for that matter."

"We have to."

"We're different."

Ruminating on their melancholy state they were silent for a few moments.

"Let's go and see the colonel."

In the meantime the battalion intelligence officer, one Lieutenant Norman Beverley, had been possessed of a similar idea. He was the 'Intelligence Officer' because he had been to Oxford. What was not generally known was he had barely scraped through getting a degree more or less at the bottom of the pile. To put it plainly, in most respects he was as dim as a TocH lamp, but had been appointed I.O. because he spoke with the equivalent of two plums in his mouth and had been to Oxford, don't you know!

He was however, entitled to one good idea in an otherwise barren life, and the one referred to above was it. As a result Haimish had a word with the brigadier, who told him to go ahead, so the first foray was planned. It was to be a company affair, around a hundred men, two thirds to surround the Kampong, another third to search it for weapons and Heihos. The battalion vehicles now having caught up, three three-tonners were to carry the troops, escorted by jeeps fitted with light machine guns. The plan was to drive out to a largish kampong called Tanjongbojo some ten miles south of Batavia, stop some two miles from the village and then foot it the rest of the way. As they had no means of previous reconnaissance the surrounding of the dwellings in the dark was going to require a considerable amount of on the spot organisation, a thought which gave Haimish some concern. The last thing he would want would be for his men to be shooting at each other in the dark. Strict orders were given therefore that there was to be no firing unless they could positively identify the target.

"Which means that if the bastards identify us first we're sitting ducks," was the general, and reasonably legitimate view.

At least the kampong was not surrounded by jungle. It lay off the road on the bank of a fairly wide river, with coconut and palm oil trees between it and the road, some two hundred yards away. Swiftly they surrounded it on its three landward sides; anyone trying to escape into the river would be taking a chance. There were water snakes in there, some of them really venomous, to say nothing of the occasional crocodile on the banks who might well relish an Indonesian breakfast.

The raid was a great success in several aspects. Firstly some twenty of the Japanese Type 38 rifles were discovered, over a dozen hand grenades, and two Nambu pistols, along with a quantity of ammunition. As a result the thirty odd men judged to be between the ages of eighteen and forty were arrested, along with the headman of the kampong, to be taken back to the security people in Batavia. However, this success was not the prime reason why the surround and search was remembered in the eyes of the squaddies who took part. Indonesian girls are in the main very beautiful. In the dawn's early light, running from their huts with next to nothing, and frequently nothing on, as imminent fear of rape or worse drove them into the centre of the village, they presented a tableau the like of which Thomas Atkins had not witnessed since the Zulu wars.

As David said to Paddy later, "And to think I didn't bring my camera!"

After the first kampong raid they made several more in different directions, but as the word got around over the next month or so they achieved less in the way of the capture of arms, but at least they imposed their presence; as a result there were far fewer incidents in Batavia itself. However, things were not improving inland. In October extremists seized Surabaya airfield some four hundred miles from Batavia on the eastern end of the main island of Java. Thirty thousand POW's and civilian internees had been assembled there, living in tents and guarded by Japanese troops, food being flown into them until shipping could be found to take them out. A few troops from an Indian regiment were in charge, some of whom, along with a British captain, had been killed in the attack.

Haimish was called to brigade HQ. When he returned he called an 'O' Group of his company commanders, along with his 2 i/c David and his RSM.

"We have a little job to do," he announced. "They are having a little problem at a place called Surabaya where the Indonesians have taken over the airfield and have killed some of our people. There are thousands of POW's and civilians congregated there; there could be a blood bath if things get worse. The original plan was for us to fly from our airfield here and drop on the Surabaya field. Then they discovered a small problem with that plan. There are only some one hundred and fifty parachutes in south east Asia, so a brigade drop is out of the question. Similarly since a battalion drop would require a minimum of six hundred with its ancillary bibs and bobs, that is out of the question. The plan therefore is that a company will drop at first light, secure the landing area, aircraft will then fly the remainder of the battalion in."

"How many aircraft are there available, sir?" David asked.

"They have six Dakotas; will carry a total of one hundred and twenty men. I propose 'A' Company to do the job, with half a dozen people to set up a signal facility and one mortar section. What's your company strength, Arnold?" he asked 'A' Company commander.

"Ninety-four this morning. We have a handful sick and six on the VD flight back to Singapore."

"Right, well charge them when they get back. We've got to stamp on this VD business, there are plenty of french letters at the MI room. No need for anyone to get the clap."

He turned to David.

"I'd like you and Mr O'Riordan to go on the jump so as to plan the distribution of the people on the planes landing after the runway has been secured by the parachutists. I shall come in on the first plane. It's roughly four hundred miles from here to Surabaya. That means if takeoff is at 0330 hours you will drop at around 0550 hours. Allowing time for refuelling and swapping crews, we should have two companies in with you during the day and the third first thing on Thursday. Dropping that early will catch them on the hop, added to which since they will never have seen a mass parachute descent before it will probably frighten the life out of them."

"Do you know what, sir? The thought of dropping on them frightens the life out of me," David replied, with a muffled 'hear, hear' coming from Paddy. Haimish smiled,

"One look at the RSM here and they will run a mile. There is one thing however that concerns me. With all those poor sex-starved camp ladies being suddenly joined by a battalion of sex-starved paratroopers anything could happen."

"And probably will, sir," Paddy concluded.

That evening 'A' Company along with David's little party from HQ Company moved out to the airfield where the six Dakotas had arrived from Singapore, complete with their parachutes. A young squadron leader in charge of the two flights unrolled two maps, one of the general area of Surabaya, the second a pre-war layout of the airfield and surrounding features.

"The weather forecast is not good," he told David, "wind should be moderate but heavy rain could be expected. Now, the airfield is due south of the town. So as to gain as much surprise as possible we will come in at low level from the north between the mainland here and Madura here. We should be on them before they know what is happening. We do not of course know what they have got in the way of anti aircraft guns, or whether they know how to use them if they have. We shall go in in line, very close together so as to get you all in as tight a drop as possible. What sort of height do you think?"

David thought for a moment.

"As low as possible, say four to five hundred feet."

"Jolly good. With a bit of luck we shall be in and gone at that level before they have a chance to load."

They all snatched a few hours' sleep after their evening meal and at 0300 were aboard their aircraft, parachutes fitted ready to go. When the squadron leader picked his way to get through the twenty heavily laden men, including David and Paddy, in the leading aircraft - David would be the first to jump – a squaddie asked him,

"Who packed our parachutes, sir?"

"I understand they were unable to find trained parachute packers in south east Asia, so they got some Jap prisoners in Changi jail to do it. I wouldn't worry, although a lot of them don't see very well, as you know." He disappeared on to the flight deck, followed by 'Ha bloody ha' from said squaddie.

The aircraft took off north out to sea, then swung east for the two-hour trip to Surabaya. They met a lot of rain. David was concerned that if the weather was too overcast they would have trouble in finding the target. He was not alone in this. Flying by dead reckoning was difficult enough over territory where you could pick out rivers, towns etc; flying over the sea was a different kettle of fish altogether.

At 0500 they had some luck in that the rain stopped. At 0530 they could see the channel between the mainland and the island of Madura. They knew where they were, although it started to rain again, but not so heavily. They turned south, put the red light on. The passengers looked up. Leaving the town on their starboard the squadron leader headed for the airfield straight ahead, the others behind him closing up. Green light on - David went, followed by Paddy and Angus so quickly after him they all three landed within fifty yards of each other, the rest of the stick being strung out across the airfield, while men from the following aircraft thudded down on the rain soaked grass, or what passes for grass in Java.

As David and Paddy were snapping out of their parachutes there was a 'candle' from number three aircraft, hitting the ground only yards away from them. A 'Roman Candle,' to give it its full name, is the occasion of a parachute malfunctioning; either the parachute does not pull out of its pack, or, if it does it twists round and round so that it will not open. This is often the result of a bad exit by the jumper in that he is spun around by the slip stream of the aircraft engine thereby winding up the rigging lines, which in turn prevents the canopy from opening. The paratroopers' song, to the tune of 'John Brown's Body,' describes it graphically.

'He lay splattered on the tarmac like a lump of strawberry jam,

And he ain't going to jump no more.'

They had no time to produce more than an automatic feeling of 'poor bastard,' when they found themselves being shot at from the airport buildings. Airfields are useful places to descend upon, no rivers, no trees, no overhead power lines, no nothing. But therein lies the rub, as our friend William S would say, there is also no cover. If someone is shooting at you all you can do is go at them, firing from the hip in the hope that they will either be hit by a lucky bullet or will get the wind up and run for it. David, Paddy and Angus did just that, and were quickly joined by a dozen others near them who had just landed and divested themselves of their parachutes. Two of the latter were Bren gunners, who along with the sub-machine Stens in the hands of the three leaders were able to make an awful lot of noise even if, from the hip, their accuracy was suspect.

Reaching the long low concrete structure which served as the terminal they quickly ejected the dozen or so defenders and put them under guard in one of the rooms. In the attack three paras had been wounded, and were being attended to by the medics, while David made a speedy reconnaissance of the buildings and immediate surroundings. He gave orders to 'A' Company officers on their defensive positions to wait, what would probably seem an eternity, before the Dakotas returned.

"Weren't there supposed to be thousands of internees and POWs here, sir?" Paddy asked.

"I assumed they were on the airfield," David replied, "they must be somewhere nearby. But first things first. We must clear those parachutes otherwise they will endanger the Dakotas landing. How many prisoners have we got?"

"About twenty, sir."

"Right, get them out with those baggage carts. If our people do it they could be shot at; if they are mixed in with the prisoners it would be less likely."

"Shall I ask for volunteers, sir?"

David thought for a moment.

"No. Ask 3 platoon officer to take ten of his men for me, and move quickly before reinforcements come in from the town."

This task took just over one nail biting hour to complete. There were one or two random shots from premises way out from the airfield, on one half of the perimeter of which there was a huge swamp which prevented any incursion from that direction. At seven o'clock they received their first attack. A Japanese armoured car, taken over by the insurgents, was nosing its way down the only road from the town to the airfield followed by a couple of dozen rifle carrying Heihos. David allowed them to get within a hundred yards, then ordered heavy fire on them added to by half a dozen mortar bombs, which although not terribly destructive do make a lot of noise. It was the first time the Heihos had been in a real fire fight;

they lost half their number, they were far from happy, they ran for cover where they could find it and stayed there.

There was a more serious attack just after nine o'clock. This time they put smoke down in front of the buildings, sent the armoured car around to the flank which poured fire into the buildings so that the insurgents could make the attack under the cover of the smoke. It was partially successful in that some of the insurgents reached the defenders, resulting in some hand to hand fighting in which the attackers had little chance. They left a lot of dead behind as they withdrew under more smoke and covering fire from the armoured car.

From ten o'clock on what was already a long morning, eyes were constantly being turned to the north for the welcome sight of the Dakotas returning, ears tuned to a fine pitch to hear the throb of those Pratt and Whitney radials powering them. David, however, was worried. What would happen if, when the six aircraft landed, the armoured car suddenly appeared among them. The Dakotas carried no armament with which to defend themselves; there could be absolute mayhem. He went on to the flat roof of the building and stared down the road towards the town. The armoured car had to approach along that road. It could not get off the road until it reached the air field perimeter because of the deep monsoon ditches on either side. He called Paddy.

"Have we any plastic explosive with us?"

"I never go anywhere without it, sir."

"You're joking."

"Not at all, not at all." He unbuttoned an ammunition pouch on his webbing and produced about a pound of standard plastic, with which all paras had been issued in Europe, but which had not been considered necessary in Java.

"And I bet a few of the old Normandy types will have done the same, sir. You can get very attached to plastic after a while."

"Have a quick recce, see if there are any other silly sods like you who would walk around with bombs in their pouches." Paddy found three!

"Major Church," David called out to 'A'Company Commander a little way away.

"Yes, David, what can I do for you?"

"Arnold, who is your best shot?"

"Oh, Livingstone by a mile."

"The range from here to fifty yards outside the perimeter gate - what do you guess?"

"Two hundred yards."

"Could your Livingstone put a round into the driver's vision slot from here?"

"How big was the slot?"

"I would think about a foot wide and six inches high."

"He could hit a half crown at that distance."

"Right, let's have him up here."

Rifleman Livingstone presented himself to David on the roof, which gave a direct line of fire down the approach road. David explained what he required.

"We can't afford to let the armoured car on to the airfield. I want you, when it reaches fifty yards from the gateway, to place as many rounds as you can in or near the driver's vision aperture. With a bit of luck you will hit him, at the least he will have to stop to adjust any periscope arrangement he may have. That will give us time to bomb him out. Mr O'Riordan."

"Yes, sir."

"While it's quiet get your three men with their bombs behind that low wall at the entrance. They can then show us how to destroy a Japanese armoured car once our friend Livingstone here has halted it."

"I'll do that, sir, it will be best if I go with them, sir won't it?" and without waiting for an answer from David, he vanished down the stairway from the roof.

"Now, Arnold, can we have two of your Bren gunners up here to fire over the heads of the bombers when they run back?"

"Will do."

It went exactly according to plan. The six Dakotas came, quickly disgorged their troops, and took off again, each of them with a bullet hole or two as they came in to land. The armoured car made its run to the gate, Livingstone made his kill, the car juddered to a stalled halt and before the body of the driver could be dragged from the driving seat and replaced Paddy and his bombers finished it off. Meanwhile the two Bren gunners on the roof plastered the Heihos following the armoured car; as a result they dived for cover again leaving the bombers to cover the two hundred yards back to the buildings in a time close to that which Jesse Owens had registered in the 1936 Olympics. Altogether, as David commented afterwards, it was a very successful little party.

But it wasn't all over yet.

* * *

Chapter Thirty

It was eight o'clock or thereabouts on Thursday the 20th September, just as Megan had at last got to bed after her night shift at Sandbury Hospital, that a somewhat liberal application of the door knocker caused her to slip on her dressing gown and run downstairs to answer it. Standing there was the smallest telegram boy she had ever seen, holding the, by now, familiar envelope containing a cable, as opposed to the dreaded buff envelope containing a telegram. She quickly opened it, although her bare feet were getting frozen, it was such a cold damp morning.

"Any reply, madam?" asked the high pitched voice.

"No, no reply. Here you are." Megan gave him a shilling from the loose change on the hallstand.

"Thank you, madam, thank you very much," and as he walked away he conjectured it must have been good news; mostly they only gave him sixpence at the most.

Megan ran back up to bed, kissing the cable over and over again. It read:

'SAILING ORDUNA 30 SEPT STOP ARR LPOOL 29 OCTOBER STOP LOVE TO

ALL STOP BRINGING CHANTEEK STOP HARRY

Reading it again she stated out loud - "They've spelt Chantek wrong," as if that was of the slightest importance compared to the rest of the contents. She excitedly telephoned Rose, who in turn telephoned her father. As she was so doing Margaret came downstairs, and waiting until Rose had completed her call asked,

"What's all the excitement about?"

"Harry will be docking at Liverpool on the 29th of October, and he is bringing Chantek."

"How lovely. I am so looking forward to meeting him." Her face lost its smile for a moment.

"I do hope he likes me."

Rose realised what was contained in that rather wistful statement. It must have been an anxiety for Margaret to realise she was taking the place of someone who was as universally loved and admired as Ruth had undoubtedly been, to wonder how she would be accepted by the family and friends, and whether there would be any hidden resentment. Fortunately, as a result of her business contacts with Fred, Ernie and Ray, she had become known to the rest of the family gradually. With Harry it would be different.

"Harry will love you as we all do, have no fear," Rose assured her.

"I do hope so. Oh, I am so pleased for Megan, she must have suffered so much these past years, as you have."

There was a mini-party at Chandlers Lodge on the Saturday, not by design, it just happened. It was Lorna Digby's birthday so she and Horry had been invited over for supper. Hugh and Cecely were staying with Charles and Jane, so they were all invited for drinks, and of course no gathering would be complete without Moira and Jack. There would have been more but Anni and Ernie, with Karl, and Rosemary were visiting Ernie's relatives in Uckfield, and Greta was at the wedding of an old Benenden friend at Eastbourne, sadly minus Stanley who was in the frozen north for a while yet.

Inevitably the conversation eventually centred on what would happen to Chantek. Hugh was able to tell them that Jane had telephoned him the estimated date of arrival, that he had been in touch with the RSPCA and they would meet the ship and take her into quarantine.

There was general concern at this.

"How long is the quarantine period?" asked a worried Megan, "she will suffer badly if it is too long."

"I'm afraid it is six months. That's the bad news. The good news is that she can be brought down here to Ashford, where they have a centre, so Harry and Megan and the children can visit her at weekends at least."

Jack intervened. "Can Harry travel down with her?"

"I don't see why not. He has to pay the transport costs and costs of housing her so I see no reason why he cannot come down from Liverpool in the same vehicle."

"Can we go and vet the quarantine centre to see it's alright, do you think, Hugh?" Fred asked.

"I can see no reason why not."

"Right, I'll organise that for next weekend. I've got some petrol."

"Perhaps you can check out the travel business while you are there. I shall be in Germany for the next two to three weeks, then I am going to call it a day at the end of the year."

Saying this he turned to Cecely who took his arm, held it tight, and kissed him lightly on the cheek.

"You all heard that, didn't you?" she asked, "hands up those who didn't." There were smiles all round but no movement of hands.

"And the time is 2135 hours, army time on the 22nd of September 1945. All agreed?"

There was a universal "Yes."

"Now, get out of that," she teased.

"I have absolutely no intention of trying," he laughingly replied.

"Well, if anyone deserves a quiet life from now on it is certainly you," Jack said seriously, "and we don't know a fraction of what you have done and the friends you have lost. I give you a toast ladies and gentlemen. To Hugh, Lord Ramsford, and to all his brave comrades of the past six years."

They all stood and drank the toast, seated themselves again with the exception of Fred who asked,

"When will you be able to tell us all you have been involved in, Hugh?"

"A little under thirty years time I believe is the current position."

"You will have to post it on to me then."

"Me too," said Jack.

"And me," from Horry.

All laughed at the grey humour. We shall not call it black humour as it was too amusing, and too obvious to be that.

It was a lovely evening, with Megan as happy as all present at the thought that soon she would be in the arms of her darling Harry, the thought of which not only knotted up her stomach, but everything else as well.

During the coming week Margaret took on the duty of finding out about the quarantine establishment, arranging for them all to visit on the following Saturday, all being Fred and Margaret in the front seats of the Rover, Megan and the three children in the back. They were warmly welcomed by the supervisor, a maiden lady of somewhat forbidding appearance which concealed an extremely kindly nature. She was probably one of those tragic middle class girls whose chances of matrimony were snatched away by the killing of a great swathe of their male contemporaries during the Great War. Officer casualties denuded both the aristocracy and middle England as nothing had ever done or hopefully ever would do again.

The centre was accepting a wide range of animals, birds, and even reptiles which largely were being brought back from all corners of the world by forces men being repatriated.

"The problems mainly are twofold," Miss Russell-Whyte told them. "Firstly the creatures they bring may be only small when they arrive, but after six months of quarantine they have often grown tremendously and become quite unsuitable as pets. Secondly although Private Atkins may love his beautiful White African parrot, his wife may take one look at it and scream her head off."

"What do you do then?" Margaret asked.

"Well, we try whenever possible to place them with private zoos. We usually have a good idea which ones are not going to be reclaimed, when their owners stop paying for their keep. Some creatures are of course in poor condition when they arrive, often having been kept in unsuitable conditions during their journey here. In the hope of their being able to be smuggled in, they are stuffed into kit bags and so on. I often wonder how many suffocated birds and animals are thrown out of railway carriage windows on the outskirts of Glasgow, Liverpool and other parts."

"So what happens to our Chantek? Can the major travel down with her?" Fred asked.

"No, that isn't possible. He will certainly not come straight home. He will be sent to an officers' discharge centre unless he is a regular officer when he will be sent to his regimental depot. I know this because we have had a number of such instances. Being discharged will only take a day after which he gets a rail travel warrant to his home town." She smiled. "I imagine at that stage of the proceedings even Chantek? - is that her name? - even Chantek will take second place! By the way, does Chantek mean anything in particular or is it just a name?"

They explained how Chantek was found, where she was found, how Harry had lived and fought in the jungle for three and a half years, and that Chantek meant 'beautiful.'

Miss Russell-Whyte was clearly moved by the story, especially when the twins told her of how they all saw daddy on the newsreel marching along with Chantek on the big parade in Singapore, and then the cinema man let everybody in to see it again. The children were bouncing on one foot after another as they excitedly recounted all this, each one waiting for the other to draw breath so that he or she could get a word in. In fact both were talking at once at one time to the amusement of them all.

"Well, you tell your daddy we shall look after Chantek as if she were our own, and you can come and see her whenever you want. Now, would you like to see the other animals?"

"Yes, please," the children all chorused.

The grown-ups were astonished at the variety of creatures assembled there, from a small brown bear, 'a gift from Russians to an officer stationed there,' a black mamba from central Africa, 'an airman who collects snakes,' to a baby crocodile from Egypt, 'that will obviously have to go to a zoo in the not too distant future.' There were jerboas from North Africa, monkeys and chimps of all descriptions, even an Arctic fox, but the animal the children loved best was a six-month-old tiger cub. It was beautiful, but they were not allowed to handle it; even now it could give a very nasty bite, to say nothing of the razor sharp claws in those feet so huge compared to the rest of its body.

They left the RSPCA centre happy that they could tell Harry how well the home his Chantek would be occupying for the next six months was run. In the meantime they would get more details as to how she would be allowed to live at Sandbury.

That evening Anni and Ernie, Moira and Jack called in at Chandlers Lodge to hear all the news of the visit to Ashford. At nine o'clock Fred switched the news on. The mellifluous tones of Stuart Hibberd commenced with describing how British parachute troops had commenced operations out of Batavia. Some casualties had been suffered, a number of prisoners had been taken, and weapons had been recovered.

Meanwhile the same programme was being heard at the Schultz home in Chingford, the same tense features receiving the news as was the case at Sandbury.

Jack Hooper and Henry Schultz evoked an almost identical response to the calm, measured announcement.

"Hasn't our David done enough without all this Dutch business?" To which, of course, there was no answer. But our David, along with sixteen hundred of his parachuting comrades were going to be called up to do a lot more over the next few months.

Susan Schultz was a little worried. Maria was now three months pregnant and in Susan's opinion her daughter was looking 'a bit peaky.' Young Henry was now fifteen months old and was, like all boys, and probably girls too, of that age, 'into everything.' Susan had found she needed to remove all her pieces of beautiful Dresden and other china and glass way out of the reach of young hands. It wasn't that her grandson was a naughty child; he seemed to live for minor adventures, like climbing into the armchair, leaning over the back and falling head first on to the carpet below.

"That's what comes of having a paratrooper for a father," was granddad Henry's comment.

The strange thing was he didn't seem to hurt himself. However, they did have to remove the fire irons after he, one morning, removed the poker from its hook and swung it round. Unfortunately he overbalanced, let go of the poker, which sailed across the hearth rug and crashed into a side lamp his grandfather used when he was reading his newspaper. Maria and Susan in the kitchen, hearing the crash, ran in to find the little lad sitting in the hearth laughing his head off until he received a scolding from his mother, the like of which he had not, up until now, experienced.

Susan Schultz therefore put Maria's peakiness down to the constant watch she had to keep to ensure young Henry didn't wreck the premises, a chore all mothers with young children have to experience. As the peakiness problem seemed not to improve, Susan suggested Maria should pay Dr Greenberg a visit, a proposal laughed off at first, but a day or so later agreed to. Dr Greenberg, their family doctor for many years, had brought Maria into the world. Now, although he should have retired the year war broke out, he was still serving his practice, 'until one of the soldier medics comes to take over.'

He checked Maria over, told her her blood pressure was a little on the high side, but considered her condition had been brought about by the emotional stress of having believed the war was all over and that her husband had survived but had now been plunged back into danger.

"I could give you a bottle of tonic," he added, "but you know as well as I do that that would be just a placebo. Keep yourself busy, write lots of letters to that handsome husband of yours, and have a word with John Jenkins, your priest in charge. He's on my panel, you know. What his bishop would say about his being treated by a Jewish doctor I can only guess."

Whether it was this little homily, or whether her mini-depression had peaked, she felt more cheerful and capable over the next few days, much to Susan's relief, until she found young Henry trying to climb from the bathroom sink out of the bathroom window, with the intention of playing on the flat roof beyond. Even then her temporary exasperation had no lasting effect.

After a long gap between receiving her Singapore letters, she at last got a batch from Java. They were light-hearted and contained a photograph he had had taken with Harry before they left Singapore. Maria telephoned Megan to tell her she would get copies done, although she was not quite sure how they could do it without a negative.

"Where is Harry now?"

"We don't know if he is coming through the Suez Canal or round the Cape. You were a sailor, you should know," she added laughingly. It seemed Megan was laughing or at least smiling all the time at present! And with good reason.

"I'll have you know I was a marine, not a sailor, and since I never saw a ship, except in the distance, I can hardly be called an authority on things nautical. Still, you know his arrival date, so it doesn't matter if he arrives via the North Pole, does it?"

"He would be very cold in that case."

"After nearly four years I think that is the most improbable state he will be in."

"Me too." The girls laughed heartily together.

Replacing the telephone Megan caught a glimpse of herself in the small mirror on the hallstand. She was now nearly thirty-three years of age. Six years of war nursing, the care and bringing up of three young children on her own, the worry of a husband in constant danger over many years had produced one or two lines on her face, and a noticeable measure of grey in her hair.

"God, I do hope he doesn't think he's come back to an old hag," she murmured to her reflection. Then she considered 'but I shall be smiling all the time so they will turn into laugh lines, and I can always tint those bits of grey.' Having convinced herself she would not be an old hag, she happily got on with her chores.

On Friday 19th October there was a party at Sandbury Hospital to bid farewell to Sister Megan Chandler. Now as you well know, hospital doctors, hospital matrons, hospital administrators, and to a lesser extent hospital nurses and ward staff are all extremely sober people. How was it then that on Saturday morning the 20th of October those who reported for duty appeared red-eyed, dry-mouthed, and afflicted with a universal malady causing them to flinch at the slightest rustle of bedclothes, to wince at the sound of a colleague's voice, to recoil from the clamorous demands of obstreperous patients and to positively cower at the ear-splitting noise of a bedpan dropped from the unsteady hands of a young probationer. It's funny really, how all the participants of such an occasion not going away, get more sloshed than the one who is leaving. It certainly was at Sandbury hospital canteen at this very special party.

In addition to it being such a memorable day, well, evening actually, the 19th of October was memorable for other more mundane plans put forward by Herbert Morrison. He announced the Nationalisation Plan. Everything was to be put into state control, and speedily too. It had all been in the Labour Party manifesto, so should have come as no surprise. When it did many people wondered whether it really would improve things, or could the government and their minions really run all the operations they were proposing to run?

Coal, gas, electricity, railways, canals, long distance road haulage, docks and harbours, were all on the immediate list. Insurance companies and banks were to follow. Jack and Fred were extremely concerned, the opinion of both of them agreeing that coal and railways could be justified but the rest of it smacked of the thin edge of communism, and as Jack said, "If they really do nationalise the banks I am off to Rhodesia." It was a good job they didn't, and, for that matter, a good job he didn't!

The days crept by. Every day, sometimes every hour, one or other of the children would ask, 'Will daddy soon be here?' or 'Where is daddy now?' or 'When shall we see Chantek?' there seemed to be no limit to the number of questions they could produce as a result of the excitement building up within them.

All the family, along with Charles, Jane and Greta, with little Sophia, met for matins on Sunday morning. When I say 'all the family' I naturally expect you to include the Hoopers and the Boltons in that category.

"He will be sailing around the north of Ireland at this very minute," Jack boomed to Megan and the children, as they walked away from the church. "Tomorrow he will land, and the next day he should be here."

Little Ceri, now almost three years old, and as big a chatterbox as any three-year-old in the fair county of Kent, if not in the country as a whole, was strangely quiet. Jack, noticing this, asked, "Like a piggy-back, Ceri?"

"Yes, please, Uncle Jack."

Jack picked her up, swung her over his head and sat her on his shoulders.

"You alright up there my love?"

"Yes thank you Uncle Jack." A few seconds later she said, "Uncle Jack, suppose daddy doesn't like me."

"Doesn't like you? He will love you to little bits." She was silent a few more seconds.

"But he knows Mark and Elizabeth, he doesn't know me."

"He knows you inside out. Your mummy has told him every single thing about you every day since you were a baby. He knows all there is to know about you."

"Even when I've been naughty?"

"I don't suppose your mummy would have told him that, and even if she did it wouldn't make any difference. You are his Ceri; he wouldn't swap you for a million pounds. Anyway, you are never naughty, your mummy told me."

Moira was listening to this dialogue, smiling widely at her huge bulky husband chatting away with this dainty little girl, both seemingly on the same wavelength. Megan joined them and knowing what a voluble little daughter she had she asked Jack what she had been telling him. Before Jack could answer Ceri told her.

"Uncle Jack says daddy wouldn't swap me for a million pounds. Is that a lot of money, mummy?"

"Your daddy wouldn't swap you for all the money in the world, neither would I."

"Neither would I," Jack chimed in.

"And neither would I," Moira added. Ceri thought again for a short while.

"Oh well, that's alright then. Uncle Jack?"

"Yes, my love."

"Why don't they ring the church bells when we leave like they do when we first come?"

She was back to normal.

* * *

Chapter Thirty-One

As soon as 'B' Company had flown in, along with Haimish, a machine gun crew and one three inch mortar section, the CO held an 'O' Group, received an appreciation of the situation from David, congratulated 'A' Company on a fine piece of work, and issued further orders. 'B' Company were to make a reconnaissance in strength towards the town centre, to find if possible where the Indonesians were holding the POW's and civilian internees. They would be supported by the mortar section whilst the machine gun people would set up a sandbagged position on the roof of the buildings with the ability to fire over the heads of any troops having to retire into the airfield.

Roger Hammick, now commanding 'B' Company, moved his men out, with orders to return immediately should they meet strong resistance to await the arrival of the rest of the battalion. They reached the outskirts of the town with no opposition. On the right-hand side of the road before them there was a number of large godowns. As they carefully approached, a door of the first one slid open a yard or so and before the leading platoon realised what was happening the door was pushed wide open and what appeared to be hundreds of females of all ages rushed out to hug and kiss them. Roger ran forward.

"Go back," he yelled. As he shouted so a burst of rifle fire came from ahead of them.

"Down," he yelled, "get down."

Two of the women and two of four platoon had been hit; the rest ran back into the shelter of the godown. "Keep those women inside," he shouted, and then,

"Five platoon, follow me."

Five platoon commander yelled for his men to charge down the road. Several more shots were fired at them, but in the meantime a Bren gun team had raced out to the left flank over open ground, and were pouring fire ahead of the charging five platoon.

After a two-hundred-yard dash Roger bellowed the order to halt and take cover, while the remainder of the company caught up. There were godowns on each side of the road here. He approached one and slid the door back; it had been bolted on the outside. As he threw the door back a smell so vile hit him that he was almost sick on the spot. Inside there were hundreds of POW's packed in like sardines.

"Wait inside," he called out, "we will have you out soon." Firing had broken out again which added emphasis to his command, but it was six platoon charging through to further clear the way ahead.

Roger wrote a message for his runner to take back to Haimish.

'Have reached first of POW's etc. Suggest we dig in here to protect them until 'C' Company arrives to push forward.'

"Barlow, take that to the CO and wait for an answer."

"Yes, sir," and Barlow clattered off up the road back to the air field.

In the meantime a scarecrow approached him from the POW godown.

"I am Colonel Abery, senior officer in the camp," he announced. Roger saluted him.

"Where are all the others, sir?"

"As far as I know there are some in the other godowns here but the bulk are in the football stadium about half a mile along here." He pointed towards the town.

"Right, well, we have another company coming in later this afternoon. When they arrive we will push on down to the stadium."

"Good show. By the way, which regiment are you?"

"The Parachute Regiment, sir."

"Never heard of it," he muttered as he turned away to rejoin his men.

Roger, listening to the conversation, could not resist following him with, "You have now, sir."

'C' Company arrived on schedule and were immediately committed to pass through 'B' to establish themselves beyond the football stadium, and dig in before it got dark. There was sporadic resistance, but it looked as though the Heihos were beginning to think that, with plane after plane coming in and disgorging well organised infantry soldiers, discretion might well be the better part of valour. As a result they retreated into the town centre.

The next morning HQ Company arrived on schedule, with the news that a Royal Navy ship would be there by mid morning, that the Dakotas would be back with food by midday and that five L.S.T.'s - tank landing craft - were coming from Singapore to transport the POW's and internees away from the island, expected the following day.

The prisoners were in an awful state. 'R' battalion medical team swiftly set up a field hospital, which was ably assisted by the sick bay personnel from the cruiser Suffolk which anchored out in the bay. A company of marines were ferried ashore to come under Haimish's command which was subjected to the usual inter-unit oratory, most of which was totally unfit for repetition in this narrative, as they passed through the ranks of the paras.

The next day the L.S.T.'s arrived with a posse of nurses and other female helpers which took over a large office block next to the football stadium which the marines cleared for them and then formed a protective screen around them.

"But who's going to protect them from the marines?" asked Roger of David, "you know what a randy lot they are."

Swiftly the very sick were loaded on to the waiting Dakotas, the airfield now deemed to be secure, and flown back to Singapore. The sick were taken on to the L.S.T.'s where they would occupy the bunks usually taken up by the tank crews when they were in transit, and finally the tank space was filled with ambulant civilians and POW's. The next day the little armada pointed its way north west. They had only removed a fraction of the numbers there, but it was a start.

HQ Company were, in the meantime, allocated the unenviable task of burying those to whom deliverance had come too late. Haimish decided that a graveyard be made on the edge of the airfield, one section for civilians, one for POW's, so that in the fullness of time the bodies could be exhumed and given proper burials in places befitting their faith, or in the case of POW's, in War Cemeteries.

They had experienced no further attacks for the past two days; furthermore early on the third day a small party of Japanese officers appeared from the town, carrying a white flag. They were taken to Haimish's HQ, bowed when presented to him, the leader offering him his sword. He spoke good English but with an American twang to it.

"I am Major Kido, sir; my troops are at your disposal."

"Where are they, major, and how many do you have?"

"We are at Gresik, twenty kilometres north of the town. We have two hundred and ten men."

"Have they kept their arms?"

"Yes, sir."

"Will you send word for them to march here to help in the defence of Surabaya so that we can evacuate the prisoners and internees. You and your second-in-command may stay here."

"Yes, sir." He turned to three of the officers and in the standard rasping voice of command which was the trademark of any Japanese to a rank beneath him, ordered them to return to the unit and bring it to Surabaya town.

As they were about to leave a small party of Indonesians appeared from the town headed by the previous mayor appointed by the Japanese commander. Major Kido, who spoke the Indonesian language, acted as interpreter.

"He says, sir, that no armed men are now in the town. He is afraid the warship will fire on them."

"Has he motor vehicles?" The major put the question to the mayor.

"We have municipal lorries."

"How many?"

"Twelve which are in working order."

"Commandeer them and send them to get your troops. Also tell him I require twenty men to come here immediately to the airfield to dig graves. They will be paid for their labour."

The major gave these orders.

The mayor and his party made the obeisance they had been accustomed to making to their conquerors over the past years, the CO telling them, through the major,

"We are not Japanese; you do not bow to us."

Whether the major was affronted by this statement it did not show; in any case Haimish couldn't have cared less.

By ten o'clock a party of some thirty Indonesians appeared who were put to continuing the work HQ company had already started, namely searching for the dead and bringing them to the airfield, and digging the graves. As each body was lowered reverently into the ground the battalion padre, Captain Evans, a Welsh rugby international in his spare time, or was, made a somewhat abbreviated committal.

"Forasmuch as it hath pleased Almighty God of his great mercy to take unto himself the soul of our dear brother (or sister) here departed, we therefore commit his (or her) body to the ground.

Earth to earth, ashes to ashes, dust to dust; in sure and certain hope of the Resurrection to eternal life, through our Lord Jesus Christ. Amen."

The padre buried over one hundred emaciated bodies in the next days. Had David and those who followed not arrived when they did who knows how many corpses they would have found.

On the tenth day of their occupation of the airfield and its immediate area south of the town, 'R' Battalion was relieved by a brigade of the Indian Army led by a battalion of the Seaforth Highlanders, who marched into the town with pipes skirling and drums beating.

"And if that doesn't frighten the life out of the bloody Indos nothing will," Paddy observed.

This gave the battalion the opportunity to regroup on the airfield ready for their next task, whatever that might be. After a week a squadron of light tanks came ashore, crewed by Sikhs. The tanks were quite small, being built for jungle use where a fifty ton Churchill would be useless. On the other hand the Sikhs were very large, which when they arrived on the airfield to the great interest of the paras, produced disbelief that three, or sometimes, four, hulking great crew members could squeeze into the small space provided and operate the driving, wireless and gunnery functions successfully. But they did, and were such genial characters, the paras immediately took to them.

Three days after their arrival the brigadier called an 'O' Group to which the Sikh's squadron commander, Major Regan, and Haimish were summoned. The orders were simple.

"You are to force your way to Jogjakarta on the south coast, secure the airfield and the port nearby so that an evacuation can take place as has been accomplished here. You will move out at dawn on the 7th of November. I will leave you, Colonel Gillespie, to sort out the details. When you have secured the airfield we shall fly you in supplies and further troops. That is all."

Haimish went back to 'R' Battalion, passed on the news to his company commanders, and handed out the maps he had been given.

"It's about two hundred miles," he guessed, "we shall be carried in lorries, which have just arrived commanded by Captain Neville here of the Royal Army Service Corps. We have just to bash on until we meet opposition, if any, and then plan our reaction on the hoof as it were. With little or no opposition we should arrive on the 9th. We shall have six tanks and some fifteen trucks, two tanks to lead, two and a small tanker after truck five, another tank after truck ten and two remaining tanks at the rear. Any questions?"

There were several questions regarding detail, after which they dispersed to get ready for the off. At dawn on the Wednesday morning, the convoy moved off. The first day's travel provided no problems. In fact passing through several larger kampongs the inhabitants turned out and waved to the passing soldiers. At five o'clock in the afternoon they came to a largish town which boasted a fair sized sports ground. Haimish, up in the leading truck and in radio contact with the British officer in the leading tank, ordered him to pull in and laager overnight here, where it would be easier to defend than if they were strung out along a highway. They had covered one hundred and twenty miles without incident.

They set off again at dawn, meeting scattered opposition as they approached Jogjakarta which was swiftly discouraged by the leading tanks giving the would-be ambushes a prolonged helping of heavy machine gun fire from their Besas. As they reached the outskirts of the town in the early afternoon they were met by a guard of honour of Japanese commanded by a colonel assisted by a private soldier with a good command of English. He explained that the town was secure but the airfield to the east and the port to the south were held by the insurgents.

"Right, we will sort the buggers out on the airfield first," Haimish decided, the translator having difficulty with the 'buggers,' interpreting it as 'villains.'

"Where are the Europeans?" Haimish asked.

"They are safe in a large office block in the city centre," was the reply, "but have very little food or medicines."

"Right. HQ Company, less mortar platoon, go with the colonel to check out the Europeans. The tanks will spearhead the attack on the airfield. When the Indos see them coming they will probably run for their lives."

And they did.

The airfield and buildings were swiftly checked; 'A' Company detached to defend them, along with two of the tanks, Haimish pointed his nose towards the docks, some five miles away. They met more serious opposition here; even so with massive covering fire from the two forward tanks, 4 platoon of 'B' Company made a spirited attack on the insurgent forces well dug in and cleared the way for the convoy to get through, losing two dead and two wounded in the process.

Upon reaching the dock area, it was only a small port, the rest of 'B' Company split up into six man patrols to search the various buildings. Mainly they consisted of small godowns, and offices, unlocked and in most cases looted. However one of the large ones was still secure, resisting all attempts to break down the solid steel entrance doors. The sergeant in charge of the patrol scratched his neck - he couldn't scratch his head since he had his helmet on. As a result of this incentive to thought he came up with the idea of putting a Piat bomb - from a sensible distance - into where the doors butted up and were firmly locked, the section he had containing the Piat man and his number two. Now, there is no doubt that a Piat bomb would do that job admirably, but, and it is a big 'but,' what if behind that door there is a store of rubber, ammunition, petrol even? It would be bonfire night in Jogjakarta, three days late it is true, since it was the 8th of November.

The sergeant then made a well known military decision, one that has been determined since long before the times of Alexander the Great, Julius Caesar and Oliver Cromwell - correction, better leave the godly Cromwell out of this.

"Shit or bust," he yelled.

They all retreated behind a neighbouring wall. The two Piat men prostrated themselves and neatly put a projectile squarely in the centre of the double doors. There was the usual loud explosion upon contact, then nothing. After a few seconds the sergeant ran to the godown, followed by the remainder of his patrol. He looked through the substantial hole and laughed his head off.

"The bleeding place is empty," he shouted.

It is peculiar that something as un-funny as that should cause a near state of hysteria among the half dozen paras, but when you are strung up, not knowing what is going to happen next, in fact not knowing whether you will still be here in five minutes' time should you be in the sights of a sniper, the nervous system does peculiar things.

With 'B' Company and two more of the tanks left to secure the docks Haimish led 'C' Company back into the town, where David and HQ Company had already been welcomed by hundreds of civilian internees and POW's. With two companies of paras and a Japanese company of some two hundred men under command the town was cleared over the next two days as aircraft arrived with much needed rice and other food for the camp people, taking the more seriously ill people back with them on the long flight to Singapore. A week later a trooper arrived at the docks and the rest of the internees were put aboard, where a large medical facility checked them, attended to their various conditions, and a catering staff fed them, little and fairly often, with the sort of food they had only dreamt about for the last three and a half years.

And that is how the fighting life of Major David Chandler, RSM Paddy O'Riordan and some of the others petered out, the younger ones to be sent to Palestine to face more trouble from both Jews and Arabs, but that is another story. Fighting flared up in many places over the next months but it was mostly quiet in 'R' Battalion's bailiewick, Paddy's comment on this state of affairs being, "They know better than to upset us, so they do."

At the end of the year they were shipped back to Singapore, where the story of 'R' Battalion came to an end. The long serving members would be going home for demobilisation, the regular soldiers returned to their parent regiments, and the young ones to the Parachute Brigade in Palestine as previously noted. 'R' Battalion had existed only for some three years yet would go down for ever in the history of the British Army.

* * *

Chapter Thirty-Two

It was a grey misty morning on Monday the 29th of October as Harry's ship was nosed into its berth in Gladstone dock at Liverpool. Harry had been told that an R.S.P.C.A. vehicle would be alongside to take his leopard down to Ashford in Kent, that he should take her off from the lower, crew gangway, and then return to be checked by the customs and immigration people with the other passengers, mainly service men and women, but including a number of civilians.

There was a great deal of hubbub on the dockside, but Harry could not see a van or truck which would be the likely vehicle to take Chantek away from him. At that thought his heart gave a wrench, and he looked down at this beautiful animal which had been such a great comfort to him for so long in such appalling circumstances. It was bad enough when he had to leave her for a week or so when they were on an operation, but to leave her now for six months would be unendurable, and if it was as bad as that for him, what would it be like for her?

The tannoy boomed.

"Major Chandler, please report to the lower gangway."

"Here it is, my precious. Now you be a good girl and I'll come and see you as soon as I can."

Chantek understood every word of course.

He went down flight upon flight of steel stairways, Chantek in her harness leading the way. The crewman guarding the exit moved swiftly out of the way when he saw a large leopard coming towards him, she looked tame enough in that harness, he thought, but he was not prepared to put it to the test by getting near her.

Waiting at the bottom of the gangway, where Harry had expected to see a burly association inspector, dressed in riot gear since he had to handle a ferocious animal, he was confronted by a charming young woman, dressed in plain tweeds. She shook hands with Harry.

"Welcome back to England, Major Chandler, I have heard of all your exploits and how you came to possess Chantek."

"Thank you, Miss?"

"Rebecca Prophett."

"Thank you, Miss Prophett. Now how would you have heard all that, I wonder?"

"From Miss Russell-Whyte at Ashford. She is my boss. She heard it from your wife and the children. Now, I must make friends with Chantek."

She produced some pieces of cold rabbit from a flat tin which had been contained in one of her capacious pockets. Chantek sniffed at the unfamiliar meat, licked the piece on offer, decided it must be alright as Harry would not let anyone give her something that wasn't alright, and whipped it into her capacious jaws.

"You liked that, didn't you, darling?" Rebecca said softly and offered her another piece. This time Chantek had no second thoughts but swiftly accepted it.

As this little episode was being played out - Harry could see Rebecca was gaining Chantek's trust whilst she was still in Harry's presence - they became the centre of attention not only from a number of people on the dockside, but also from hundreds of passengers leaning over the ship's side from the various decks. At last Rebecca slowly moved to stroke Chantek's head and jowls to gasps of astonishment from those watchers nearby.

"I think she will be alright now, major, let's put her in the car." She led Harry to a large shooting brake, opened up the back doors to reveal a pair of wire mesh double doors opening from a spacious cage. These she opened.

"Up you come, my beauty," Harry said. Chantek, thinking she was going somewhere with Harry, readily jumped up into the cage, sniffed around the blankets on the floor and settled herself down. Harry fondled her; Rebecca closed the cage doors, and then the car doors. There was a burst of applause from the onlookers, smilingly acknowledged by the couple.

"She will be fine," she said.

"How will you get her out?" Harry asked. It had occurred to him that after a two-hundred-and-fifty mile journey Chantek might not be in too good a humour and might very well show it!

"No problem," Rebecca replied "the complete cage comes out and we put it against her new home, open the doors and leave her to it. I shall see her every day. She'll not be lonely."

"Thank you, Rebecca, thank you very much. I shall sleep easier now I know she is in such good hands." They shook hands and Chantek started her journey to the south of England, thoroughly puzzled as to why Harry was not with them but reasonably satisfied she was in good hands with this lady who was obviously a friend of Harry's.

Harry disembarked just before eleven o'clock that morning, carrying a large suitcase full of goodies he had been able to buy in Singapore, another box from the hold 'not wanted on voyage,' to be sent on by Carter Patterson. He had been unable to telephone from the ship, queues at the few lines available being miles long by the time he got back from seeing Chantek off. Having got to Liverpool Lime Street he found a London train waiting to leave in five minutes, so he had no opportunity to telephone until he reached Euston - and then he had to queue!

All day long Megan had been on tenterhooks waiting for this call. 'Suppose the ship is a day late - could easily happen' she considered. She even went to the extent of leaving the lavatory door open when she had to go so that she would hear the bell. What she would have done had she been summoned halfway through the operation I leave to you to decide.

At 5.05pm the summons she had been waiting for all day came. The short conversation which ensued was so disjointed it would be as well not to try and detail it; the gist of it being Harry was on his way to the Officer's Reception Depot at Guildford, would phone from there and would be home tomorrow. It was difficult to say more when there was a queue a mile long waiting to use the blasted phone, none of whom was the slightest bit concerned that this twit up the front was having the first conversation with his wife for nearly four years.

That evening they enjoyed their first conversation in years, Harry anxious to say hello to the children, Megan anxious to know what happened to Chantek. They all went to bed eventually in a cloud, impatient for the morrow to come.

Harry found himself to be a bit of an unusual case to the officer in charge of leave entitlement prior to discharge. As a matter of course he was entitled to fourteen days' disembarkation leave and twenty eight days' discharge leave. Then it was established he had received no leave entitlement since the beginning of 1942. At ten days for each three months he was due a total of one hundred and sixty days. Altogether therefore he could still wear his uniform for another six months or more, during which time he would be paid although discharged. To the captain totting this all up Harry said, in his usual bantering manner,

"Gosh, money for old rope, what?" to which the captain replied, having Harry's service record before him,

"For what you have done for us all, sir, you should get the Crown Jewels."

For one of the few times in his life Harry was left with no answer. Eventually he managed to say, "That's very kind of you," afterwards thoroughly appreciating in his own mind the plaudit of one, who judging by his campaign ribbons, had also been around a bit before he landed this desk job.

By midday, all the formalities completed, and Harry having been given his cardboard box containing his demob suit, overcoat, shoes, socks and trilby hat, he said goodbye to the army, made his way back to London to collect his gear from the left luggage at Victoria, and at last settled back in his first class compartment, one of the few privileges of being an officer.

Just after three o'clock that afternoon the station hire-car pulled up outside the house that he had dreamt about so many times in so many places. It was obvious that Megan had been keeping a watchful eye through the curtains, since, as the car came to a stop, the front door opened and a neat, trim figure hurtled down the garden path to throw herself into the arms of her darling Harry. However, two untoward things happened. Firstly, Harry was wearing the bush hat with which he had been issued for the parade in Singapore. This is a high crowned, wide brimmed piece of apparel designed to keep the sun and rain off the head and face of the wearer. It is not designed to be suddenly dislodged by the head of an excited female endeavouring to kiss and hug its wearer. It therefore ended up in the ground where a breeze moved it under the car.

These things happen at sudden reunions.

The second untoward happening was that the three children, the twins having been kept from school to welcome their daddy, had chased after their mother, but little Ceri, running faster than her legs were designed to carry her, fell over. Crying more through exasperation at being last to meet her daddy rather than through any real hurt, she was picked up, given a big kiss, and was better immediately.

The driver, in the meantime having rescued Harry's hat and dumped his considerable amount of baggage in the front passageway, was paid off, tipped handsomely and drove away, leaving the family to be what they had dreamt of being for so long - a family.

The next day they were to make their way to Chandlers Lodge in the morning and stay for lunch. Margaret was just a little apprehensive as to how Harry would feel toward her, but Rose, suspecting this, had told her that Harry would 'love her to bits,' like they all did. The twins were walked to school by their dad, and as they left the front gate each holding one of their daddy's hands, Megan watched from the doorway and had to turn back into the house in tears at the emotion of seeing her darling Harry at last there to be with his family, and for the children to have a father to play with and look up to. Their main question, time and again of course 'When shall we see Chantek?' They settled on Saturday after telephoning Miss Russell-Whyte to enquire whether Chantek had arrived safely, and to make sure they could visit.

They arrived at Chandlers Lodge at around eleven o'clock, Harry pushing the pushchair with Ceri safely strapped in it. There was of course a great welcome from Rose and from his father, who had come up from the factory to greet him. Margaret was introduced and received a big hug and a kiss which put her fears to rest.

"Well, let's have a look at you," Fred announced as Harry took his hat and coat off - it was very cold to him after years almost on the equator. "You haven't lost any weight that I can see, mainly I suppose because you were always like me, all steel and whipcord. Your hair isn't quite so dark ..."

Harry butted in.

"What you mean is I'm now ash-blonde like May West - right?" He turned to Margaret. "It's the fashion these days, isn't it, Margaret?"

"Oh, definitely, I'm thinking of going that way myself."

Harry was captivated by the soft American accent. He had feared his new stepmother might be possessed of one of those strident deliveries one heard on the silver screen from time to time. 'Enough to turn milk sour,' had been his opinion expressed on occasion.

"Well, if it's alright by you, we intend to have a welcome home party on Saturday night. Everybody wants to see you."

Harry turned to Megan. "What about the children?" he asked.

Again Megan had that surge of emotion that Harry was thinking first about his family before himself. She covered it with a little cough before saying, "The twins can go to Nanny, they love going there with John. Ceri can come here and sleep in her cot we keep here."

"Right, we shall look forward to that."

They left soon after midday. As they walked back Harry asked, "Could you now take the pushchair love. I would like to go and see mum's grave."

"You wouldn't want me to come with you?"

"No, you go on, I'll not be long."

He found the plot where Ruth, Pat and Lady Halton had been laid to rest. Death to him over the past three and a half years had been commonplace, mainly hideous death; in the cases of the two comrades he had had to dispatch, abhorrent and ghastly. Here death was peaceful and serene, the autumn leaves drifting down from the three oak trees which bordered that side of the churchyard making a counterpane to cover the graves. He stood with head bowed for several minutes, then turning to leave saw Canon Rosser standing a few yards away.

"It's Harry, isn't it?" he stated, not questioned. "Welcome home Harry, welcome home. Have you time for a glass of sherry? My gaffer would like to say hello."

"That would be most acceptable padre, thank you very much, and thank you for all the help you have been to the family through these years. Rose and David have both told me of how you comforted them and many others as well I wouldn't mind betting."

"Yes, we've seen a lot of sorrow. Still no more of that, it is really great to see you back. Now, what about this leopard of yours? We all saw you on the cinema screen you know, on a Sunday too. I didn't dare tell the bishop I had been to a cinema on a Sunday; I would have been cashiered!"

When Harry arrived back for lunch at the cottage, he kissed Megan, who laughingly said, "It's not only the churchyard you've been to."

"All you can smell is ecclesiastical sherry forced down my unwilling throat by Canon Rosser. He sends his kind regards."

Later that afternoon Rose telephoned Megan, some arrangements they had made two or three weeks before now having to be rescheduled.

"Harry looked well," Rose reflected, "mind you with that tan anyone would look well, wouldn't they?"

Megan laughed a somewhat 'cat that ate the cream' sort of laugh.

"When Harry came back from Dunkirk your mother rang me the next day asking after his health. I remember very clearly replying I was most pleased to report that despite what Harry may or may not have been through, there was nothing wrong with his health. I can now report to you, that between you and me, if anything his health has improved despite all he has been through. Now, what do you make of that?"

"Well, would you like me to take the children for a couple of weeks while you lock all the doors and pull the curtains?"

"If it wasn't for the local authorities finding out and charging me with negligence I would definitely not hesitate."

Saturday came, and the visit to Ashford to see Chantek. With Ernie and Anni and young David, Jack, Moira and young John, Margaret and Fred of course, along with Rose and young Jeremy, all anxious to see Chantek in the flesh, Harry decided to hire one of the small charabancs from the local coach firm. They left at nine thirty for the twenty-five-mile trip to Ashford, and were therefore in the quarantine centre by quarter past ten. They were met by Rebecca.

"She has been pacing up and down for the past hour," the party was told.

"How could she have known?" asked an incredulous Jack.

Harry replied that he had been on a six or seven day operation on many occasions. She always knew when he was on the way back. He approached the large enclosure where she was housed. She rushed to the door, then rushed away, rolled over and over then rushed to the door again. Rebecca gave Harry her body lead. He opened the front of the security vestibule and closed the door behind him, then opened the inner door to let himself in to the enclosure. Chantek ran at him, put her paws up on to his shoulders, and nuzzled his suit. Dropping to her feet again she hurtled around the wire perimeter, returning to rub against his legs while he slipped the lead on.

"Now, my precious, simmer down and come and meet all your new friends."

She understood perfectly of course, every word he said.

Outside the enclosure they all took turns to pet her, although young Jeremy and David, Anni's boy, were a little hesitant. Harry had been a little worried that too much attention all at once might upset her. After all, if a leopard is upset, if only momentarily and not too intensely, she could do some damage. He kept a tight hold on her, which was in fact not required - she lapped up the attention.

At length it was time to go home. Harry thanked Rebecca for looking after Chantek so well, Rebecca replying it was a team effort, all the staff so intrigued by the story behind this beautiful creature.

"She's our star guest," she added, "you see, they are all only our guests. Every week we lose one or two as their quarantine period is up, except that is for those that conveniently get forgotten, then we have either to place them in a zoo or have them put down. But that won't happen to you my darling, will it?"

As she said that last sentence Megan joined them, and as Harry led Chantek to her cage she asked, "Were you talking of my husband then? I have no intention of having him put down just yet."

Rebecca smiled at her and replied,

"Neither would anyone in their right mind. I think he's gorgeous; it must have been awful for you all those years. The soldiers get medals for being away; surely their wives should get a medal for having to carry on alone."

"I'm inclined to agree with you, although being in the Chandler family I have never been entirely alone, and I daresay there are some wives who set out not to be alone for long. We have had several in our maternity ward whose husbands have been abroad for a year or more."

Infidelities and hasty war-time marriages resulted in 1946 showing a monumental increase in divorce, the people concerned being as much casualties of war in most cases as any other.

On Monday, bonfire night, Harry made his first visit to the factory. Astonished at the way it had grown he was fearful it had outgrown him. His father had deliberately not asked thus far whether he had any plans. After all, he had a long leave to enjoy with his wife and children; there would be plenty of time to plan in the New Year. It was Harry himself who raised the question, on returning to Fred's office after having toured the workshops and been greeted by the handful of workers and staff who knew him in 1939.

"Where do you think I will fit in dad?"

Fred's usually impassive face broke into a wide grin.

"So you are coming back are you?"

"Of course, I've been dreaming of it for six years and more."

"Right. Then I will tell you. Sir Jack and I have discussed it. I am going to retire within the next year and you will understudy me until then, and then take over."

"What about Ernie?"

"Ernie will be M.D. of Sandbury Engineering, Ray M.D. of Sandbury Plastics. We are going to form a company to make caravans so will have to appoint an M.D. for that. The whole shebang will be run by Sandbury Holdings, with you as M.D. and Sir Jack and me as joint Chairmen."

Harry's reply said it all.

"Blimey."

He thought for a moment, then putting forward another question, asked,

"What about David?"

"We don't know what David will want to do. For all we know he may want to stay in the army, or become a parson, we just do not know. My feeling is that as his father-in-law owns a sizeable commercial vehicle business, and is about my age, David may be tempted to take that over. It's a sure-fire growth area, or will be, that's for certain."

Harry was silent for several long seconds.

"And to think, just over ten years ago, we were on a farm," he was silent again for a short while, "and it's all down to David originally isn't it?"

Fred smiled in reply, and nodded.

He went back to Margaret early that evening, held her close, and told her,

"Harry is going to take over. I shall retire next year, and for the rest of my days I shall do everything in my power to make you and our little one enjoy a peaceful and enjoyable life."

"Well, we certainly shall not have a peaceful life this evening," Margaret replied, "that sounds like the first arrivals."

A huge bonfire had been built over the past three weeks in Chandlers Lodge back garden. The extended Chandler family were all to come for the most monumental firework night any of the younger ones had ever seen. Harry had been universally voted as i.c. fireworks, "Don't want everybody letting them off, do we?" Jack had declared, to everyone's agreement. It was a somewhat misty evening but dry. The bonfire was rather slow in coming to life, but when it did, lit up the faces of the youngsters, and if the truth was known excited the faces of a number of their elders as well. It was proof positive that peacetime had really come.

The children went to bed tired and happy that night, looking forward to the next big event on their calendar - Christmas.

So too were Fred and Margaret, the latter watching the bonfire party from a comfortable upright chair in a warm upstairs bedroom. Fred had suggested it would be 'taking a chance', as he put it, if she went out into the cold with the others; she could easily stumble on the uneven ground, and it was not worth risking that, nor getting a cold, when she only had six weeks to go. Ray Osbourne's wife, June, too was pregnant, and although not as advanced as Margaret elected to stay with her.

"When does Ray come home?" Margaret asked.

Ray had left for America in early October to study the developing plastics industry there. Originally scheduled for a month's stay he had cabled he was extending his trip for two weeks, so much had been laid on for him to see by the commercial attaché at the British Embassy.

"He should be back at the end of the month. I just hope he brings us back a few cases of goodies for Christmas. Who would have thought that with the war over we would be more heavily rationed than we were back in 1941?"

Yet this was the case, a situation which caused considerable confusion to the British who, having won the war as they thought, were now having to pull in their belts so that the Germans did not starve in this first terrible winter they were to endure, with no hope whatsoever of the population explosion in the west, due to the millions of refugees, being able to get food from their new, eastern communist neighbours.

"Ray is so looking forward to building this plastics company, and it is all down to his meeting with Harry. Do you know, half the people you meet seem to have their present good fortune arrive as a result of contact in one way or another with the Chandlers."

"What about you?" asked Margaret, thinking to find the exception to that statement.

"Me too. If my mother hadn't lived in one of your husband's flats, I wouldn't have met Ray."

"I didn't know that."

"Yes. Ray was negotiating with her to take it over when I arrived and saw she was crying. I was immediately up in arms thinking he had been bullying her, when all the time he had been so kind she was crying with gratitude. And the rest, as they say, is history."

The days passed slowly on towards Christmas, Margaret having weekly visits from Doctor John as she always called John Power. On Sunday 16th of December she began to feel not well, Fred immediately saying he would call John straight away.

"Like your lot, he will charge double time for Sundays," she said, "leave it until tomorrow, I am sure it's only something trivial."

Fred smiled at her whimsically. Since however she still felt 'not up to par' as she put it, he telephoned early on Monday, left for the factory at Margaret's insistence - 'Rose will be here' - with the plea that Rose should telephone him as soon as John had made his visit. John was not entirely happy when he examined her.

"Your blood pressure is up a bit too high," he pronounced. "I think I will get you into hospital." He booked a side ward, sent an ambulance for her, and at four o'clock that afternoon she was admitted.

And then the 'not so well' symptoms disappeared. As Margaret said, when Fred and Rose visited her that evening.

"I really do feel an absolute fraud."

"Better to be safe than sorry," Fred replied. "John doesn't flap; he wouldn't have taken up bed space if he had not been concerned. Anyway he's going to keep you in a for a couple of days to make sure whatever it was doesn't repeat itself. I told him it was probably those six pickled onions you ate with your supper on Saturday night, and do you know he believed me for a moment or two!"

The couple of days passed, Margaret came home, but two days later was rushed back in again and on Christmas Eve produced a bonny little girl weighing six pounds seven ounces, to the wholehearted congratulations of, not only the extended family, but also dozens of people she didn't even know, but who knew of her.

On Christmas Day Margaret was allowed to see visitors, 'but not too many' warned Sister. It is difficult to describe how Margaret felt. Happy? It was a great deal more than that. Blessed? Yes, but doubly so if there is a superlative to describe that. Fortunate? Oh! yes, so very fortunate. At a time of life when many women look ahead to their children growing away from them, she would have the thrill of the experience of watching her little girl grow up. The birth itself had been somewhat prolonged and she had suffered, but now all that was forgotten.

As she lay in her bed, tired after the visitors had all gone, she marvelled at the chain of events which had brought her here. A routine visit to a small country factory, small compared to the G.E.C.'s, A.E.I.'s, and other giants she had been to, along with a pig of a man who hardly gave her the time of day, resulted in her meeting and being attracted to a man so different in every way to the moron accompanying her. Admittedly their baby was an 'accident' but, as she looked at the cot beside her bed, what a wonderful, wonderful accident that was. She drifted off to sleep, to be awakened by the Irish nurse, already claiming a proprietary interest in the little one, with,

"Feeding time for my little darlin'."

They went home on New Year's Eve, the family having the happiness of having them, at the same time remembering with sadness the loss of dear Ruth three years earlier.

1946 produced the coldest winter in the recorded history of England. Week after week the snow lay on the ground. Coal was rationed. In the country wood was burnt, but in the cities where trees were sparse many municipal fences disappeared, park seats vanished, anything that would burn was burnt. This was what David was to come home to.

* * *

Chapter Thirty-Three

Early in January 1946 David and Paddy, now housed out at Nee Soon where Harry had first been stationed when he arrived back in 1941, decided to take a trip into Singapore town to a favourite watering hole they had discovered in Orchard Road, called 'The Princes Bar.' It served excellent Chinese food, and was frequented mainly by middle ranking officers along with a fair number of prosperous looking Chinese civilians, the males generally approaching, or already arrived at, middle age. Strangely enough their female companions all seemed to be half their age. As Paddy commented, "Do you think they are their daughters?"

David had grinned.

"I hardly think hard-headed Chinese businessmen would waste the sort of money they are spending, on their daughters," he suggested.

As they sat at the bar conjecturing the relationships, a voice behind them, accompanied by a heavy hand placed on a shoulder of each, declared,

"This I do not believe, what the devil are you two doing here?"

The two paras swung round on their swivel seats, instantly sliding off to confront the colonel they had worked for when they dropped into Yugoslavia back in 1942, except that he was now in civilian clothes and accompanied by an attractive lady, mid-forties David judged.

"What the devil are you two doing here? Darling, this is Major Chandler and Mr O'Riordan who were the two valiant trail blazers sent to suss out our friend Marshall Tito, each winning an MC in the process."

Mrs Hopgood shook hands with the pair.

"The questions are, sir, firstly what are you doing here, and secondly why are you slumming in a low dive like this? I would have thought you would be firmly anchored in the Raffles. But, please, do sit down, Mrs Hopgood, what would you care to drink?"

The drinks question taken care of, David received replies to his questions.

"Well, I have now reached the dizzy heights of brigadier and I am here to rebuild the Malay Regiment. I am looking for someone to command the first battalion along with two more company commanders. Now, I awoke in the middle of last night and had a blinding flash of inspiration. I thought young Chandler would make a good colonel for the first battalion, and Mr O'Riordan, duly commissioned, would make a jolly good company commander. Now, what do you think of that?"

David looked at Paddy. Paddy looked at David. They spontaneously shook their heads.

"Sir," replied David, "with your extremely elegant and refined wife present we would be totally unable to tell you what we think of that."

The brigadier and his wife laughed their heads off.

"Well, as my father always told me, you can't expect to win them all."

"Sir, we were just about to eat. Would you both care to join us?"

They had a most pleasant meal together, after which David and Paddy hired a taxi to Nee Soon, whilst the brigadier and Mrs Hopgood returned to their new married quarters at the same Alexandra married quarters David had occupied when they first came to Singapore - now, of course, suitably refurbished and staffed as befits the occupation by a brigadier and his lady wife.

The next morning, the 10th of January, they were notified they were on the list to be repatriated. They would sail on 'The Brittanic,' sister ship of 'The Mauritania,' on the 15th of January to arrive at Liverpool on the 5th of February.

The voyage home was one of sheer luxury compared to most of the past six years and more. David and Paddy each had their own cabin, David being a field officer and Paddy being an RSM The food and service were probably not quite up to the thirties' peace-time standard, but nevertheless were not very far from it. The ship was huge, so huge in fact that at one point in the Suez Canal it was scraping the bottom, becoming almost stuck at one section. They were told later it was the largest ship thus far to have negotiated the canal, the canal itself, ten years later, to become another battlefield upon which the paras would make their presence felt.

The Brittanic was held up from docking for a day, sitting at the mouth of the River Mersey whilst a couple of thousand home-hungry passengers champed at the bit at seeing the lights of Seaforth and New Brighton shining in the distance. Equally those at home, literally sitting by the telephone waiting for it to produce the news that their parting was over, became despondent at its continued silence, since there were no means of telephoning until they docked.

"Be patient," Mr Schultz told Maria, "it is common for ships to have to wait to dock, especially big ships like The Brittanic, they cannot be berthed any old place."

Maria was now eight months pregnant. She worried that her ungainly appearance, particularly the extra weight she appeared to have put on around her face and neck would be so unsightly to her darling David. Furthermore, he had been away for months and would doubtless need her badly; how could she overcome that? Her mother had reassured her, when Maria had remarked to her, 'what will David think when he sees me waddling along?' Realising the reason behind that, and knowing it also contained the fear that she could not welcome a husband home as she would like to and as he would have been dreaming about since he was torn from her, she assured her daughter.

"He will be happy just to be with you again, do not fear about that my love, and to be with you when the little one arrives."

At ten o'clock on Thursday 7th February the telephone shrilled out.

"We are landing today, they have just connected the land-lines, and Paddy had a fight with two RAF blokes to get this one. I shall go to Guildford apparently to be discharged; Paddy has to go to Winchester. I shall be home tomorrow sometime, and will ring you this evening with more exact details. I have to go now, there's a queue a mile long for this phone. Bye bye, darling."

Maria had no chance to say a word of welcome!

Through the snow and ice-covered countryside Paddy and David travelled to Waterloo together, then separated when David alighted at Guildford. They hugged each other, others in the compartment somewhat nonplussed at the sight of a major and an RSM clinching in that manner in public, and in uniform too!

And so David ended his active soldiering career on Thursday 7th February 1946, although he had the leave entitlement for his active service in Java and the standard disembarkation leave. He was entitled to be described as 'Major Chandler,' but like most Second World War officers below the rank of colonel, he did not give effect to that right.

He arrived back at Chingford just as the Schultz family were having tea. His first words to Maria were, "You look wonderful," which pronouncement caused her to burst into tears.

"What have I said?" he laughingly asked of his mother-in-law.

As she hugged him in welcome, she told him that Maria had feared he would think she was unlovely. Shaking hands with Henry Schultz, he took young Henry up, settling him in one arm, put his arm around Maria, kissed her on the cheek, and posing as for a family group asked, "Where's the camera?" followed by,

"And I repeat, you look wonderful."

That night as they lay in bed together they were silent for a while until Maria, snuggling her face into David's shoulders whispered,

"I have the impression you are more than pleased to be home."

He held her a little closer.

"It will keep, it will keep."

On Saturday they went to Sandbury to meet David's new stepsister, now some six weeks old, and then on Sunday Harry took him and the twins and Ceri to see Chantek while Maria rested at Chandlers Lodge. Harry had ordered one of the new Morris Oxfords when he arrived home, which were as from the previous December now being released on to the UK market, and was fortunate in getting a cancelled order, otherwise there would have been a four month wait.

It was while the brothers were at Ashford that Maria suddenly started having the first indications she was going to produce an early grandchild for Mr and Mrs Chandler, now sitting beside her on the settee in some disquiet. She and David had determined to drive back to Chingford that evening, Fred putting forward the view that might be unwise. David was due back at about five o'clock. When he did arrive he agreed with his father they should stay overnight - if it was a false alarm they would go back in the morrow.

It wasn't!

On Monday morning 11th February at a little after four o'clock, Maria was taken to Sandbury hospital, put in the same ward that Margaret had so recently vacated, and later that evening presented the family with another little female to add to the clan.

"So what do we call her?" David asked. In the short time he had been home they had not discussed names, thinking they had plenty of time, without remembering that nature sometimes plays some funny tricks on all of us!

"I like Ann," Maria replied, "just Ann."

"Ann Chandler - sounds perfect to me," and Ann Chandler it was, who grew up with Mary Chandler, her aunt, older by a couple of months, to be almost as sisters together.

It was agreed that the two babies would be christened by Canon Rosser at four o'clock on Easter Sunday, a huge gathering then to take place at Chandlers Lodge for the rest of the day. At a little after nine o'clock Jack called for order.

"Ladies and gentlemen. This is the first occasion upon which we have all been able to be together, as we are now, for many years. Upon the occasion of our two new additions to the Chandler family - our family that is, we are all one family together - I would like to express the hope that we may look forward to a world where such terrible times as we and others have experienced will never again take place. In our small community we are saddened by the loss of our dear Jeremy, our Pat, and the passing of our beloved Ruth. We mourn the passing of our great friends Colonel Tim, Jim Napier and Lady Halton, along with Nigel Coates who few of us knew, but of whose suffering we know so much. They will always be in our thoughts, they will never be forgotten.

"We must also be aware of the courage of the serving members of our family, David, Harry and Mark, along with our extended family of Stanley, Oliver, Lord Ramsford, and his son Charlie. Each and every one of those mentioned has performed deeds of valour of which we know little or nothing. Maybe we shall be able to prise that knowledge out of them over the coming years. I suspect we shall be astonished at what we shall discover.

"In conclusion, ladies and gentlemen, we, the allies, have won the war at a great price. May we now have the intelligence to win the peace so that such a cataclysmic disaster cannot happen again to devastate the lives of our two little ones whose christening we have solemnized today."

With that fervent desire, we end the story of The Chandlers and their life and times during what is regarded as the most significant period of the history of our country. What would life have been like if the allies had not won the war? How much more suffering would there have been if Hiroshima and Nagasaki not been sacrificed?

So many 'ifs.'

* * *

POSTCRIPT 2006

It is now sixty years since we concluded the story of The Chandlers. A million and a quarter words were written about them, their activities and other people connected with them, or having dealings in one way or another with them. It would be interesting to know how their lives developed, since they are, in the main, ordinary people, many of whom carried out extraordinary deeds.

THE CHANDLER FAMILY

FRED CHANDLER

Fred was born in 1880. He retired at the end of 1946, handing the reins over to Harry, of whom more later. He and Margaret in due course settled into a wonderfully companionable life together, enjoying watching and taking an active part in the growing up of little Mary. They travelled a great deal, as soon as it was possible, until in 1953 when Fred was 73, he suffered a stroke. He slowly recovered over the next year but in early 1955 he was stricken again and died as a result.

Margaret and Fred had ten happy and loving years together, free of major worries and the dangers of war. At Fred's funeral so many people attended they were standing at the end and along the sides of the nave, itself of considerable spaciousness. He was laid to rest in the family plot next to Ruth.

What a varied life he had experienced! By today's standards his education, ending abruptly as it did on his fourteenth birthday, was rudimentary. Yet he quickly realised that education does not end when you leave school. In fact it has been said that education is what you have when you have forgotten all you were taught. That statement is good cause for debate no doubt. He joined the army in boy's service, where he studied further, and at the age of eighteen had won his Army first class certificate of education. He was sent to India and spent nearly a year fighting the insurgents up in Waziristan before his battalion was sent to the South African War, known as the Boer War. A spell in Ireland after that, and then the

Mons retreat and the hell of the trenches, about which you will have read in previous volumes, along with his spell in Woolwich Arsenal after he was invalided from the army. His work on Sir Oliver Routledge's farm and the rest of his life chronicled in 'The Chandlers,' brings in full circle a lifetime of hard work, incredible danger, devotion to duty, love and happiness, and just reward.

As Sir Jack said when, at his funeral service, he gave his eulogy to his great friend, "They broke the mould when they made Fred Chandler." With which sentiment all agreed who knew him.

MARGARET CHANDLER

Margaret was fifty-one when Fred died. She was desolate at his loss, but deeply grateful for being given the years she had spent with him. When she was low in spirits she wished so hard that she could have spent longer with him, but then chided herself that many people, particularly in wartime do not have ten long years together. Look at poor Rose and Jeremy, Moira and her first husband and thousands upon thousands of others she knew not. That self-admonishment may have been deserved, she thought, but it gave her little comfort.

Gradually, however, the hurt grew less, though it never disappeared. She threw herself into doing voluntary work, and with that and her care of little Mary she obtained reasonable fulfilment. In 1959, some four years after Fred's death, she found herself part of a small delegation of Sandbury residents to visit the County Council offices at Maidstone to contest a road widening plan being put forward at the approaches to Sandbury. The meeting went on all day. She was not concerned too much about getting home to look after fourteen-years-old Mary, who attended a day school at Sandbury, since they had employed a housekeeper-cum-cook, who would be there to greet her.

She had noticed that a military-looking man, one of the planning people, had given her several intense looks. She was not unduly perturbed at this; after all, at the ripe old age of fifty five, it was not something which happened every hour on the hour. It would be fair to say that although she was perhaps a trifle flattered, she was also somewhat amused. At the conclusion of the meeting he approached her, away from the others.

"Mrs Chandler, would you care to have dinner with me this evening?"

Margaret was somewhat taken aback at the directness of the approach.

"I'm sorry Mr ..., again I'm sorry I'm afraid I don't even know your name."

"Bowman, Mrs Chandler, Major Peter Bowman."

"Well I'm sorry Major Bowman, but I have a daughter at home waiting to have dinner with me."

"Well, perhaps another time. I will telephone you if I may," and without waiting for a yea or nay he turned away.

When she arrived home Harry was there. She told him of the incident. The next day he telephoned a very good friend of his in the planning department to 'get the low-down' on this major. He established that the major had been a major in the Home Guard, was known as 'The Groper' in the Town Hall, and had a wife and four kids. Harry expressed his grateful thanks, decided not to tell Margaret, but did telephone the major. When he was put through he just said,

"Mr Groper, I'm sorry, Major Groper. I am Harry Chandler. I just want you to know that if you try and contact my step-mother again in any way, I will come to Maidstone Town Hall and I will belt the life out of you in front of all your colleagues. Do you clearly understand me, Major Groper?"

There was no reply, except for the faint click of a receiver being replaced. Margaret had no further approach, swiftly forgetting he ever existed. She lived on until 1980, dying of renal failure after a short illness.

MARY CHANDLER

We have heard only of the birth of Margaret's daughter; she has formed little part of our chronicles. However, she was a bright child, did well at school, was able to go to university where she studied law, got a first class degree and was taken into chambers. Then she threw it all up to be a show-jumper; she had been riding since she was three. She has now celebrated her sixtieth birthday and still rides to hounds.

There could be a good story there?

HARRY CHANDLER

Harry was forty five when his father died and he found himself at the head of a very sizeable group of companies. In addition to the manufacturing concerns, they had acquired, soon after the war ended, sizeable packets of land in Kent and Sussex and had a professional land agent to run that side of the business. With the children growing up he and Megan had bought a larger house in five acres of grounds out towards Mountfield named Blendon House. Apart from this substantial dwelling his only extravagance was the possession of a vintage Bentley, used only on high days and holidays, his normal carriage to and from the factory being a modest Ford. In 1950 he and Megan, along with Ray Osborne and June, made the journey to France to visit Madame Duchesne and her daughters who had so kindly cared for them during their bridge blowing exploits. Madame and one of the daughters, Jeanne, newly married to a strapping ex-soldier who had been a prisoner of war in Germany for five years, would not speak of the other daughter except to say that she married a German and now lived in Bremen.

They visited the little school and church where the nuns and the padre had given Harry the pews for seating the wounded he was ferrying back to Dunkirk in his lorries. Alas, the padre had been part of the Resistance, had been captured and shot along with thirty others in the district. His pretty nun was still there though, ten years older, but still pretty!

That same year Matthew Lee came to England along with his wife and two children and was invited to stay. He had specialised in paediatrics in Singapore after the war, and was now taking up a consultant's post at Great Ormond Street. After Singapore's independence he stayed on in England, living in London but spending frequent weekends with Harry, where he renewed his friendship with Chantek, of which more later.

Harry and Matthew both died in the same year as Margaret, 1980, Harry being seventy years old and Matthew suffering a fatal heart attack at the age of sixty.

MEGAN CHANDLER

Despite her closeness with death in her years at Sandbury hospital, the deaths in the same year of her great friend Margaret followed by that of Matthew, for whom she had great affection, and culminating in the loss of her darling husband, brought on a great depression. She therefore decided to move from Blendon House back into Sandbury to be closer to her friends and relatives, where she lived on for another ten years.

MARK CHANDLER

The elder of Megan and Harry's twins - by thirty-five minutes - turned out to be the playboy of the Chandler clan. He was clever at school, good at sport, especially cricket, where he played as an amateur in Kent second eleven, and in the first team from time to time. He had no financial worries having received a substantial bequest from his grandfather to be made available to him on his twenty-first birthday. This was partly in cash, partly in shares, the shares to be sold back to the family should he wish to part with them. In his cricket he was a very useful fast bowler, although like the rest of his living, erratic at times.

He bought a secondhand M.G. Midget, and promptly crashed it. A new Riley went the same way, although on this occasion he did not get off scot-free, being badly cut and bruised and furthermore causing the left arm of his very dishy blonde companion to be broken. An interesting aside to this incident is that when the young lady was admitted to hospital it was found she was wearing no underwear. They should have looked in Mark's right hand jacket pocket.

In 1972 at the age of thirty-five, three major events happened to him in the space of one month. Firstly, he was arrested for 'driving under the influence,' secondly he was dropped from the Kent team, thirdly he met Claire Bruton and married her within a couple of months at a Register Office with none of the family present - not even his twin sister! The marriage lasted precisely two years, fortunately not producing offspring to argue about. In 1975 he decided to emigrate to Australia where at the age of thirty-nine he was killed in a road accident. The woman he was living with at the time organised the funeral arrangements, writing to his father a week later asking to be reimbursed for the money it had cost her, which Harry settled immediately.

The family were distraught. There was nothing spiteful or ill-natured about Mark, he was to a certain extent a victim of the irresponsible times in which he lived. John Hooper, his great schoolboy friend - almost a brother to him - was very sad about, what he considered to be the waste of a good life.

ELIZABETH CHANDLER

Elizabeth stayed on into the sixth form but decided against going to university. At a party at Blendon House in 1955 she found herself talking to a rather charming lady about what she was going to do, or rather about the quandary she was in as to what to do. She had got good 'A' levels in literature and history.

"Why not try journalism?" the lady asked. "We have a need for active young people with your qualifications." She handed Elizabeth her card, which showed she was a member of the family which owned the Kent Messenger, a very old established county newspaper.

"Go and see Mr Moss at Aylesford. I'll tell him to get his secretary to contact you with a time."

And that is how Elizabeth got started. She spent five years with the Kent Messenger, then moved on to the Daily Telegraph, a spell with the Sunday Telegraph, then with 'The Old Thunderer' until she retired aged sixty in 1997.

Although she had a number of relationships she seemed never to be in any one place at any one time after she left the Kent Messenger, so as to put down any roots. As a result she never married - until the year she retired, which was in fact the reason for her retirement. Visiting Sandbury she encountered John Hooper again, he having lost his wife to cancer several years before. He had known and loved Elizabeth since they were children. It was natural they should wed.

CERI CHANDLER

Perhaps because he saw nothing of Ceri's babyhood and first years, she became the apple of her father's eye, after Megan of course. He never lost the great love he had always shared with Megan.

From her earliest days Ceri had said she was going to be a nurse 'like mummy.' She did in fact become a doctor, having studied at the Victoria Infirmary in Glasgow, becoming an ardent support of Queens Park football club whose Hampden Park Stadium was nearby.

Unlike her brother and sister before her, in 1961 she met a young Scottish student at medical college and never looked seriously at any other would-be suitor. They were married five years later. Ceri had decided she would be a GP, whilst Alex, her husband, decided to stay on at the Victoria Infirmary to aim for a consultancy. They set up home at Newton Mearns, a very pleasant rural suburb, where Ceri took up the post of junior doctor in an old established practice in the town. They had three children. Alex died at the early age of fifty seven in 1999 after which Ceri moved back to Blendon House carrying out locum work in the district, where she still lives.

ROSE LAURENSON nee CHANDLER and MARK

Rose, until 1965, lived the life 'following the drum.' Her husband Mark served as a major in the City Rifles in Germany for three years, then in Libya in considerable luxury for a little over a year. He was promoted to lieutenant colonel and Rose found herself in a different world altogether when he was posted as military attaché to the embassy in Warsaw for two years. Her sigh of relief when that tour of duty was up could have been heard back in Sandbury. She then sampled the fleshpots of Washington where Mark was called upon to perform similar duties as in Warsaw, the main difference being their car was not followed bumper to bumper as it had been whenever they had emerged from the embassy in Warsaw.

In 1954 Mark was given command of the battalion of City Rifles which had been sent to Malaya for what was never known as a 'war,' but has always been named 'The Emergency.' Rose was based in Singapore where Mark could join her during his spells out of the jungle, in the Alexandra married quarters, where her brother David had been billeted nine years before. This posting left Mark with a profound admiration for Harry and his men as he re-trod some of the ground Harry had covered in those years raiding the Japs.

Following this they returned to England where Mark had spells at Tidworth, Catterick and in Horse Guards, as a full colonel, retiring in 1965. They came back to Chandlers Lodge, living a quiet country life with Margaret, who died in 1980, and where they still live.

JEREMY CARTWRIGHT

When Rose, his mother, and his step-father took up their station in Germany, Jeremy was nearly six years old, and went with them, attending the military families' school. In Libya he attended a private school with other British ex-pats' children. He was ten years old when his step-father was posted to Warsaw; as a result he was boarded at Cantelbury College, where his father, grandfather, and Uncle David had been educated before him, spending weekends at Chandlers Lodge, and school holidays at Romsey with his grandparents.

When his grandparents died in the 1960s he had just left university and was following in his grandfather's footsteps in the City. With the exception of a bequest to his mother from their estate, he was the sole beneficiary, which made him very wealthy indeed. He continued his work in the Square Mile, but at the same time founded a youth centre in a very deprived area of Southwark, in south London, along with a young persons' refuge adjacent to it. This area was becoming the centre of the London drugs scene from the mid-sixties onwards. The young woman he employed to run the refuge left to marry, the newlyweds then having arranged to leave for Australia. The manager of the centre advertised the vacancy, but received few applications for a post involving 'druggies' in an area far removed from the more salubrious parts of London and Home Counties. When they at last totalled four, the manager telephoned Jeremy, who asked to sit in on the selection of the new refuge leader.

On a wet and miserable afternoon Jeremy took a cab over to Southwark, little knowing his destiny was to be determined in the next few hours. He was twenty five years of age, had played the upper-crust field, but as yet had not found the girl of his dreams. The last of the four applicants was a Miss Nita Jones, with a degree in social sciences, a pleasant no-nonsense way of speaking, twenty-three years of age, and lovely with it!! She got the job, Jeremy found she shared his love of opera, they went to Covent Garden a week later, and that was that.

They were married in 1968, had two children and now live quietly back in the grandparents' original home in Romsey.

SIR JACK and LADY HOOPER

Jack and Moira both retired in early 1946, although Jack retained his directorships in the Sandbury group of companies, as well as the chairmanship of the family commodities business now returned to the City. Rather than send John away to Harrow, as they had originally intended, they decided he would be a weekly boarder at Cantelbury, coming home most weekends. They immersed themselves in the social life of the district and the county, remaining close all their days to Fred and Margaret, Harry and Megan, David and Maria.

When Fred died in 1955, Jack called the family together to garner ideas regarding a permanent memorial to his great friend. After a number of suggestions Harry produced the answer. Up until now the local branch of the British Legion met in the club room at 'The Angel.' New owners had taken over with the sad passing of John Tarrant, and they had plans to move more up-market; at the same time the Legion had been attracting more members and needed larger premises. Harry proposed therefore that Sir Jack head a committee to raise the necessary funds to build and equip a single story club room on a piece of land adjacent to the Sandbury apartments, owned by Sandbury Properties, the latter to donate the land and start the campaign off with a donation of one thousand pounds. The suggestion was taken up with enthusiasm, the British Legion contacted, outline planning approval obtained, and Sir Jack set about organising the design and facilities for what was to be known as 'The Fred Chandler Memorial Hall.' Opened by General Sir Frederick Earnshaw, in addition to club facilities for ex-servicemen, it had a 'band room' at the rear of the building, well sound-proofed, to train young men, and much later young women, as military musicians. A second fund was instigated to buy the instruments necessary for such a band from Boosey and Hawkes, it becoming known as the 'Chandler British Legion Band.'

Sir Jack died in his sleep in 1960 at the age of seventy-three, Moira in 1963 at the age of sixty-nine, and were both very greatly missed.

ERNIE BOLTON, ANNI, KARL and ROSEMARY

There must be few people who work for one firm all their working lives. Ernie Bolton was one such person. In 1984 when he retired he had served Sandbury Engineering, now one of the largest agricultural equipment and service engineers in the south of England, for no less than nearly fifty years. He had lived through, what was without doubt, the most revolutionary times in the history of agriculture, the complete transition from manual labour to machines, forecast so perceptibly by Fred and Sir Jack back in the thirties.

Ernie made his one endeavour not to be just abreast of developments, but to be ahead of them, frequently to instigate them, until his name became the voice of authority in the industry. Manufacturers came to him when seeking advice on a project, knowing that there would be no way their trade secrets would be passed on to others. Users came to him for impartial advice on the best pieces of plant to suit their particular land, or pocket. The owner of a large farm in Sussex came to Sandbury one day, at the end of their discussions remarking, "I can always get an honest answer from you."

Ernie replied, "Well, sir, you see, I was trained by the Chandlers."

Anni and Ernie had three children, David, Ruth and Harry, all named after members of their great mentors, the Chandler family. Two years after the war they made the sad trip to Dachau where they laid flowers in memory of Trudi, Anni's mother. This act, whilst poignant in itself, succeeded in drawing a line under their grieving. They had visited the place where Trudi had so evilly been incarcerated and where she had met her death, even though they had had no grave at which to pray for the repose of her soul.

They flew to Canada to visit Ernie's sister Deborah and her husband Alec, now possessed of a family of four children, 'although one of them looks a bit like that window cleaner who calls' had joked the irrepressible Alec.

Karl went back to Ulm with Rosemary in 1950 and was able to establish his rights over the property he owned there before the war, to sell in a swiftly rising market and invest the proceeds in blue chip German companies until such time as they could be sold and the money transmitted to his bank in Sandbury. He died in his early seventies in 1963, Rosemary following him two years later.

THE CREW FAMILY

The Earl of Otbourne and Gloria had a short, but wonderfully content life together. They knew when they were first wed that they would not enjoy years of companionship and love as they could have done had they met at an earlier age. As a result they were seldom apart, and again seldom took part in occasions where they had to share their togetherness with other people. Christopher was so happy that his son, Lord Ramsford, had at last found fulfilment with marrying Cecely, along with the great pride in his grandson Charlie and his beautiful wife Emma and their three children. The line was secure for at least three more generations. The Earl died aged eighty in 1952, three years before his great friend Fred Chandler. Gloria stayed on at Ramsford Grange, where she was joined by Charlie and Emma and the children as we shall see.

Hugh Ramsford and Cecely, now the Earl and Countess of Otbourne, elected not to live at Ramsford, but lived in town or in Scotland, where Hugh had now inherited his uncle's estates. He therefore suggested that Charlie should take over Ramsford Grange. Charlie never fully recovered from the ghastly wound he had received in Normandy, Emma being firmly of the opinion that he would be much better off in the country than in town. As a result of his wound, unlike his father he was unable to ride to hounds, otherwise he and Emma played the part nobly of the squire, throwing themselves into the life of Ramsford and the county generally, nurturing and gradually adding to the estate so as to provide the wherewithal to keep Ramsford Grange at its immaculate level, despite the ruinous taxation by successive county, district and government money grabbers intent on levelling down everything in sight.

Sadly Charlie did not make old bones, as his premature death was described in the village. A simple fall from a ladder on to a cobbled yard in the stable block at The Grange resulted in a reopening of his internal surgery, which in turn produced massive infection from which he did not, could not, recover. He was just forty-four years of age. Emma did not remarry, but stayed on in the big house, proving to be a thoroughly competent chatelaine until her eldest son could take over. In this she was assisted, whenever she called for help or guidance, by her father-in-law, who with Cecely was a tower of strength in their mutual grief. Emma is now eighty-two years of age and, in the opinion of her nearest and dearest, and many others probably, as lovely as ever.

Hugh and Cecely travelled to Malaya as soon as it was possible. They had already instructed solicitors named Rintoul in Kluang to ensure Cecely's property in Muar and in Kuala Lumpur was rebuilt, although the apartment in K.L. needed little doing to it other than some repair and considerable redecoration. There was the inevitable tearful welcome from Ah Chin and his rapidly increasing family, the excited stories from some of the children about the major with the 'enormous' leopard which they petted and finally the story of how the great big sergeant major had flattened the two men who tried to steal tuan's house. They had taken an enlarged framed photograph of Harry with Megan and the children, and with Chantek stretched out on a carpet in front of them. It would become, next to his family, Ah Chin's most treasured possession.

Hugh died aged seventy-six in 1972; Cecely lived on at The Grange with Emma until she too passed away some ten years later.

The current Earl of Otbourne is a chip off the old block, the Ramsford estates being in good and reliable hands as his brilliant handling of its present affairs, despite the problems he had with the antics of his siblings, clearly show. He followed in the footsteps of his great-grandfather - Christopher - in his love of the orchids at Ramsford Grange, considerably extending the glass-houses so that after a few years they became a tourist attraction, producing an always welcome addition to the estate's income. He married late and has two sons, one at Eton, one at Sandhurst, the one at Sandhurst being the absolute double of his grandfather, Charlie.

THE von HASSELLBEKS

When the war ended in the spring of 1945 the south western district of Germany where Konrad and Elizabeth von Hassellbek lived was occupied by the French, who behaved abominably. A large proportion of the force was of colonial troops; in the Neustadt district mainly Senegalese. Their officers seemed to have little control over their excesses. Rape was common, despite the fact that the Allied High Command had ordered the ' no fraternisation ban.' Eventually the new German authorities protested vehemently to General Eisenhower at the excesses these people were committing, theft, assaults, drunkenness, even murder, so that the French were forced to do something about it. Nevertheless, no woman would appear on the streets on her own even in daylight, and at night few men either.

Things improved by the end of the year with the arrival of more French nationals, replacing the north and west Africans; even so there was a great deal of animosity, more so than in the other sectors.

Inge was sentenced to ten years for war crimes, but in common with most of those whose evil deeds did not include actual murder, was released after a little over three years in 1950. She had not, until her release, contacted her parents, although they, and Dieter, had written to her in prison. Upon her being discharged, she telephoned her mother, who immediately pleaded with her to come home, at least for a while. Technically she was still married to Himmler's nephew, although he, despite the fact he had escaped incarceration, had not contacted her in any way during her trial or imprisonment.

At thirty years old Inge therefore arrived at Neustadt into the welcoming arms of her mother and father, but where there had been the beauty and freshness of an extremely attractive young woman in the thirties, fear and disillusionment, combined with prison life, had left lines on that beautiful face and grey hair where there had been a glorious gold. However, she kept a low profile; got a post in a local pharmaceutical company where her natural ability soon secured her promotion to a well paid position, divorced her husband, but never remarried.

When Konrad died in 1961 he had willed the house at Neustadt to Dieter. He and Rosa, along with his mother and sister, lived on there. His mother died three years later after her husband; the other three are still alive. As soon as it was practicable, they visited David and the Chandlers in England, the visits being reciprocated many times. Dieter and Rosa had three children, who in turn became great friends of the Chandlers, coming to love England almost as much as their own beautiful homeland, as a result of many visits.

And that just about brings it all to a close.

"WHAT'S THAT? HOW ABOUT WHO? WHO? OH, YES. PADDY AND DAVID - I had forgotten about them."

PADDY O'RIORDAN

When Paddy left the army in March 1946 he and Mary paid a day long visit to David and Maria at Chingford.

"Now that you have no defaulters to bash, what do you think of doing?" David asked.

"Well, sir," Paddy replied, out of habit.

"SIR? We are civilians now, so you can cut that out."

Paddy grinned. "That's going to be an awful difficult thing to remember, so it is," nearly adding 'sir' again. "Anyway, Mary and me said a long time ago that we would like to get a pub, not just a drinking pub you understand, but with her experience a pub which would serve good food. Do you know, sir - there, I've done it again - do you know David, apart from the old coaching inns there's hardly a pub which serves anything beyond cheese rolls and pickles. We've found a small free-house out on the A418 towards Thame which we understand is coming up for sale, plenty of room at the front for cars, and room at the back to put a single storey restaurant. I've had my war gratuity, and my twenty-one years service gratuity, and as a Warrant Officer Class One, thanks to you, they are well worth having. I put aside all my pay I didn't draw when we were in Yugoslavia and then again in Indonesia, that's nigh on a year's money altogether, so all in all that's a fair amount. Eamonn, Mary's father, has kept back their wedding present until we were settled, that's a thousand pounds, so we've got enough to buy the place and move in. Eamonn is very friendly with Mr Cole, Barclay's manager and he will let us have money to refurbish the place - he's been to see it and likes the idea."

He sat back. "What do you think of it, sir?"

"I think it's a great idea, sir."

"Oh, I'm sorry, but it's going to take some getting used to, this David business."

"One alteration I would suggest to the plans."

"What would they be."

"Leave the bank out of it. Borrow what money you need from me on as long a term as you like and at no interest. That way you will save a lot on bank charges and interest, and if you need some extra facility in a hurry for any reason the bank will be knocking on your door to give it to you. You see, Country Style has been earning me money all through the war so I'm not short of a bob or two."

"Do you mean that?" Mary asked incredulously.

"Of course I do."

She got up and went over to David, giving him a big, big kiss, with the inevitable caution from Maria, "Be careful, you don't know where he's been."

"Well, that's me settled, what about you? Have you decided anything yet?" Paddy asked.

"The short answer to that is 'no.' I'm going to give it another couple of weeks."

Mary asked what his choices were.

"Well, there's a good Evening News stand for sale outside Chigwell station. They need a potman at the Forest Arms, so I saw advertised in the saloon bar window. I once told my dad I could always be a road sweeper, but he said I would fall off the broom within an hour. Do you know, that was nearly ten years ago when he said that, and I still haven't got a proper job."

"For what you and Paddy have done in the past six years and more you should be entitled not to have to do a stroke for the rest of your days," Mary stated forcefully.

"We were only two among millions," David replied thoughtfully, "the aircrews, the submariners, the jungle fighters, the list is endless."

David was symptomatic of many many thousands of young men in their twenties who had never had a decision-making civilian job, but had rapidly been put into positions of responsibility for the life or death of sometimes a hundred or more of their fellow men, then been jettisoned back into a world of entirely different values. The necessity of starting off once again at the bottom of the ladder, of learning a different code, of having on occasion to kowtow to people he would not have made a lance-corporal a year or two ago. It was extremely difficult, needing a new kind of resilience, a tough flexibility.

They said their goodbyes to Mary and Paddy, happy for them in their facing their exciting challenges. Paddy lived to enjoy thirty six years of life as 'mine host,' Mary surviving him by another five years, dying in 1987.

DAVID, MARIA AND THE SCHULTZ'S

As we have seen, David, having been thrust from a life of action, decision and danger over the past six years, found it extremely difficult to decide upon how to contend with this new world of domesticity, safety and to a certain extent undistinguished living. There had been a cachet in being a decorated officer in a crack regiment; now he was to be plain Joe Bloggs in amongst all the other Joe Bloggs. On the credit side, no one would, hopefully, be shooting at him any more, he would not be required to carry sixty pounds weight of army rubbish for miles on end to no good purpose, and he would sleep at night with his gloriously unclothed and welcoming Maria. With that thought alone he established he was better off as a civvy.

But what to do?

He told himself he was lucky to have a choice. He listed this in his mind.

1) He could join the Sandbury Group. A place would be found for him. A niggle at the back of his mind said, 'I don't want a place to be <u>found</u> for me.'

2) He could take advantage of the army scheme of placing ex-officers in universities to obtain degrees they had forgone in joining the forces. Yes, but what degree, what university, and would he be separated from his family again for three years?

3) He could develop 'Country Style.' There was a good deal of money in the kitty to enable him to branch out into country type towns, and in this enterprise doubtless Maria could join him, and Sandbury Properties would finance any building requirements.

4) There was always the Evening News stand at Chingford station. A bit 'parky' this time of year but only for four hours a day.

Up until now Henry Schultz had not mentioned any plans he might have. He was firmly established in the commercial vehicle business, had been disappointed his son Cedric had shown no interest in becoming part of it before he was so tragically killed at Calais but recognised fully his son's entitlement to choose his own calling. He was now fifty-six years old, and hoping to enjoy a decade of travel and social activities denied the world in general since the thirties, before he finally retired to his pipe and slippers.

It was at a recent trade conference he was approached by a director of Jaguar Cars, a gentleman he had known for many years and with whom he had worked on several trade charities and in a government enquiry.

"Mr Schultz, we want to set up a sales and service outlet for our cars somewhere in your locality. Any ideas as to who might be able to co-finance such an operation? You must know most people in the district. He would, of course, have to be prepared to run the show," he added.

Henry's mind went into top gear.

"Leave it with me, Mr Anstruther; I think I may be able to suggest something there. May I telephone you in the next couple of days?"

"By all means. We are anxious to get things going. We have a site in mind out on the Epping Road at Buckhurst Hill; there's a lot of money out there and into Essex, and Jaguars would sell well."

That evening Henry approached David.

"David my boy, would you be interested in running a Jaguar sales and service main dealership?"

"Those beautiful cars? Who wouldn't? But if I'm not being rude, what is your connection with Jaguar? You are in the commercial vehicle business."

"I have good friends in many places." He went on to describe the proposed set-up, that he would be supplying half the finance for the project with the prospect of buying the remainder of the shares in five years' time, that David would be the managing director, he and a representative from Jaguar being co-chairmen. They would employ a sales director and a works director with experience of quality cars.

Henry added, "Oh, and of course, a Jaguar motor car goes with the job."

David laughed. "Well, if I had suffered any doubts, that fact would have settled it completely."

"So you would be interested?"

At that point Maria and her mother joined them. Maria asked, "Interested? Interested in what?"

Her father explained the proposal he had made to David, David watching her face for signs of the reception she was giving it.

"But David has had no experience in the motor trade."

Maria, stating the obvious, had only expressed what had been going on in David's mind, up until now not having been put into words since surely Henry would have realised that and catered for it.

"No problem there. Whilst the dealership is being built and equipped he will be spending most of his time at the factory and at other dealerships. He is, after all, a trained engineer. He will just need product knowledge and the know-how of the Jaguar sales and service procedure, warranty obligations and so forth."

Maria turned to David, "I think it would be wonderful working with such beautiful machines."

"So do I, darling, so do I."

David built the dealership up over the years enjoying the excitement of the 'E' types. the luxury of the 2.4s and its larger version. They built a beautiful house on the outskirts of Epping to which all the family came from time to time, along with Paddy and his brood, Dieter and Rosa and their children.

In 1954 Paddy and David each received an extremely formal looking letter from 'The Embassy of the Socialist Republic of Yugoslavia.' It stated simply:

The President of the Socialist Republic of Yugoslavia requests the presence of .... (either David or Paddy) at an investiture in the Presidential Palace in Belgrade on the 12th of June 1954 to receive:

The Order of the Partisan Star. First Class

The Order of Bravery Medal

for services to the Partisans during the War of National Liberation.

It was signed by the Yugoslav Ambassador to the Court of St James. A separate letter gave details regarding travel arrangements, and the invitation included for the recipient's wife and immediate family to be invited to the ceremony. There was one problem. The invitation stipulated 'Uniform or Morning Dress,' the latter causing Paddy to comment 'they're getting posh in their old age,' and the former seeming to have shrunk considerably since they were carefully put away eight years before. However, one of Paddy's customers was a master tailor who performed the miracle of getting them to fit once again, albeit expressing the view there would be little room for further expansion to take up any increasing muscularity.

They joined a dozen or so other prospective recipients of honours or awards at London Heathrow, were flown to Belgrade, where they were met by a posse of military and civilian government personnel, directed to their coach and taken to their hotels. David's and Paddy's group were told the coach would collect them for the investiture on the morrow.

The organisation was immaculate. Marshall Tito gave a short address thanking all those brave soldiers who came to the aid of the Partisans in their hour of need, after which the names were called. First were those to be awarded 'The Order of the Partisan Star First Class.' These, with the exception of David and Paddy, were mainly senior officers, since the award was for 'leadership skills and special merit in the face of the enemy.' However, the Marshall said to each of them, through his interpreter, "We meet again in very different circumstances, do we not?"

The second award, the 'Order of Bravery Medal,' did not produce as many recipients, and only one other who had been previously decorated, since this medal was for exceptional conduct in battle. Few who were nominated for it lived to receive it.

At the reception that evening David, Paddy and their wives were standing in a group when a Yugoslav general came towards them accompanied by a very attractive female officer, these latter two smiling broadly. David immediately recognised them. "Livia, Comrade Mavric" he exclaimed, "how wonderful to see you again." He clasped Livia in a big hug while Paddy shook hands vigorously with the general. Livia was the attaché they were afforded when they were dropped into Yugoslavia way back in 1942. She marched every inch with them, fought every battle with them until they were transferred to the south. Comrade Todor Mavric, now a general, was their partisan commander.

"Do you remember what you said to me when we parted?" asked the general, with Livia translating.

"I do, General, I remember it clearly."

The general turned to Maria and Mary, with again Livia translating. He said, "Your husbands told me that a part of their hearts would always remain in Yugoslavia. I knew they would come back again one day."

They flew back home laden with photographs of the occasion pictured with the President, the general and Livia; surely all life would be an anti-climax after that. In the luggage of both David and

Paddy the general had organised the hotel staff to slip a bottle of slivovitz, with a note saying, 'To remind you of part of your heartland.'

David and Maria are now in their eighties living the gentle life on the outskirts of Epping Forest, like the rest of us at that age wondering what the world is coming to!!

THE END

Well, not quite.

These six volumes, around a million and a quarter words, half as long again as War and Peace (albeit division three from a literary point of view compared to our Leo), have not been accomplished without the help of many and varied people and organisations upon whom I have descended for research purposes.

However, before I give you details of those you must know of two ladies without whom none of these stories would have seen the light of day. Every word was originally written in longhand, longhand being the rather kindly description of the hieroglyphics my ball-point pen leaves on the paper. These, combined with constant erasures, alterations, interjections, etc, without doubt left the understanding of the readings on the walls of the ancient Egyptian temples a piece of cake in comparison.

Volume one was deciphered and put into print by my dear friend RITA CARTER who lives in Bournemouth. As a result of the work now being legible I was able to show it to certain people to get a view as to its quality, or lack of. The general opinion was 'well I have read worse.' So I started volume two.

My grateful thanks therefore, Rita, for your starting the long journey travelled by The Chandlers through World War Two, and for your constant encouragement since those early days.

The remaining volumes were mysteriously transmogrified by LIAN BECKETT into a magic machine I was told in my ignorance was called a computer. This apparatus was so clever it could sing the National Anthem in Mandarin Chinese if called upon so to do, or so I was assured. Well, I have not yet lost all my marbles so I must say I thought that would be somewhat unlikely. However, when I saw a small disc upon which there were over half a million words, and which produced the next three volumes, I began to believe what I had been told. It was obvious they had come a long way since I mastered the wind-up gramophone.

Lian has worked like a Trojan without ever tearing her hair out at the sudden descent of another one hundred pages of scribble through her letter box, or bashing Natalie and Alister in frustration at trying to decode the runic symbols imprinted thereon. Her ideas on presentation have been invaluable, so to you, Lian, my very, very, grateful thanks.

Now to the volumes, but first the front covers.

FRONT COVERS

Volume One   The school featured on the front cover is a view of Eltham College, kindly provided by David Jones, one time the head of the junior school and now, in retirement, making a wonderful job of marshalling the school archives.

Volume Two   The main part of the picture is a photograph of men wading to the boats at the miracle of Dunkirk.

Volume Three   The name of the unfortunate airman at the point of being beheaded is not known. He was an Australian, that is all that is known. This bestial behaviour was common on the part of the so-called 'samurai warriors.'

Volume Four   In contrast to the picture on volume three, here we have the serene beauty of Leading Wren Veronica Owen. She was one of the team working in Fort Southwick, deep in the bowels of Portsdown Hill at Portsmouth. Her job was to code or decode messages between the fleet at sea and the naval command ashore. She was one who worked through the build-up of the massive fleet which eventually took our troops to Normandy.

Volume Five   The magnificent shires of the Hop Fields at peaceful Beltring in Kent contrast the picture of Pegasus Bridge where the 6th Airborne Division fought the first battles in the dark hours of D-Day.

<u>Volume Six</u>   Reversing our previous settings of showing life at home in the top diagonal and the fighting Chandlers in the lower diagonal we have reversed the setting on the cover of volume six. The upper picture, a painting by Geoff Otway of Major Jack Watson M.C. leading men across the DZ on the Rhine Drop, an action in which David and Paddy are featured in the book. The lower picture explains itself -Victory at last!

THE RESEARCHED

VOLUME ONE

In volume one I needed to know what a mortgage would cost in 1933. The Chief of the Woolwich Building Society, Don Kirkham no less, gladly provided this for me. Nothing beats going straight to the top! I required details of farm tractors again at that time. The Ford Motor Company, per Anis Collett and Paul Beard, sent me so much detail on their Fordson models I could have written a small book on those alone - a prime example of how people and firms reacted to someone they had never heard of in all their lives!

There was one exception to this. I needed to know the exchange rate of pounds to French francs and German marks in May 1935. I approached 'The Financial Times,' they will be sure to know, I thought. I was told by their representative they could provide the answer at a cost of thirty pounds. Despite the fact I told them I was a struggling writer in a lonely, candle-lit, freezing cold garret, they insisted on their pound of flesh, or thirty pounds to be precise. I referred the gentleman to a well-known taxidermist's near their offices.

Having had this temporary setback I thought, 'Go to the top again,' so I telephoned the Bank of England, well, as Harry Chandler was to say in later pages, 'Shit or bust.' I was directed to a charming young lady, Elaine Howell, responsible for their archives, and I can positively affirm she was most definitely not one of the archives, so much so that I wondered several times later what sort of excuse I could manufacture to telephone the Bank of England yet again! The answer to my problem was swiftly given and it cost me only the price of a telephone call!

Sadly three of my friends who helped me have since died. Harold Salmon, who owned the famous department store, Cuff's, in Woolwich, which was featured in the story. Dr Frank Luckett who guided me on matters medical, and the Rev Derek Baker, a saintly man if ever there was one, who gave me advice and opinions whenever I asked.

My thanks too go to Major Cassidy at the Royal Greenjackets Museum at Winchester for help in details of the book's mythical 'City Rifles,' modelled on our mutual regiment, the Rifle Brigade.

All the information provided in respect of the Royal Army Service Corps, Harry's regiment, in this and succeeding volumes was provided by my late brother Alec who served for three long years in the Western Desert with General Wavell and then General Montgomery.

Finally I needed to know the position regarding Anni, arriving here as a refugee from Germany. I wrote to what was then the Immigration and Nationality Department at Croydon. Despite the fact it was clearly pointed out to them that this was with reference to a character in a novel, I received a most detailed and courteous reply from Emma de-la-Haye in the Policy Division. Answering all my queries and providing information about other aspects of naturalisation, she added 'Applicants are also required to be of good character, have an adequate knowledge of the English language and would be required to take an oath of allegiance to the King.'

Things seem to have changed since then.

VOLUME TWO

Sundry calls during the writing of this volume resulted firstly from the Motor Cycle Museum in the Midlands being very helpful in supplying me with information about the German Zundapp which was powered by a British 'Rudge' power unit. Charlie Crew comes into the story and was modelled on an old Octu friend of mine who rejoiced in the name of Tony Cave-Brown-Cave, later to become a hero in the war against the Japanese in Burma. All casualty figures and other day by day diary information was gleaned from Keesing's Directory, an absolutely endless mine of information ranging from verbatim reports by ministers from the Ministry of Food, to such epics as 'Orders in Council' to alter the dates you were allowed to shoot grouse, and on to the state of the weather in Patagonia. Each annual volume comprises some six thousand pages. Now that is what I call a 'read.'

At this point I introduced the Earl of Otbourne's hobby of cultivating, if that is the correct word, orchids. I have a friend, Arthur Wyatt, a surgeon of considerable repute, but also an acknowledged authority on the growing of orchids. My thanks go to him for the highly technical know-how on this subject, reproduced in the story.

In addition, Arthur gave me advice on numerous occasions on medical matters, how long 'rigor mortis' lasts and so on. A useful chap to have around!

VOLUME THREE

In this volume I was again so surprised at the help I received from a very large concern, in this case British Airways. I wished to know how Cecely and the children could fly to Britain from Singapore. Whilst the war had not started in the Far East it was raging in the Mediterranean and in Europe generally. I was directed to the Archives department where a gentleman whose name I cannot now find in my records went into detail with me of the 'Horseshoe Route' all of which is contained in the book.

At this time Maria joined the Wrens. I am indebted to Margaret Harrison, of Henley on Thames, herself a wartime member of that illustrious sorority, who provided me with all the background to life therein.

I obtained a great deal of the details of the Partisan movement in Yugoslavia in which David and Paddy became involved from a wonderful little book by Velimir Vuksic, published by Osprey, people who produce fabulous accounts of campaigns, equipment etc of many different armies throughout the world.

In volume three Fred is awarded the OBE. My friend Ian Adams, also from Henley on Thames, helped me here by researching the order of procedure of honours and awards. Ian spent his early life, after we had together ceased to be shot at by various nationalities around the world, on a gold mine in West Africa, so was able to give me chapter and verse on such installations which I used to good effect in a later volume. I suppose you could call him a mine of information (people have died for less than that.)

Sadly, one dear friend, who was responsible for providing me with all my Chinese names, is no longer with us. Jean Starkey from Pantymwyn in North Wales had a Chinese daughter-in-law living in Singapore who she, so kindly, contacted on my behalf. After all, names of overseas people do not readily come to mind, particularly oriental ones, and I had to be furnished with a substantial number once Harry joined Force 136. We miss Jean greatly.

VOLUME FOUR

Three of my recipients for grateful thanks in this volume are ladies. Firstly Helge Phillips. I wished to include a beautiful German song which had stayed in my otherwise extremely suspect memory since my schooldays. Gabrielle, a Munich student sings it as she dies, having been arrested by the Gestapo. Being far from word-perfect I asked Helge if she knew it; she in turn went to considerable trouble in contacting literary friends in Munich who provided 'Das Zerbrochene Ringlein' for me, written by Joseph von Eichendorff (1788-1857). It really was a masterpiece of scholarly detective work on her, and her friends' part.

The second lady is Diane Burkinshaw from Walsingham in Norfolk. Her husband Philip, in addition to being an old wartime comrade of mine, badly wounded in Normandy, was a District Officer in Gambia after the war - real 'Sanders of the River' stuff! Diane acquired a leopard cub, whose mother had been shot, and brought it up as a pet until it was fully grown. It was this true story which produced 'Chantek' for 'The Chandlers,' and which a number of people have said they found most appealing. We shall have the full account of Diane and 'Barra,' as the real leopard was named, in my next book, a miscellany of stories, poems, and so on, now being prepared.

My third lady is a reverend lady, Reverend Claire Wilson of the parish of Chingford in Essex. Reverend Claire gave me considerable help in a number of matters ecclesiastical, and the details of St Peter and St Paul's Church in Chingford where David and Maria were married. This included such diverse questions as the possibility of a catholic being a god-parent to a protestant, the baptism of infants as distinct from babies, and sundry other matters of religion which have cropped up in a number of the volumes from time to time. She too, as a matter of coincidence, has written a beautiful tract which will join Diane in the miscellany.

My fourth thank you goes to another member of the cloth, one Reverend Bob Cheadle from Newcastle under Lyme. In a former life Bob was, would you believe, a glider pilot! Now paratroopers are generally regarded as a bit round the twist, jumping out of airplanes. They on the other hand are firmly convinced that people who fly in gliders need their heads examined, and the people who fly them should without doubt be certified. I ask you - would you go a couple of thousand feet up without an engine? I rest my case.

Reverend Bob gave me invaluable help in the detail of the flying functions, particularly of the Hamilcar glider, which are included in this volume. I can inform you with confidence he has now returned to sanity, with the aside from his delightful wife Mary - 'more or less!"

My final thanks regarding this volume go to my friend Lieutenant-Commander John Mons-White for all the 'inside information,' as one might describe it, regarding David and Paddy's submarine trip. John was himself a submariner; another breed whose sanity must compare with Reverend Bob above. It would take an elephant to drag me into one.

VOLUME FIVE

In this volume we were brought face to face (that can't be right?) with crocodiles and snakes, particularly the reticulated python, the latter in my opinion being utterly beautiful! The research for this was carried out by my daughter and son-in-law, Ann and Bryan Lambert of Bickerton in Cheshire. They surfed the internet for me, a task quite beyond my intelligence, and produced excellent results which I was able to incorporate into the story, thus proving the old adage 'it's not what you know, it's who you know.' Many thanks, you two, the only problem being I now have an urgent desire to know a great deal more about these reptiles, particularly water snakes, which I knew next to nothing about prior to your efforts.

In volume five, and elsewhere, accounts were given of the shelling of 'Hell-Fire Corner,' that part of Kent from Folkestone round to Margate. Like most people I had knowledge that it had taken place but nothing of the detail. I therefore contacted Deal Library, which I found later was in fact the recipient of one of those long-range monsters, along with the pub on the other side of the road! I spoke to a delightful young lady named Dawn, who gave me the lead on books relating to both the shelling and the nearby coalmines at Betteshanger. It was another example of help despite the fact the knowledge gained was to be used in 'just a novel.'

Here I must mention my friend Alan Heaviside who comes from Durham and was himself a miner in his early days. He was the person who gave me the real nitty-gritty regarding life in the pit, particularly the episode of the roof fall in this volume. My son-in-law Bryan also gave help here in researching the efforts of the 'Bevin Boys' on his magic machine. I am indebted to both of them for what I thought was a particularly realistic picture of life underground.

My final thank you in respect of this volume is another friend from Durham, Regimental Sergeant Major Andrew Gavaghan. He is an authority on regimental traditions of the British Army, that is those county regiments which existed after WW2 but which now sadly have all been amalgamated. In this case a member of the Cameronians, the Scottish Rifles, had died when his parachute had failed to open. Andy provided all the detail of how a funeral of a soldier in that regiment would take place, the detail of which very greatly added to the poignancy of the story.

VOLUME SIX

We covered a lot of ground in this volume. My first thank you must go again to Phil Burkinshaw. The story of Paddy's patrol over the River Maas into German territory was based on a very hairy expedition, led by Phil and described in detail in his book 'Alarms and Excursions.' Phil was mentioned in despatches for this escapade.

We move now to Australia in 1945 where Charles Coates has ended up in Brisbane having been rescued from a Jap camp. He had to get to Fremantle to join a ship back to England. How? I contacted my friend Dennis Palmer in Canberra, working on the assumption that, as he was a retired judge, if he didn't know he would certainly know people who did know. (They're a knowledgeable lot in Australia despite what followers of cricket believe). Dennis contacted an organisation called the 'Rail Resource Centre' where a gentleman named Cris Harding gave him chapter and verse, although again Dennis had told him the information was required for a novel. A most interesting thing was that apparently there were three different gauges on the permanent way resulting in several changes of train. Another nugget of information I acquired, from Dennis' wife Phyllis, was that Nullarbor, the immense plain one has to cross to get to Perth from the east, was aborigine for 'no trees.'

My next thank you would have been to my great friend Captain John Bury; sadly we lost him this year (2006). From the very beginning in volume one, if I needed to know anything about ships, tides, or matters nautical of any description he was always there to solve the problem. He served at sea all through the war, on one occasion being the officer of the watch, I believe that was the proper name, forgive me if I'm wrong, he saw a torpedo coming towards them from straight ahead. It passed only a few feet down the side of the ship as they watched it pass. Those Merchant Navy chaps earned their corn, day after day, night after night, never knowing when they were going to be blasted by a totally unseen enemy.

My next thank you is to my dear friend Alison Kemsley of Malpas in Cheshire. She helped me in two respects. Firstly by operating her magic machine so that I received chapter and verse on gypsies, their origins and customs. As a result I was able to build into the story the gypsy wedding paragraph. Along with the other information she gleaned there would be enough to start another book. Now, there's a thought!

Secondly - there are no limits to her research abilities - she was able to get me details of the Berlin occupied zones as at the end of World War Two, including a street plan and the position of the eventual Berlin wall. As a result I was able to plan the exact route that Dieter took to escape from the Soviets to the American sector. I had been wondering how the devil I was going to get him back into the arms of his beloved - Alison provided the answer!

Finally, I must thank two more people, one for the second time.

Firstly, the gentleman who has read, altered, suggested, struck out, used gallons of red ink, wept tears, used language of which few of us would know the meaning, eventually to put into some sort of readability (readability? - no such word in the dictionary he will maintain - more red ink!) each manuscript as it thudded on to his desk. I refer to Graham Coles my editor and proof reader. If ever there was a medal for conspicuous application in the face of literary incompetence, he would get it with swords and oak leaves. So thank you, Graham.

My last word must go to my old comrade Ian Adams who has given me enormous encouragement in the form of a size ten pointed-toed shoe strategically placed upon my person at frequent intervals. This, with a degree of power designed to lend persuasiveness, has ensured that nothing short of earthquake or flood has kept me away from my desk at the times when I should have been there.

The telephone rings.

"Why were you not at your desk?"

"I went for a pee."

"You are not allowed to pee in writing time."

What with him and Graham I would be better off back in the army!!

And this really is

THE END